W9-CKL-093

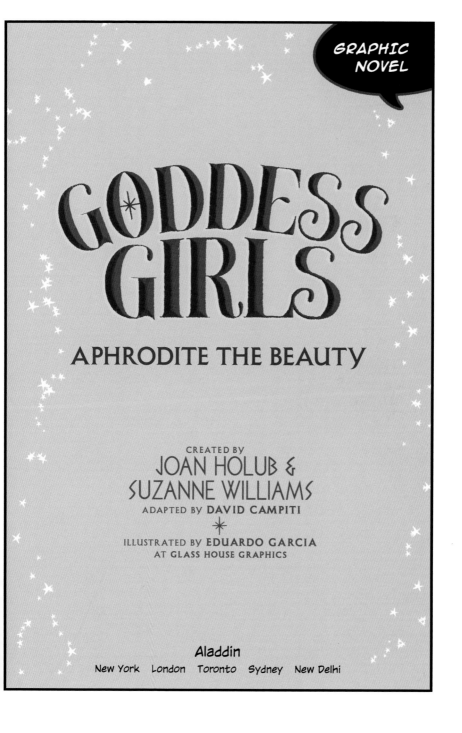

GRAPHIC NOVEL

GODDESS GIRLS

APHRODITE THE BEAUTY

CREATED BY
JOAN HOLUB &
SUZANNE WILLIAMS
ADAPTED BY DAVID CAMPITI

*

ILLUSTRATED BY EDUARDO GARCIA
AT GLASS HOUSE GRAPHICS

Aladdin
New York London Toronto Sydney New Delhi

THIS BOOK IS A WORK OF FICTION. ANY REFERENCES TO HISTORICAL EVENTS, REAL PEOPLE, OR
REAL PLACES ARE USED FICTITIOUSLY. OTHER NAMES, CHARACTERS, PLACES, AND EVENTS ARE
PRODUCTS OF THE AUTHOR'S IMAGINATION, AND ANY RESEMBLANCE TO ACTUAL EVENTS OR PLACES
OR PERSONS, LIVING OR DEAD, IS ENTIRELY COINCIDENTAL.

ALADDIN
AN IMPRINT OF SIMON & SCHUSTER CHILDREN'S PUBLISHING DIVISION
1230 AVENUE OF THE AMERICAS, NEW YORK, NEW YORK 10020
FIRST ALADDIN EDITION AUGUST 2022
TEXT COPYRIGHT © 2022 BY JOAN HOLUB AND SUZANNE WILLIAMS
COVER ILLUSTRATION BY JOÃO ZOD
ILLUSTRATIONS COPYRIGHT © 2022 BY GLASS HOUSE GRAPHICS
ART BY EDUARDO GARCIA. ADDITIONAL ART BY JOÃO ZOD, MARCOS CORTEZ, AND NOZA.
LETTERING BY MARCOS INOUE. ART SERVICES BY GLASS HOUSE GRAPHICS.
ALL RIGHTS RESERVED, INCLUDING THE RIGHT OF REPRODUCTION IN WHOLE OR IN PART IN ANY
FORM. ALADDIN AND RELATED LOGO ARE REGISTERED TRADEMARKS OF SIMON & SCHUSTER, INC.
FOR INFORMATION ABOUT SPECIAL DISCOUNTS FOR BULK PURCHASES, PLEASE CONTACT
SIMON & SCHUSTER SPECIAL SALES AT 1-866-506-1949 OR BUSINESS@SIMONANDSCHUSTER.COM.
THE SIMON & SCHUSTER SPEAKERS BUREAU CAN BRING AUTHORS TO YOUR LIVE EVENT. FOR MORE
INFORMATION OR TO BOOK AN EVENT CONTACT THE SIMON & SCHUSTER SPEAKERS BUREAU AT
1-866-248-3049 OR VISIT OUR WEBSITE AT WWW.SIMONSPEAKERS.COM.
THE ILLUSTRATIONS FOR THIS BOOK WERE RENDERED DIGITALLY.
THE TEXT OF THIS BOOK WAS SET IN FONT ANIME ACE 2.0 BB AT 6.5 POINTS OVER
7.5 POINT LEADING AND STEINANTIK AT 10 POINTS OVER 11 POINT LEADING.
MANUFACTURED IN CHINA 0522 SCP
2 4 6 8 10 9 7 5 3 1
LIBRARY OF CONGRESS CONTROL NUMBER 2021945035
ISBN 978-1-5344-7393-5 (HC)
ISBN 978-1-5344-7392-8 (PBK)
ISBN 978-1-5344-7394-2 (EBOOK)

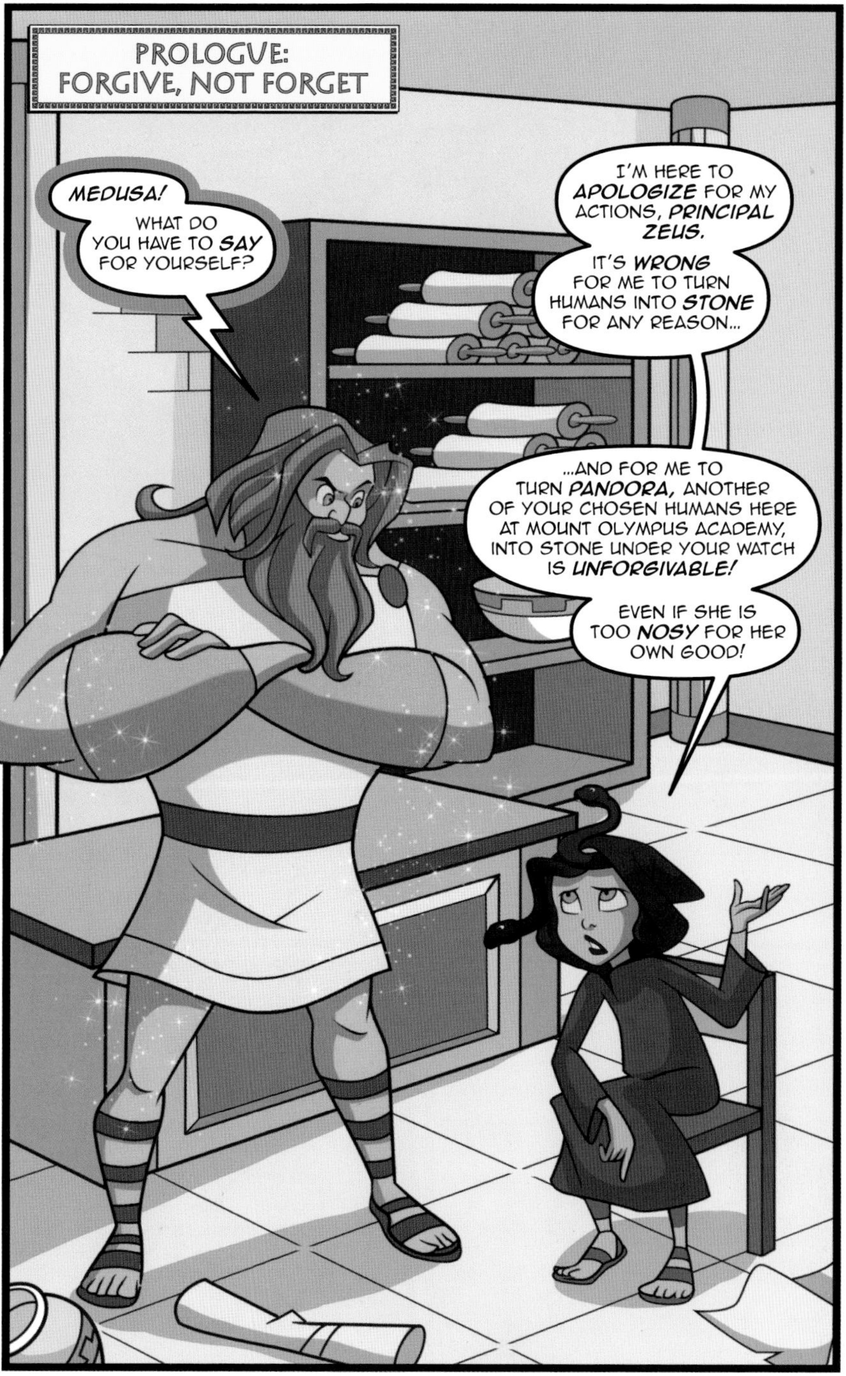
PROLOGUE: FORGIVE, NOT FORGET
MEDUSA! WHAT DO YOU HAVE TO SAY FOR YOURSELF?
I'M HERE TO APOLOGIZE FOR MY ACTIONS, PRINCIPAL ZEUS.
IT'S WRONG FOR ME TO TURN HUMANS INTO STONE FOR ANY REASON...
...AND FOR ME TO TURN PANDORA, ANOTHER OF YOUR CHOSEN HUMANS HERE AT MOUNT OLYMPUS ACADEMY, INTO STONE UNDER YOUR WATCH IS UNFORGIVABLE!
EVEN IF SHE IS TOO NOSY FOR HER OWN GOOD!

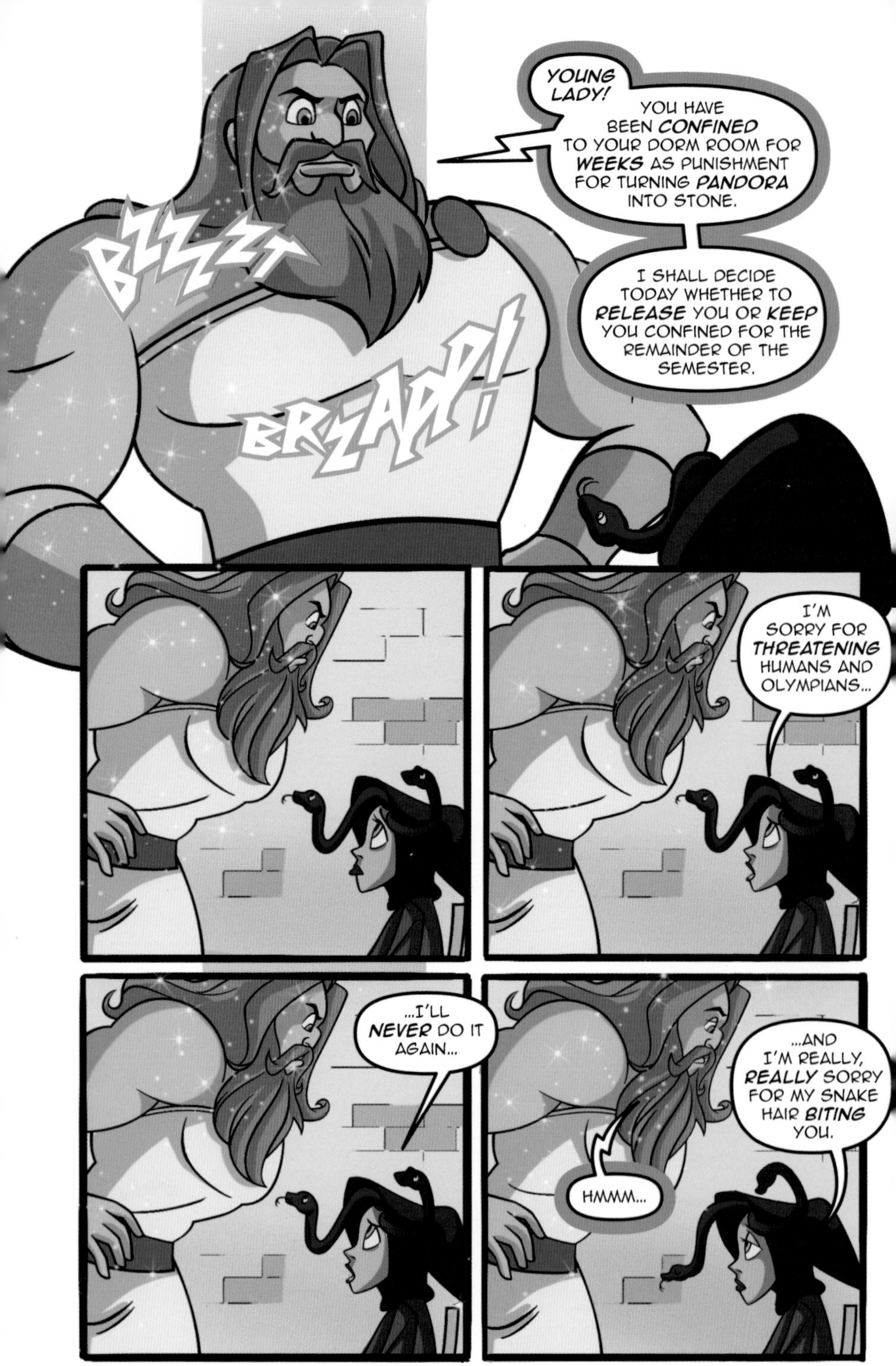

YOUNG LADY! YOU HAVE BEEN CONFINED TO YOUR DORM ROOM FOR WEEKS AS PUNISHMENT FOR TURNING PANDORA INTO STONE.
I SHALL DECIDE TODAY WHETHER TO RELEASE YOU OR KEEP YOU CONFINED FOR THE REMAINDER OF THE SEMESTER.
BZZZZT
BRZAPP!
I'M SORRY FOR THREATENING HUMANS AND OLYMPIANS...
...I'LL NEVER DO IT AGAIN...
...AND I'M REALLY, REALLY SORRY FOR MY SNAKE HAIR BITING YOU.
HMMM...

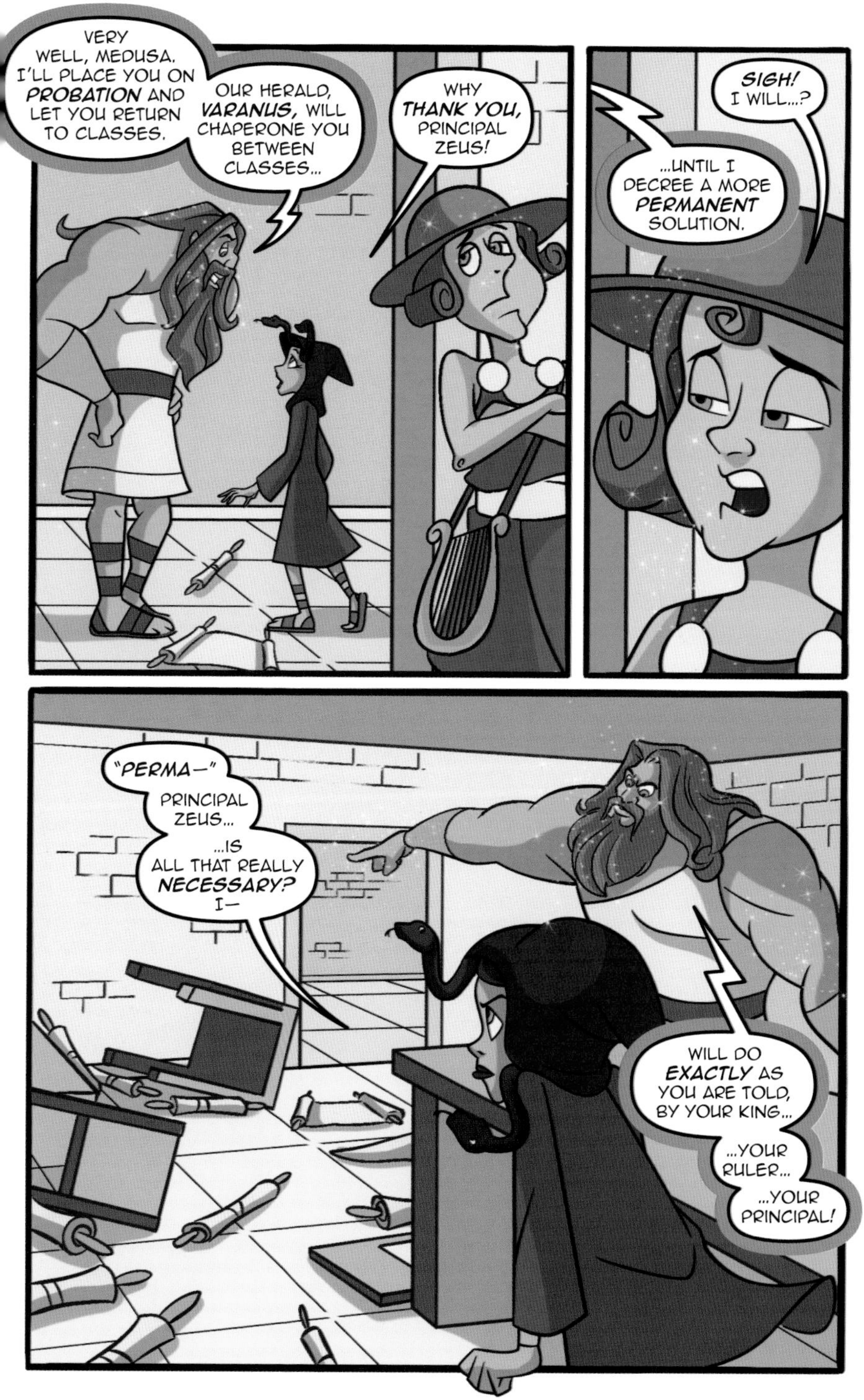
VERY WELL, MEDUSA. I'LL PLACE YOU ON PROBATION AND LET YOU RETURN TO CLASSES.
OUR HERALD, VARANUS, WILL CHAPERONE YOU BETWEEN CLASSES...
WHY THANK YOU, PRINCIPAL ZEUS!
...UNTIL I DECREE A MORE PERMANENT SOLUTION.
SIGH! I WILL...?
"PERMA—"
PRINCIPAL ZEUS...
...IS ALL THAT REALLY NECESSARY? I—
WILL DO EXACTLY AS YOU ARE TOLD, BY YOUR KING...
...YOUR RULER...
...YOUR PRINCIPAL!

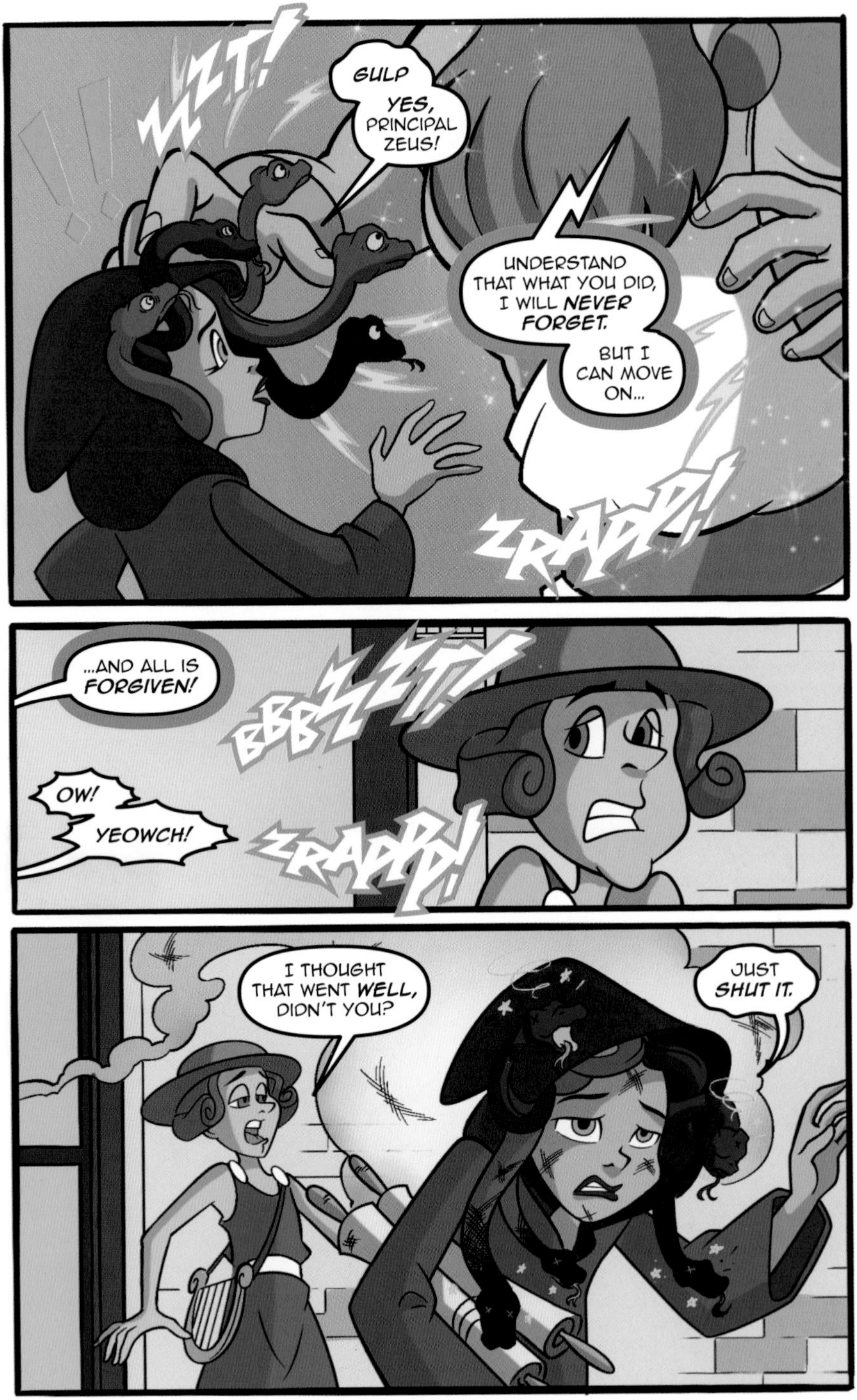

BZZZT!
GULP
YES, PRINCIPAL ZEUS!
UNDERSTAND THAT WHAT YOU DID, I WILL NEVER FORGET.
BUT I CAN MOVE ON...
ZRAPPP!
...AND ALL IS FORGIVEN!
BBBZZZT!
OW!
YEOWCH!
ZRAPPP!
I THOUGHT THAT WENT WELL, DIDN'T YOU?
JUST SHUT IT.

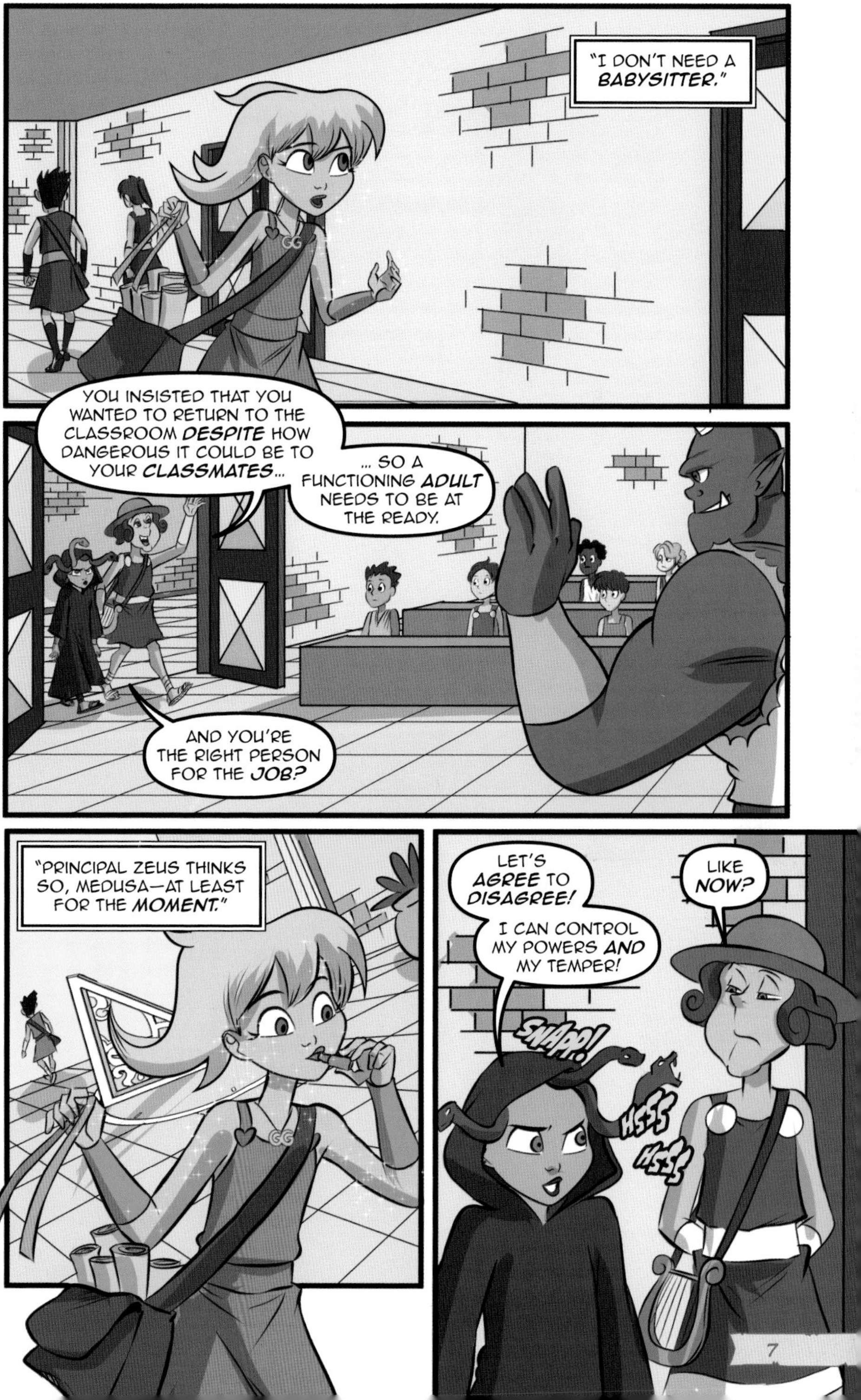
"I DON'T NEED A BABYSITTER."
YOU INSISTED THAT YOU WANTED TO RETURN TO THE CLASSROOM DESPITE HOW DANGEROUS IT COULD BE TO YOUR CLASSMATES...
... SO A FUNCTIONING ADULT NEEDS TO BE AT THE READY.
AND YOU'RE THE RIGHT PERSON FOR THE JOB?
"PRINCIPAL ZEUS THINKS SO, MEDUSA—AT LEAST FOR THE MOMENT."
LET'S AGREE TO DISAGREE!
I CAN CONTROL MY POWERS AND MY TEMPER!
LIKE NOW?
SNAP!
HSSS
HSSS

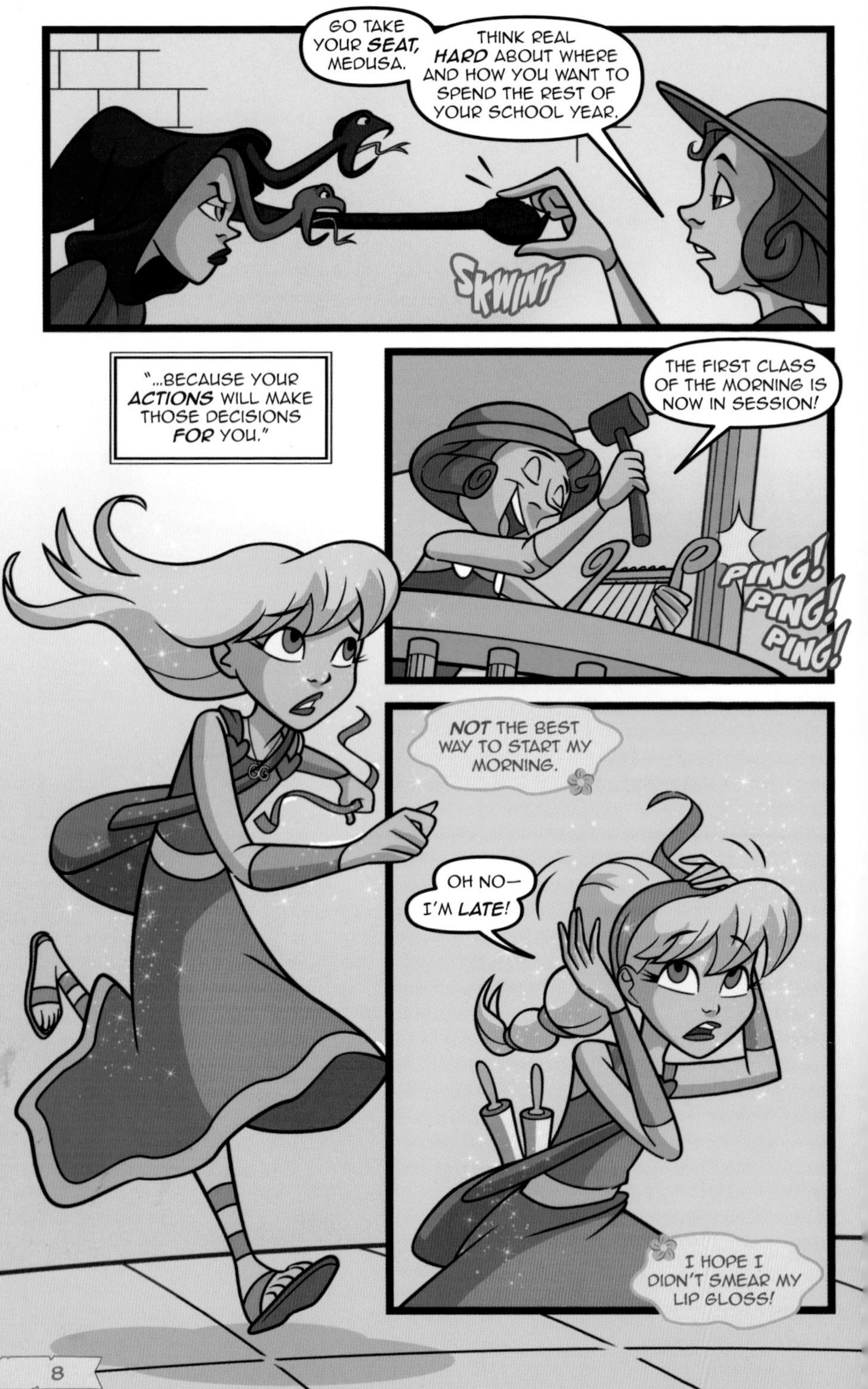
GO TAKE YOUR SEAT, MEDUSA.
THINK REAL HARD ABOUT WHERE AND HOW YOU WANT TO SPEND THE REST OF YOUR SCHOOL YEAR.
SKWINT
"...BECAUSE YOUR ACTIONS WILL MAKE THOSE DECISIONS FOR YOU."
THE FIRST CLASS OF THE MORNING IS NOW IN SESSION!
PING! PING! PING!
NOT THE BEST WAY TO START MY MORNING.
OH NO— I'M LATE!
I HOPE I DIDN'T SMEAR MY LIP GLOSS!

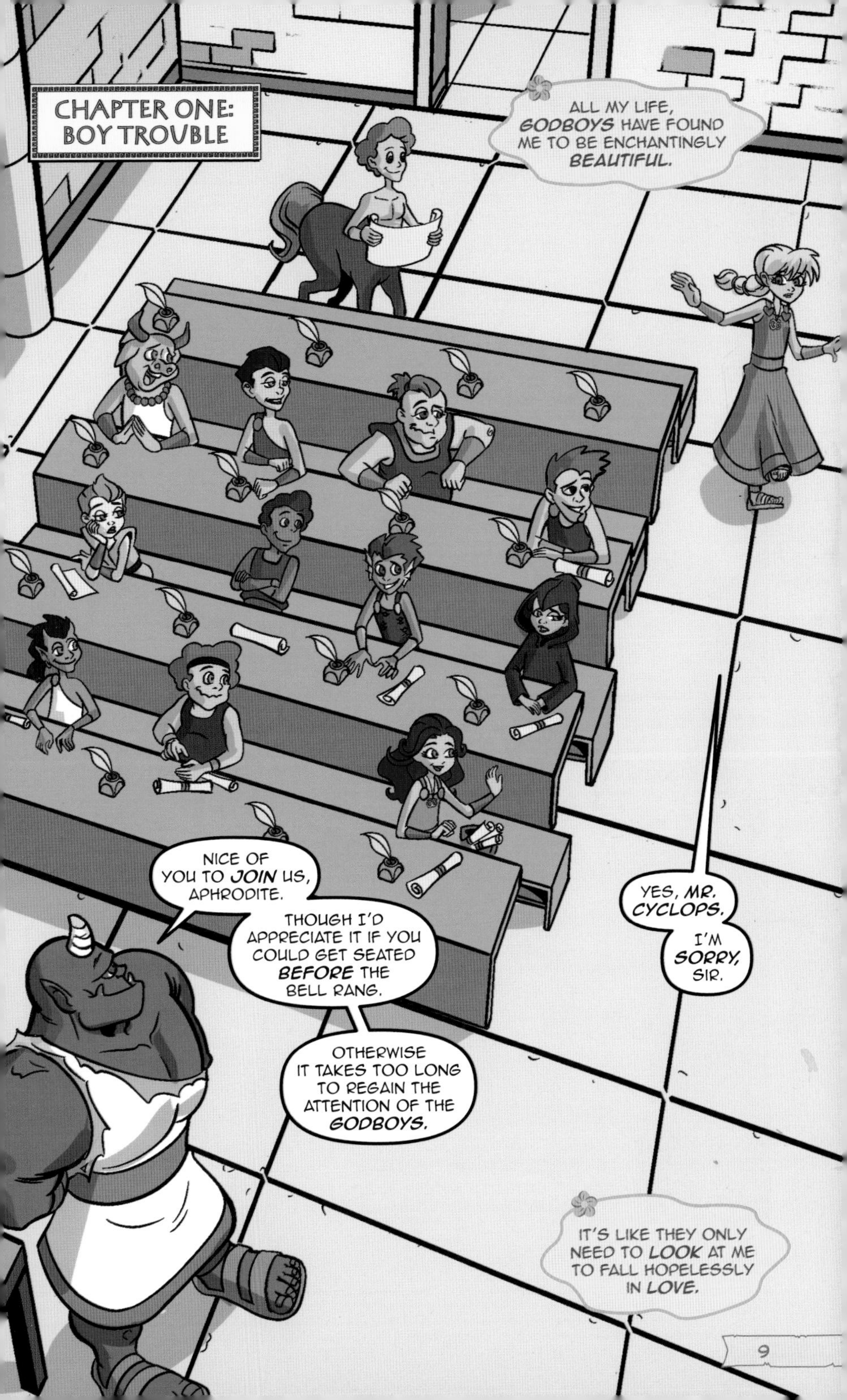

CHAPTER ONE: BOY TROUBLE
ALL MY LIFE, GODBOYS HAVE FOUND ME TO BE ENCHANTINGLY BEAUTIFUL.
NICE OF YOU TO JOIN US, APHRODITE.
THOUGH I'D APPRECIATE IT IF YOU COULD GET SEATED BEFORE THE BELL RANG.
OTHERWISE IT TAKES TOO LONG TO REGAIN THE ATTENTION OF THE GODBOYS.
YES, MR. CYCLOPS.
I'M SORRY, SIR.
IT'S LIKE THEY ONLY NEED TO LOOK AT ME TO FALL HOPELESSLY IN LOVE.

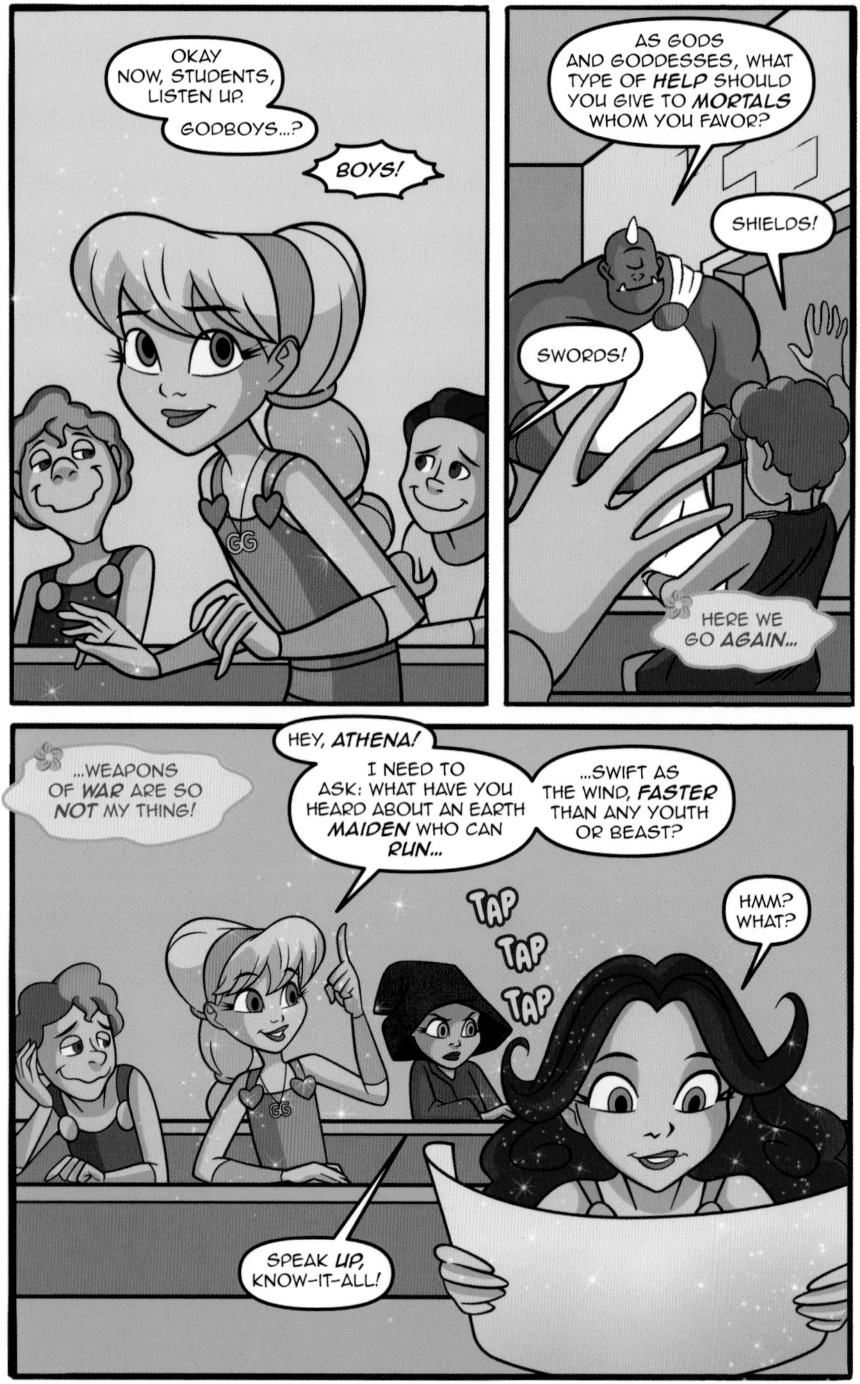
OKAY NOW, STUDENTS, LISTEN UP.
GODBOYS...?
BOYS!
AS GODS AND GODDESSES, WHAT TYPE OF HELP SHOULD YOU GIVE TO MORTALS WHOM YOU FAVOR?
SHIELDS!
SWORDS!
HERE WE GO AGAIN...
...WEAPONS OF WAR ARE SO NOT MY THING!
HEY, ATHENA! I NEED TO ASK: WHAT HAVE YOU HEARD ABOUT AN EARTH MAIDEN WHO CAN RUN...
...SWIFT AS THE WIND, FASTER THAN ANY YOUTH OR BEAST?
TAP TAP TAP
HMM? WHAT?
SPEAK UP, KNOW-IT-ALL!

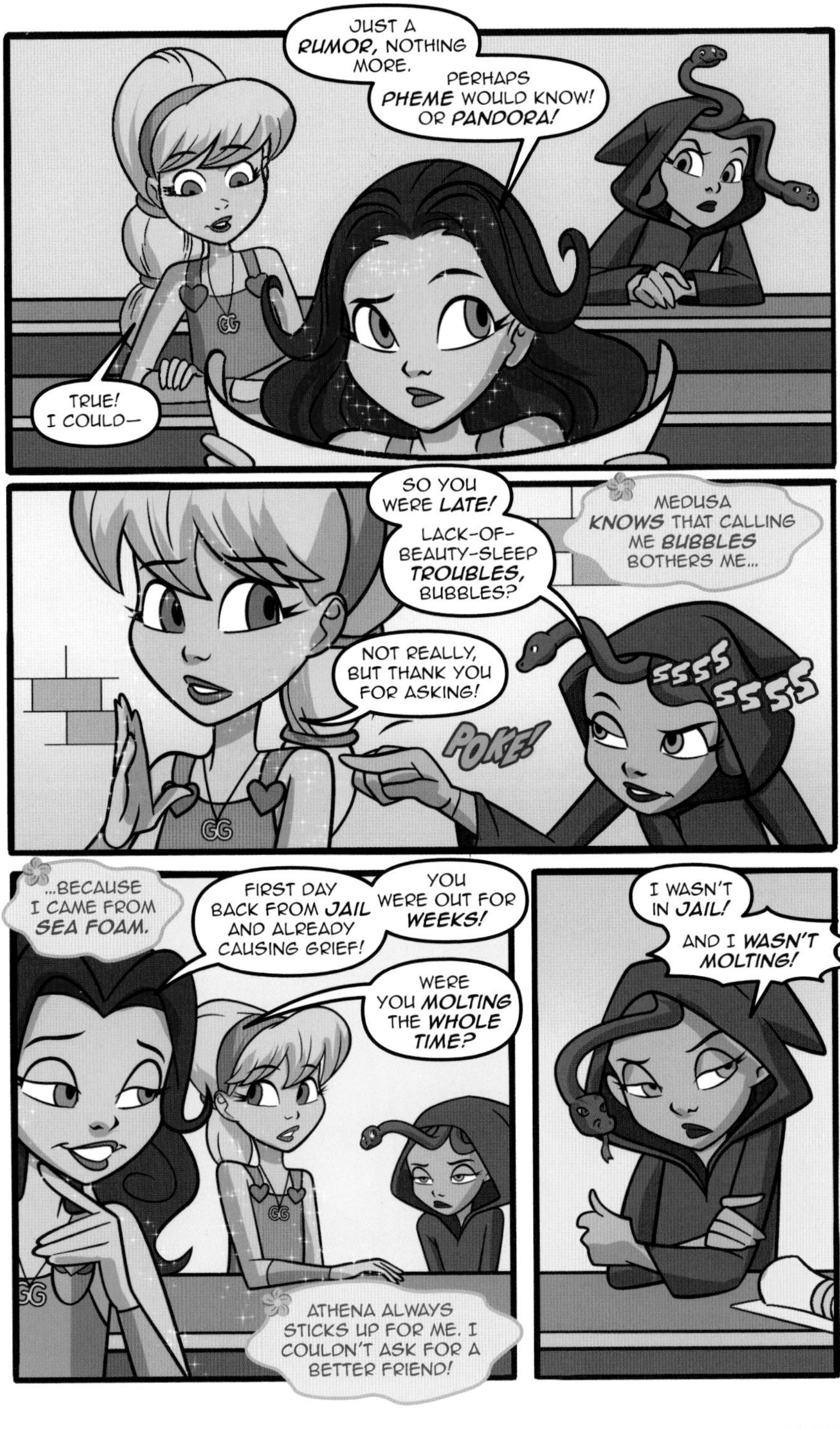

JUST A RUMOR, NOTHING MORE.
PERHAPS PHEME WOULD KNOW! OR PANDORA!
TRUE! I COULD—
SO YOU WERE LATE!
LACK-OF-BEAUTY-SLEEP TROUBLES, BUBBLES?
MEDUSA KNOWS THAT CALLING ME BUBBLES BOTHERS ME...
NOT REALLY, BUT THANK YOU FOR ASKING!
SSSS SSSS
POKE!
...BECAUSE I CAME FROM SEA FOAM.
FIRST DAY BACK FROM JAIL AND ALREADY CAUSING GRIEF!
YOU WERE OUT FOR WEEKS!
WERE YOU MOLTING THE WHOLE TIME?
ATHENA ALWAYS STICKS UP FOR ME. I COULDN'T ASK FOR A BETTER FRIEND!
I WASN'T IN JAIL!
AND I WASN'T MOLTING!

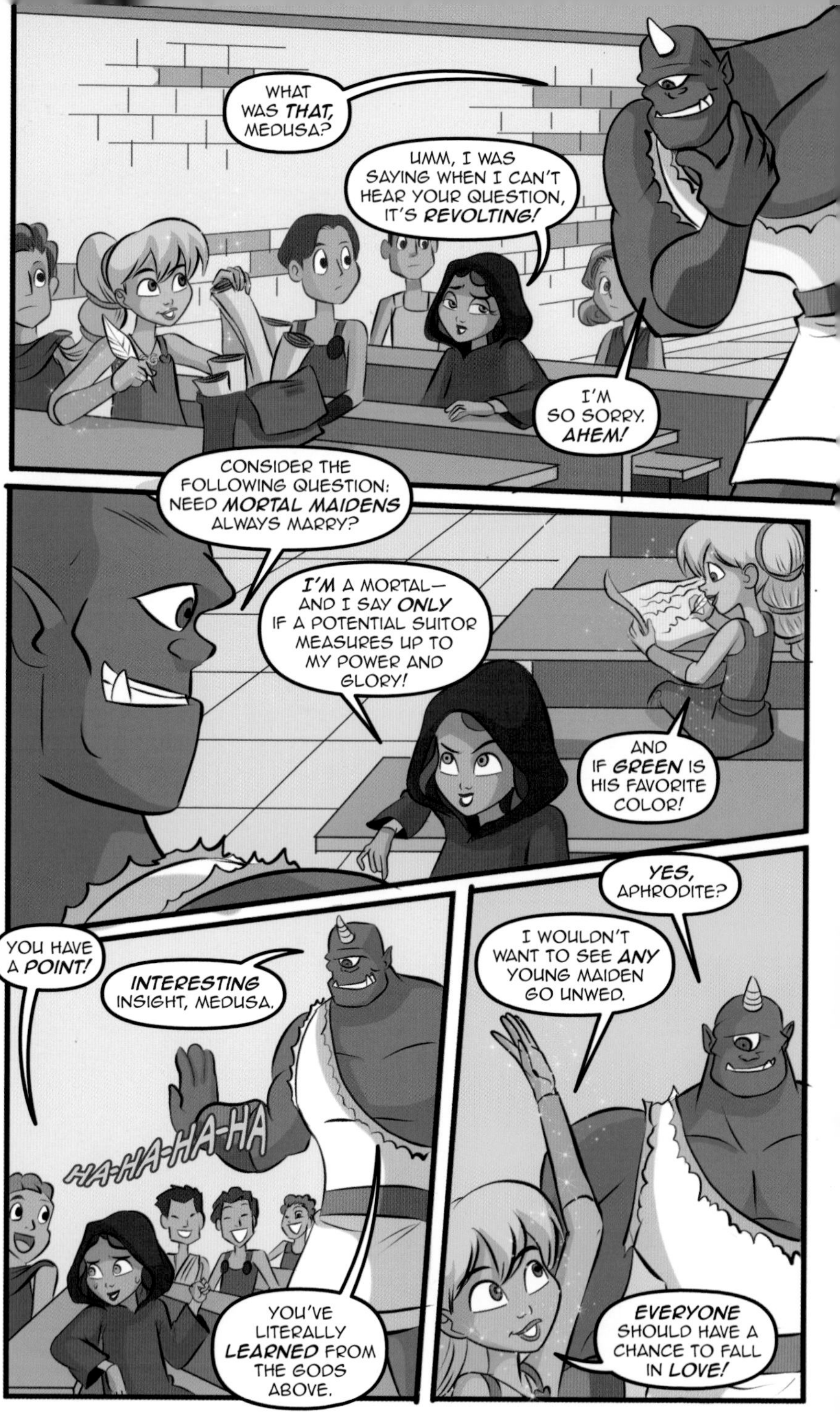
WHAT WAS THAT, MEDUSA?
UMM, I WAS SAYING WHEN I CAN'T HEAR YOUR QUESTION, IT'S REVOLTING!
I'M SO SORRY. AHEM!
CONSIDER THE FOLLOWING QUESTION: NEED MORTAL MAIDENS ALWAYS MARRY?
I'M A MORTAL— AND I SAY ONLY IF A POTENTIAL SUITOR MEASURES UP TO MY POWER AND GLORY!
AND IF GREEN IS HIS FAVORITE COLOR!
YOU HAVE A POINT!
INTERESTING INSIGHT, MEDUSA.
HA-HA-HA-HA
YOU'VE LITERALLY LEARNED FROM THE GODS ABOVE.
YES, APHRODITE?
I WOULDN'T WANT TO SEE ANY YOUNG MAIDEN GO UNWED.
EVERYONE SHOULD HAVE A CHANCE TO FALL IN LOVE!

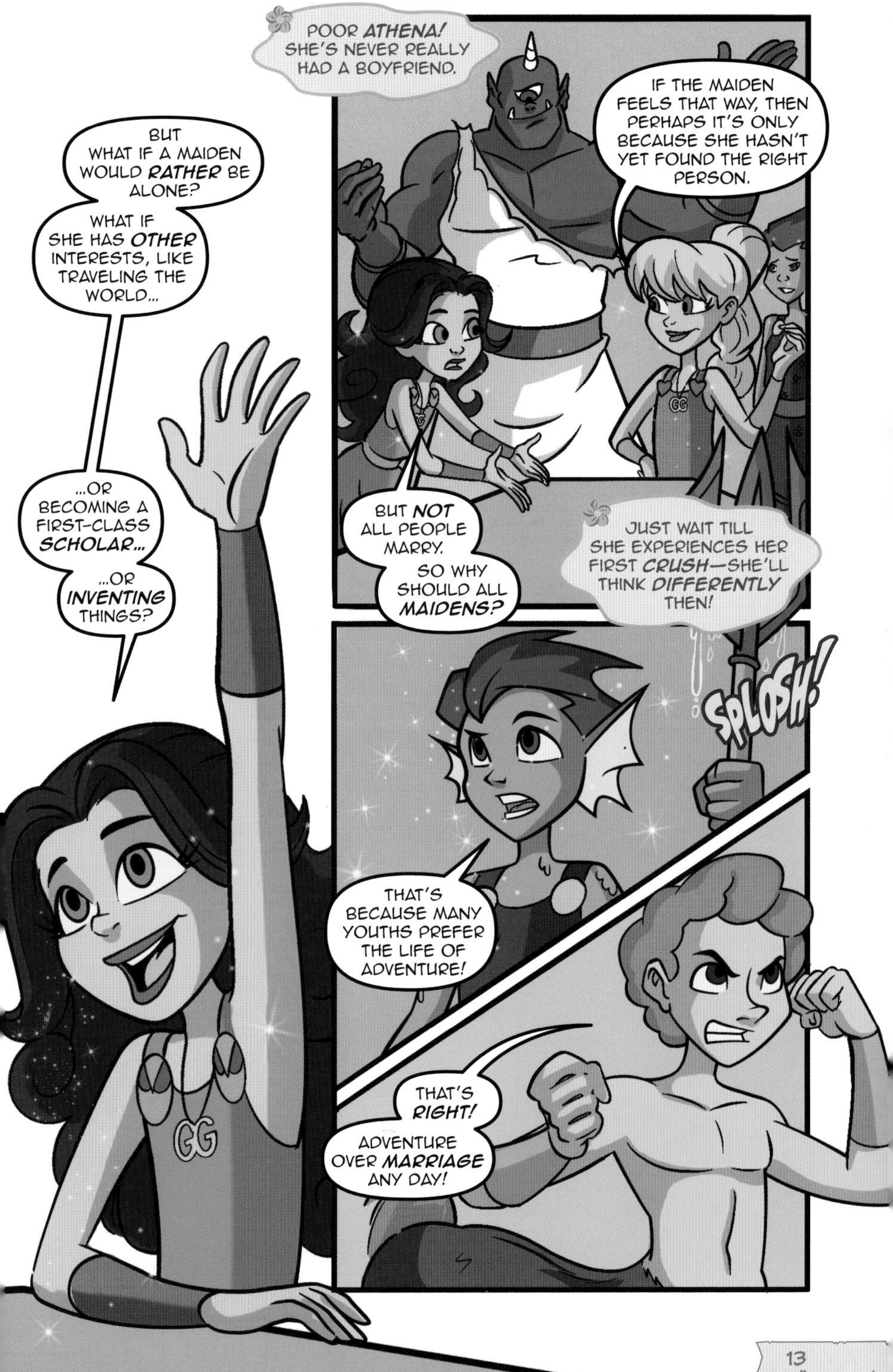
POOR ATHENA! SHE'S NEVER REALLY HAD A BOYFRIEND.
IF THE MAIDEN FEELS THAT WAY, THEN PERHAPS IT'S ONLY BECAUSE SHE HASN'T YET FOUND THE RIGHT PERSON.
BUT WHAT IF A MAIDEN WOULD RATHER BE ALONE?
WHAT IF SHE HAS OTHER INTERESTS, LIKE TRAVELING THE WORLD...
...OR BECOMING A FIRST-CLASS SCHOLAR...
...OR INVENTING THINGS?
BUT NOT ALL PEOPLE MARRY.
SO WHY SHOULD ALL MAIDENS?
JUST WAIT TILL SHE EXPERIENCES HER FIRST CRUSH—SHE'LL THINK DIFFERENTLY THEN!
SPLOSH!
THAT'S BECAUSE MANY YOUTHS PREFER THE LIFE OF ADVENTURE!
THAT'S RIGHT!
ADVENTURE OVER MARRIAGE ANY DAY!

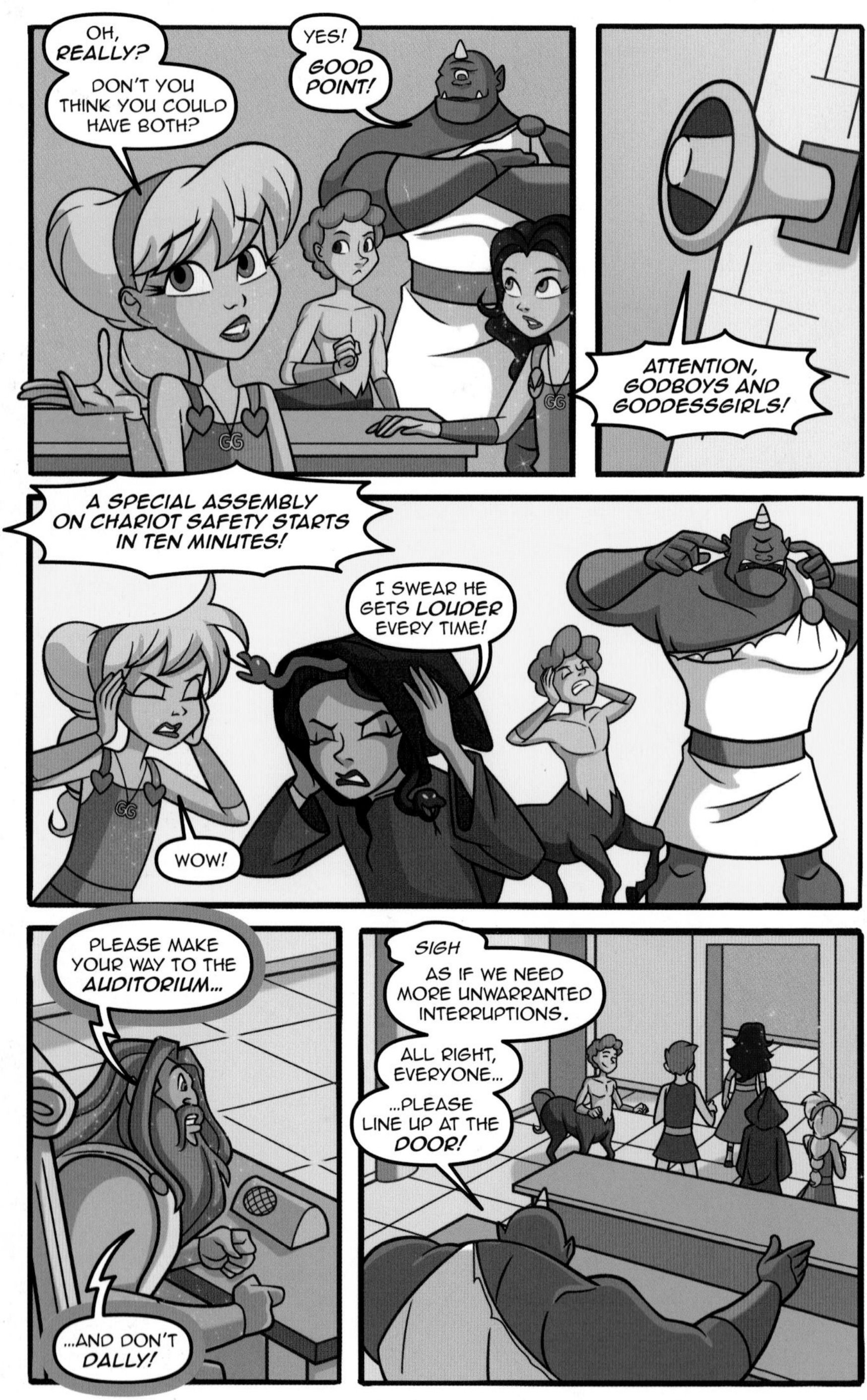
OH, REALLY?
DON'T YOU THINK YOU COULD HAVE BOTH?
YES! GOOD POINT!
ATTENTION, GODBOYS AND GODDESSGIRLS!
A SPECIAL ASSEMBLY ON CHARIOT SAFETY STARTS IN TEN MINUTES!
I SWEAR HE GETS LOUDER EVERY TIME!
WOW!
PLEASE MAKE YOUR WAY TO THE AUDITORIUM...
...AND DON'T DALLY!
SIGH
AS IF WE NEED MORE UNWARRANTED INTERRUPTIONS.
ALL RIGHT, EVERYONE...
...PLEASE LINE UP AT THE DOOR!

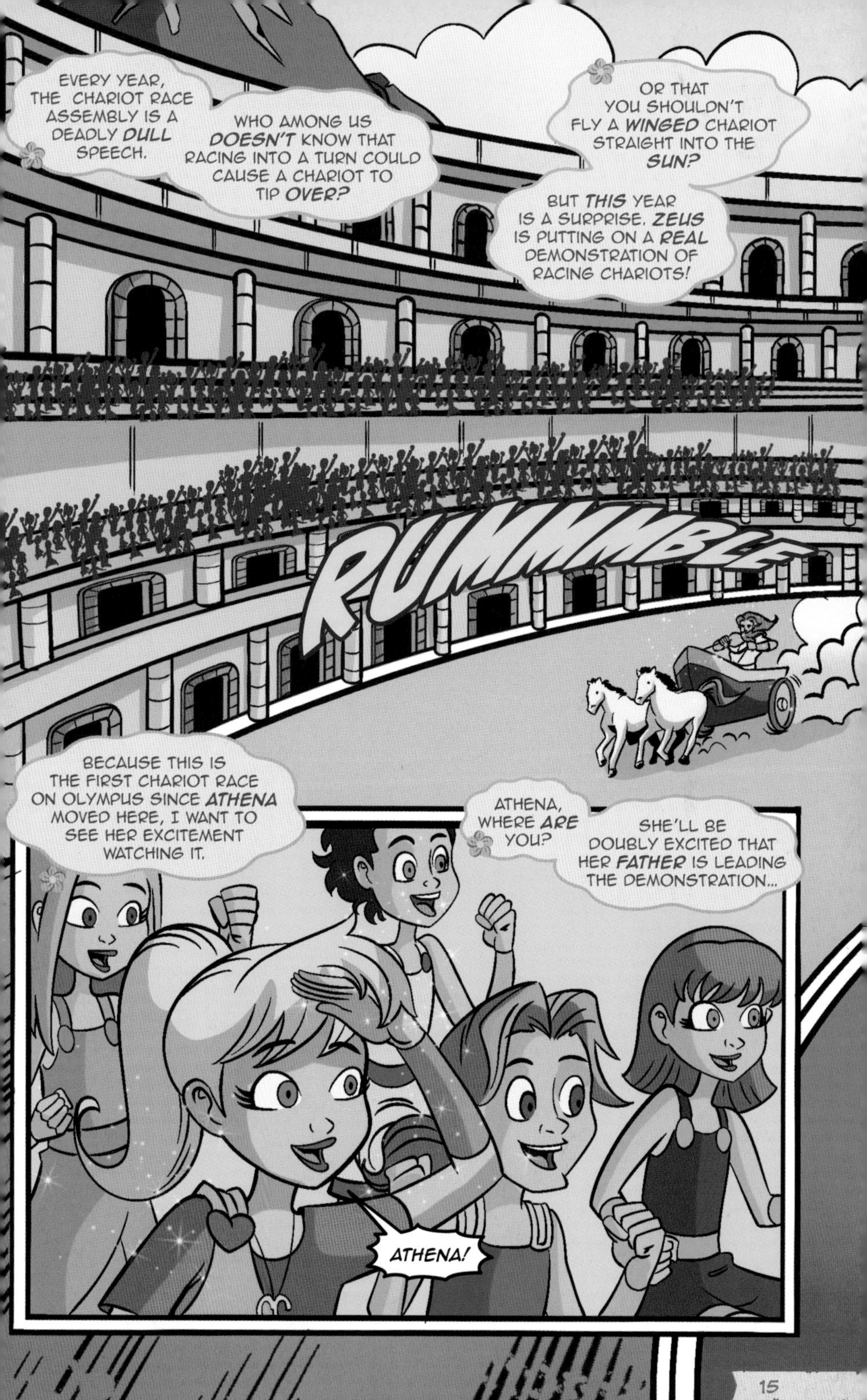

EVERY YEAR, THE CHARIOT RACE ASSEMBLY IS A DEADLY DULL SPEECH.
WHO AMONG US DOESN'T KNOW THAT RACING INTO A TURN COULD CAUSE A CHARIOT TO TIP OVER?
OR THAT YOU SHOULDN'T FLY A WINGED CHARIOT STRAIGHT INTO THE SUN?
BUT THIS YEAR IS A SURPRISE. ZEUS IS PUTTING ON A REAL DEMONSTRATION OF RACING CHARIOTS!
RUMMMBLE
BECAUSE THIS IS THE FIRST CHARIOT RACE ON OLYMPUS SINCE ATHENA MOVED HERE, I WANT TO SEE HER EXCITEMENT WATCHING IT.
ATHENA, WHERE ARE YOU?
SHE'LL BE DOUBLY EXCITED THAT HER FATHER IS LEADING THE DEMONSTRATION...
ATHENA!

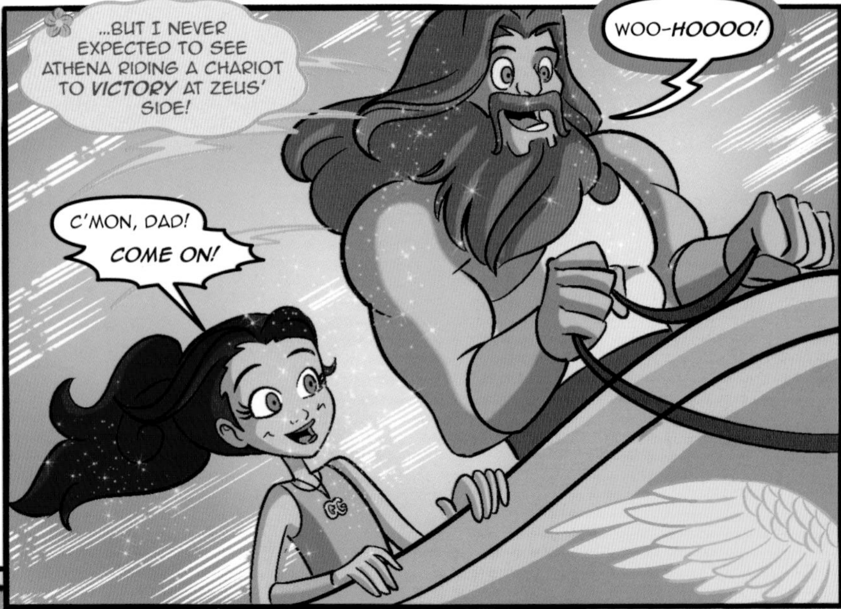
...BUT I NEVER EXPECTED TO SEE ATHENA RIDING A CHARIOT TO VICTORY AT ZEUS' SIDE!
WOO-HOOOO!
C'MON, DAD! COME ON!

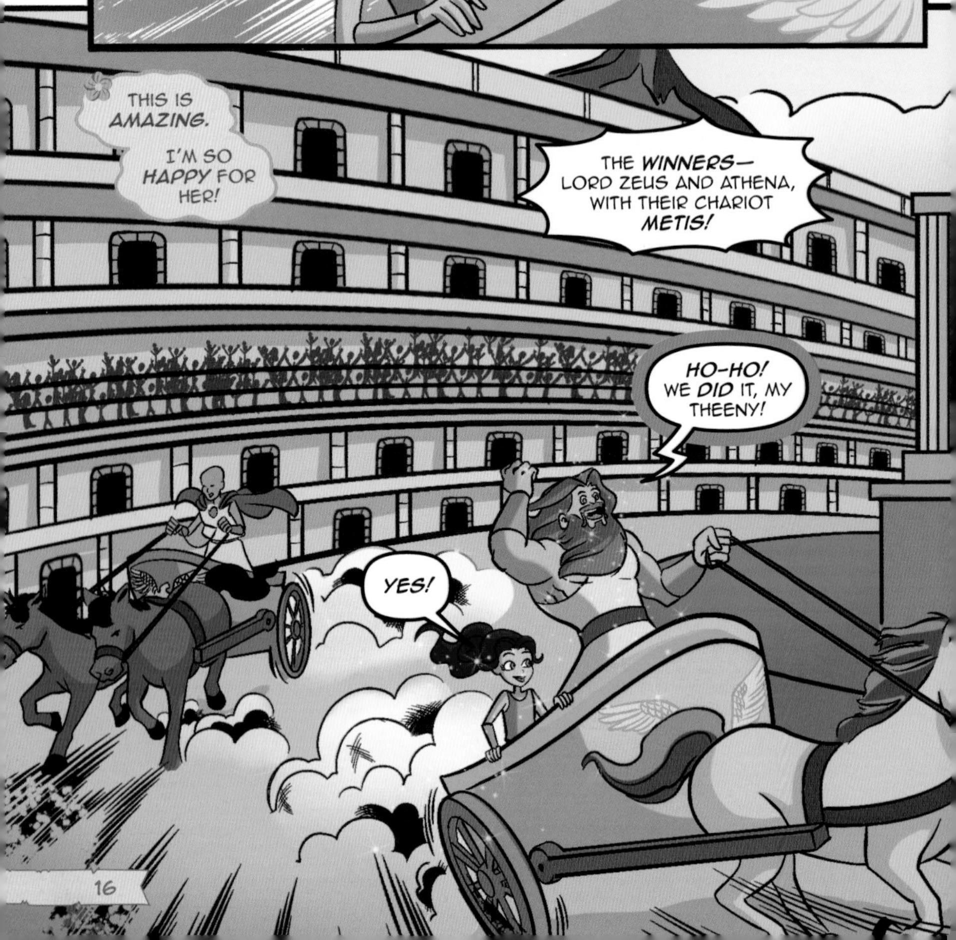
THIS IS AMAZING.
I'M SO HAPPY FOR HER!
THE WINNERS— LORD ZEUS AND ATHENA, WITH THEIR CHARIOT METIS!
HO-HO! WE DID IT, MY THEENY!
YES!

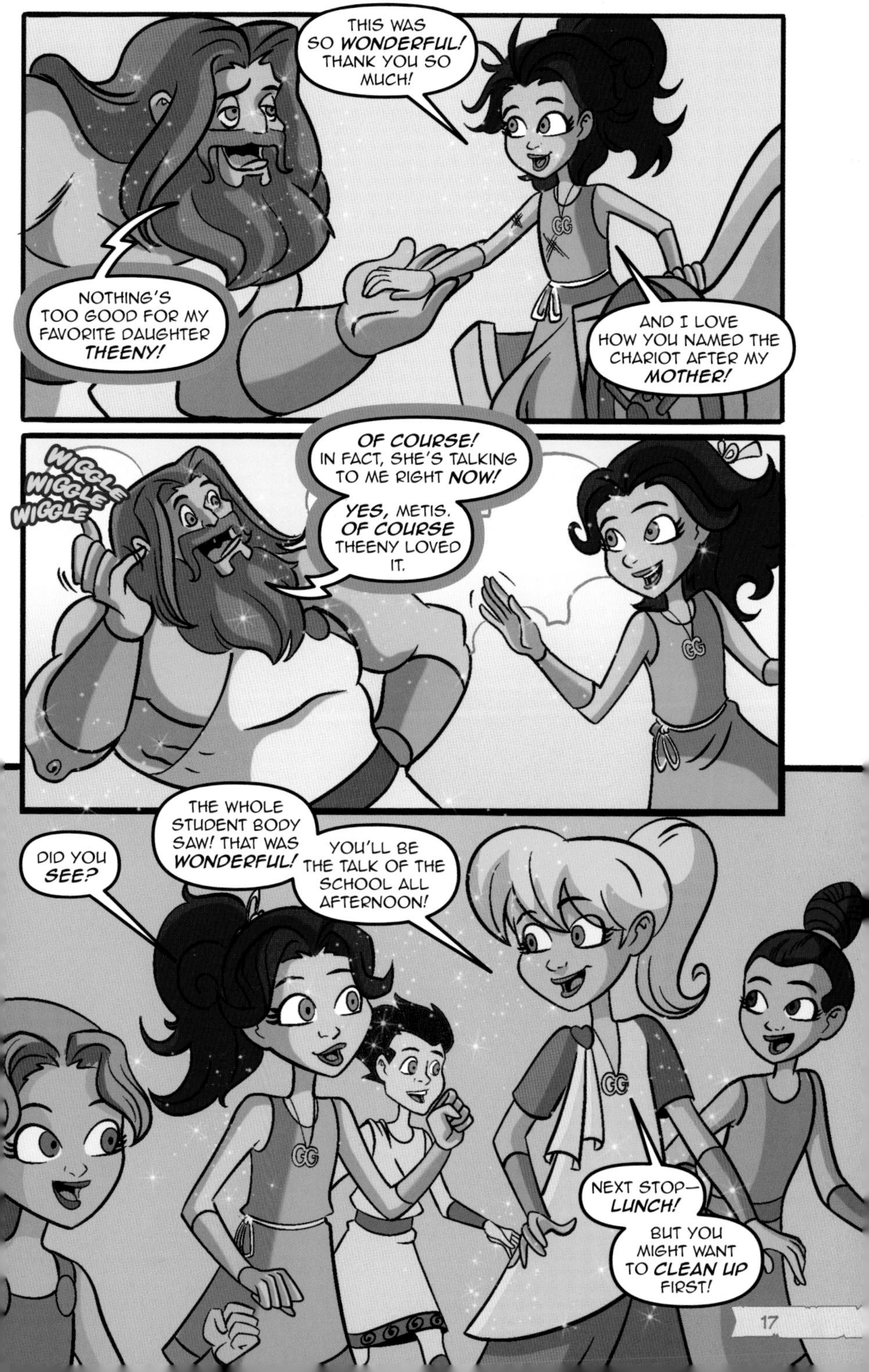
THIS WAS SO WONDERFUL! THANK YOU SO MUCH!
NOTHING'S TOO GOOD FOR MY FAVORITE DAUGHTER THEENY!
AND I LOVE HOW YOU NAMED THE CHARIOT AFTER MY MOTHER!
WIGGLE WIGGLE WIGGLE
OF COURSE! IN FACT, SHE'S TALKING TO ME RIGHT NOW!
YES, METIS. OF COURSE THEENY LOVED IT.
DID YOU SEE?
THE WHOLE STUDENT BODY SAW! THAT WAS WONDERFUL!
YOU'LL BE THE TALK OF THE SCHOOL ALL AFTERNOON!
NEXT STOP— LUNCH!
BUT YOU MIGHT WANT TO CLEAN UP FIRST!

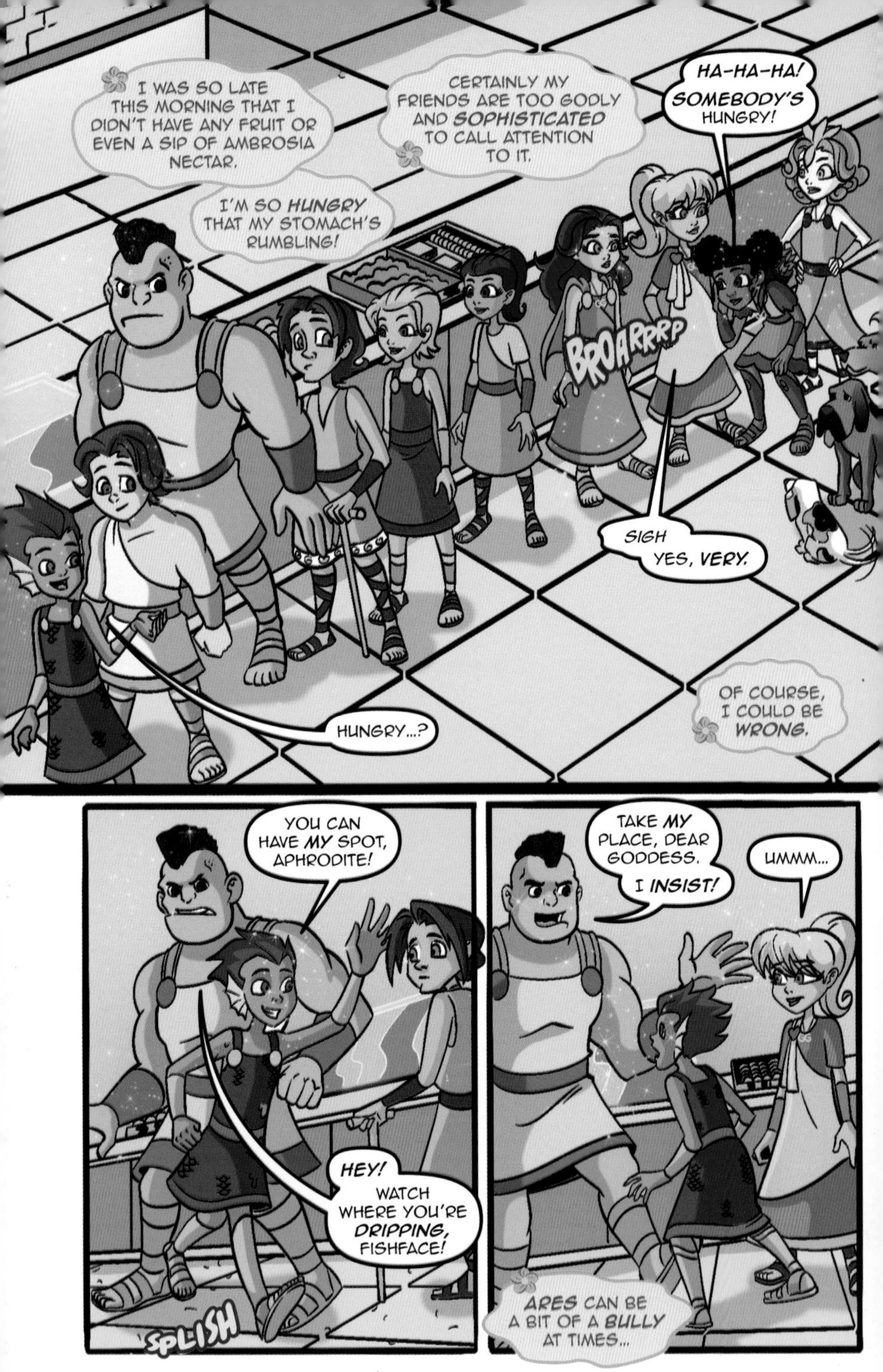
I WAS SO LATE THIS MORNING THAT I DIDN'T HAVE ANY FRUIT OR EVEN A SIP OF AMBROSIA NECTAR.
I'M SO HUNGRY THAT MY STOMACH'S RUMBLING!
CERTAINLY MY FRIENDS ARE TOO GODLY AND SOPHISTICATED TO CALL ATTENTION TO IT.
HA-HA-HA! SOMEBODY'S HUNGRY!
BROARRRP
SIGH YES, VERY.
HUNGRY...?
OF COURSE, I COULD BE WRONG.
YOU CAN HAVE MY SPOT, APHRODITE!
HEY! WATCH WHERE YOU'RE DRIPPING, FISHFACE!
SPLISH
TAKE MY PLACE, DEAR GODDESS. I INSIST!
UMMM...
ARES CAN BE A BIT OF A BULLY AT TIMES...

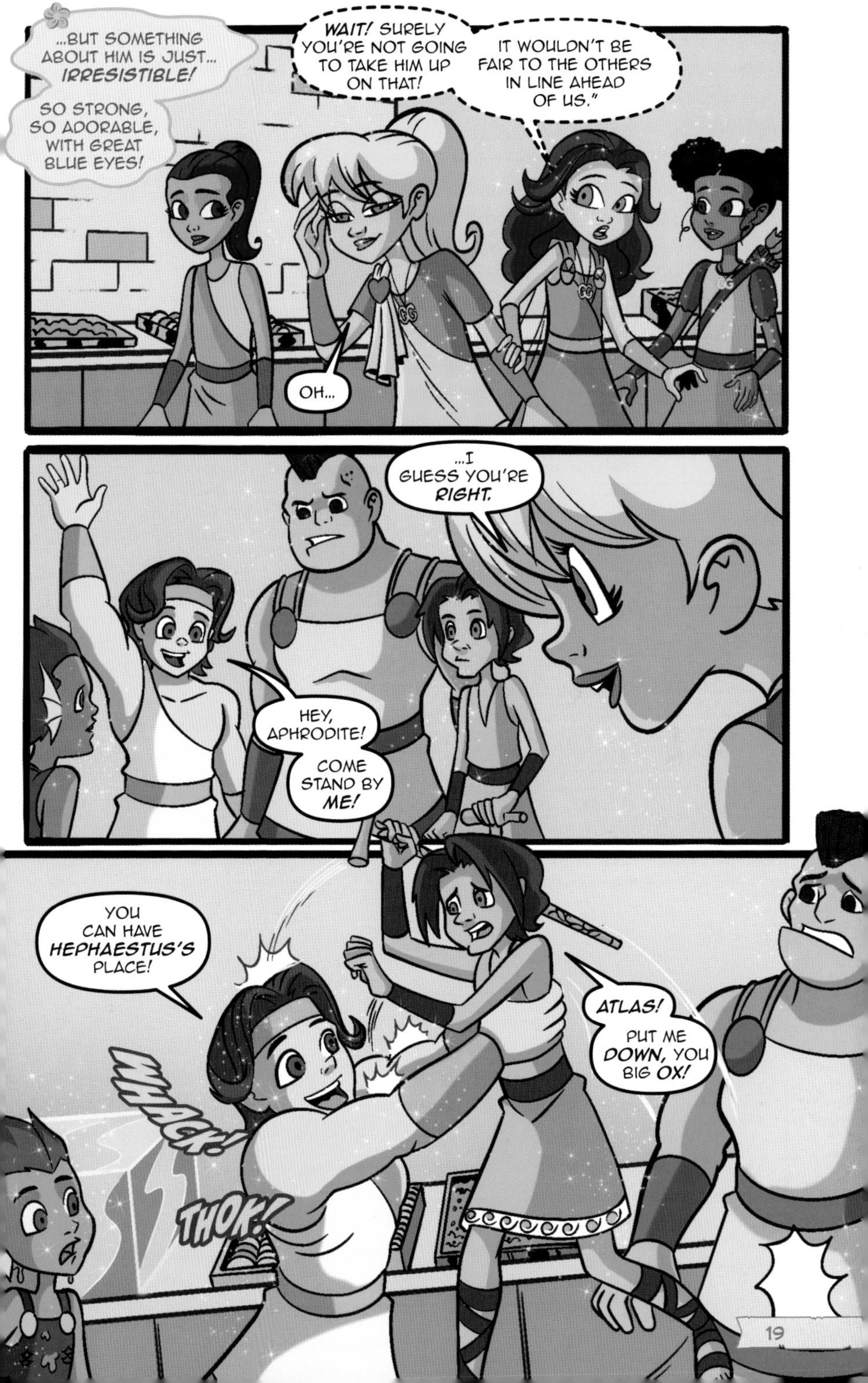
...BUT SOMETHING ABOUT HIM IS JUST... IRRESISTIBLE!
SO STRONG, SO ADORABLE, WITH GREAT BLUE EYES!
WAIT! SURELY YOU'RE NOT GOING TO TAKE HIM UP ON THAT!
IT WOULDN'T BE FAIR TO THE OTHERS IN LINE AHEAD OF US."
OH...
...I GUESS YOU'RE RIGHT.
HEY, APHRODITE!
COME STAND BY ME!
YOU CAN HAVE HEPHAESTUS'S PLACE!
ATLAS!
PUT ME DOWN, YOU BIG OX!
WHACK!
THOK!

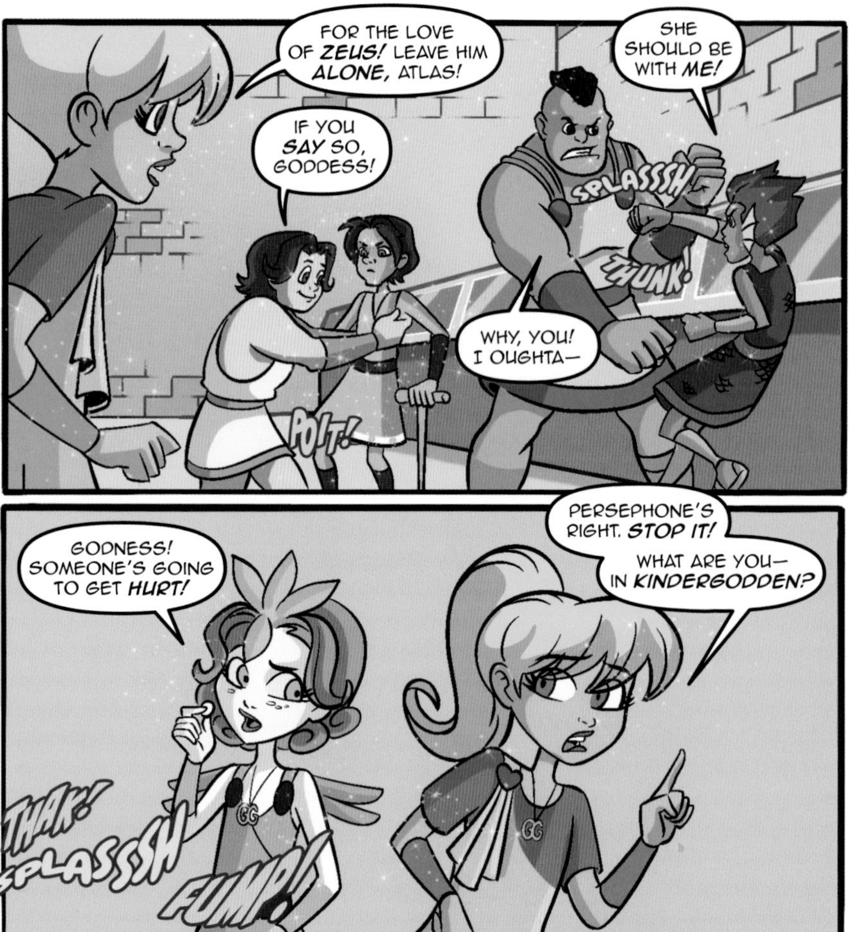
FOR THE LOVE OF ZEUS! LEAVE HIM ALONE, ATLAS!
SHE SHOULD BE WITH ME!
IF YOU SAY SO, GODDESS!
SPLASSSH
THUNK!
WHY, YOU! I OUGHTA—
POIT!
GODNESS! SOMEONE'S GOING TO GET HURT!
PERSEPHONE'S RIGHT. STOP IT!
WHAT ARE YOU— IN KINDERGODDEN?
THAK!
SPLASSSH
FUMP!
I APPRECIATE YOUR OFFERS, BUT I'LL WAIT MY TURN...
...JUST LIKE EVERYONE ELSE!
MAN OH MAN...
ALL RIGHT.
SPLISH

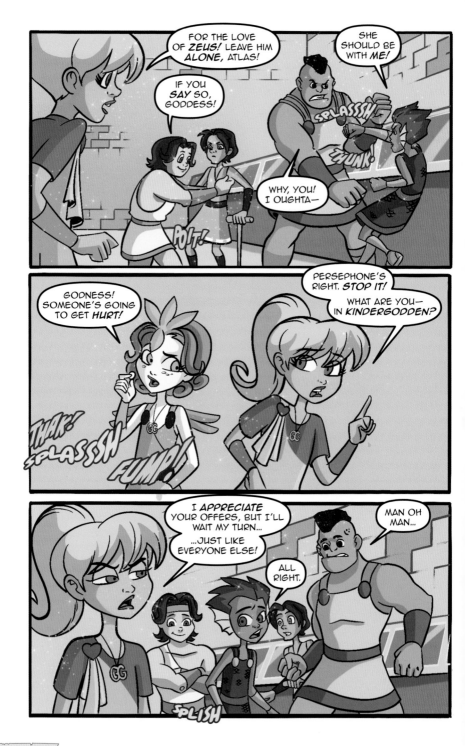

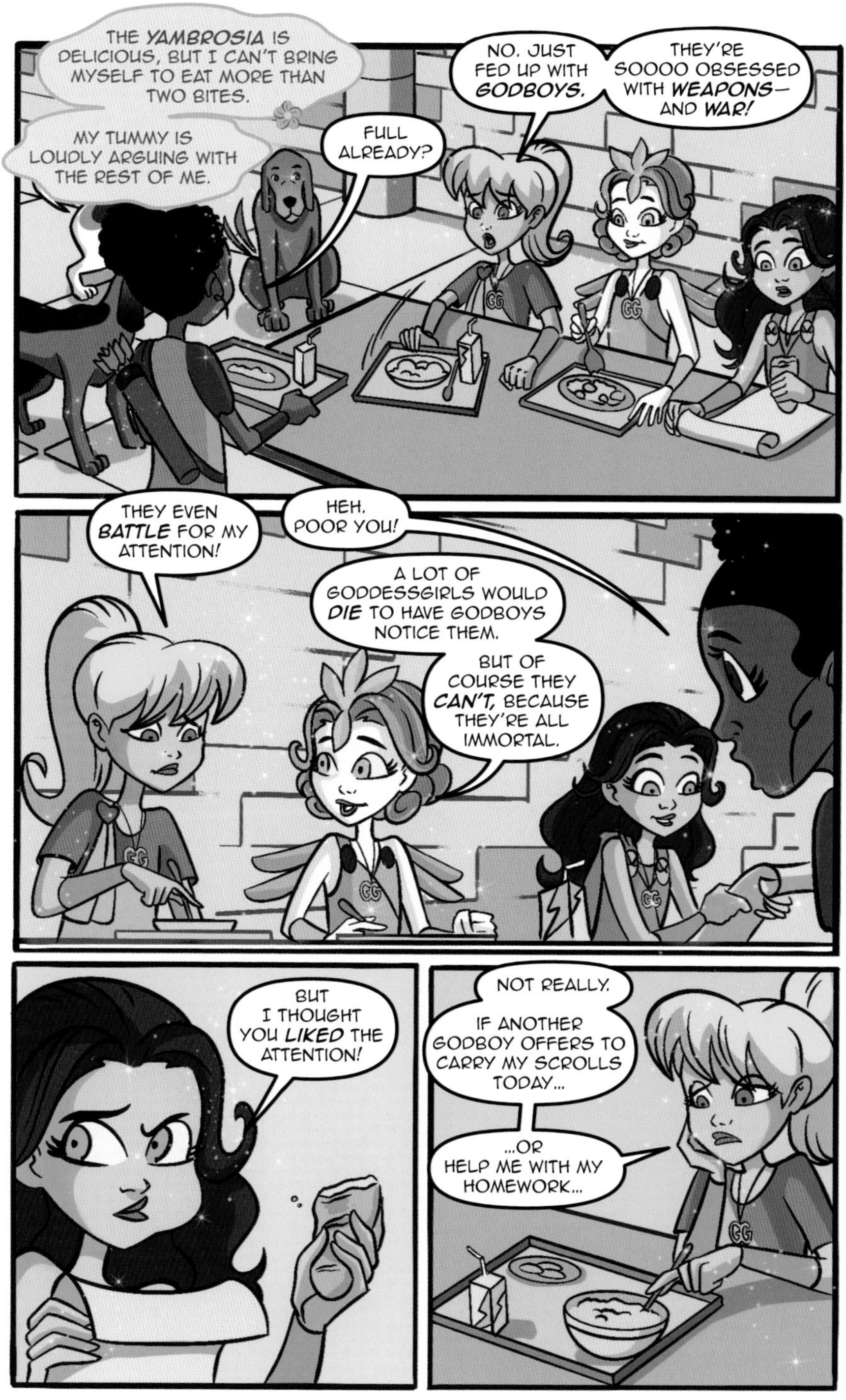
THE YAMBROSIA IS DELICIOUS, BUT I CAN'T BRING MYSELF TO EAT MORE THAN TWO BITES.
MY TUMMY IS LOUDLY ARGUING WITH THE REST OF ME.
FULL ALREADY?
NO. JUST FED UP WITH GODBOYS.
THEY'RE SOOOO OBSESSED WITH WEAPONS— AND WAR!
THEY EVEN BATTLE FOR MY ATTENTION!
HEH. POOR YOU!
A LOT OF GODDESSGIRLS WOULD DIE TO HAVE GODBOYS NOTICE THEM.
BUT OF COURSE THEY CAN'T, BECAUSE THEY'RE ALL IMMORTAL.
BUT I THOUGHT YOU LIKED THE ATTENTION!
NOT REALLY.
IF ANOTHER GODBOY OFFERS TO CARRY MY SCROLLS TODAY...
...OR HELP ME WITH MY HOMEWORK...

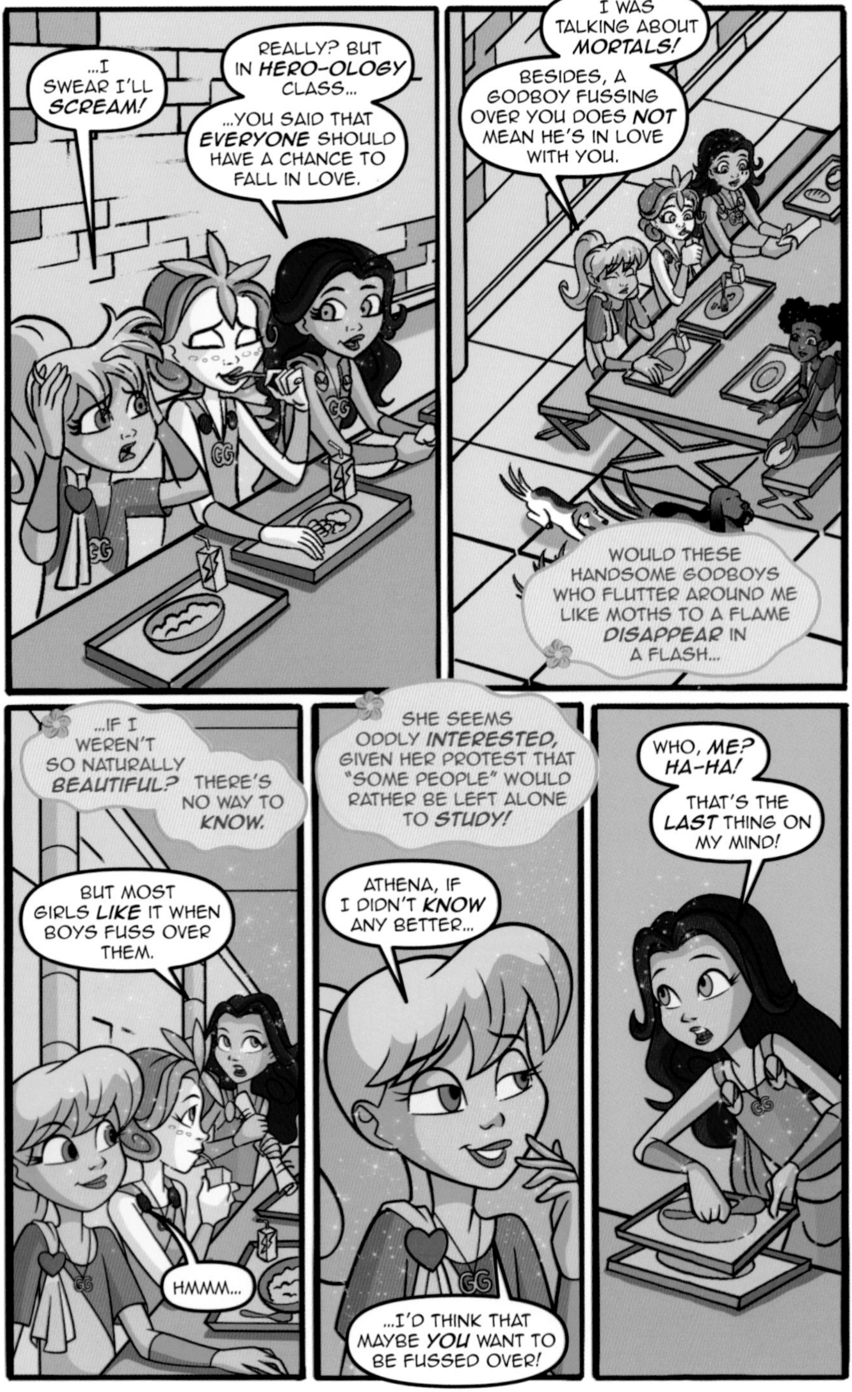
...I SWEAR I'LL SCREAM!
REALLY? BUT IN HERO-OLOGY CLASS...
...YOU SAID THAT EVERYONE SHOULD HAVE A CHANCE TO FALL IN LOVE.
I WAS TALKING ABOUT MORTALS!
BESIDES, A GODBOY FUSSING OVER YOU DOES NOT MEAN HE'S IN LOVE WITH YOU.
WOULD THESE HANDSOME GODBOYS WHO FLUTTER AROUND ME LIKE MOTHS TO A FLAME DISAPPEAR IN A FLASH...
...IF I WEREN'T SO NATURALLY BEAUTIFUL? THERE'S NO WAY TO KNOW.
BUT MOST GIRLS LIKE IT WHEN BOYS FUSS OVER THEM.
HMMM...
SHE SEEMS ODDLY INTERESTED, GIVEN HER PROTEST THAT "SOME PEOPLE" WOULD RATHER BE LEFT ALONE TO STUDY!
ATHENA, IF I DIDN'T KNOW ANY BETTER...
...I'D THINK THAT MAYBE YOU WANT TO BE FUSSED OVER!
WHO, ME? HA-HA!
THAT'S THE LAST THING ON MY MIND!

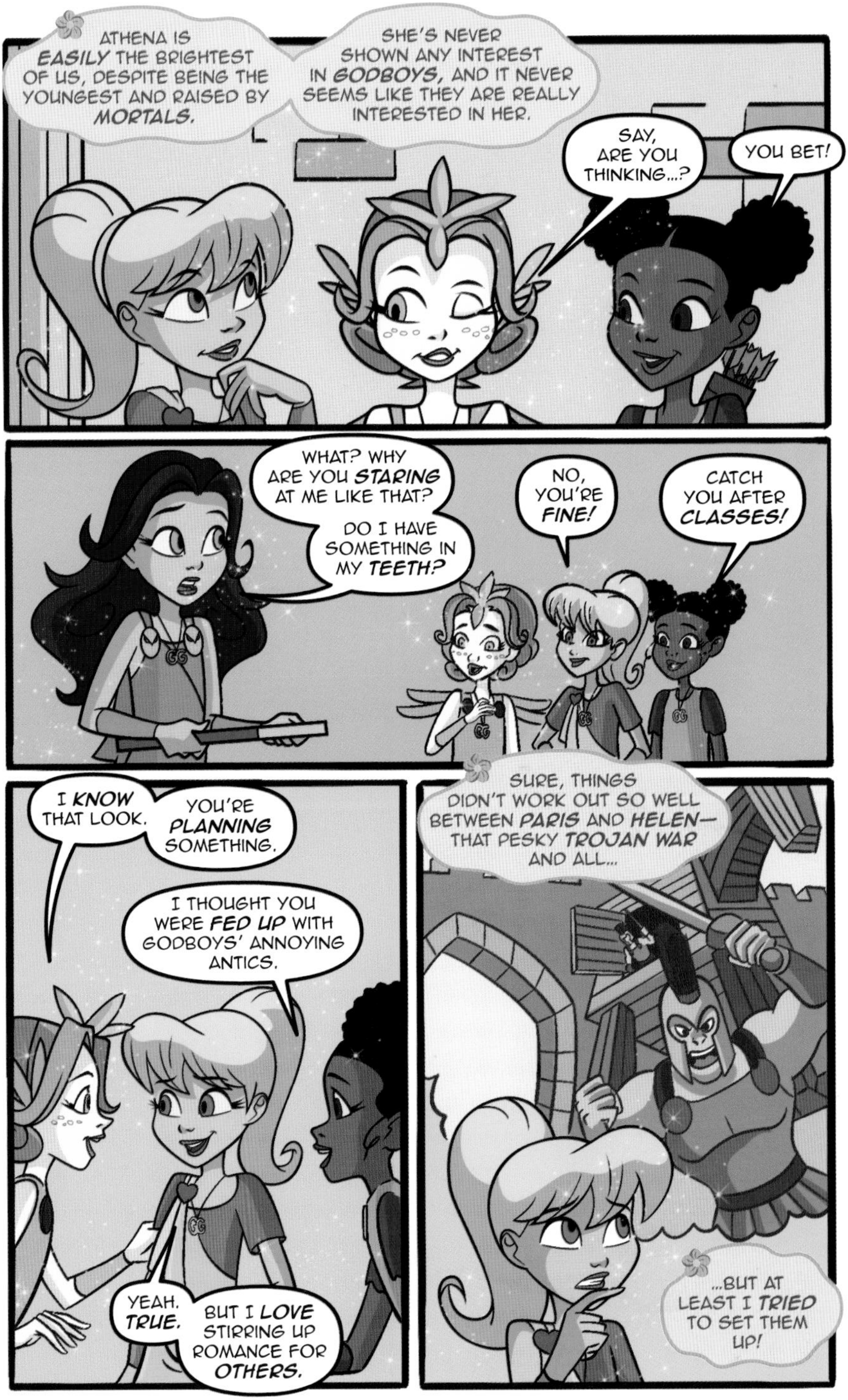
ATHENA IS EASILY THE BRIGHTEST OF US, DESPITE BEING THE YOUNGEST AND RAISED BY MORTALS.
SHE'S NEVER SHOWN ANY INTEREST IN GODBOYS, AND IT NEVER SEEMS LIKE THEY ARE REALLY INTERESTED IN HER.
SAY, ARE YOU THINKING...?
YOU BET!
WHAT? WHY ARE YOU STARING AT ME LIKE THAT?
DO I HAVE SOMETHING IN MY TEETH?
NO, YOU'RE FINE!
CATCH YOU AFTER CLASSES!
I KNOW THAT LOOK.
YOU'RE PLANNING SOMETHING.
I THOUGHT YOU WERE FED UP WITH GODBOYS' ANNOYING ANTICS.
YEAH. TRUE.
BUT I LOVE STIRRING UP ROMANCE FOR OTHERS.
SURE, THINGS DIDN'T WORK OUT SO WELL BETWEEN PARIS AND HELEN—THAT PESKY TROJAN WAR AND ALL...
...BUT AT LEAST I TRIED TO SET THEM UP!

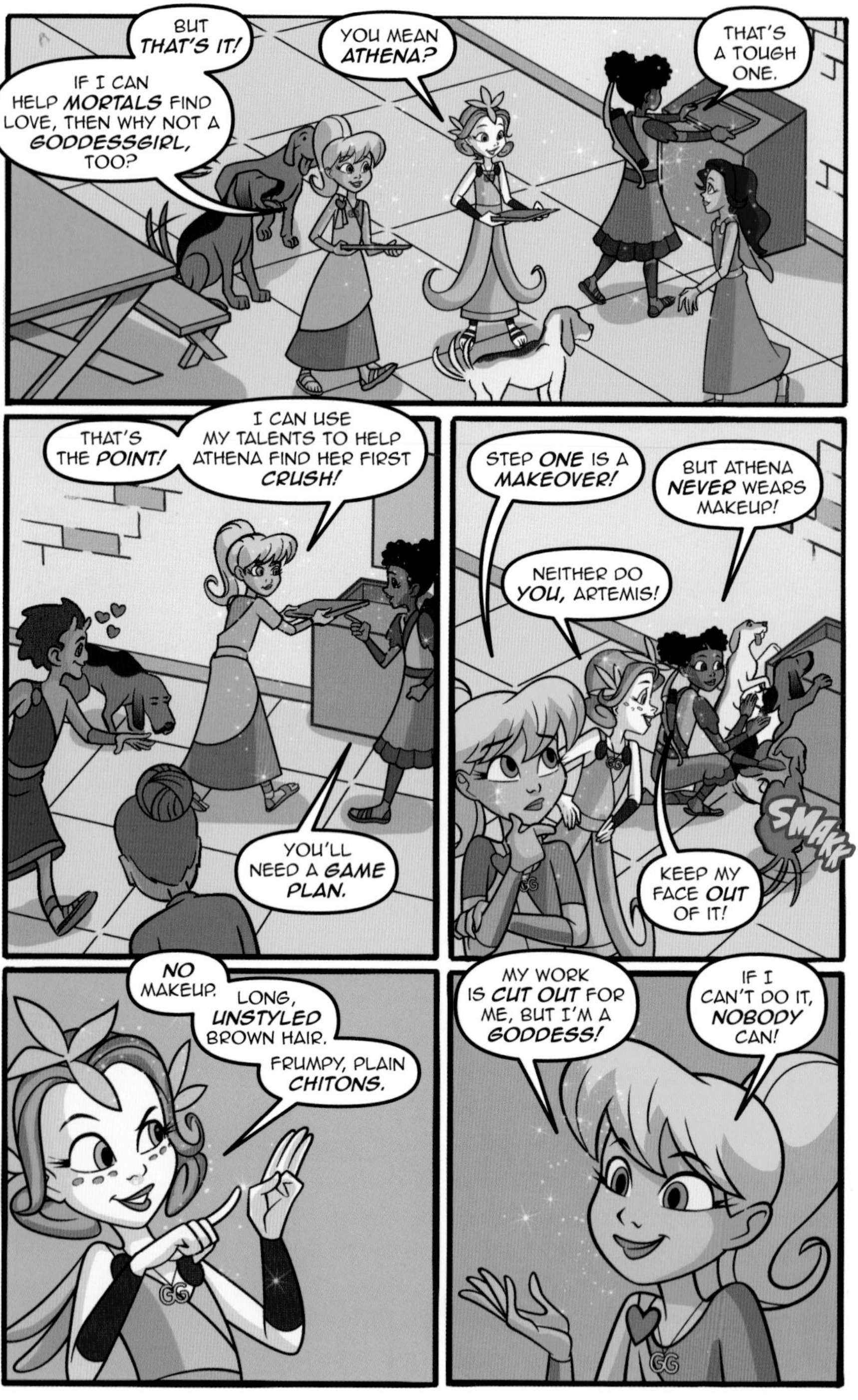
BUT THAT'S IT!
IF I CAN HELP MORTALS FIND LOVE, THEN WHY NOT A GODDESSGIRL, TOO?
YOU MEAN ATHENA?
THAT'S A TOUGH ONE.
THAT'S THE POINT!
I CAN USE MY TALENTS TO HELP ATHENA FIND HER FIRST CRUSH!
YOU'LL NEED A GAME PLAN.
STEP ONE IS A MAKEOVER!
BUT ATHENA NEVER WEARS MAKEUP!
NEITHER DO YOU, ARTEMIS!
SMAKK
KEEP MY FACE OUT OF IT!
NO MAKEUP.
LONG, UNSTYLED BROWN HAIR.
FRUMPY, PLAIN CHITONS.
MY WORK IS CUT OUT FOR ME, BUT I'M A GODDESS!
IF I CAN'T DO IT, NOBODY CAN!

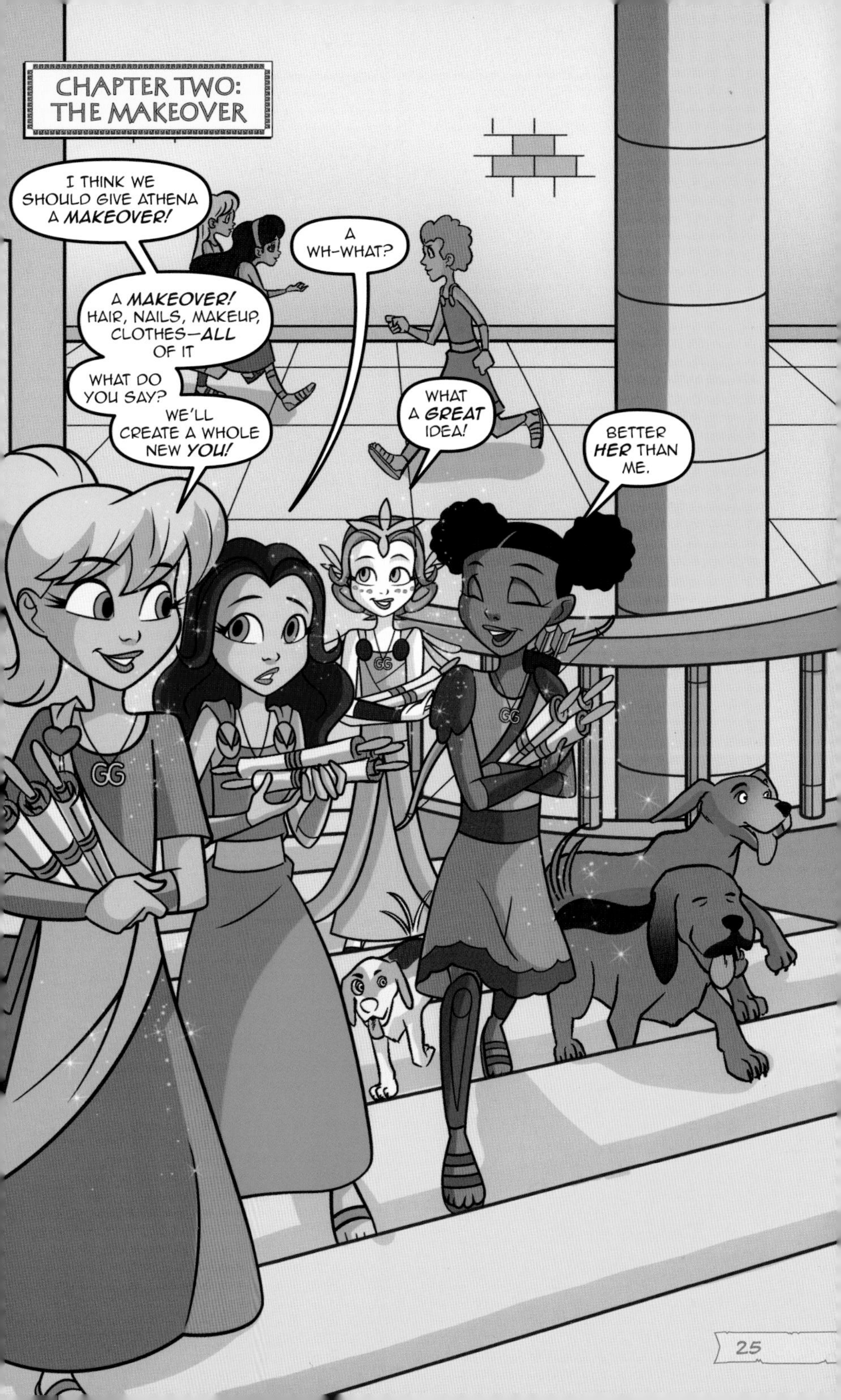
CHAPTER TWO: THE MAKEOVER
I THINK WE SHOULD GIVE ATHENA A *MAKEOVER!*
A WH-WHAT?
A *MAKEOVER!* HAIR, NAILS, MAKEUP, CLOTHES—*ALL* OF IT
WHAT DO YOU SAY?
WE'LL CREATE A WHOLE NEW *YOU!*
WHAT A *GREAT* IDEA!
BETTER *HER* THAN ME.

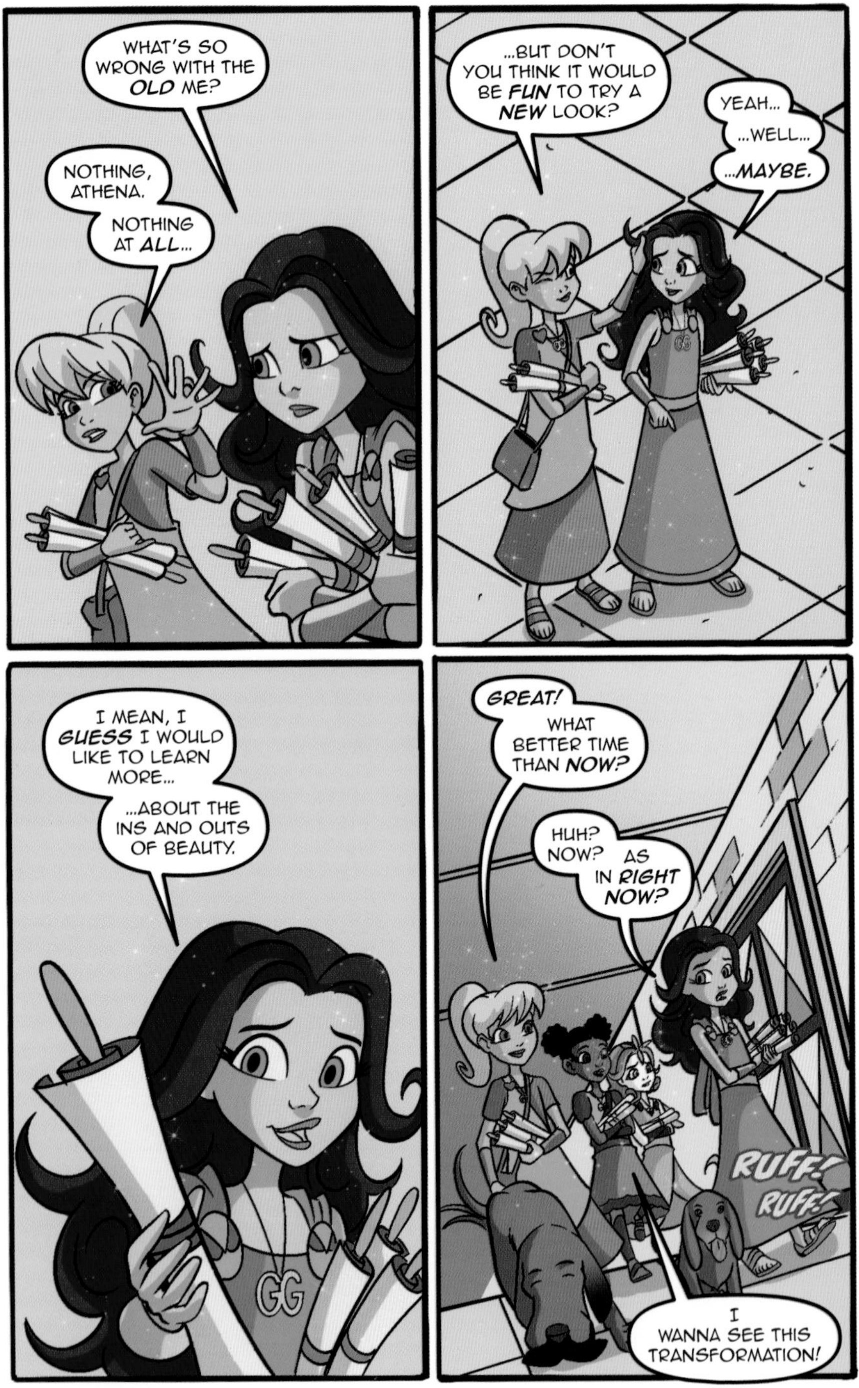

WHAT'S SO WRONG WITH THE OLD ME?
NOTHING, ATHENA.
NOTHING AT ALL...
...BUT DON'T YOU THINK IT WOULD BE FUN TO TRY A NEW LOOK?
YEAH...
...WELL...
...MAYBE.
I MEAN, I GUESS I WOULD LIKE TO LEARN MORE...
...ABOUT THE INS AND OUTS OF BEAUTY.
GREAT!
WHAT BETTER TIME THAN NOW?
HUH? NOW?
AS IN RIGHT NOW?
RUFF!
RUFF!
I WANNA SEE THIS TRANSFORMATION!

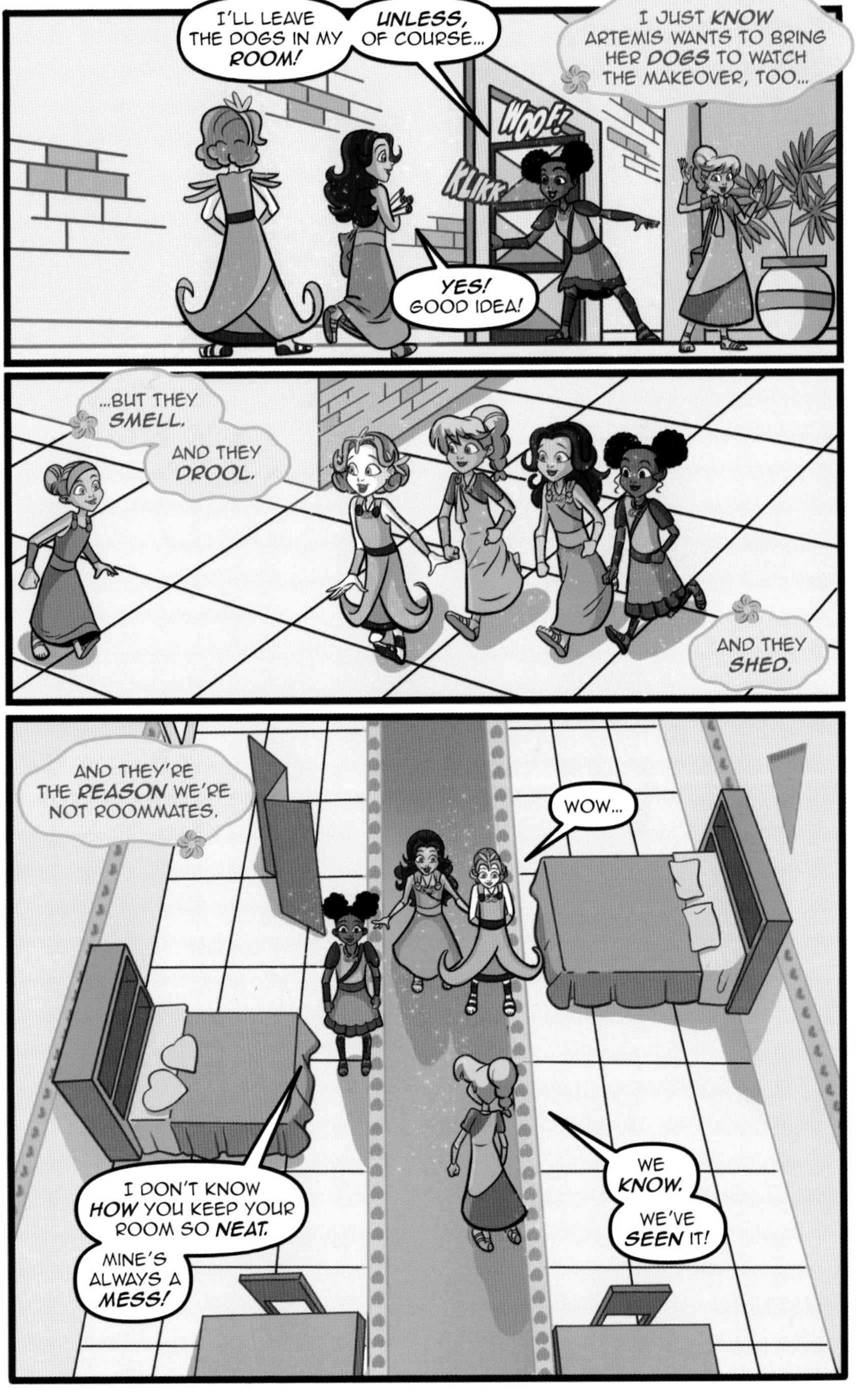
I'LL LEAVE THE DOGS IN MY ROOM!
UNLESS, OF COURSE...
I JUST KNOW ARTEMIS WANTS TO BRING HER DOGS TO WATCH THE MAKEOVER, TOO...
WOOF!
KLIKK
YES! GOOD IDEA!
...BUT THEY SMELL.
AND THEY DROOL.
AND THEY SHED.
AND THEY'RE THE REASON WE'RE NOT ROOMMATES.
WOW...
I DON'T KNOW HOW YOU KEEP YOUR ROOM SO NEAT.
MINE'S ALWAYS A MESS!
WE KNOW.
WE'VE SEEN IT!

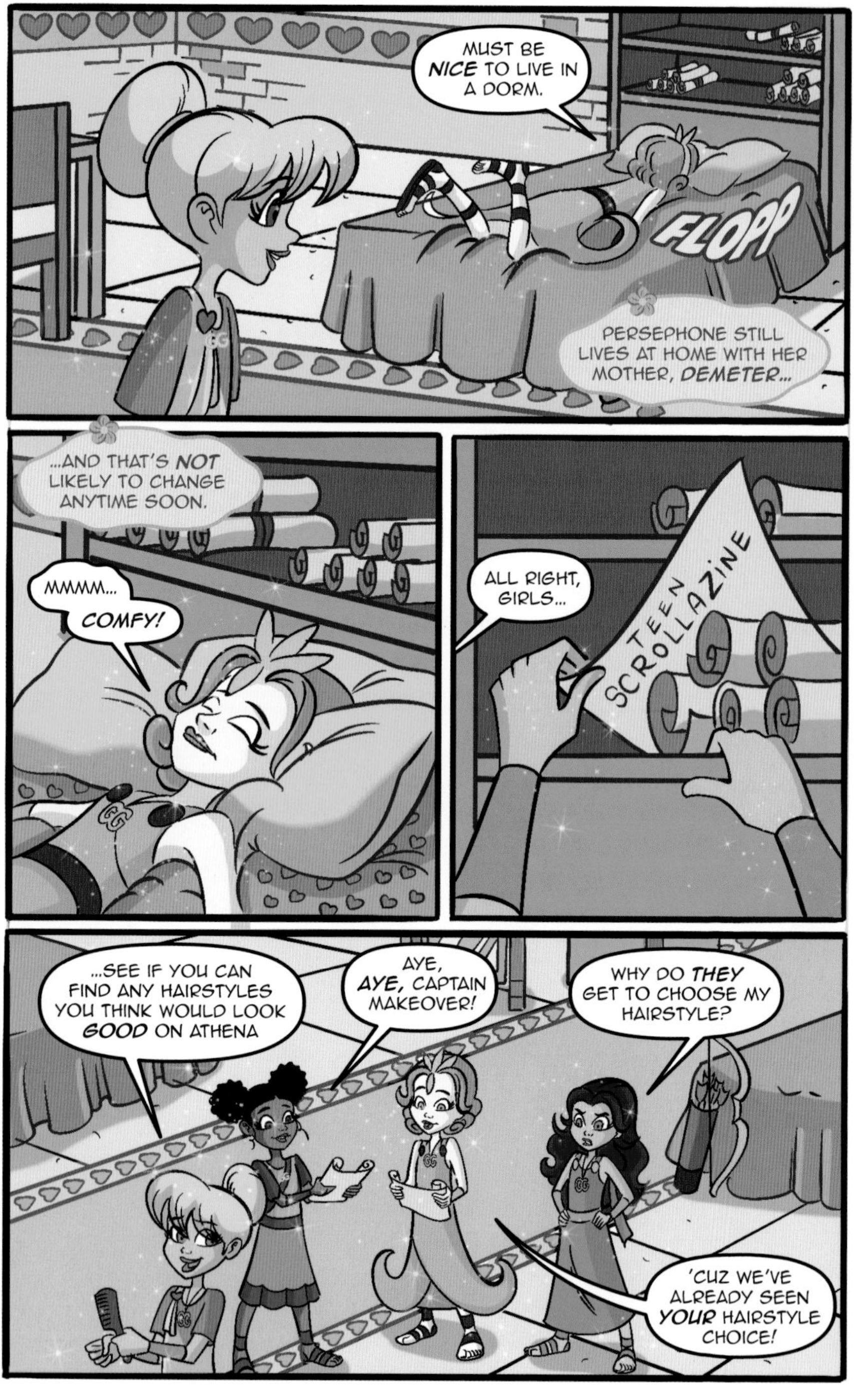
MUST BE NICE TO LIVE IN A DORM.
FLOPP
PERSEPHONE STILL LIVES AT HOME WITH HER MOTHER, DEMETER...
...AND THAT'S NOT LIKELY TO CHANGE ANYTIME SOON.
MMMM... COMFY!
ALL RIGHT, GIRLS...
TEEN SCROLLAZINE
...SEE IF YOU CAN FIND ANY HAIRSTYLES YOU THINK WOULD LOOK GOOD ON ATHENA
AYE, AYE, CAPTAIN MAKEOVER!
WHY DO THEY GET TO CHOOSE MY HAIRSTYLE?
'CUZ WE'VE ALREADY SEEN YOUR HAIRSTYLE CHOICE!

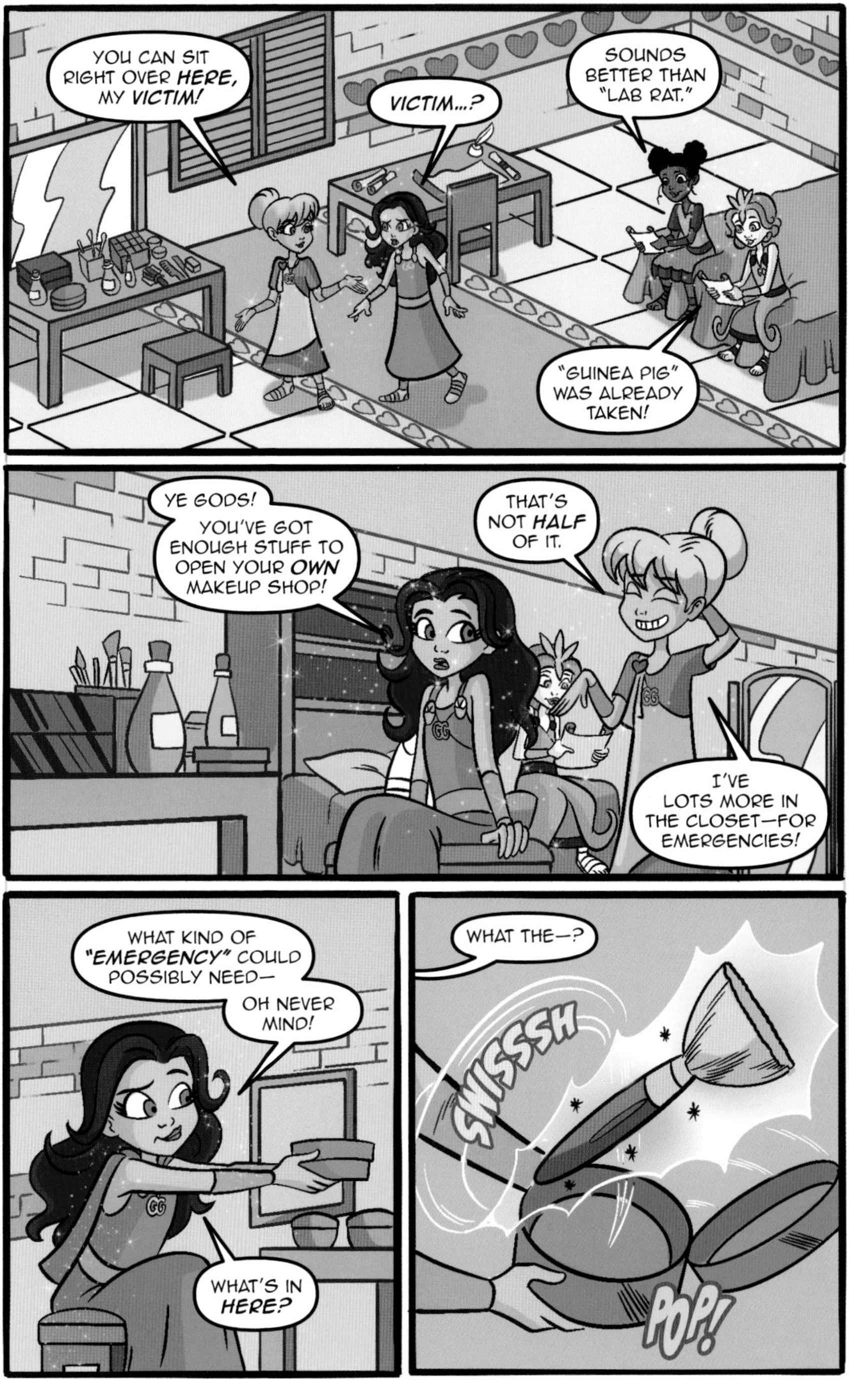
YOU CAN SIT RIGHT OVER HERE, MY VICTIM!
VICTIM...?
SOUNDS BETTER THAN "LAB RAT."
"GUINEA PIG" WAS ALREADY TAKEN!
YE GODS!
YOU'VE GOT ENOUGH STUFF TO OPEN YOUR OWN MAKEUP SHOP!
THAT'S NOT HALF OF IT.
I'VE LOTS MORE IN THE CLOSET—FOR EMERGENCIES!
WHAT KIND OF "EMERGENCY" COULD POSSIBLY NEED—
OH NEVER MIND!
WHAT'S IN HERE?
WHAT THE—?
SWISSSH
POP!

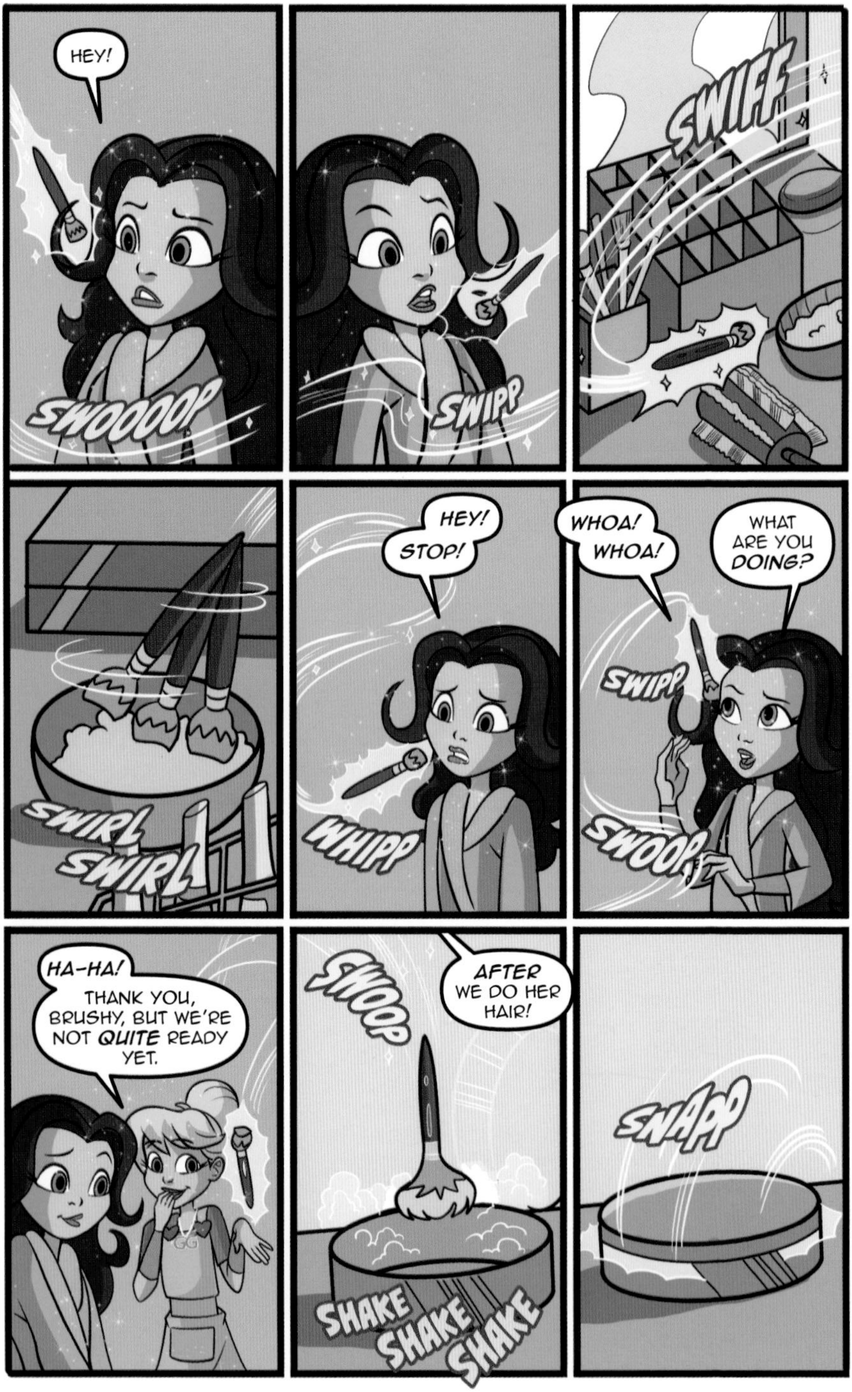
HEY!
SWOOOOP
SWIPP
SWIFF
SWIRL
SWIRL
HEY! STOP!
WHIPP
WHOA! WHOA!
WHAT ARE YOU DOING?
SWIPP
SWOOP
HA-HA! THANK YOU, BRUSHY, BUT WE'RE NOT QUITE READY YET.
SWOOP
AFTER WE DO HER HAIR!
SHAKE
SHAKE
SHAKE
SNAPP

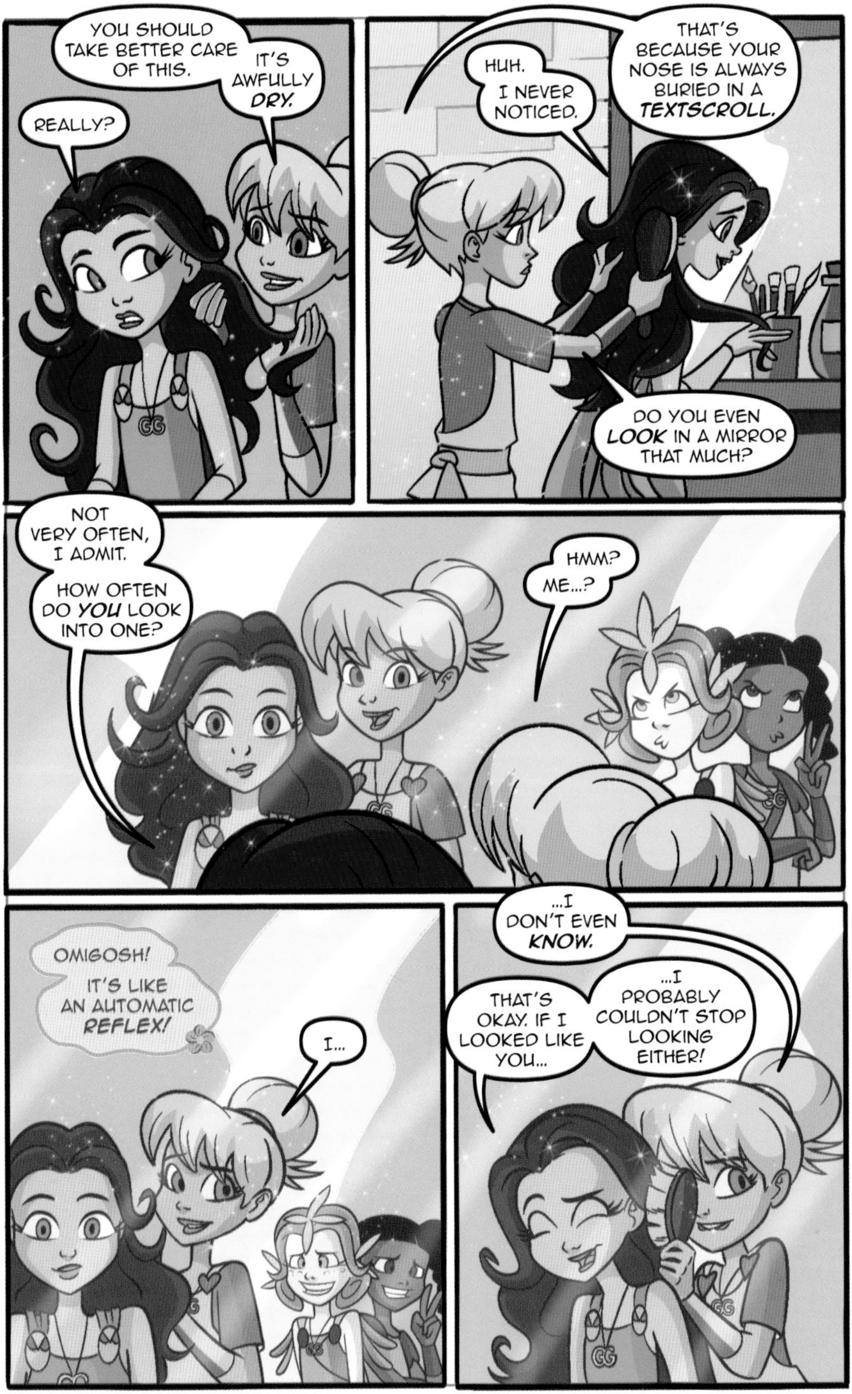

YOU SHOULD TAKE BETTER CARE OF THIS.
IT'S AWFULLY DRY.
REALLY?
HUH. I NEVER NOTICED.
THAT'S BECAUSE YOUR NOSE IS ALWAYS BURIED IN A TEXTSCROLL.
DO YOU EVEN LOOK IN A MIRROR THAT MUCH?
NOT VERY OFTEN, I ADMIT.
HOW OFTEN DO YOU LOOK INTO ONE?
HMM? ME...?
OMIGOSH! IT'S LIKE AN AUTOMATIC REFLEX!
I...
...I DON'T EVEN KNOW.
THAT'S OKAY. IF I LOOKED LIKE YOU...
...I PROBABLY COULDN'T STOP LOOKING EITHER!

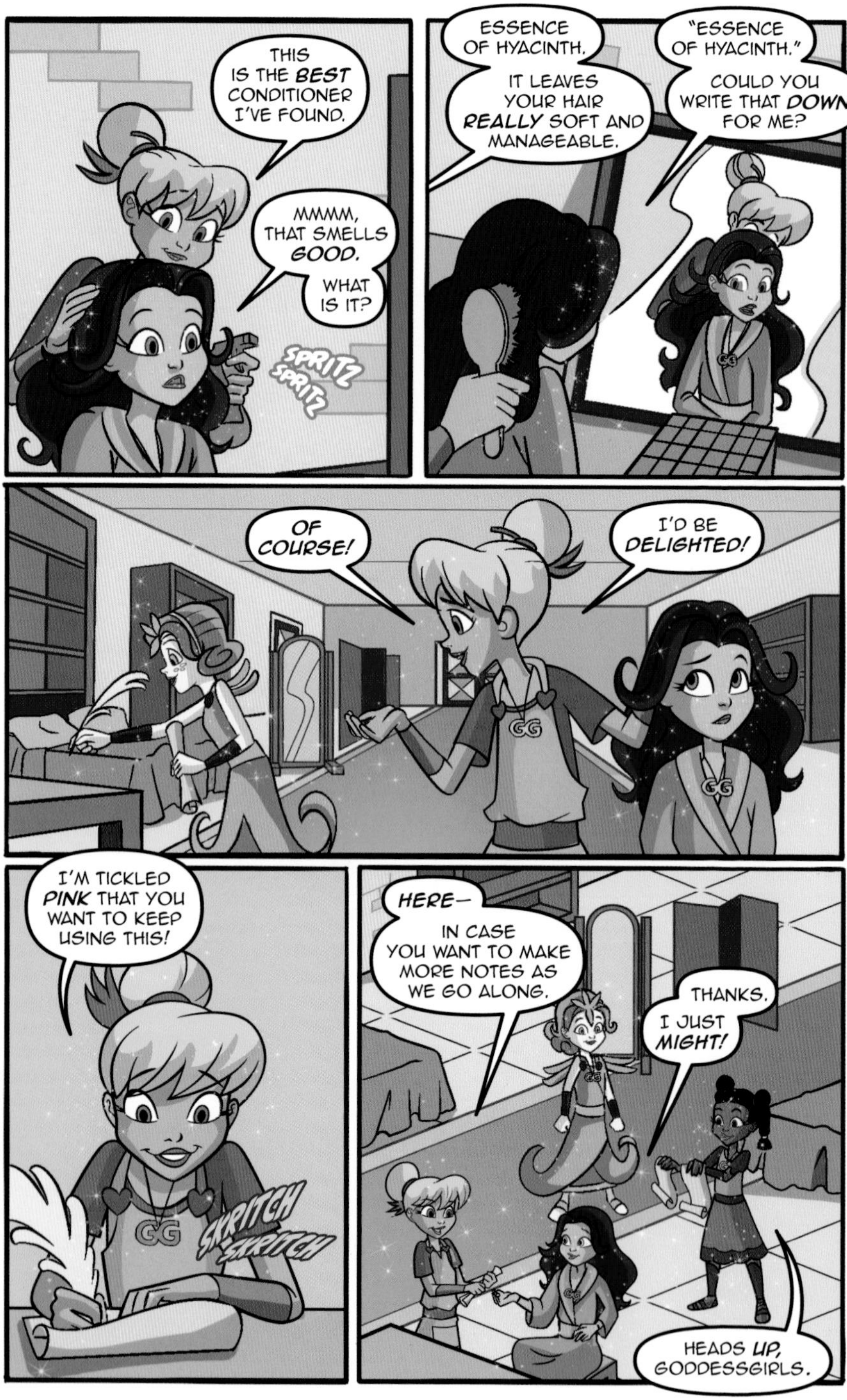

THIS IS THE BEST CONDITIONER I'VE FOUND.
MMMM, THAT SMELLS GOOD.
WHAT IS IT?
SPRITZ SPRITZ
ESSENCE OF HYACINTH.
IT LEAVES YOUR HAIR REALLY SOFT AND MANAGEABLE.
"ESSENCE OF HYACINTH."
COULD YOU WRITE THAT DOWN FOR ME?
OF COURSE!
I'D BE DELIGHTED!
I'M TICKLED PINK THAT YOU WANT TO KEEP USING THIS!
SKRITCH SKRITCH
HERE—
IN CASE YOU WANT TO MAKE MORE NOTES AS WE GO ALONG.
THANKS.
I JUST MIGHT!
HEADS UP, GODDESSGIRLS.

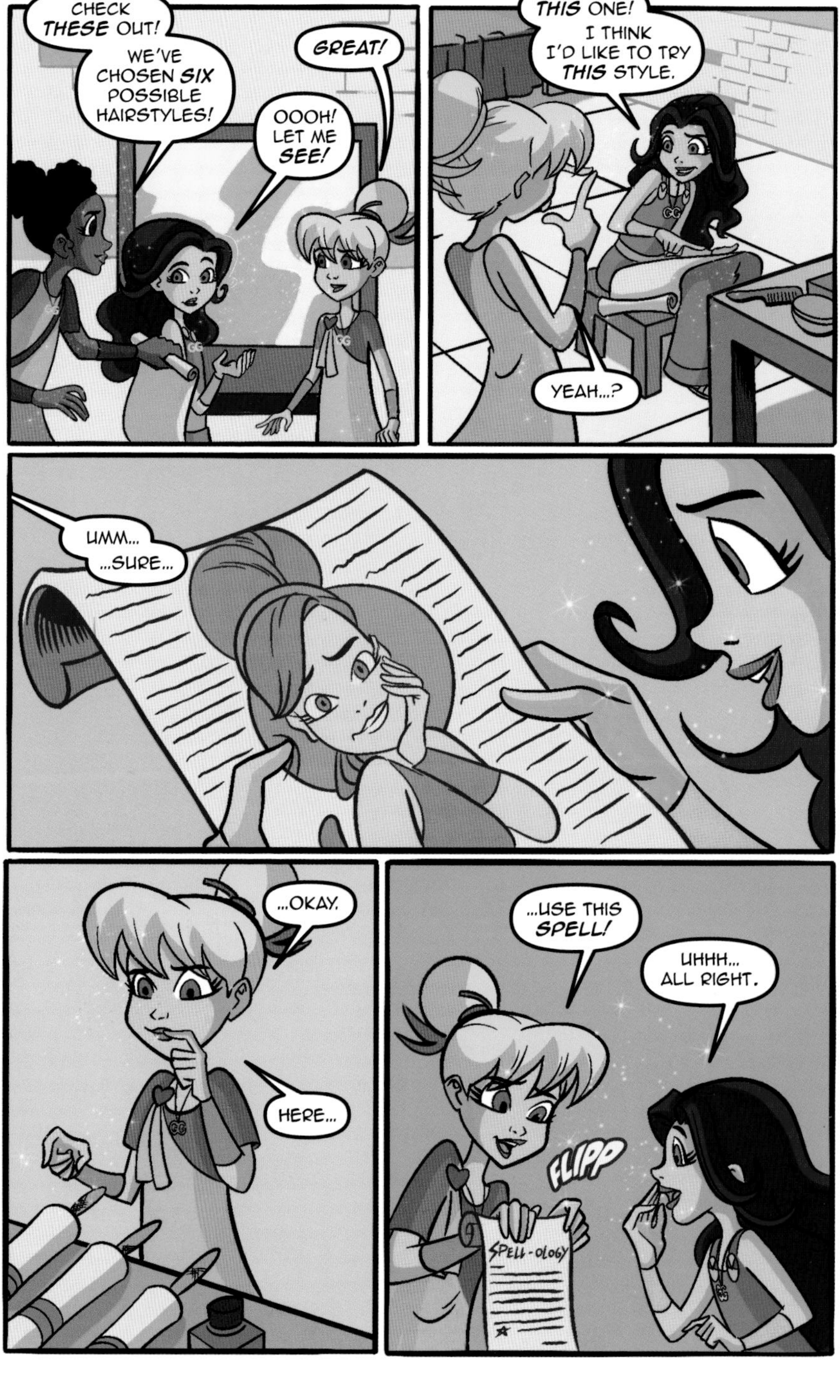
CHECK THESE OUT!
WE'VE CHOSEN SIX POSSIBLE HAIRSTYLES!
OOOH! LET ME SEE!
GREAT!
THIS ONE!
I THINK I'D LIKE TO TRY THIS STYLE.
YEAH...?
UMM... ...SURE...
...OKAY.
HERE...
...USE THIS SPELL!
UHHH... ALL RIGHT.
FLIPP
SPELL-OLOGY

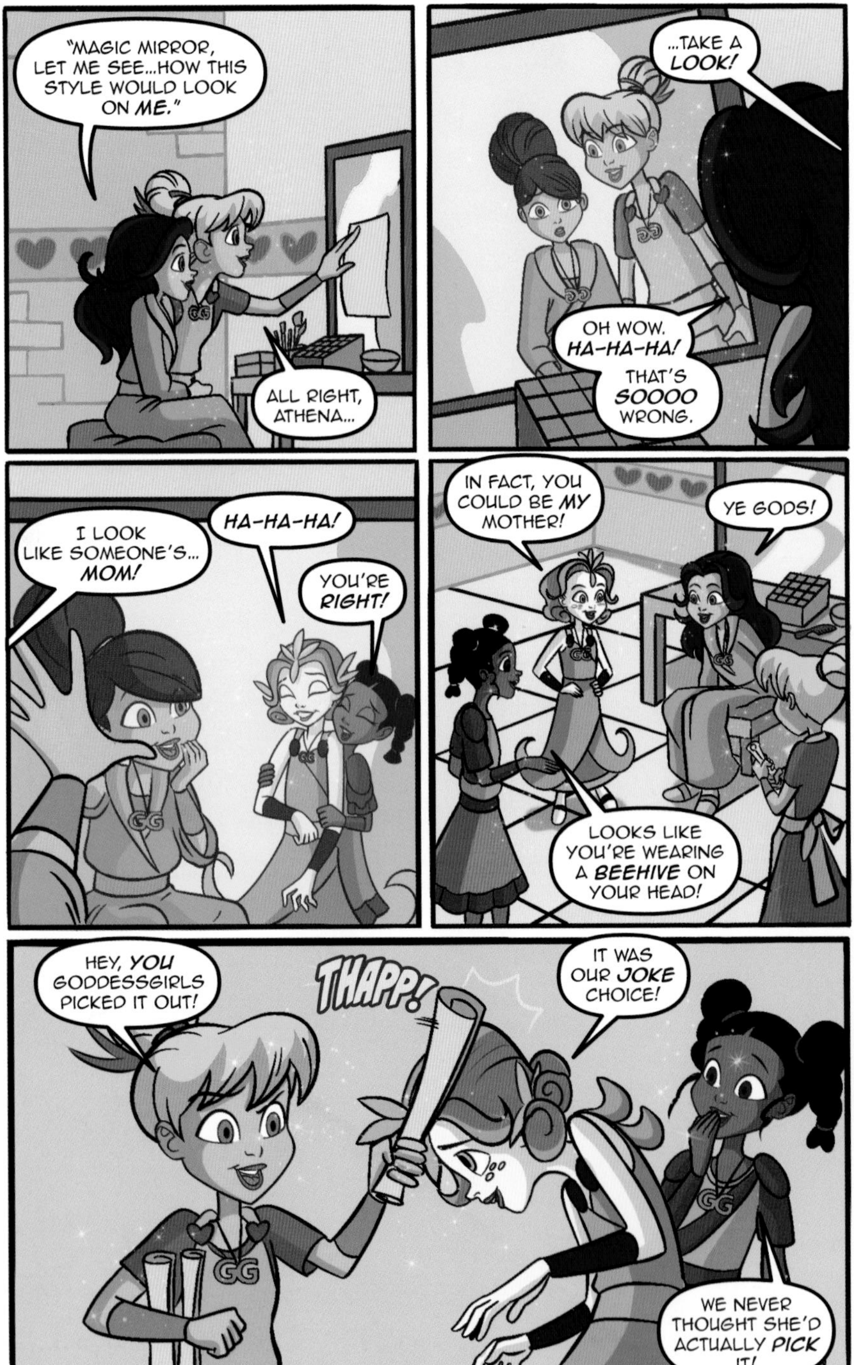
"MAGIC MIRROR, LET ME SEE...HOW THIS STYLE WOULD LOOK ON ME."
ALL RIGHT, ATHENA...
...TAKE A LOOK!
OH WOW. HA-HA-HA! THAT'S SOOOO WRONG.
I LOOK LIKE SOMEONE'S... MOM!
HA-HA-HA!
YOU'RE RIGHT!
IN FACT, YOU COULD BE MY MOTHER!
YE GODS!
LOOKS LIKE YOU'RE WEARING A BEEHIVE ON YOUR HEAD!
HEY, YOU GODDESSGIRLS PICKED IT OUT!
THAPP!
IT WAS OUR JOKE CHOICE!
WE NEVER THOUGHT SHE'D ACTUALLY PICK IT!

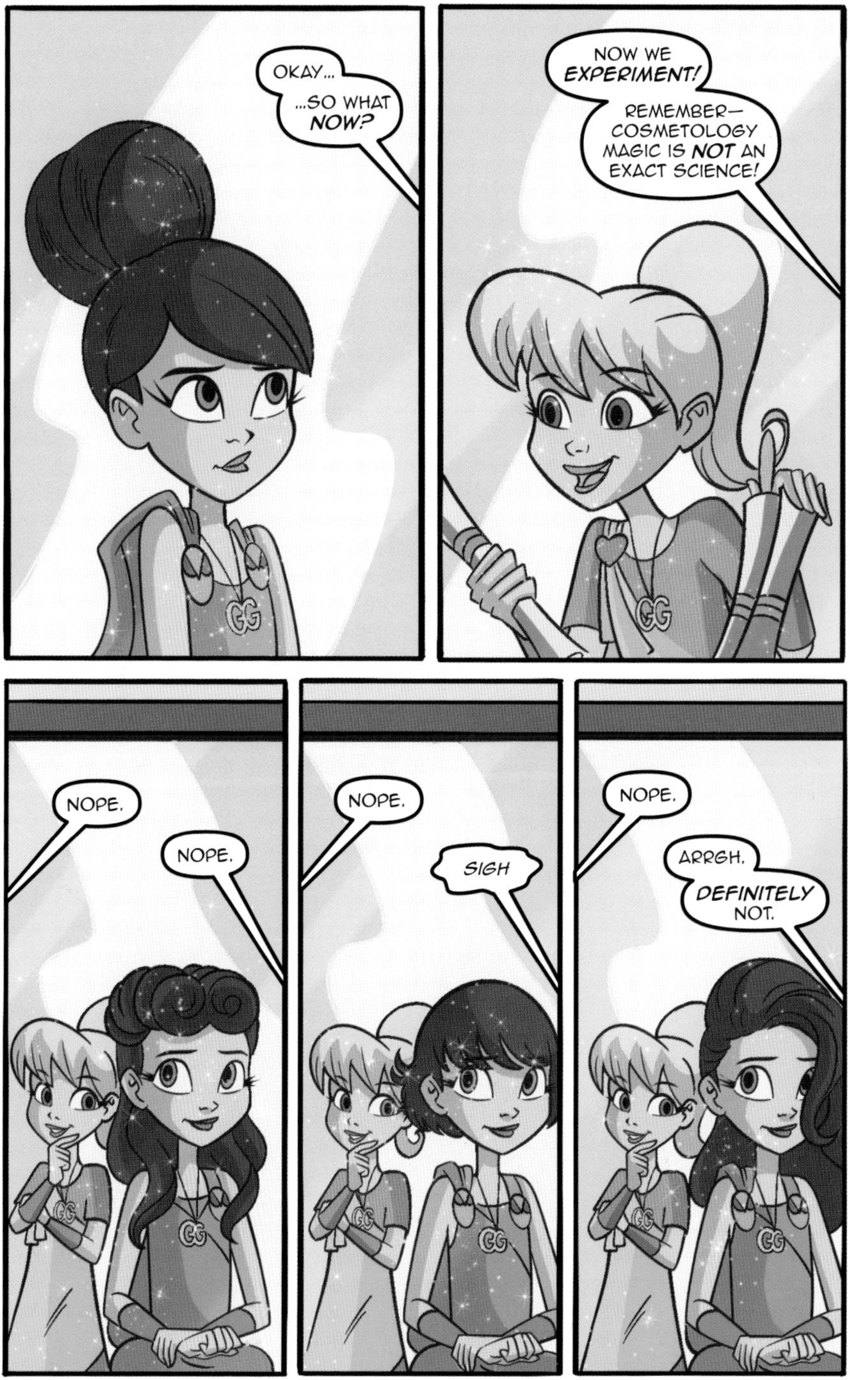
OKAY...
...SO WHAT NOW?
NOW WE EXPERIMENT!
REMEMBER— COSMETOLOGY MAGIC IS NOT AN EXACT SCIENCE!
NOPE.
NOPE.
NOPE.
SIGH
NOPE.
ARRGH.
DEFINITELY NOT.

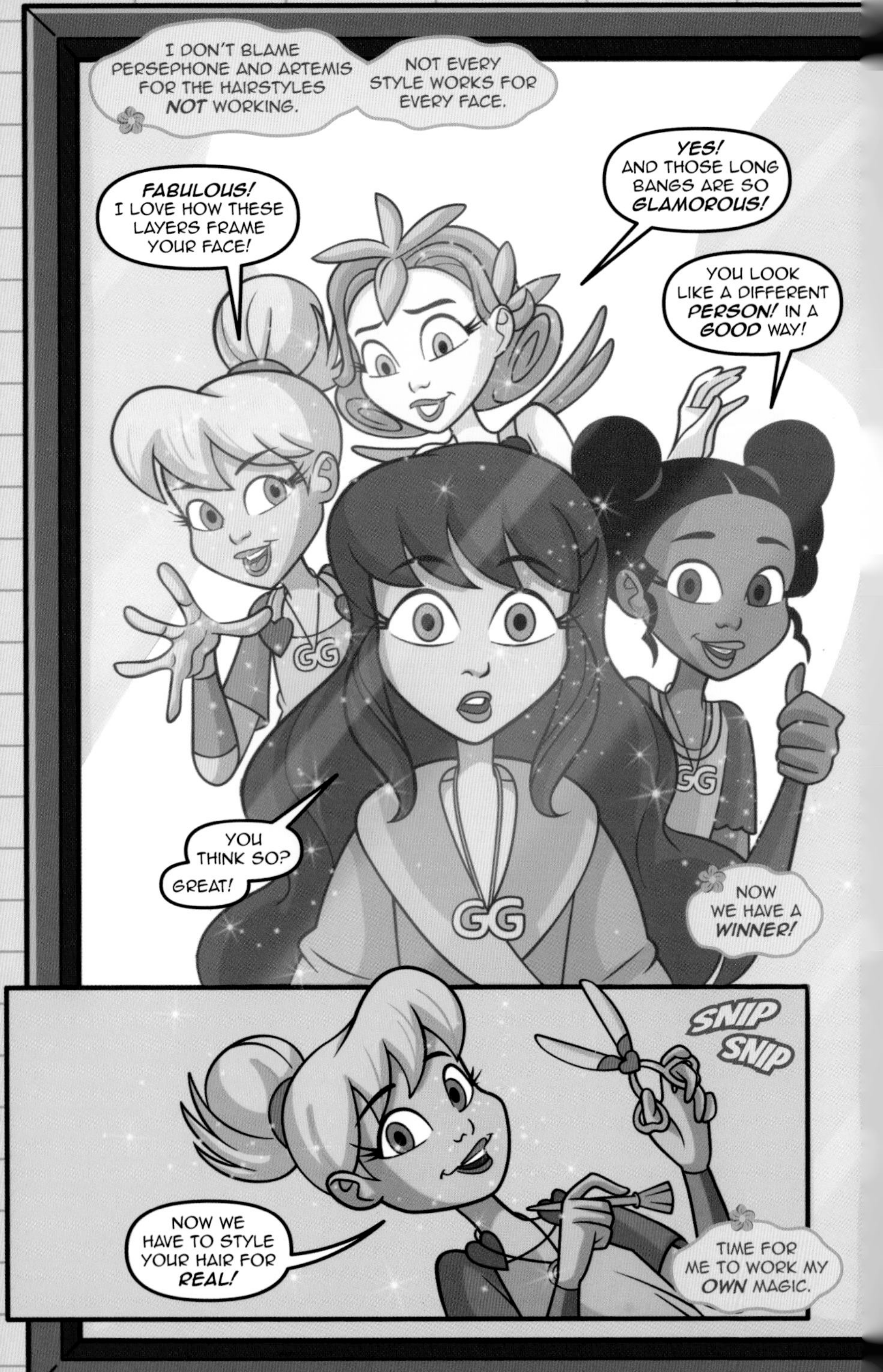
I DON'T BLAME PERSEPHONE AND ARTEMIS FOR THE HAIRSTYLES *NOT* WORKING.
NOT EVERY STYLE WORKS FOR EVERY FACE.
FABULOUS! I LOVE HOW THESE LAYERS FRAME YOUR FACE!
YES! AND THOSE LONG BANGS ARE SO *GLAMOROUS!*
YOU LOOK LIKE A DIFFERENT *PERSON!* IN A *GOOD* WAY!
YOU THINK SO?
GREAT!
NOW WE HAVE A *WINNER!*
SNIP SNIP
NOW WE HAVE TO STYLE YOUR HAIR FOR *REAL!*
TIME FOR ME TO WORK MY *OWN* MAGIC.

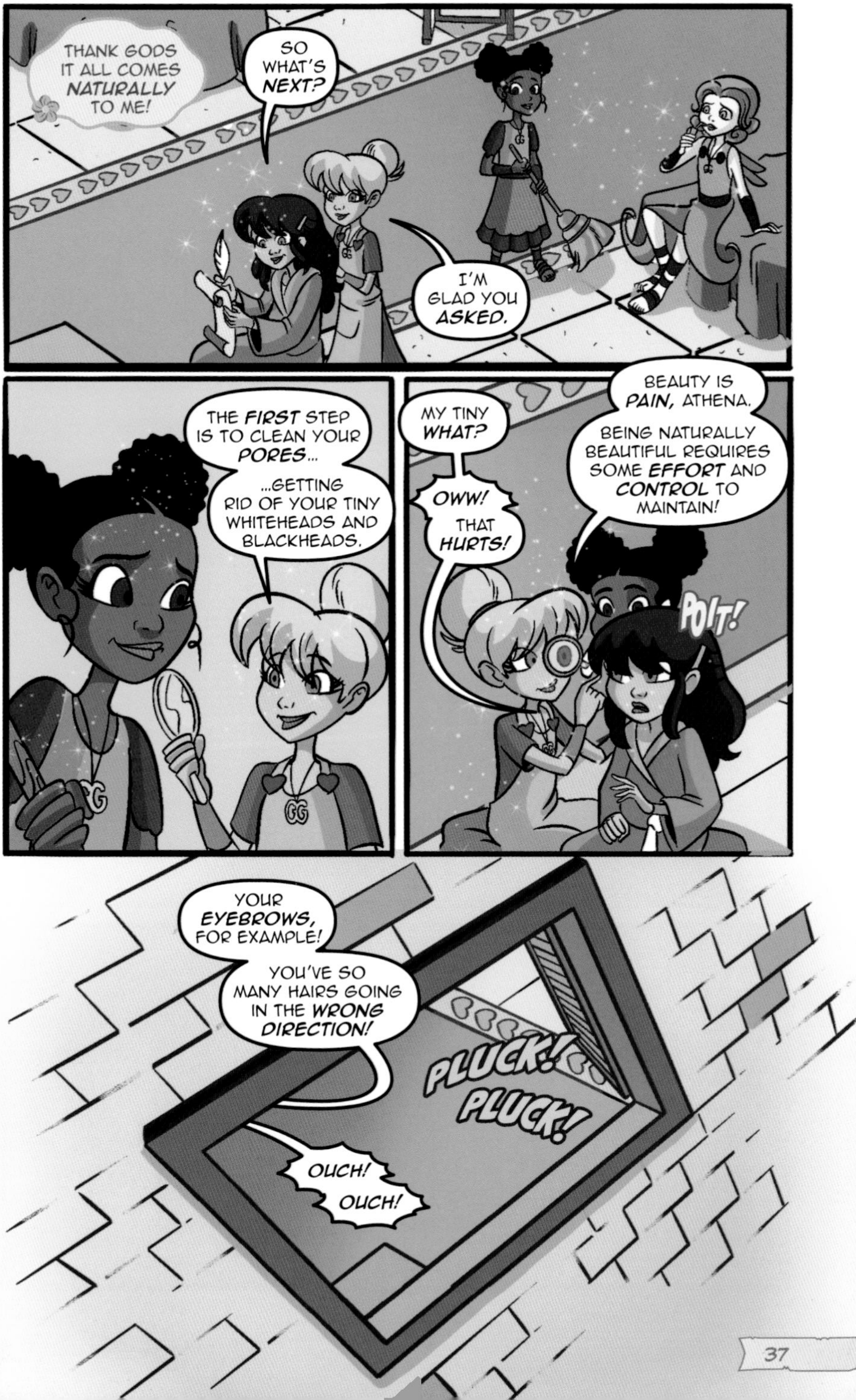
THANK GODS IT ALL COMES NATURALLY TO ME!
SO WHAT'S NEXT?
I'M GLAD YOU ASKED.
THE FIRST STEP IS TO CLEAN YOUR PORES...
...GETTING RID OF YOUR TINY WHITEHEADS AND BLACKHEADS.
MY TINY WHAT?
OWW! THAT HURTS!
BEAUTY IS PAIN, ATHENA.
BEING NATURALLY BEAUTIFUL REQUIRES SOME EFFORT AND CONTROL TO MAINTAIN!
POIT!
YOUR EYEBROWS, FOR EXAMPLE!
YOU'VE SO MANY HAIRS GOING IN THE WRONG DIRECTION!
PLUCK! PLUCK!
OUCH! OUCH!

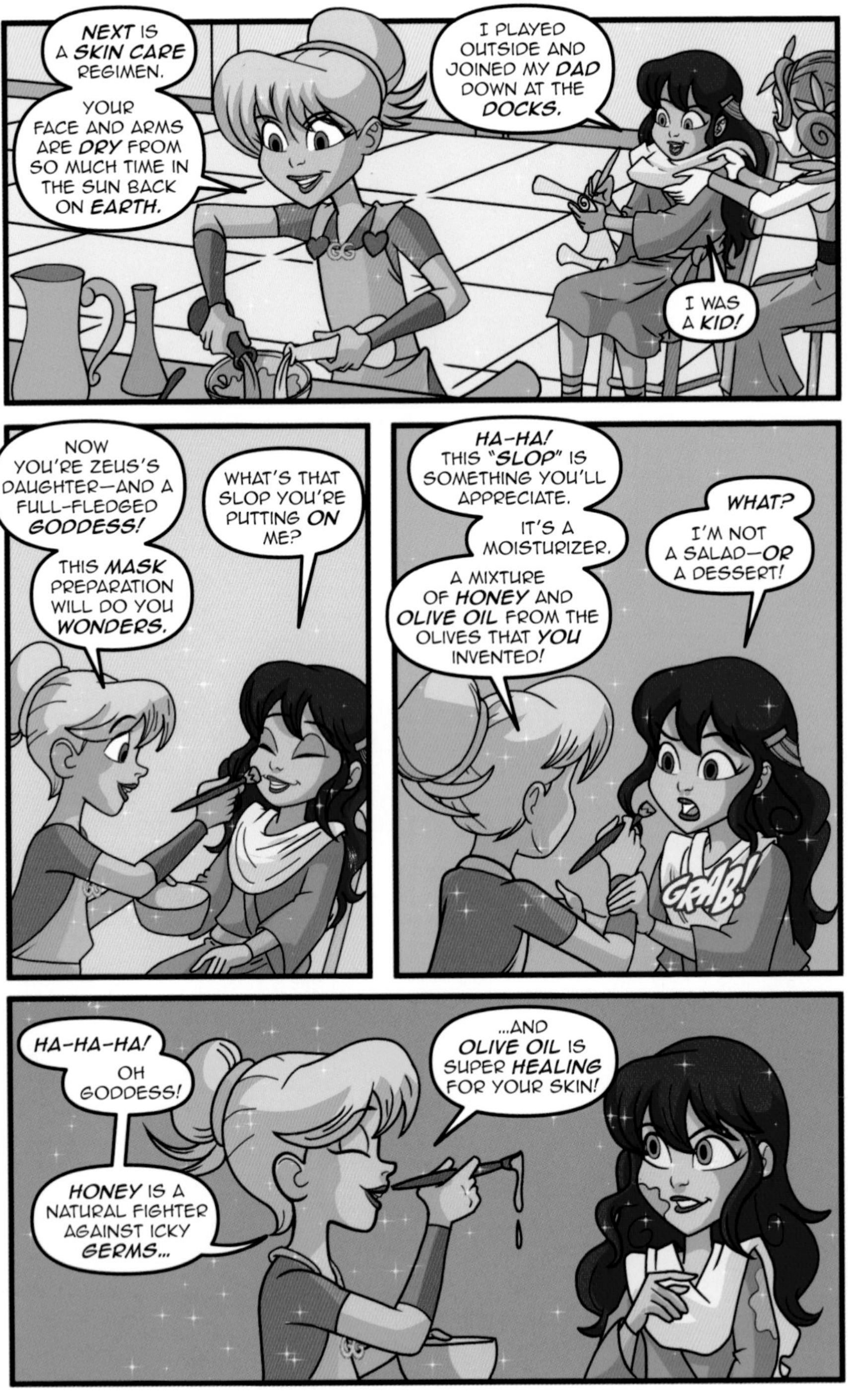

NEXT IS A SKIN CARE REGIMEN.
YOUR FACE AND ARMS ARE DRY FROM SO MUCH TIME IN THE SUN BACK ON EARTH.
I PLAYED OUTSIDE AND JOINED MY DAD DOWN AT THE DOCKS.
I WAS A KID!
NOW YOU'RE ZEUS'S DAUGHTER—AND A FULL-FLEDGED GODDESS!
THIS MASK PREPARATION WILL DO YOU WONDERS.
WHAT'S THAT SLOP YOU'RE PUTTING ON ME?
HA-HA! THIS "SLOP" IS SOMETHING YOU'LL APPRECIATE.
IT'S A MOISTURIZER.
A MIXTURE OF HONEY AND OLIVE OIL FROM THE OLIVES THAT YOU INVENTED!
WHAT? I'M NOT A SALAD—OR A DESSERT!
GRAB!
HA-HA-HA! OH GODDESS!
HONEY IS A NATURAL FIGHTER AGAINST ICKY GERMS...
...AND OLIVE OIL IS SUPER HEALING FOR YOUR SKIN!

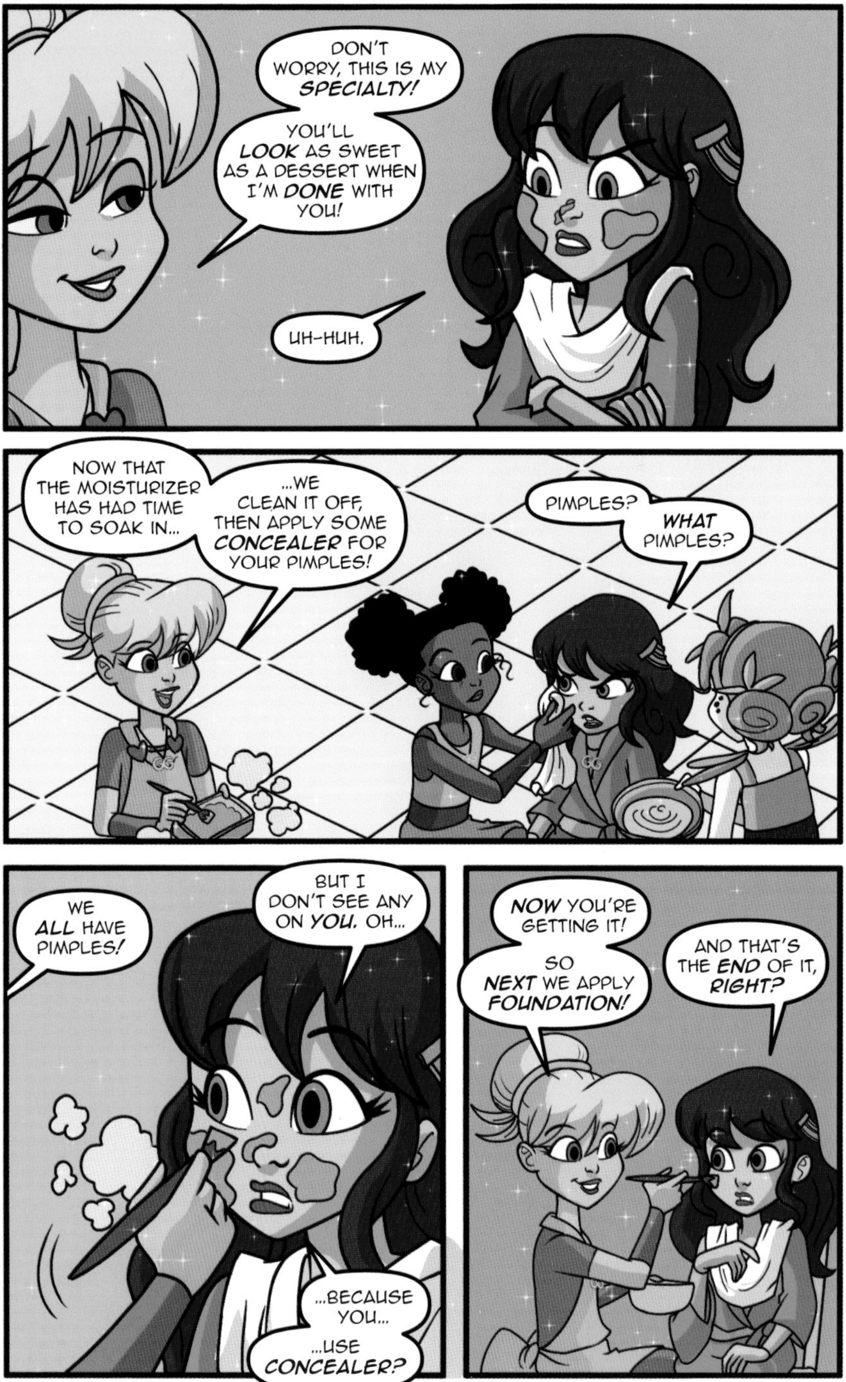

DON'T WORRY, THIS IS MY SPECIALTY!
YOU'LL LOOK AS SWEET AS A DESSERT WHEN I'M DONE WITH YOU!
UH-HUH.
NOW THAT THE MOISTURIZER HAS HAD TIME TO SOAK IN...
...WE CLEAN IT OFF, THEN APPLY SOME CONCEALER FOR YOUR PIMPLES!
PIMPLES?
WHAT PIMPLES?
WE ALL HAVE PIMPLES!
BUT I DON'T SEE ANY ON YOU. OH...
...BECAUSE YOU...
...USE CONCEALER?
NOW YOU'RE GETTING IT!
SO NEXT WE APPLY FOUNDATION!
AND THAT'S THE END OF IT, RIGHT?

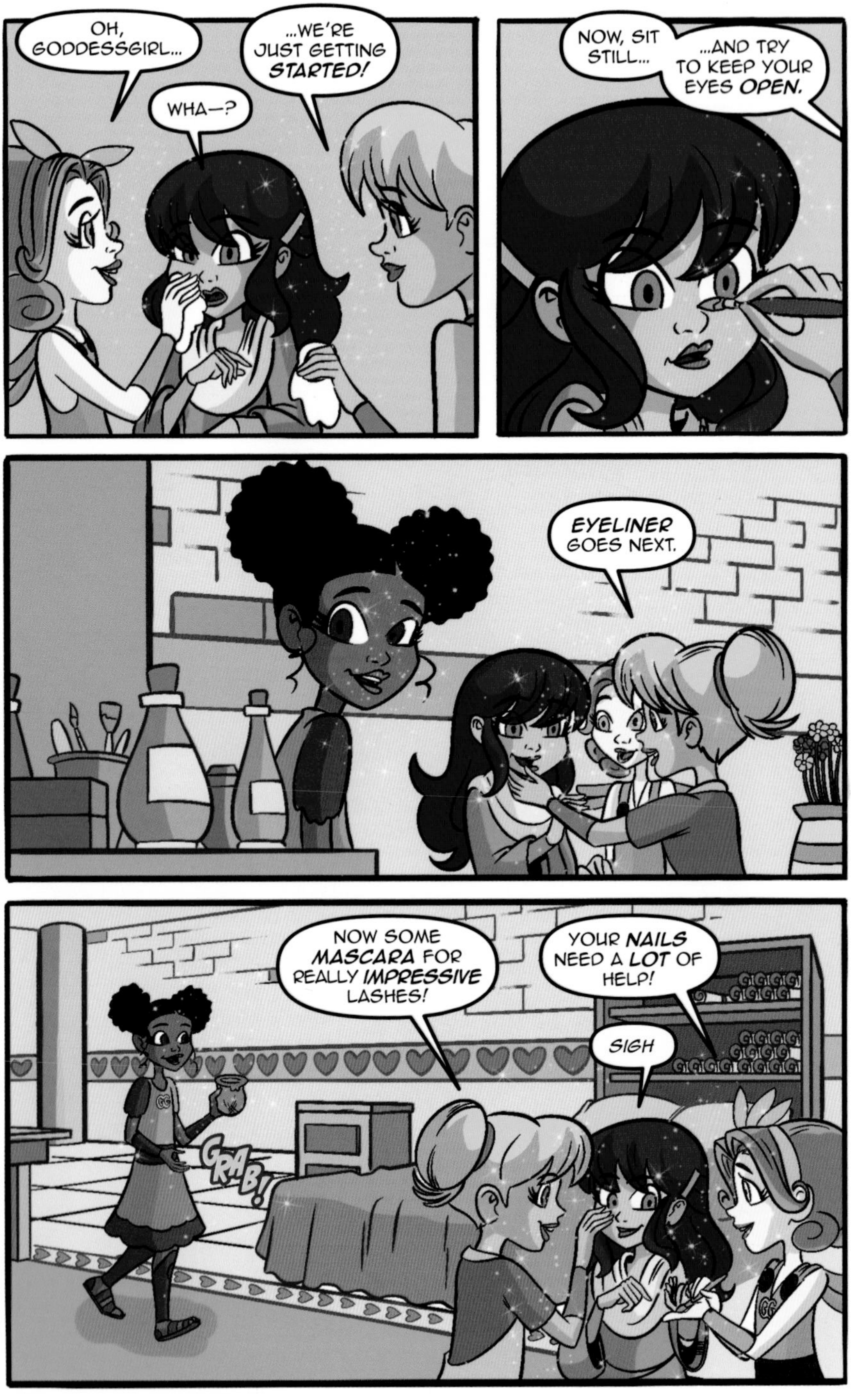
OH, GODDESSGIRL...
WHA—?
...WE'RE JUST GETTING STARTED!
NOW, SIT STILL...
...AND TRY TO KEEP YOUR EYES OPEN.
EYELINER GOES NEXT.
NOW SOME MASCARA FOR REALLY IMPRESSIVE LASHES!
YOUR NAILS NEED A LOT OF HELP!
SIGH
GRAB!

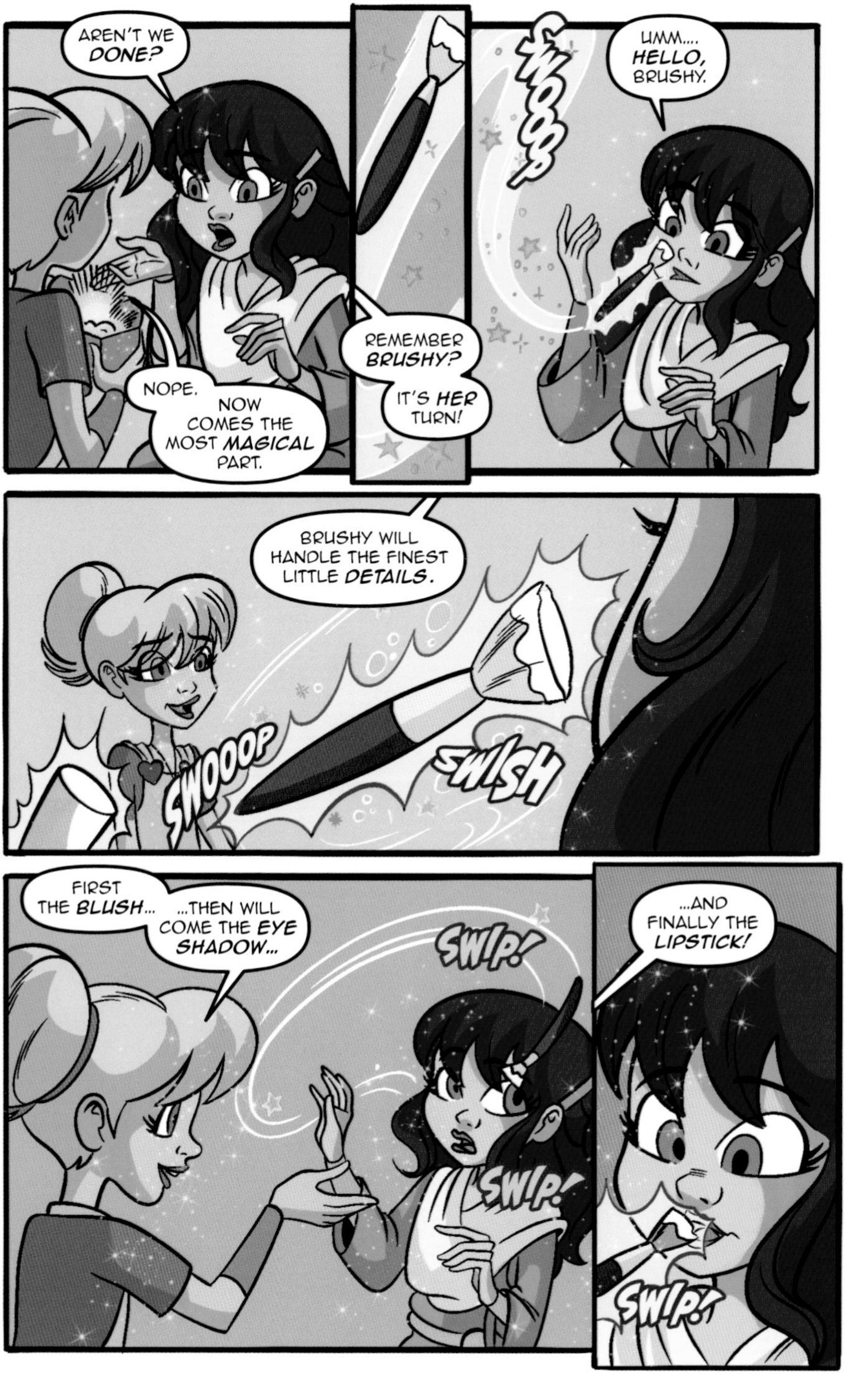
AREN'T WE DONE?
NOPE.
NOW COMES THE MOST MAGICAL PART.
REMEMBER BRUSHY?
IT'S HER TURN!
SWOOOP
UMM.... HELLO, BRUSHY.
BRUSHY WILL HANDLE THE FINEST LITTLE DETAILS.
SWOOOP
SWISH
FIRST THE BLUSH...
...THEN WILL COME THE EYE SHADOW...
SWIP!
SWIP!
...AND FINALLY THE LIPSTICK!
SWIP!

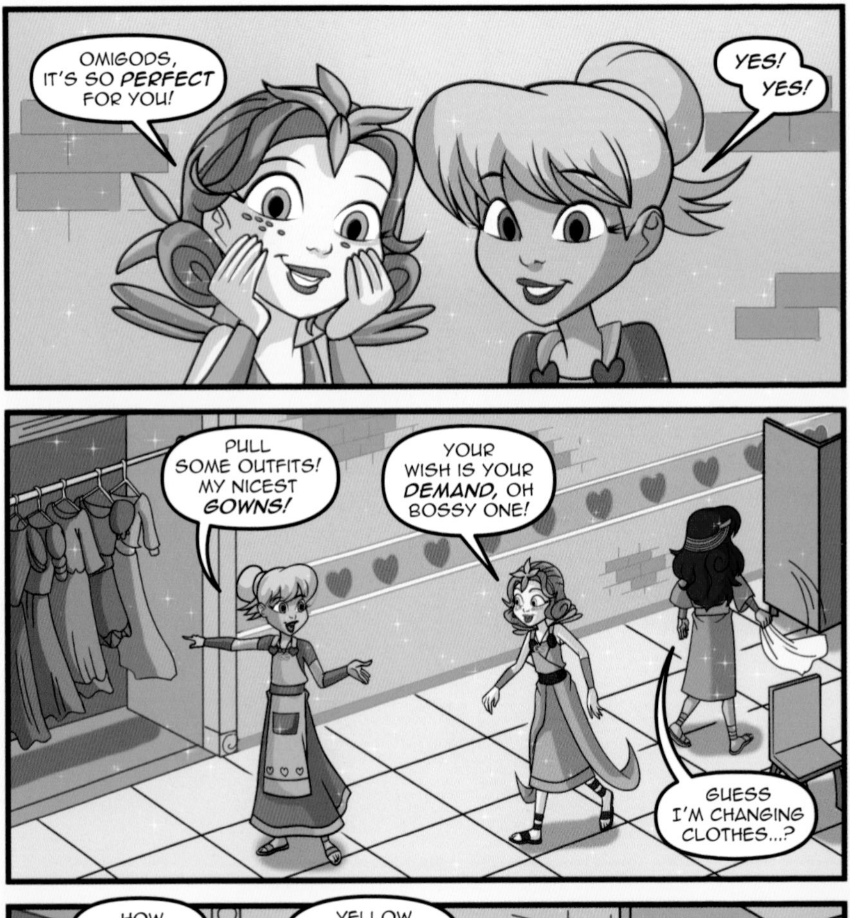

OMIGODS, IT'S SO **PERFECT** FOR YOU!
YES! YES!
PULL SOME OUTFITS! MY NICEST **GOWNS!**
YOUR WISH IS YOUR **DEMAND,** OH BOSSY ONE!
GUESS I'M CHANGING CLOTHES...?
HOW ABOUT **THIS** ONE?
YELLOW LOOKS GREAT ON **YOU,** PERSEPHONE...
...BUT IT DOESN'T **QUITE** SUIT ATHENA. IT'S ALL ABOUT **TONES.**
HEY.
I'M RIGHT **HERE.**
REMEMBER?

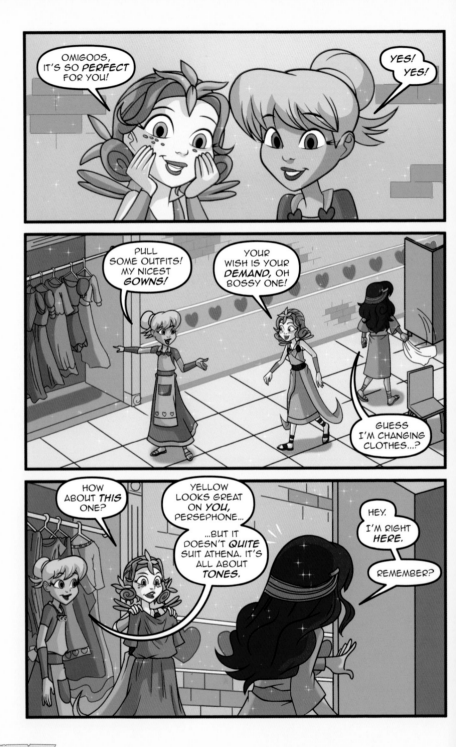

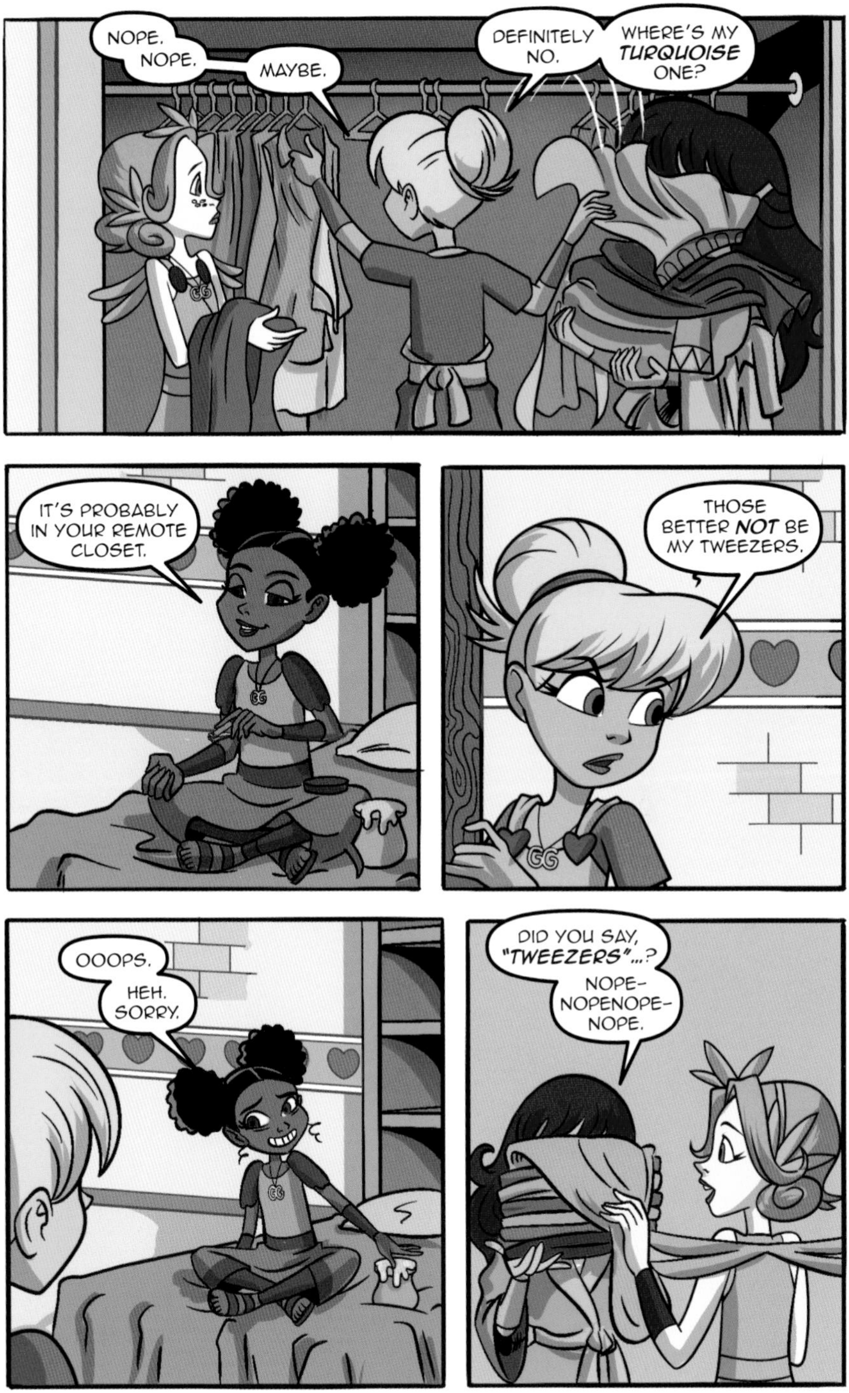

NOPE.
NOPE.
MAYBE.
DEFINITELY NO.
WHERE'S MY *TURQUOISE* ONE?
IT'S PROBABLY IN YOUR REMOTE CLOSET.
THOSE BETTER **NOT** BE MY TWEEZERS.
OOOPS.
HEH. SORRY.
DID YOU SAY, ***"TWEEZERS"***...?
NOPE-NOPENOPE-NOPE.

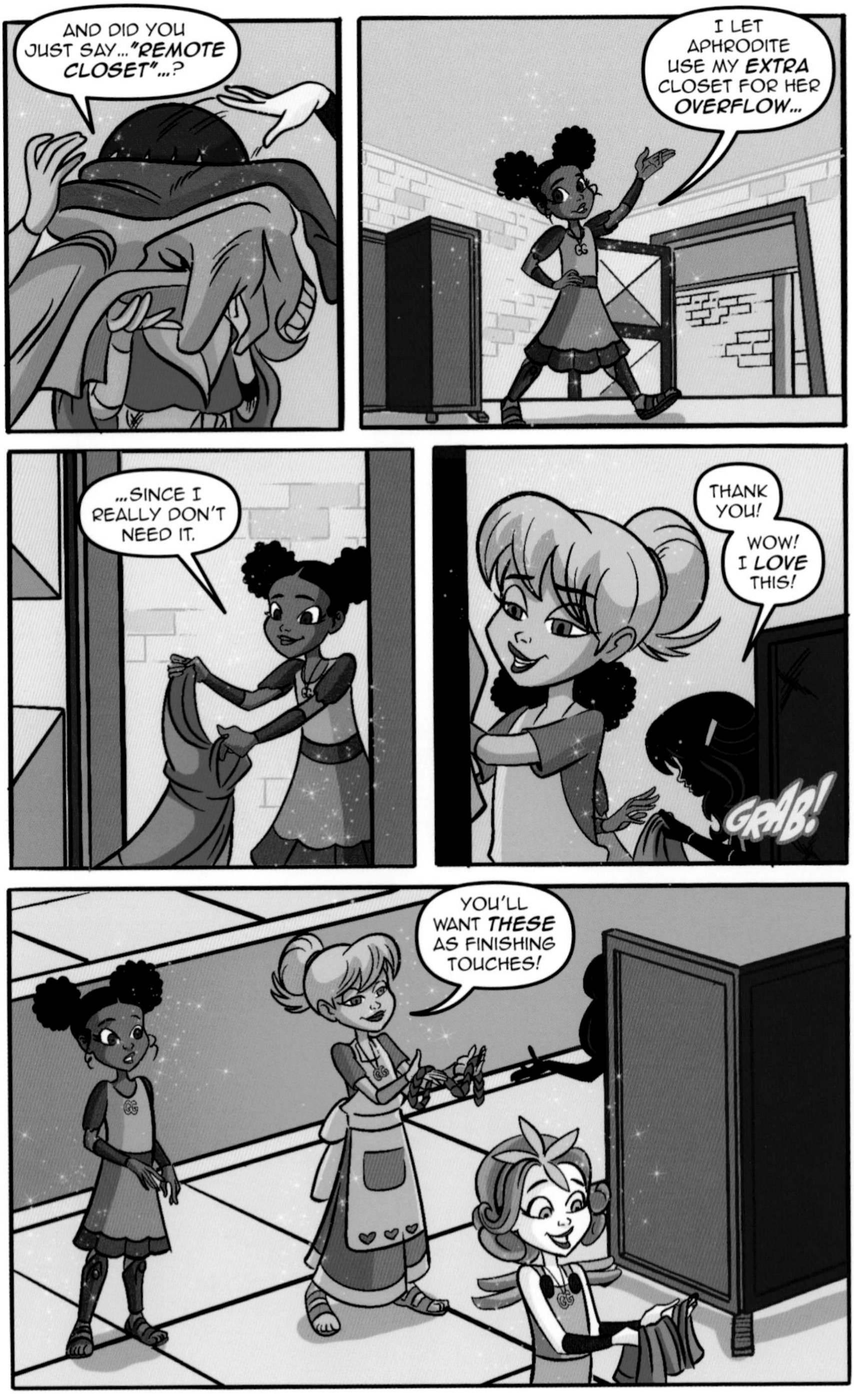
AND DID YOU JUST SAY..."REMOTE CLOSET"...?
I LET APHRODITE USE MY EXTRA CLOSET FOR HER OVERFLOW...
...SINCE I REALLY DON'T NEED IT.
THANK YOU!
WOW! I LOVE THIS!
GRAB!
YOU'LL WANT THESE AS FINISHING TOUCHES!

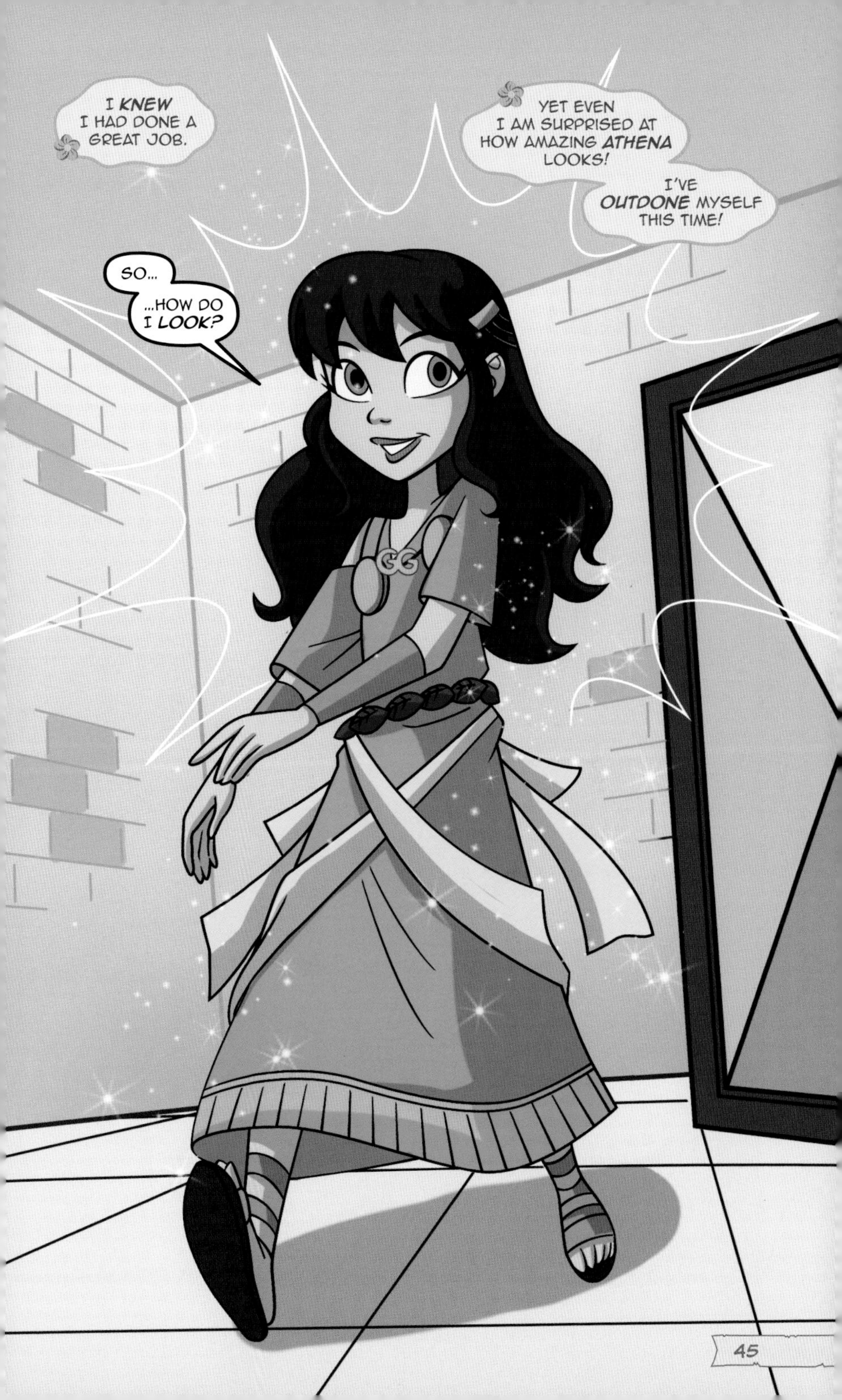

I KNEW I HAD DONE A GREAT JOB.
YET EVEN I AM SURPRISED AT HOW AMAZING ATHENA LOOKS!
I'VE OUTDONE MYSELF THIS TIME!
SO...
...HOW DO I LOOK?

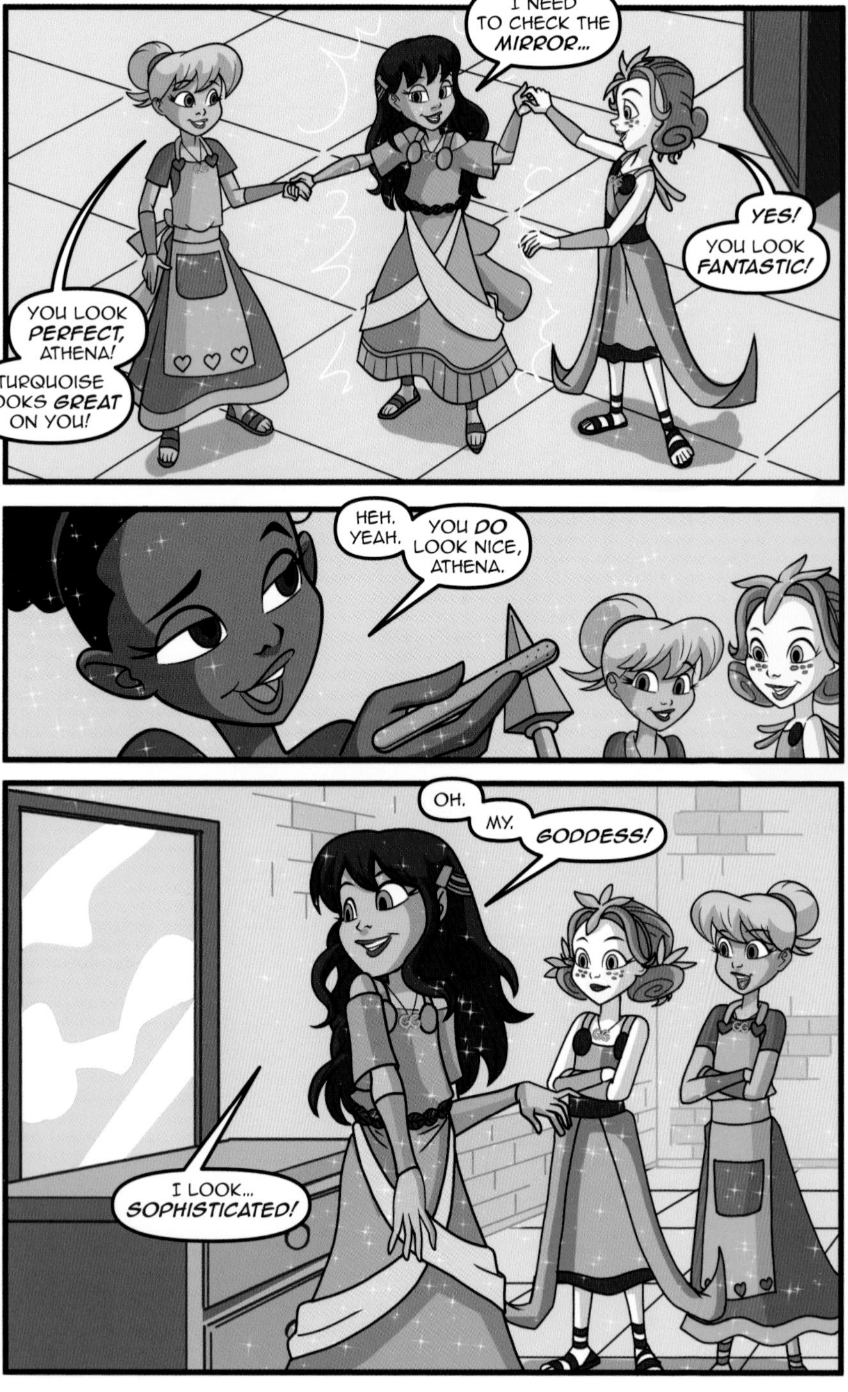
I NEED TO CHECK THE MIRROR...
YES! YOU LOOK FANTASTIC!
YOU LOOK PERFECT, ATHENA!
TURQUOISE LOOKS GREAT ON YOU!
HEH. YEAH.
YOU DO LOOK NICE, ATHENA.
OH.
MY.
GODDESS!
I LOOK... SOPHISTICATED!

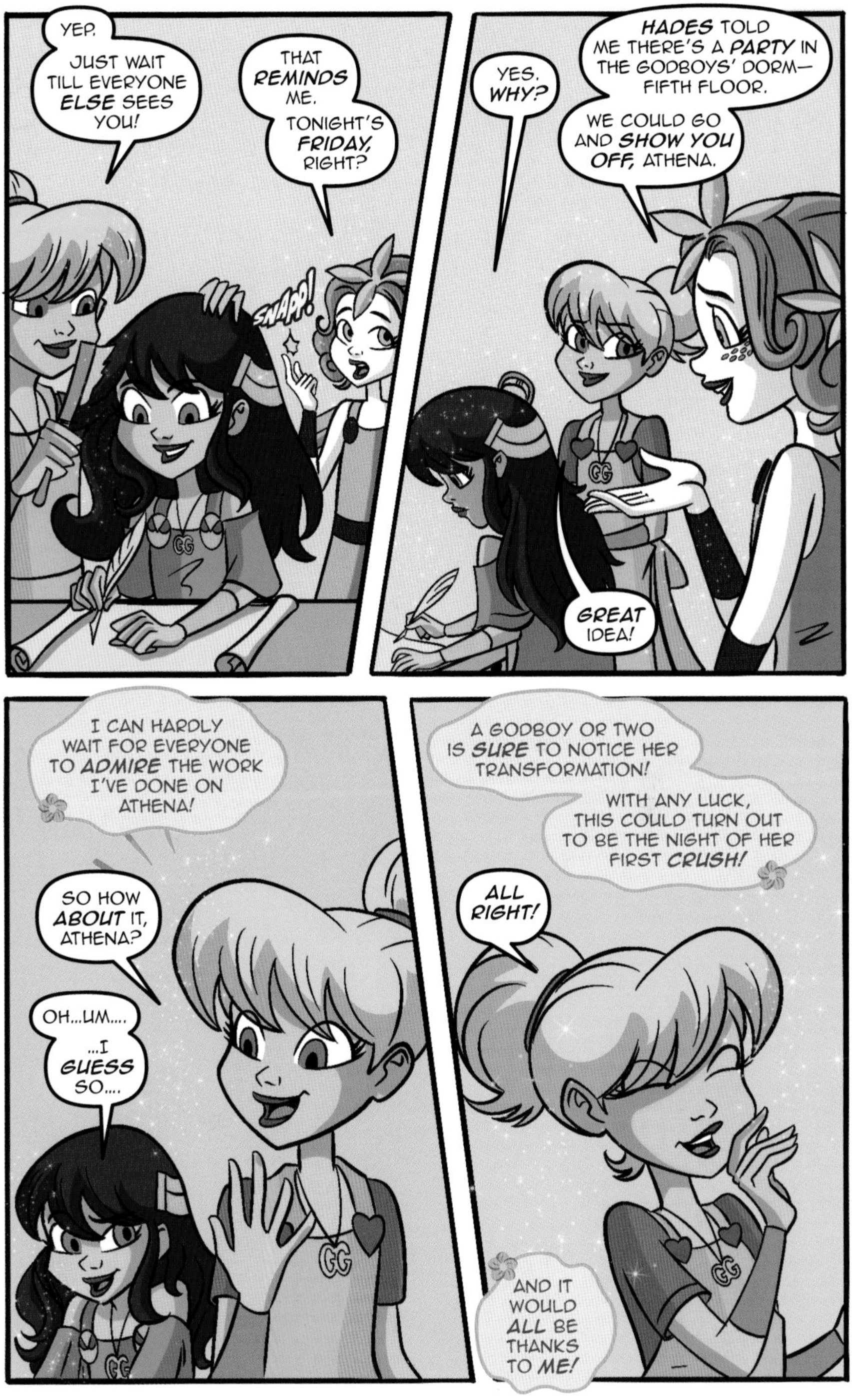
YEP.
JUST WAIT TILL EVERYONE ELSE SEES YOU!
THAT REMINDS ME.
TONIGHT'S FRIDAY, RIGHT?
SNAPP!
YES. WHY?
HADES TOLD ME THERE'S A PARTY IN THE GODBOYS' DORM—FIFTH FLOOR.
WE COULD GO AND SHOW YOU OFF, ATHENA.
GREAT IDEA!
I CAN HARDLY WAIT FOR EVERYONE TO ADMIRE THE WORK I'VE DONE ON ATHENA!
SO HOW ABOUT IT, ATHENA?
OH...UM....
...I GUESS SO....
A GODBOY OR TWO IS SURE TO NOTICE HER TRANSFORMATION!
WITH ANY LUCK, THIS COULD TURN OUT TO BE THE NIGHT OF HER FIRST CRUSH!
ALL RIGHT!
AND IT WOULD ALL BE THANKS TO ME!

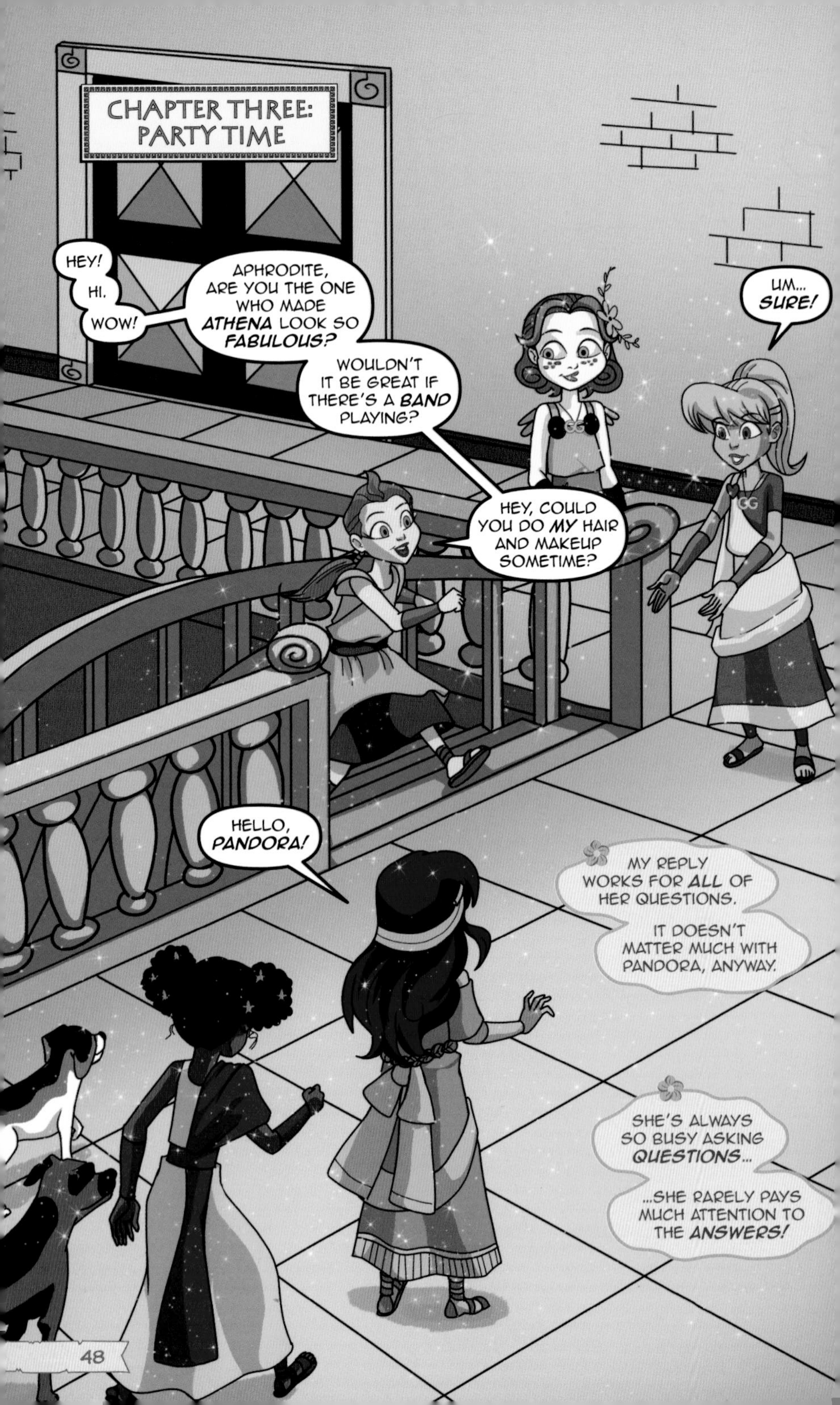
CHAPTER THREE:
PARTY TIME
HEY!
HI.
WOW!
APHRODITE, ARE YOU THE ONE WHO MADE ATHENA LOOK SO FABULOUS?
WOULDN'T IT BE GREAT IF THERE'S A BAND PLAYING?
HEY, COULD YOU DO MY HAIR AND MAKEUP SOMETIME?
UM... SURE!
HELLO, PANDORA!
MY REPLY WORKS FOR ALL OF HER QUESTIONS.
IT DOESN'T MATTER MUCH WITH PANDORA, ANYWAY.
SHE'S ALWAYS SO BUSY ASKING QUESTIONS...
...SHE RARELY PAYS MUCH ATTENTION TO THE ANSWERS!

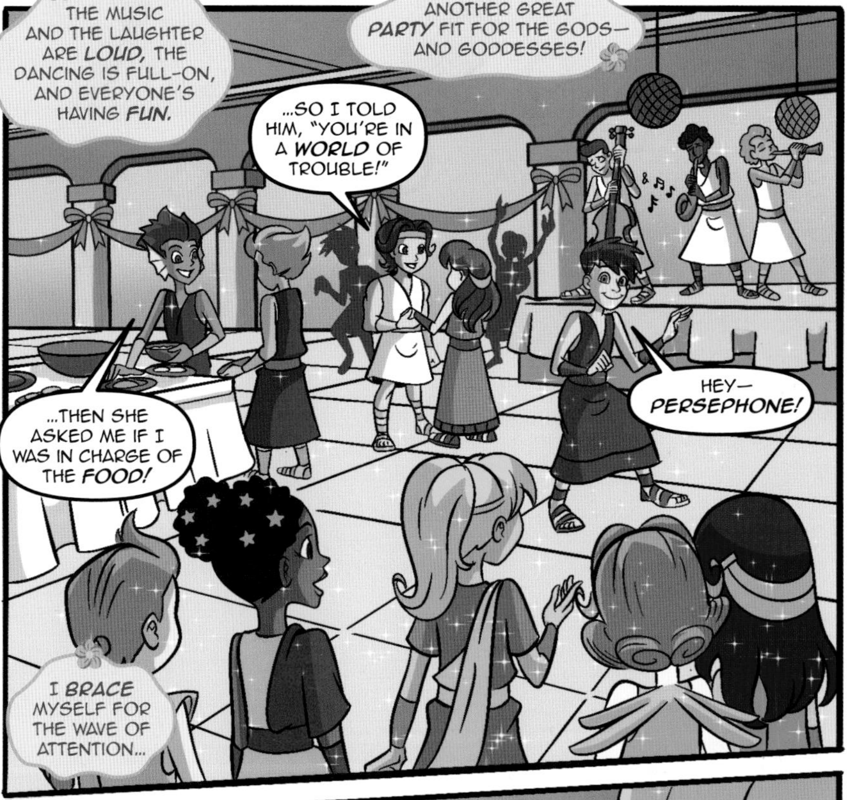
THE MUSIC AND THE LAUGHTER ARE LOUD, THE DANCING IS FULL-ON, AND EVERYONE'S HAVING FUN.
ANOTHER GREAT PARTY FIT FOR THE GODS—AND GODDESSES!
...SO I TOLD HIM, "YOU'RE IN A WORLD OF TROUBLE!"
...THEN SHE ASKED ME IF I WAS IN CHARGE OF THE FOOD!
HEY—PERSEPHONE!
I BRACE MYSELF FOR THE WAVE OF ATTENTION...

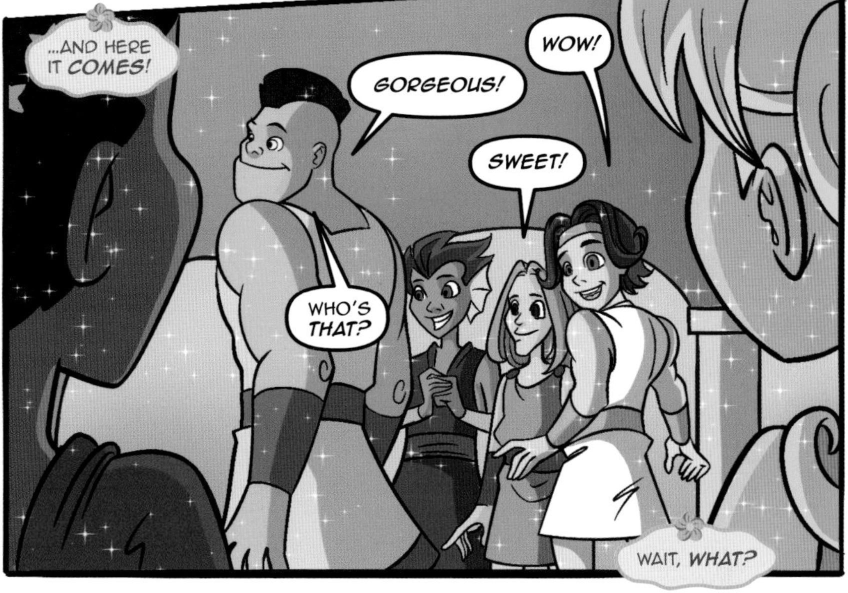
...AND HERE IT COMES!
GORGEOUS!
WOW!
SWEET!
WHO'S THAT?
WAIT, WHAT?

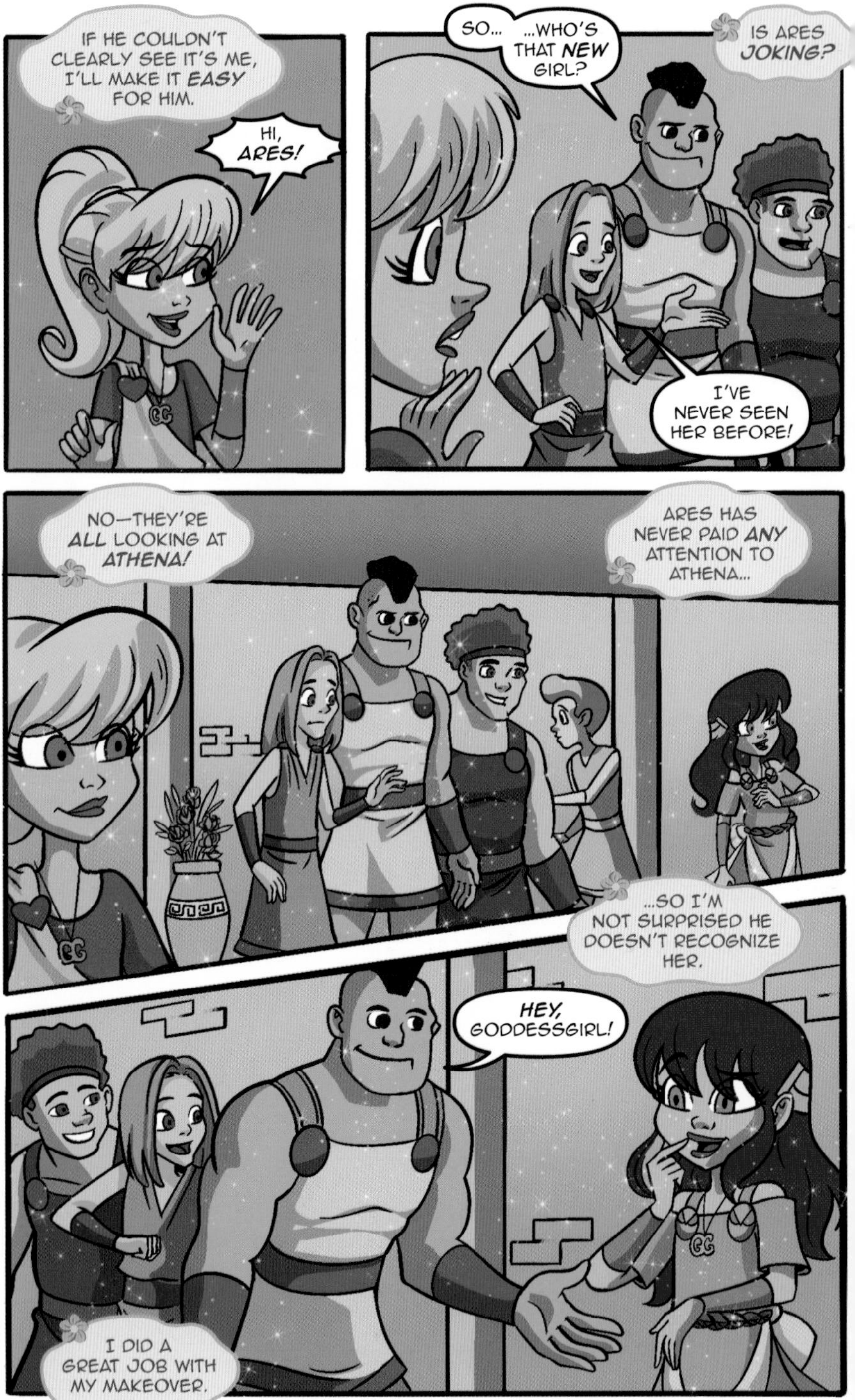
IF HE COULDN'T CLEARLY SEE IT'S ME, I'LL MAKE IT EASY FOR HIM.
HI, ARES!
SO... ...WHO'S THAT NEW GIRL?
IS ARES JOKING?
I'VE NEVER SEEN HER BEFORE!
NO—THEY'RE ALL LOOKING AT ATHENA!
ARES HAS NEVER PAID ANY ATTENTION TO ATHENA...
...SO I'M NOT SURPRISED HE DOESN'T RECOGNIZE HER.
HEY, GODDESSGIRL!
I DID A GREAT JOB WITH MY MAKEOVER.

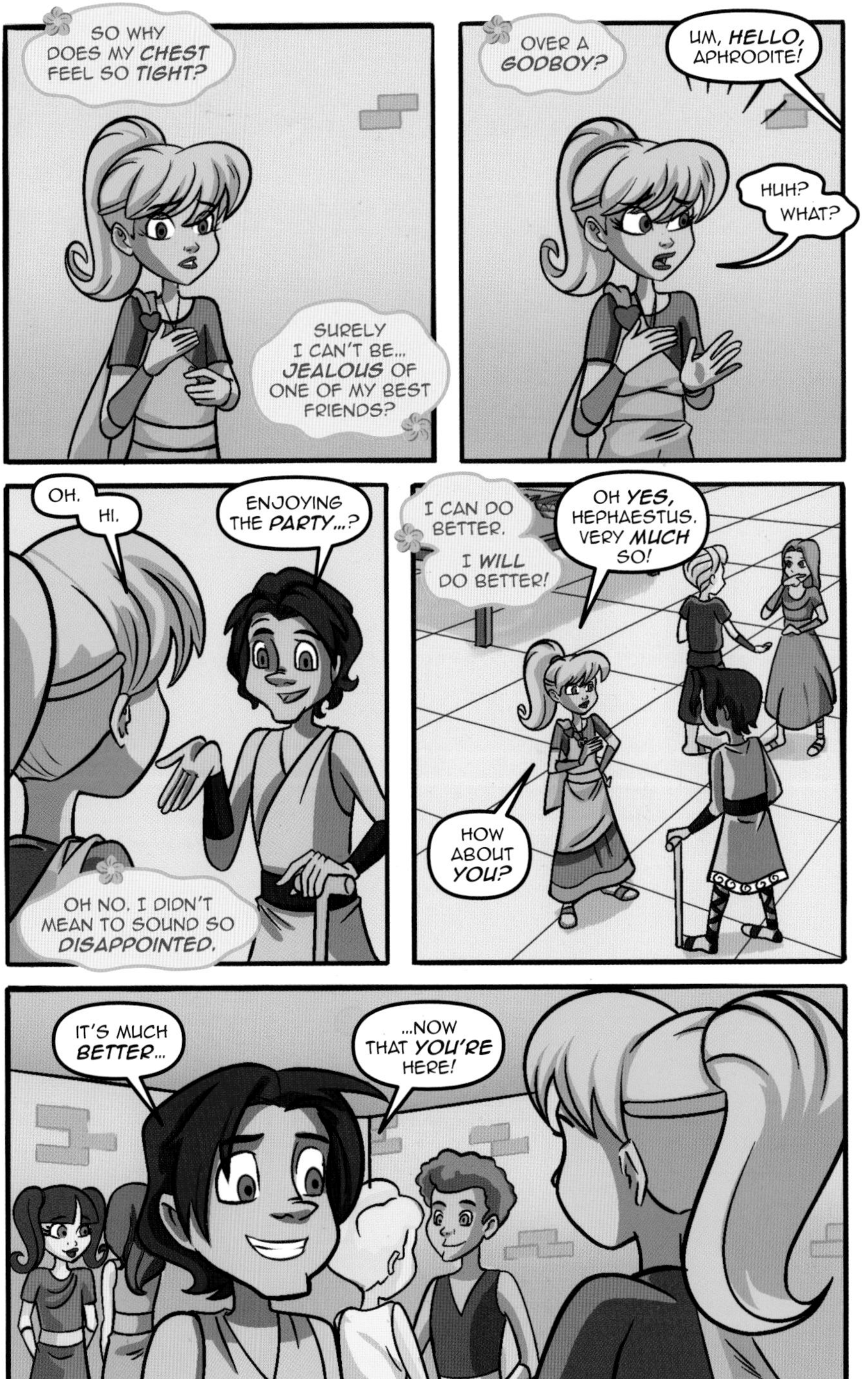
SO WHY DOES MY CHEST FEEL SO TIGHT?
SURELY I CAN'T BE... JEALOUS OF ONE OF MY BEST FRIENDS?
OVER A GODBOY?
UM, HELLO, APHRODITE!
HUH? WHAT?
OH. HI.
ENJOYING THE PARTY...?
OH NO. I DIDN'T MEAN TO SOUND SO DISAPPOINTED.
I CAN DO BETTER.
I WILL DO BETTER!
OH YES, HEPHAESTUS. VERY MUCH SO!
HOW ABOUT YOU?
IT'S MUCH BETTER...
...NOW THAT YOU'RE HERE!

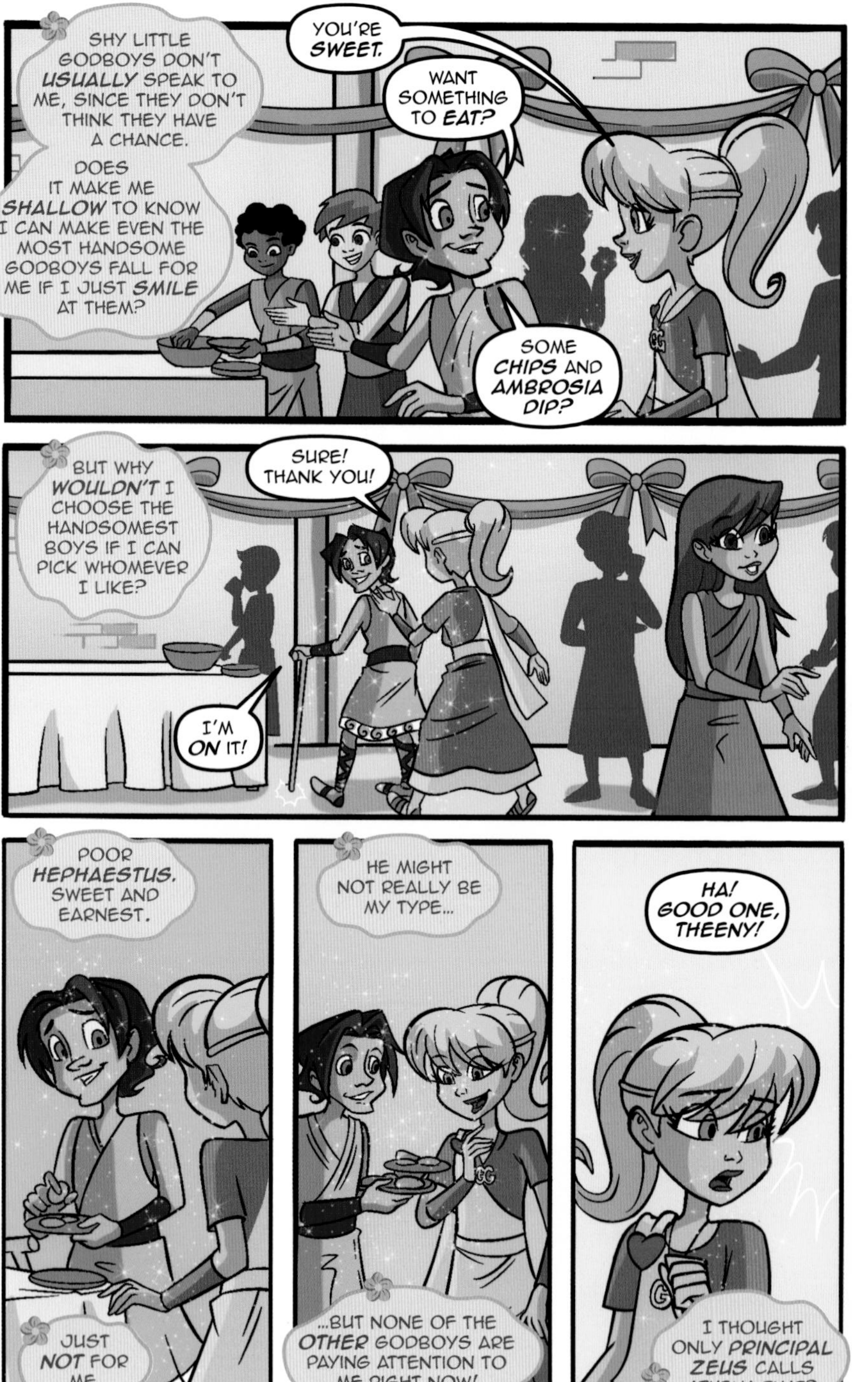

SHY LITTLE GODBOYS DON'T USUALLY SPEAK TO ME, SINCE THEY DON'T THINK THEY HAVE A CHANCE.
DOES IT MAKE ME SHALLOW TO KNOW I CAN MAKE EVEN THE MOST HANDSOME GODBOYS FALL FOR ME IF I JUST SMILE AT THEM?
YOU'RE SWEET.
WANT SOMETHING TO EAT?
SOME CHIPS AND AMBROSIA DIP?
BUT WHY WOULDN'T I CHOOSE THE HANDSOMEST BOYS IF I CAN PICK WHOMEVER I LIKE?
SURE! THANK YOU!
I'M ON IT!
POOR HEPHAESTUS. SWEET AND EARNEST.
JUST NOT FOR ME.
HE MIGHT NOT REALLY BE MY TYPE...
...BUT NONE OF THE OTHER GODBOYS ARE PAYING ATTENTION TO ME RIGHT NOW!
HA! GOOD ONE, THEENY!
I THOUGHT ONLY PRINCIPAL ZEUS CALLS ATHENA THAT?

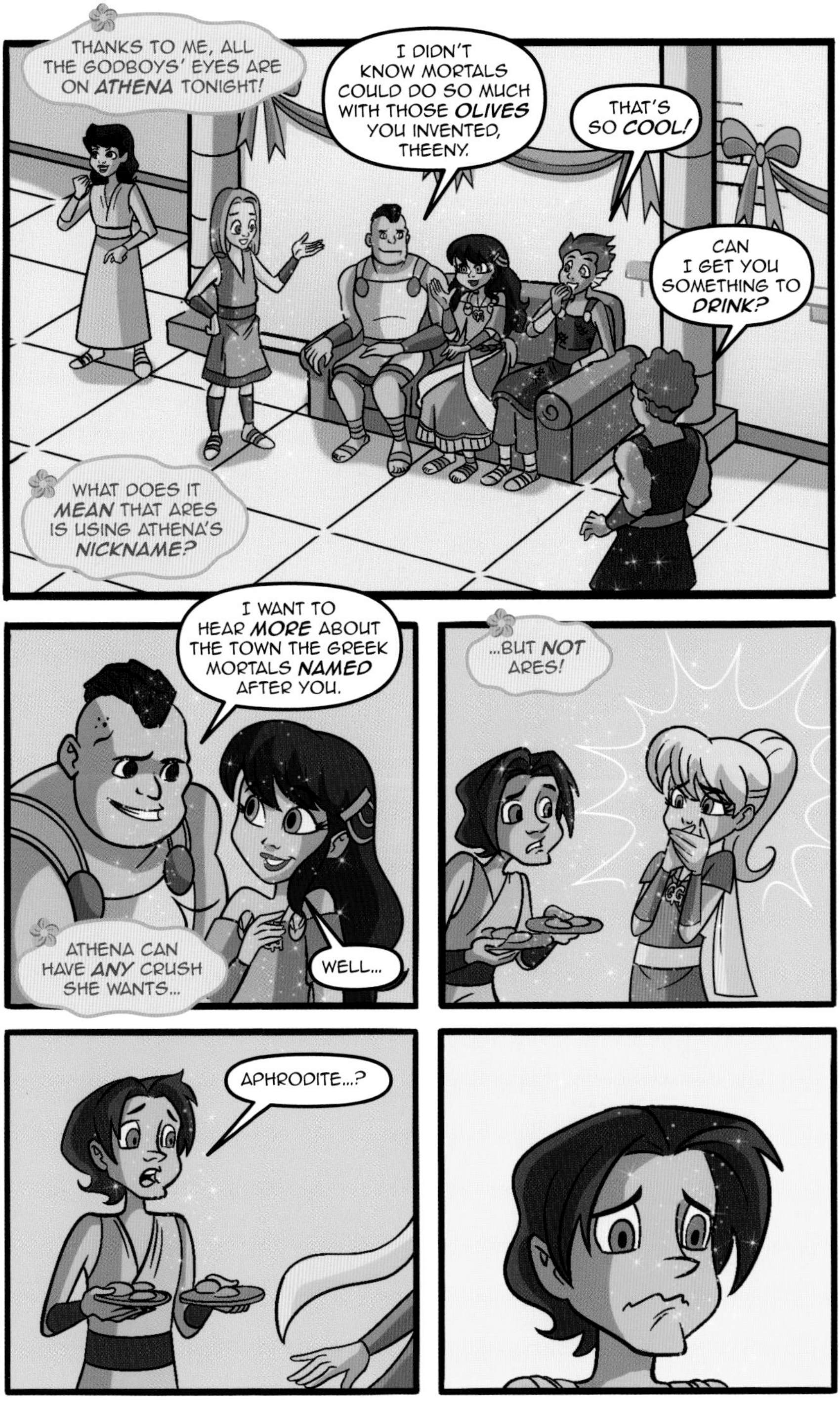
THANKS TO ME, ALL THE GODBOYS' EYES ARE ON ATHENA TONIGHT!
I DIDN'T KNOW MORTALS COULD DO SO MUCH WITH THOSE OLIVES YOU INVENTED, THEENY.
THAT'S SO COOL!
CAN I GET YOU SOMETHING TO DRINK?
WHAT DOES IT MEAN THAT ARES IS USING ATHENA'S NICKNAME?
I WANT TO HEAR MORE ABOUT THE TOWN THE GREEK MORTALS NAMED AFTER YOU.
ATHENA CAN HAVE ANY CRUSH SHE WANTS...
WELL...
...BUT NOT ARES!
APHRODITE...?

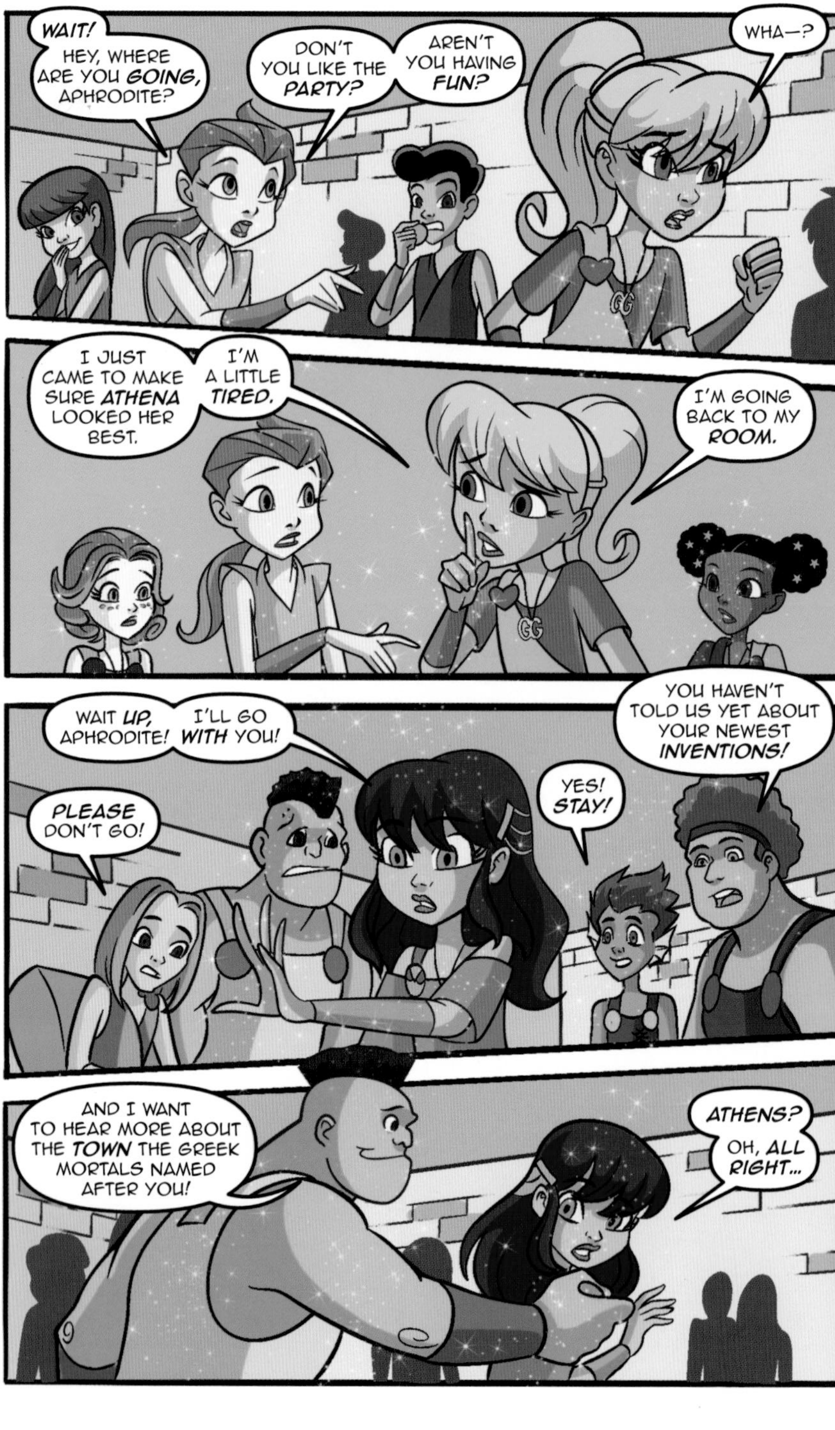
WAIT! HEY, WHERE ARE YOU GOING, APHRODITE?
DON'T YOU LIKE THE PARTY?
AREN'T YOU HAVING FUN?
WHA—?
I JUST CAME TO MAKE SURE ATHENA LOOKED HER BEST.
I'M A LITTLE TIRED.
I'M GOING BACK TO MY ROOM.
WAIT UP, APHRODITE!
I'LL GO WITH YOU!
PLEASE DON'T GO!
YES! STAY!
YOU HAVEN'T TOLD US YET ABOUT YOUR NEWEST INVENTIONS!
AND I WANT TO HEAR MORE ABOUT THE TOWN THE GREEK MORTALS NAMED AFTER YOU!
ATHENS?
OH, ALL RIGHT...

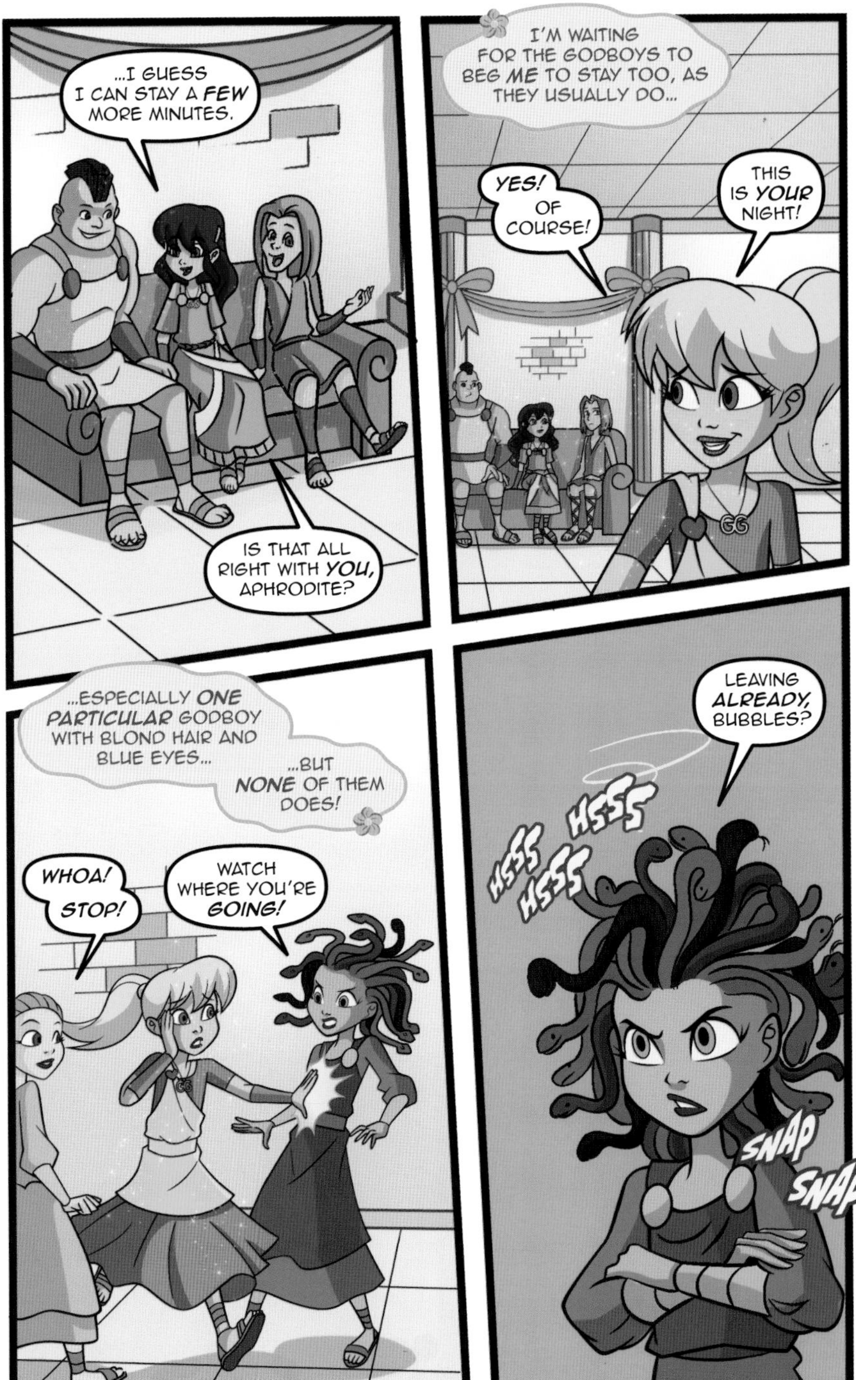
...I GUESS I CAN STAY A FEW MORE MINUTES.
IS THAT ALL RIGHT WITH YOU, APHRODITE?
I'M WAITING FOR THE GODBOYS TO BEG ME TO STAY TOO, AS THEY USUALLY DO...
YES! OF COURSE!
THIS IS YOUR NIGHT!
...ESPECIALLY ONE PARTICULAR GODBOY WITH BLOND HAIR AND BLUE EYES...
...BUT NONE OF THEM DOES!
WHOA! STOP!
WATCH WHERE YOU'RE GOING!
LEAVING ALREADY, BUBBLES?
HSSS HSSS HSSS
SNAP SNAP

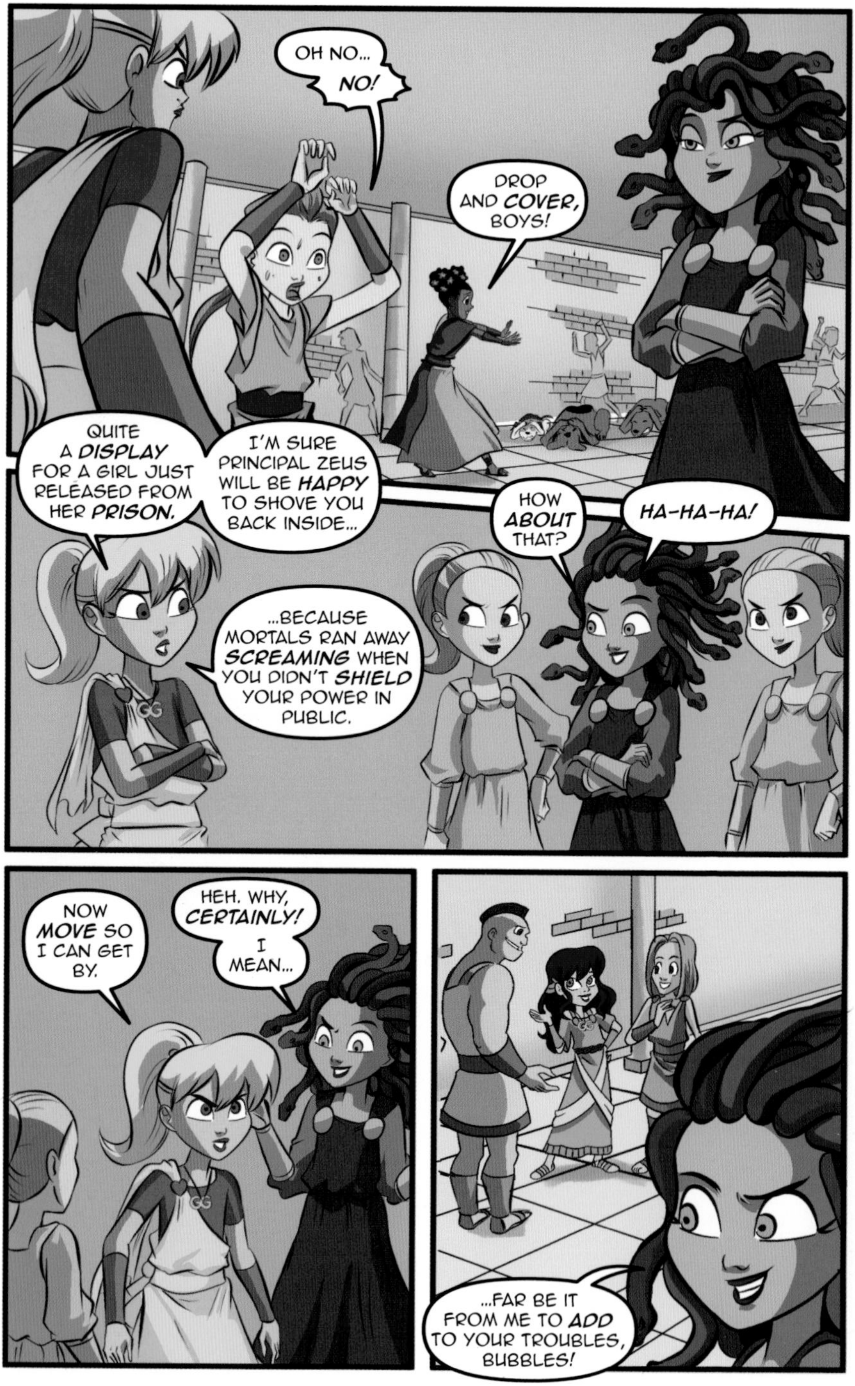
OH NO... NO!
DROP AND COVER, BOYS!
QUITE A DISPLAY FOR A GIRL JUST RELEASED FROM HER PRISON.
I'M SURE PRINCIPAL ZEUS WILL BE HAPPY TO SHOVE YOU BACK INSIDE...
...BECAUSE MORTALS RAN AWAY SCREAMING WHEN YOU DIDN'T SHIELD YOUR POWER IN PUBLIC.
HOW ABOUT THAT?
HA-HA-HA!
NOW MOVE SO I CAN GET BY.
HEH. WHY, CERTAINLY!
I MEAN...
...FAR BE IT FROM ME TO ADD TO YOUR TROUBLES, BUBBLES!

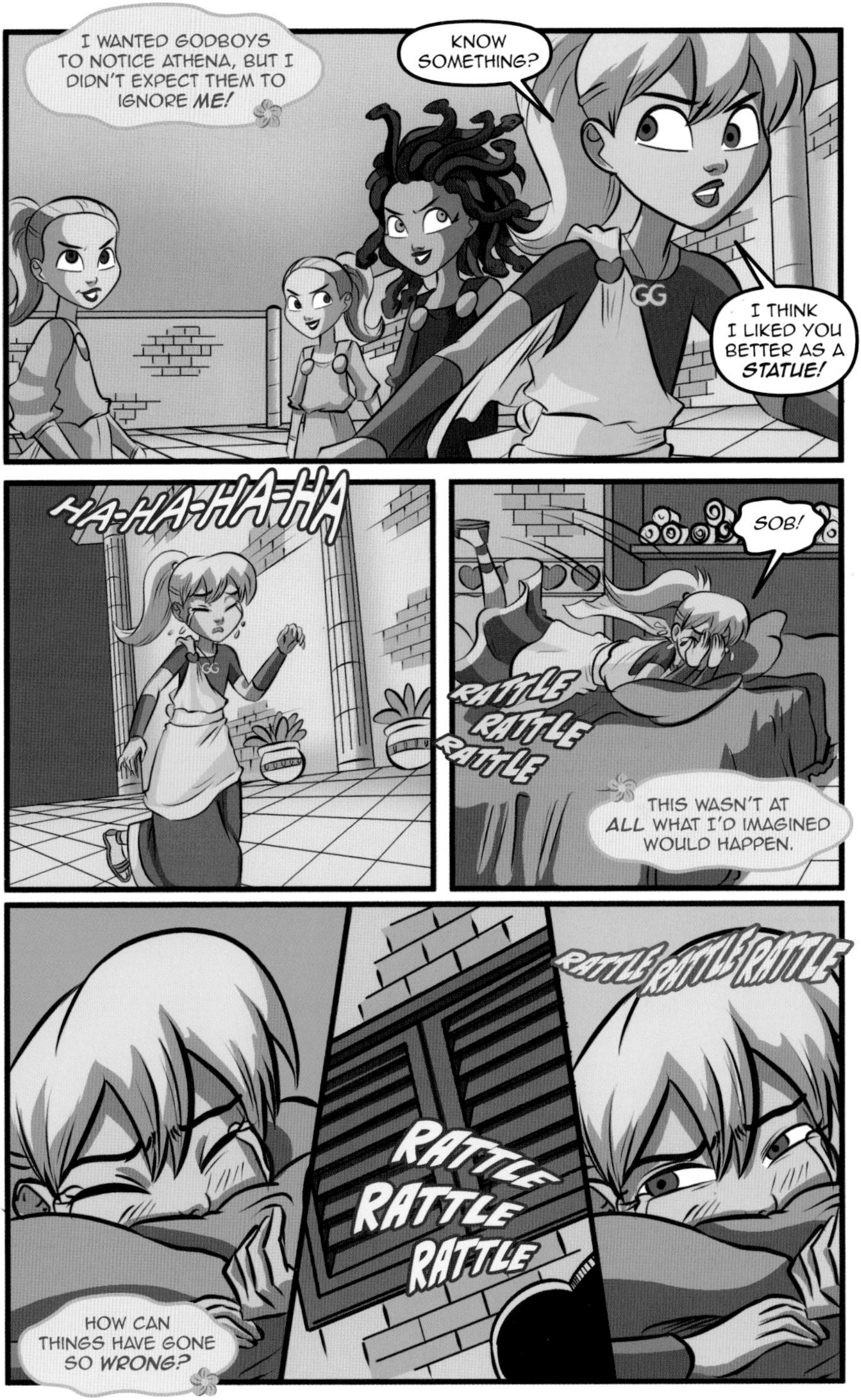
I WANTED GODBOYS TO NOTICE ATHENA, BUT I DIDN'T EXPECT THEM TO IGNORE *ME!*
KNOW SOMETHING?
I THINK I LIKED YOU BETTER AS A *STATUE!*
HA-HA-HA-HA-HA
SOB!
RATTLE RATTLE RATTLE
THIS WASN'T AT *ALL* WHAT I'D IMAGINED WOULD HAPPEN.
RATTLE RATTLE RATTLE
RATTLE RATTLE RATTLE
HOW CAN THINGS HAVE GONE SO *WRONG?*

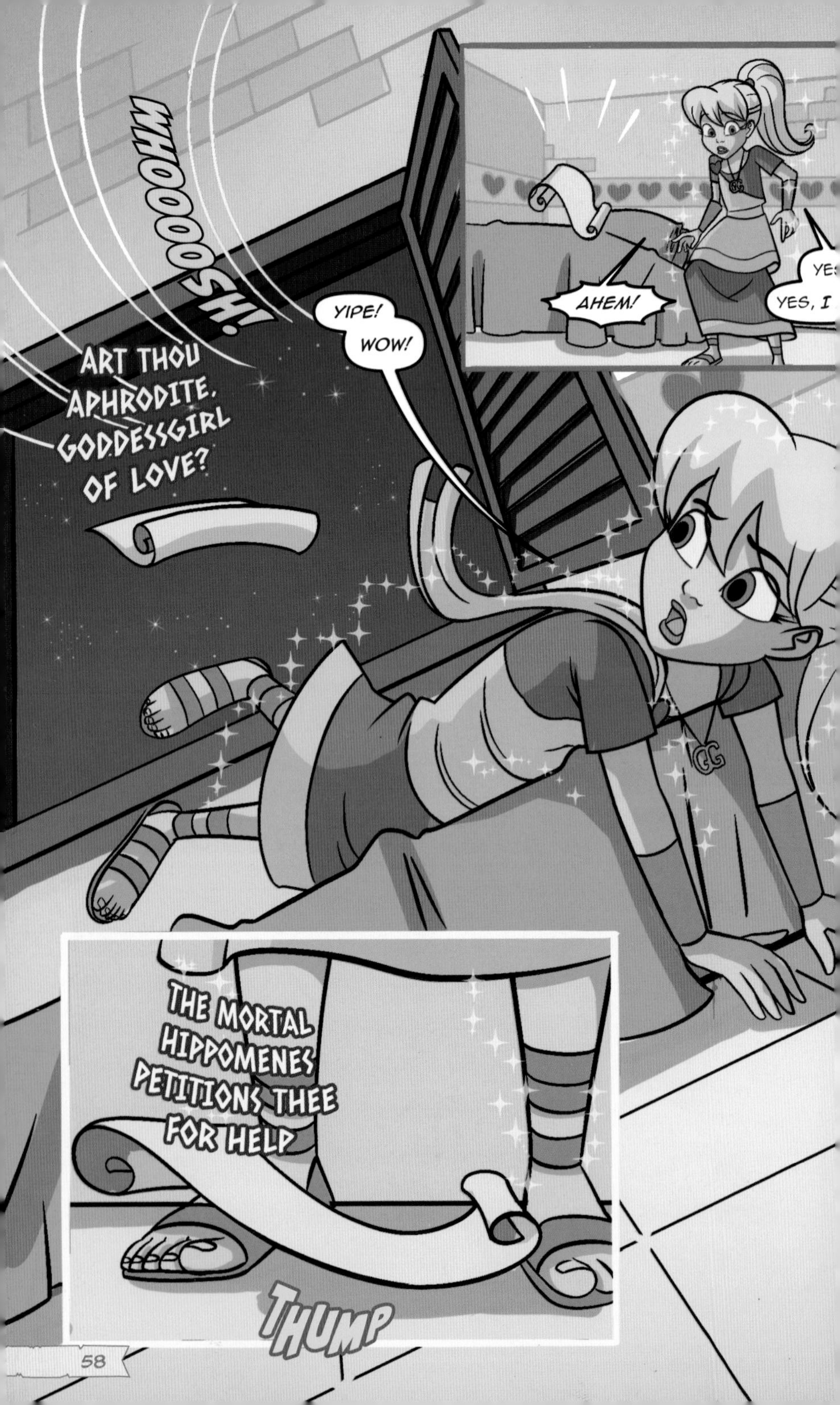
AHEM!
YES, I
WHOOOOSH!
ART THOU APHRODITE, GODDESSGIRL OF LOVE?
YIPE! WOW!
THE MORTAL HIPPOMENES PETITIONS THEE FOR HELP
THUMP

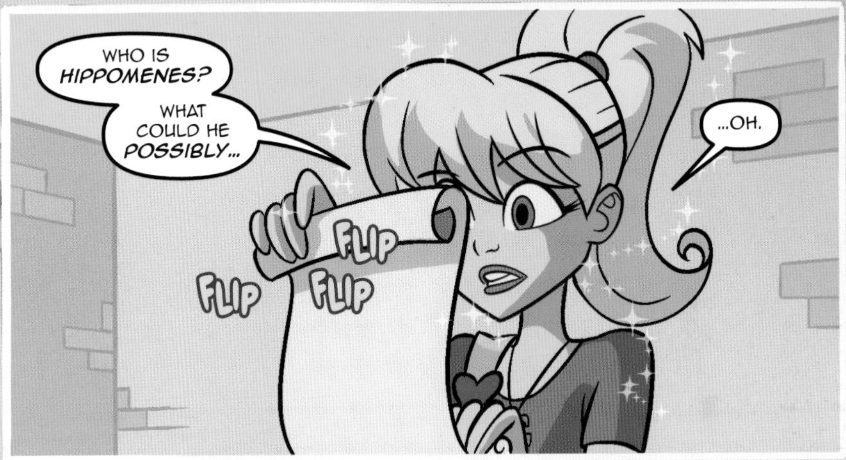
WHO IS HIPPOMENES? WHAT COULD HE POSSIBLY...
FLIP FLIP FLIP
...OH.

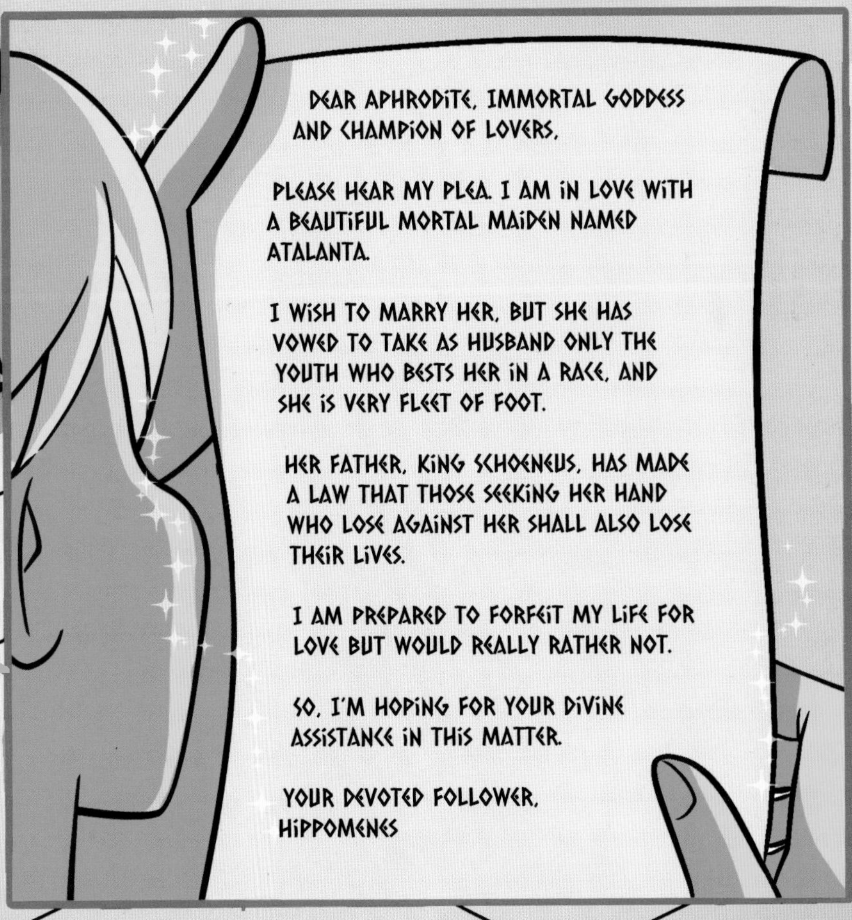
DEAR APHRODITE, IMMORTAL GODDESS AND CHAMPION OF LOVERS,
PLEASE HEAR MY PLEA. I AM IN LOVE WITH A BEAUTIFUL MORTAL MAIDEN NAMED ATALANTA.
I WISH TO MARRY HER, BUT SHE HAS VOWED TO TAKE AS HUSBAND ONLY THE YOUTH WHO BESTS HER IN A RACE, AND SHE IS VERY FLEET OF FOOT.
HER FATHER, KING SCHOENEUS, HAS MADE A LAW THAT THOSE SEEKING HER HAND WHO LOSE AGAINST HER SHALL ALSO LOSE THEIR LIVES.
I AM PREPARED TO FORFEIT MY LIFE FOR LOVE BUT WOULD REALLY RATHER NOT.
SO, I'M HOPING FOR YOUR DIVINE ASSISTANCE IN THIS MATTER.
YOUR DEVOTED FOLLOWER,
HIPPOMENES

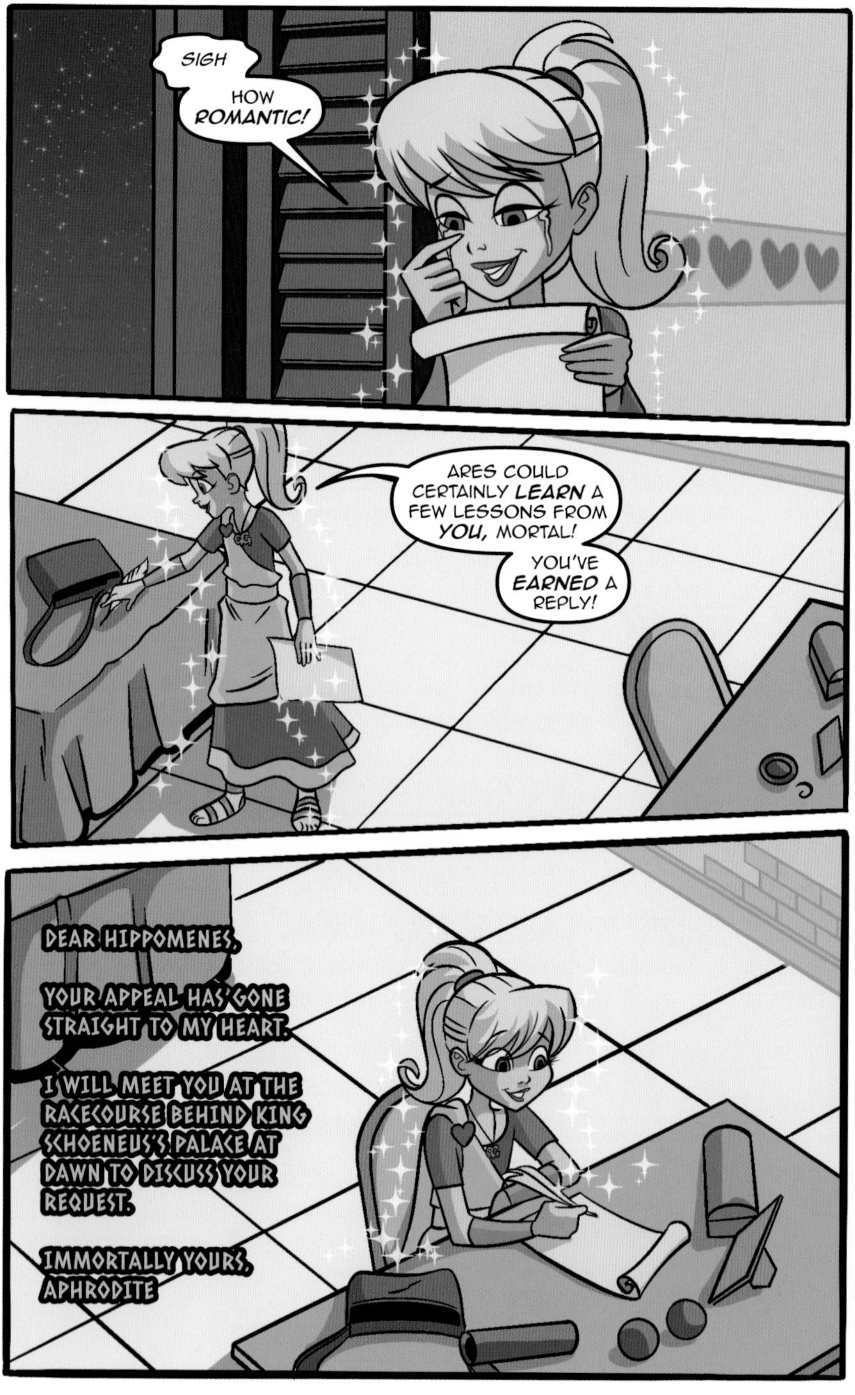

SIGH
HOW ROMANTIC!
ARES COULD CERTAINLY LEARN A FEW LESSONS FROM YOU, MORTAL!
YOU'VE EARNED A REPLY!
DEAR HIPPOMENES,
YOUR APPEAL HAS GONE STRAIGHT TO MY HEART.
I WILL MEET YOU AT THE RACECOURSE BEHIND KING SCHOENEUS'S PALACE AT DAWN TO DISCUSS YOUR REQUEST.
IMMORTALLY YOURS,
APHRODITE

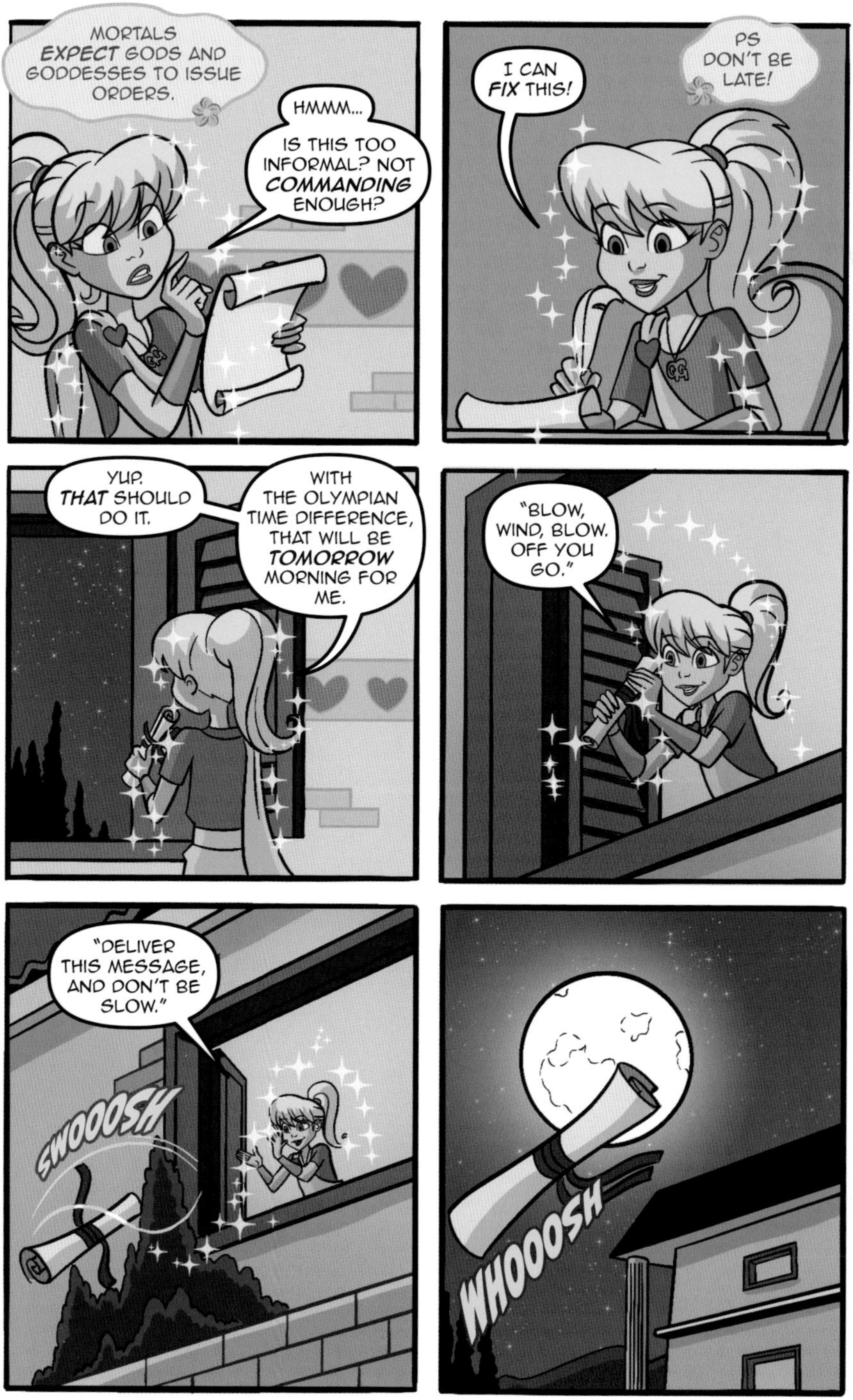
MORTALS EXPECT GODS AND GODDESSES TO ISSUE ORDERS.
HMMM...
IS THIS TOO INFORMAL? NOT COMMANDING ENOUGH?
I CAN FIX THIS!
PS DON'T BE LATE!
YUP. THAT SHOULD DO IT.
WITH THE OLYMPIAN TIME DIFFERENCE, THAT WILL BE TOMORROW MORNING FOR ME.
"BLOW, WIND, BLOW. OFF YOU GO."
"DELIVER THIS MESSAGE, AND DON'T BE SLOW."
SWOOOSH
WHOOOSH

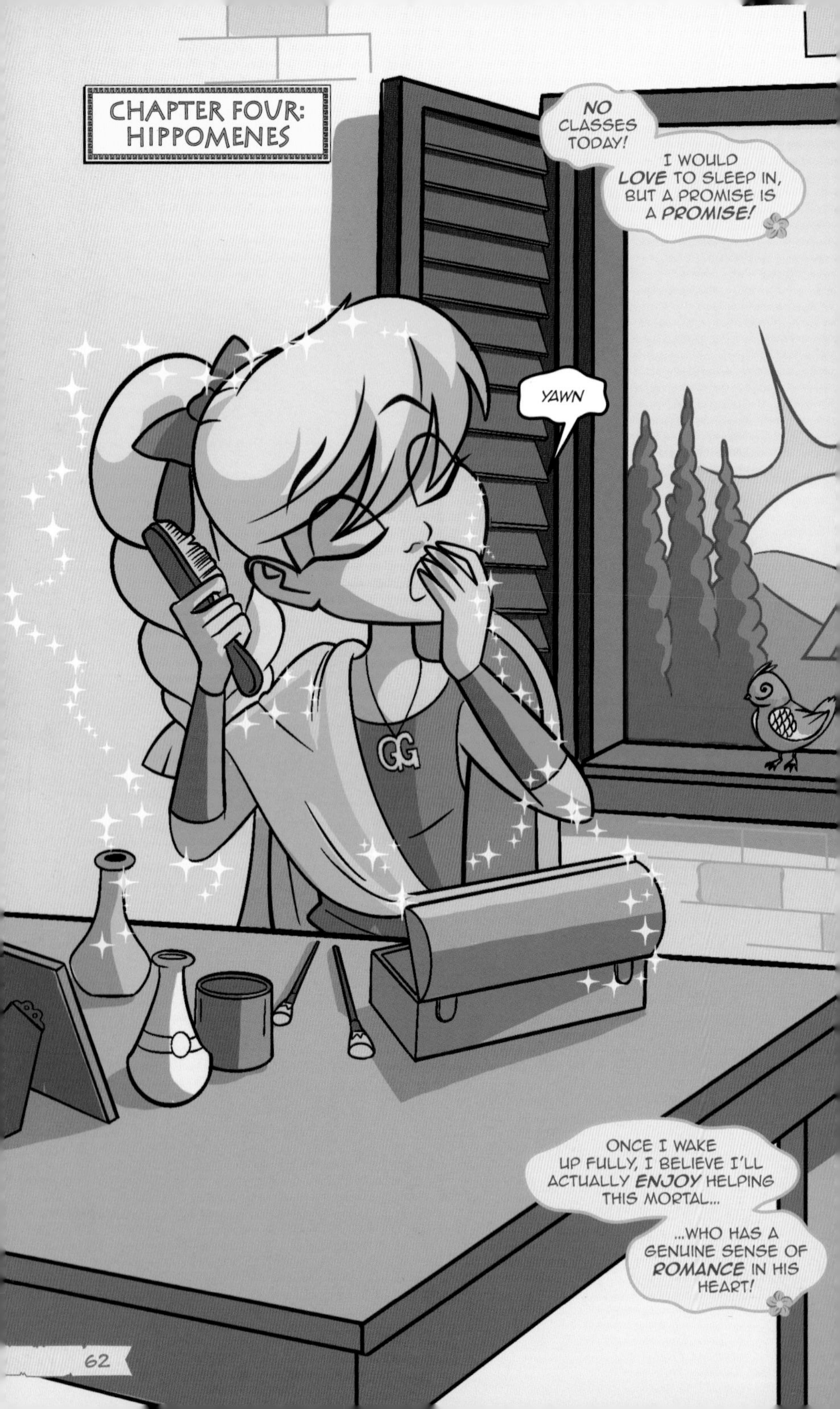
CHAPTER FOUR: HIPPOMENES
NO CLASSES TODAY!
I WOULD LOVE TO SLEEP IN, BUT A PROMISE IS A PROMISE!
YAWN
ONCE I WAKE UP FULLY, I BELIEVE I'LL ACTUALLY ENJOY HELPING THIS MORTAL...
...WHO HAS A GENUINE SENSE OF ROMANCE IN HIS HEART!

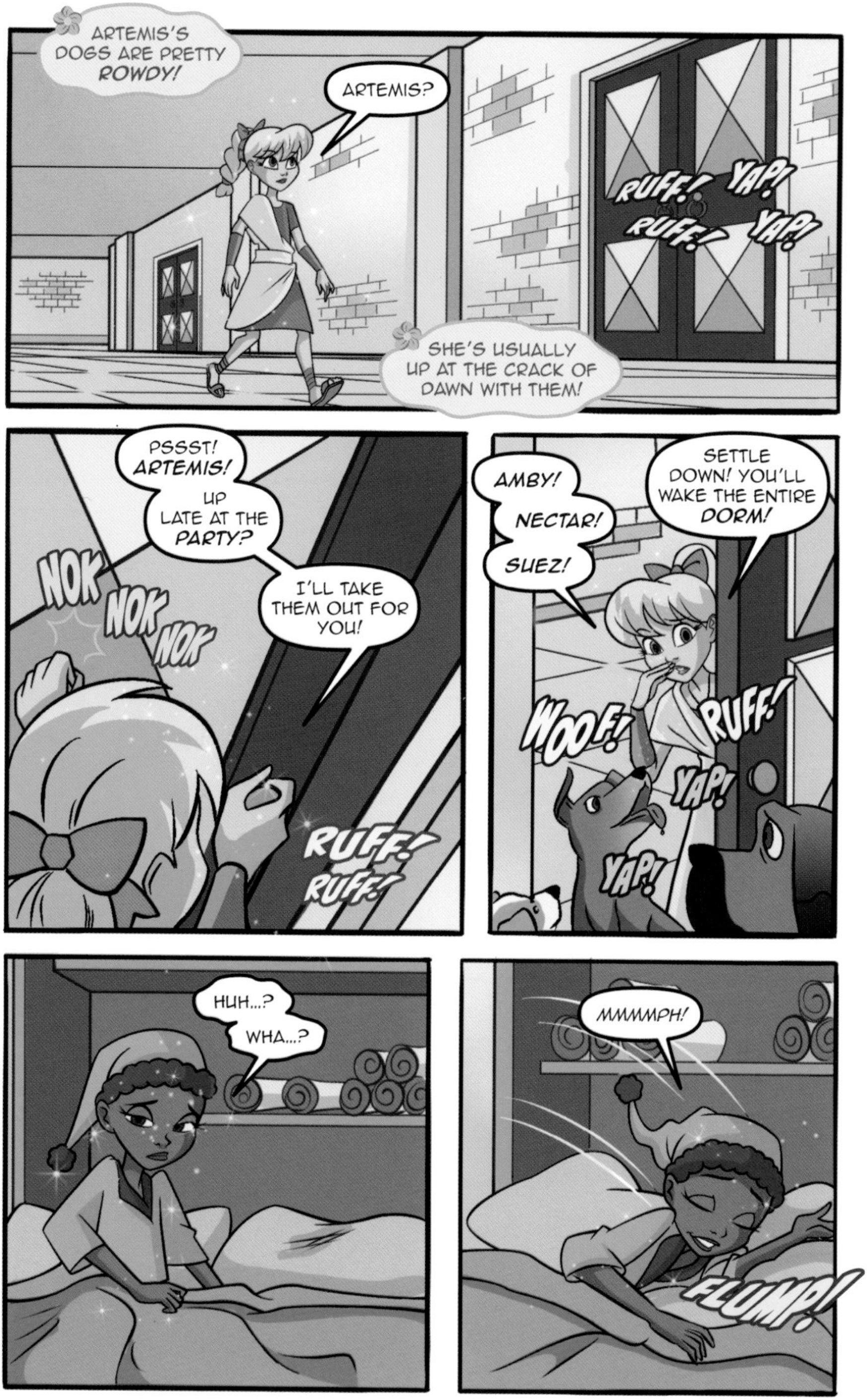
ARTEMIS'S DOGS ARE PRETTY ROWDY!
ARTEMIS?
RUFF! YAP!
RUFF! YAP!
SHE'S USUALLY UP AT THE CRACK OF DAWN WITH THEM!
PSSST! ARTEMIS!
UP LATE AT THE PARTY?
I'LL TAKE THEM OUT FOR YOU!
NOK NOK NOK
RUFF! RUFF!
AMBY!
NECTAR!
SUEZ!
SETTLE DOWN! YOU'LL WAKE THE ENTIRE DORM!
WOOF! RUFF!
YAP!
YAP!
HUH...?
WHA...?
MMMMPH!
FLUMP!

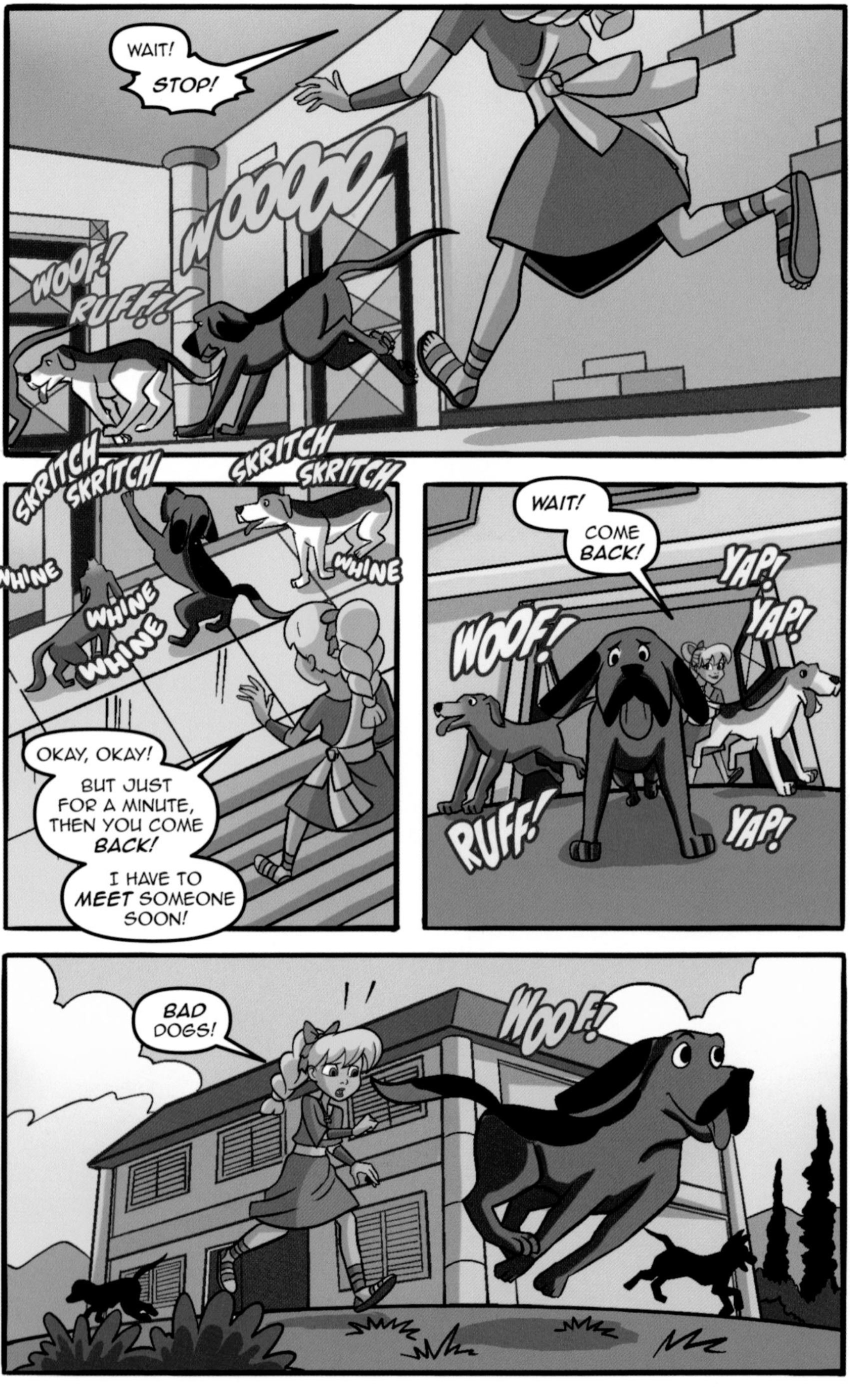
WAIT!
STOP!
WOOOOO
WOOF!
RUFF!!
SKRITCH
SKRITCH
SKRITCH
SKRITCH
WHINE
WHINE
WHINE
WHINE
OKAY, OKAY!
BUT JUST FOR A MINUTE, THEN YOU COME BACK!
I HAVE TO MEET SOMEONE SOON!
WAIT!
COME BACK!
YAP!
YAP!
WOOF!
RUFF!
YAP!
BAD DOGS!
WOOF!

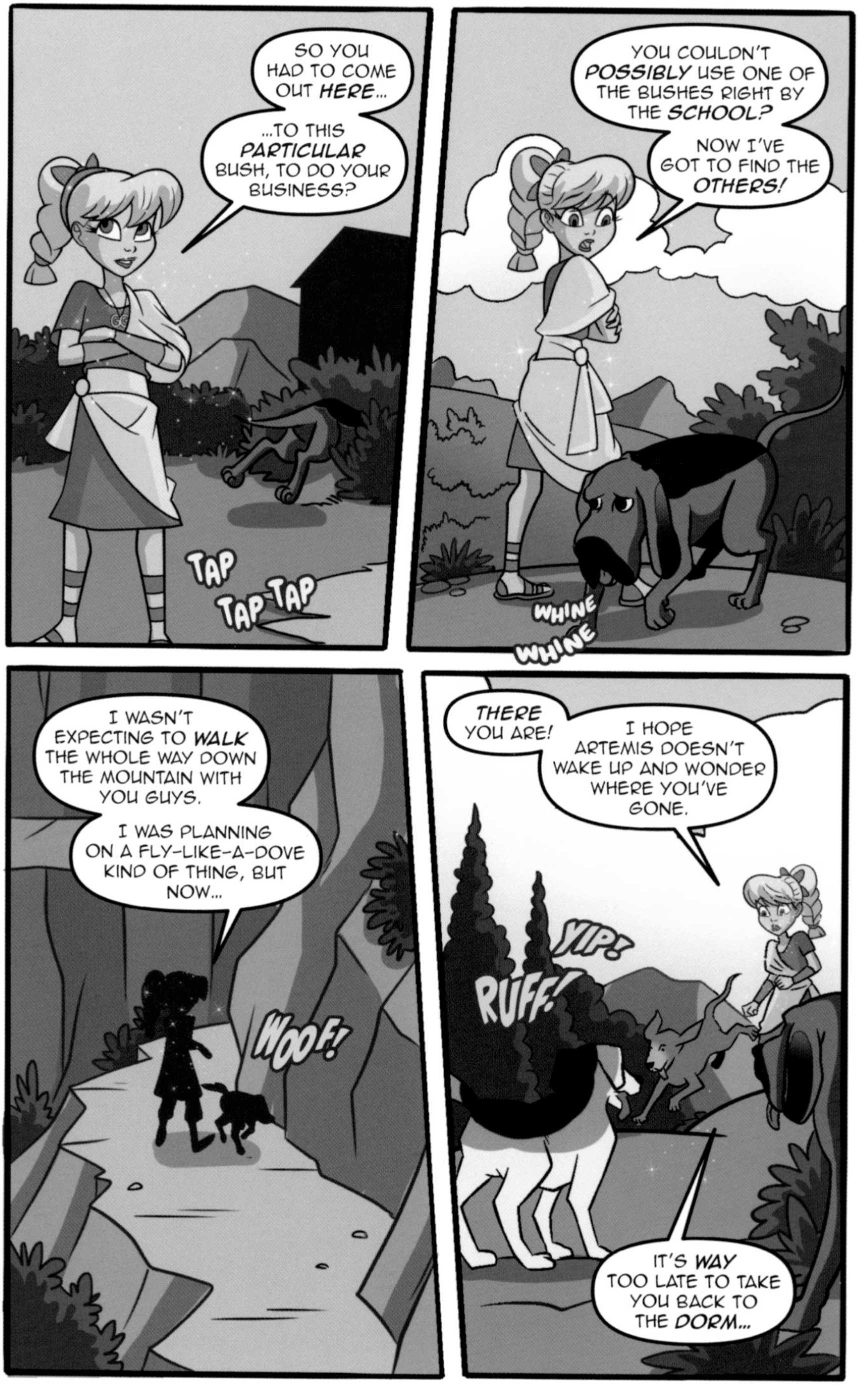

SO YOU HAD TO COME OUT HERE...
...TO THIS PARTICULAR BUSH, TO DO YOUR BUSINESS?
TAP
TAP TAP
YOU COULDN'T POSSIBLY USE ONE OF THE BUSHES RIGHT BY THE SCHOOL?
NOW I'VE GOT TO FIND THE OTHERS!
WHINE
WHINE
I WASN'T EXPECTING TO WALK THE WHOLE WAY DOWN THE MOUNTAIN WITH YOU GUYS.
I WAS PLANNING ON A FLY-LIKE-A-DOVE KIND OF THING, BUT NOW...
WOOF!
THERE YOU ARE!
I HOPE ARTEMIS DOESN'T WAKE UP AND WONDER WHERE YOU'VE GONE.
YIP!
RUFF!
IT'S WAY TOO LATE TO TAKE YOU BACK TO THE DORM...

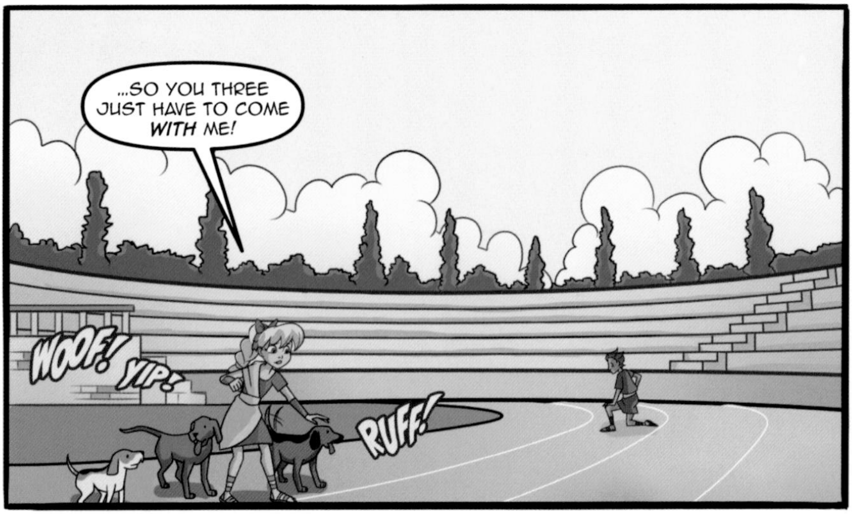
...SO YOU THREE JUST HAVE TO COME WITH ME!
WOOF! YIP!
RUFF!

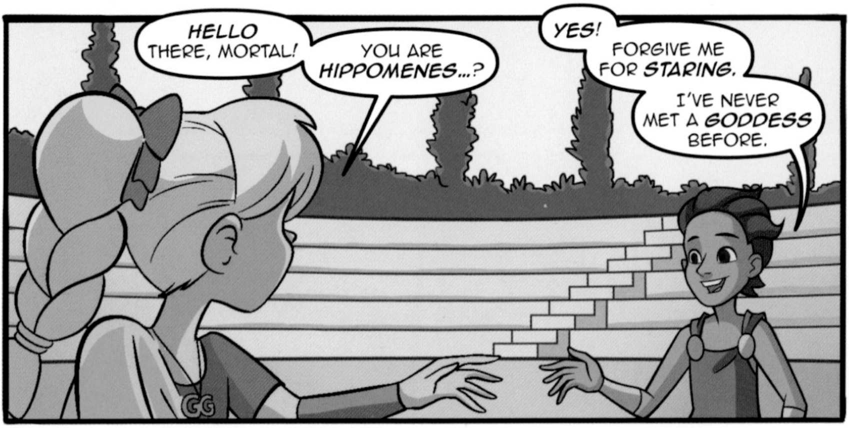
HELLO THERE, MORTAL!
YOU ARE HIPPOMENES...?
YES!
FORGIVE ME FOR STARING.
I'VE NEVER MET A GODDESS BEFORE.

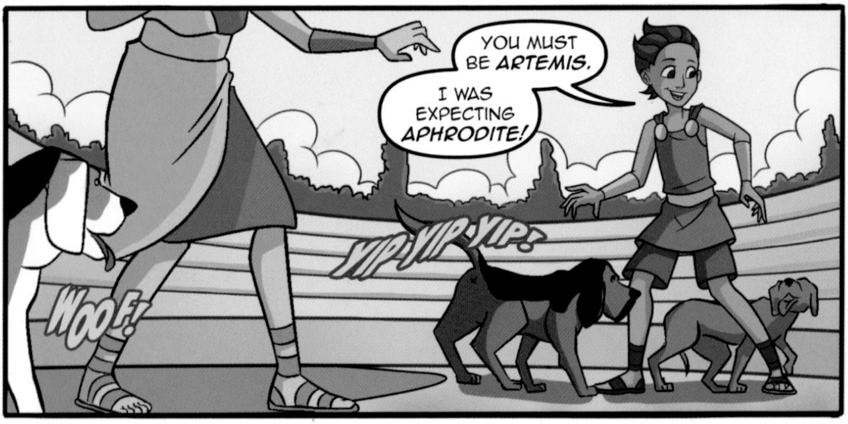
YOU MUST BE ARTEMIS.
I WAS EXPECTING APHRODITE!
YIP-YIP-YIP!
WOOF!

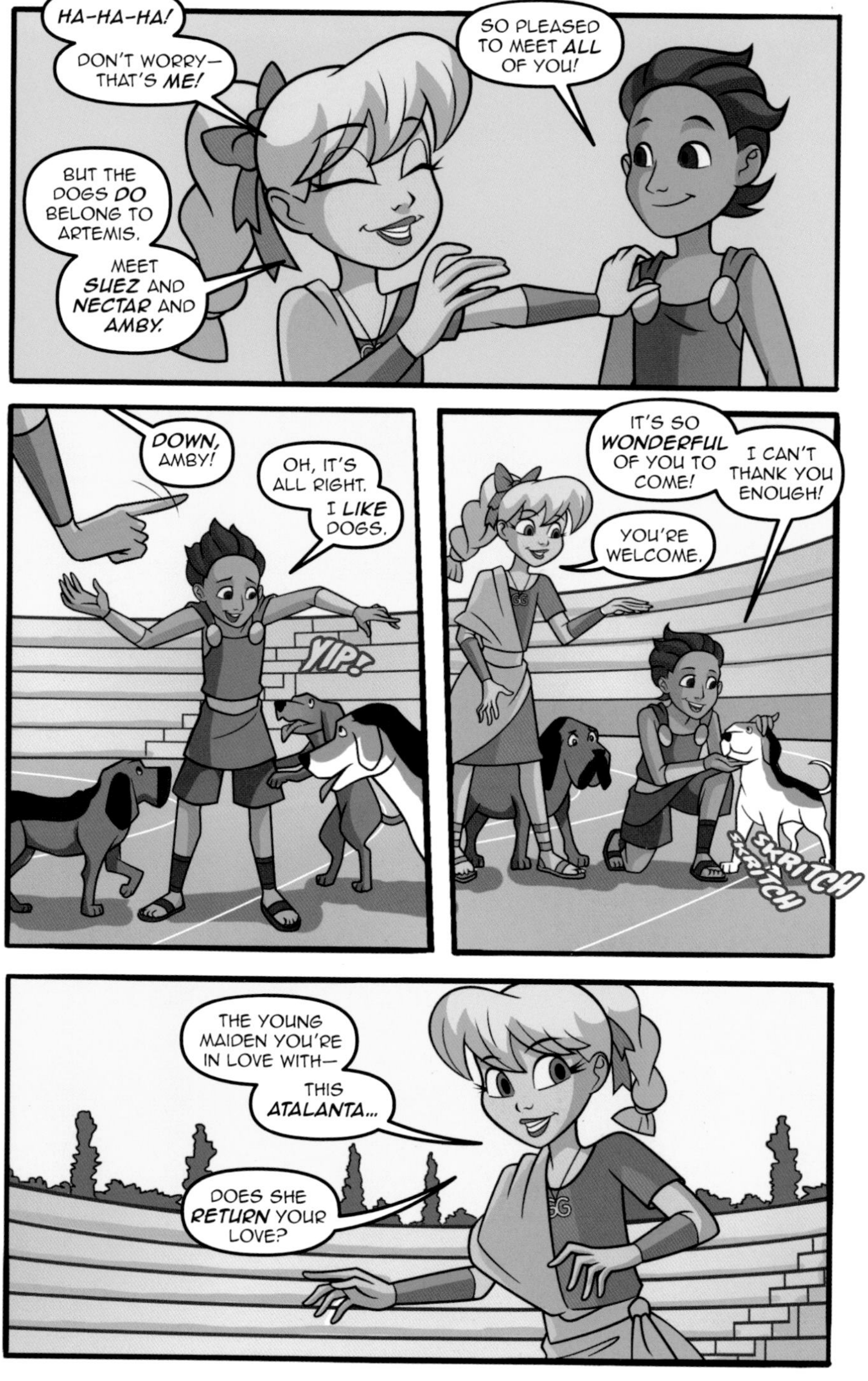
HA-HA-HA!
DON'T WORRY— THAT'S ME!
SO PLEASED TO MEET ALL OF YOU!
BUT THE DOGS DO BELONG TO ARTEMIS.
MEET SUEZ AND NECTAR AND AMBY.
DOWN, AMBY!
OH, IT'S ALL RIGHT.
I LIKE DOGS.
YIP!
IT'S SO WONDERFUL OF YOU TO COME!
I CAN'T THANK YOU ENOUGH!
YOU'RE WELCOME.
SKRITCH
SKRITCH
THE YOUNG MAIDEN YOU'RE IN LOVE WITH—
THIS ATALANTA...
DOES SHE RETURN YOUR LOVE?

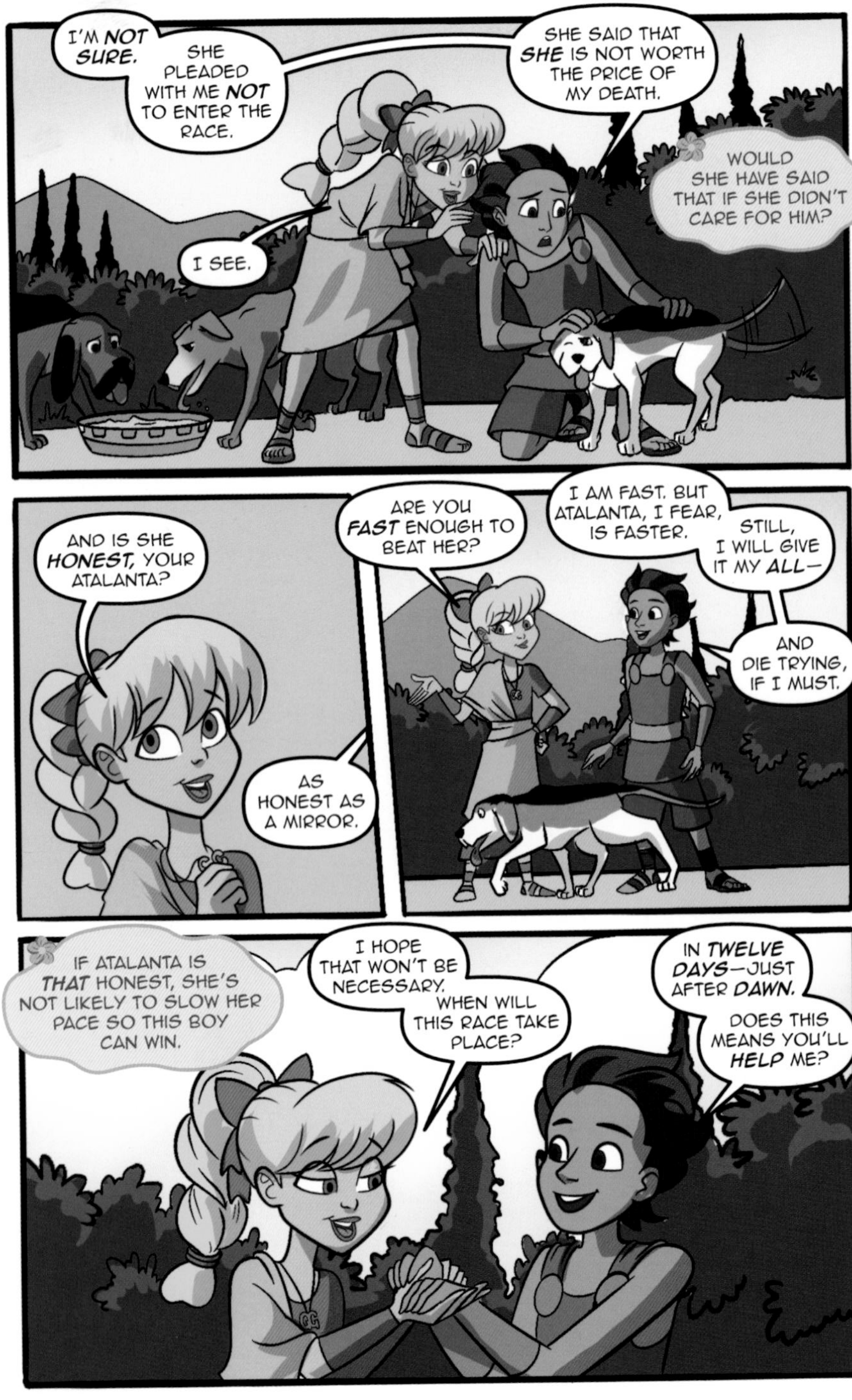

I'M NOT SURE.
SHE PLEADED WITH ME NOT TO ENTER THE RACE.
SHE SAID THAT SHE IS NOT WORTH THE PRICE OF MY DEATH.
I SEE.
WOULD SHE HAVE SAID THAT IF SHE DIDN'T CARE FOR HIM?
AND IS SHE HONEST, YOUR ATALANTA?
AS HONEST AS A MIRROR.
ARE YOU FAST ENOUGH TO BEAT HER?
I AM FAST. BUT ATALANTA, I FEAR, IS FASTER.
STILL, I WILL GIVE IT MY ALL—
AND DIE TRYING, IF I MUST.
IF ATALANTA IS THAT HONEST, SHE'S NOT LIKELY TO SLOW HER PACE SO THIS BOY CAN WIN.
I HOPE THAT WON'T BE NECESSARY.
WHEN WILL THIS RACE TAKE PLACE?
IN TWELVE DAYS—JUST AFTER DAWN.
DOES THIS MEANS YOU'LL HELP ME?

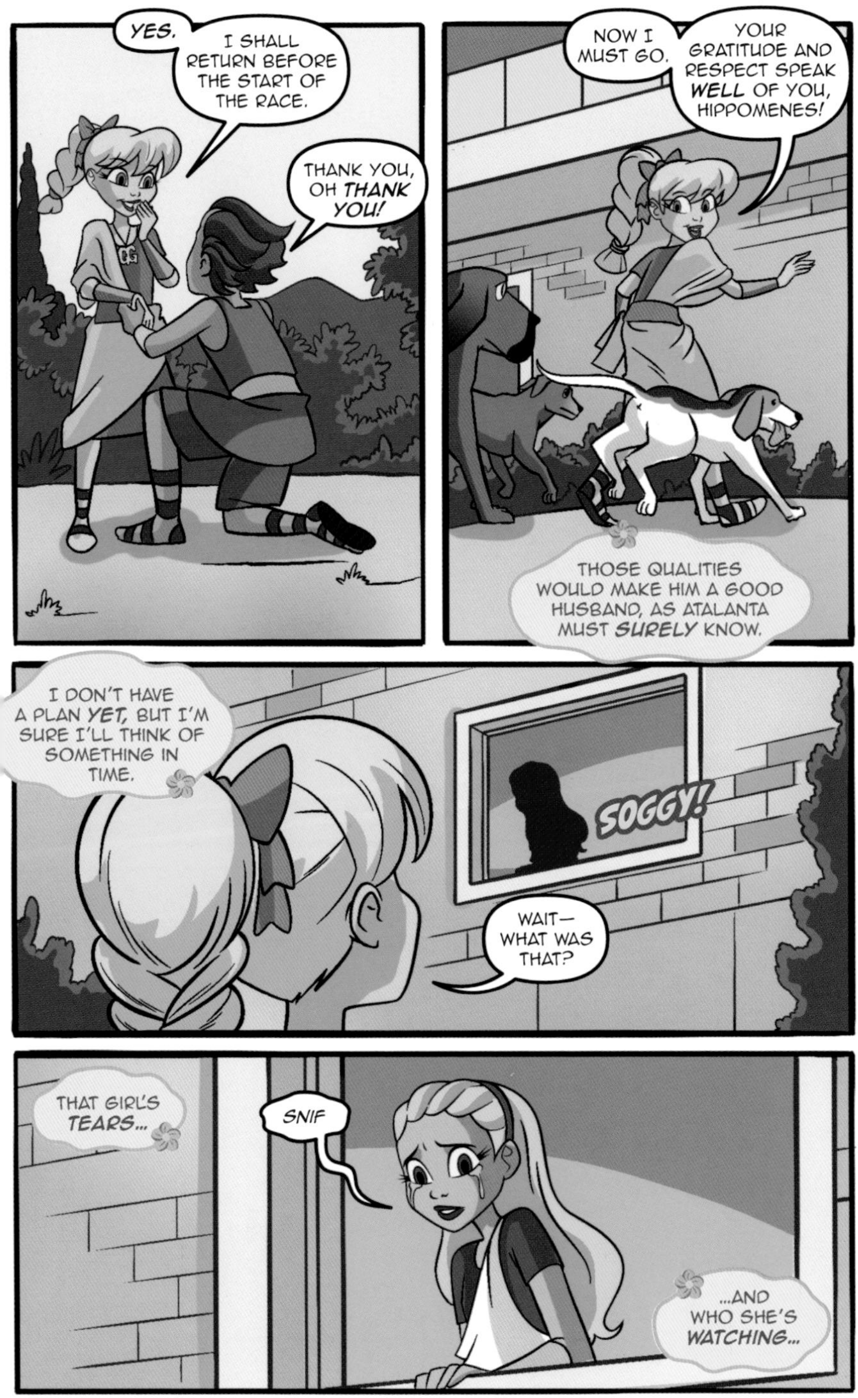
YES.
I SHALL RETURN BEFORE THE START OF THE RACE.
THANK YOU, OH THANK YOU!
NOW I MUST GO.
YOUR GRATITUDE AND RESPECT SPEAK WELL OF YOU, HIPPOMENES!
THOSE QUALITIES WOULD MAKE HIM A GOOD HUSBAND, AS ATALANTA MUST SURELY KNOW.
I DON'T HAVE A PLAN YET, BUT I'M SURE I'LL THINK OF SOMETHING IN TIME.
SOGGY!
WAIT— WHAT WAS THAT?
THAT GIRL'S TEARS...
SNIF
...AND WHO SHE'S WATCHING...

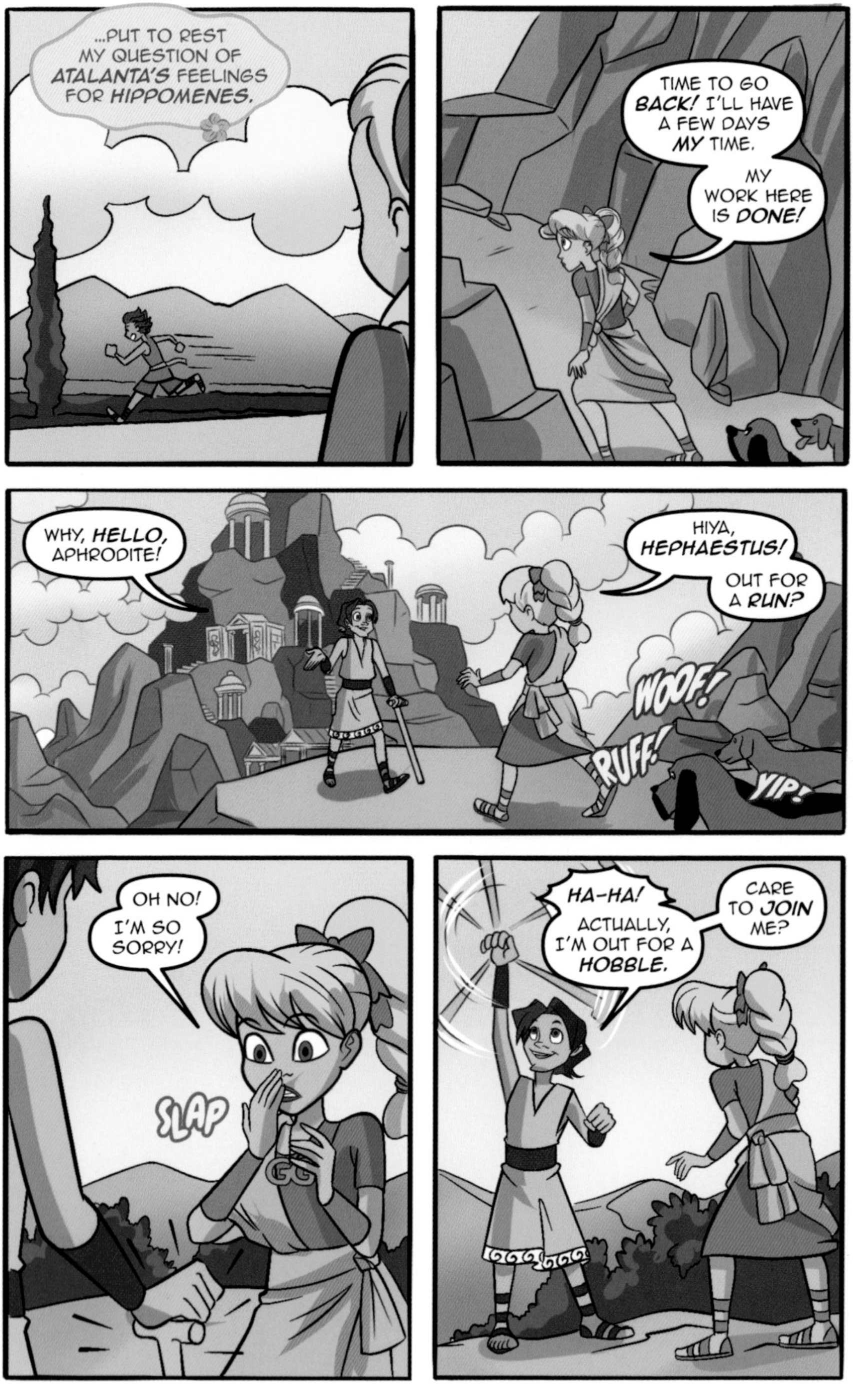
...PUT TO REST MY QUESTION OF ATALANTA'S FEELINGS FOR HIPPOMENES.
TIME TO GO BACK! I'LL HAVE A FEW DAYS MY TIME.
MY WORK HERE IS DONE!
WHY, HELLO, APHRODITE!
HIYA, HEPHAESTUS!
OUT FOR A RUN?
WOOF!
RUFF!
YIP!
OH NO! I'M SO SORRY!
SLAP
HA-HA!
ACTUALLY, I'M OUT FOR A HOBBLE.
CARE TO JOIN ME?

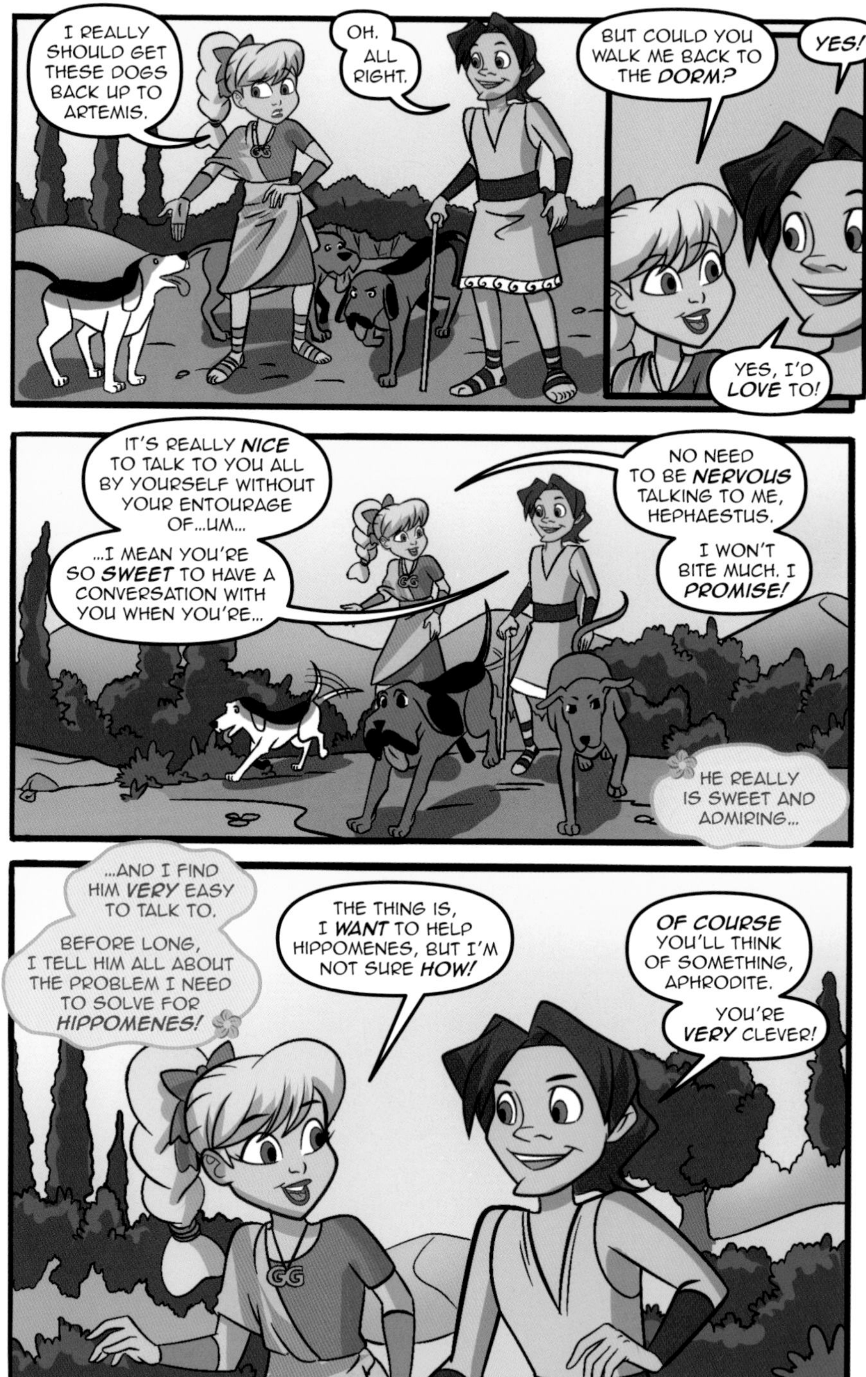

I REALLY SHOULD GET THESE DOGS BACK UP TO ARTEMIS.
OH. ALL RIGHT.
BUT COULD YOU WALK ME BACK TO THE *DORM?*
YES!
YES, I'D *LOVE* TO!
IT'S REALLY *NICE* TO TALK TO YOU ALL BY YOURSELF WITHOUT YOUR ENTOURAGE OF...UM...
...I MEAN YOU'RE SO *SWEET* TO HAVE A CONVERSATION WITH YOU WHEN YOU'RE...
NO NEED TO BE *NERVOUS* TALKING TO ME, HEPHAESTUS.
I WON'T BITE MUCH. I *PROMISE!*
HE REALLY IS SWEET AND ADMIRING...
...AND I FIND HIM *VERY* EASY TO TALK TO.
BEFORE LONG, I TELL HIM ALL ABOUT THE PROBLEM I NEED TO SOLVE FOR *HIPPOMENES!*
THE THING IS, I *WANT* TO HELP HIPPOMENES, BUT I'M NOT SURE *HOW!*
OF COURSE YOU'LL THINK OF SOMETHING, APHRODITE.
YOU'RE *VERY* CLEVER!

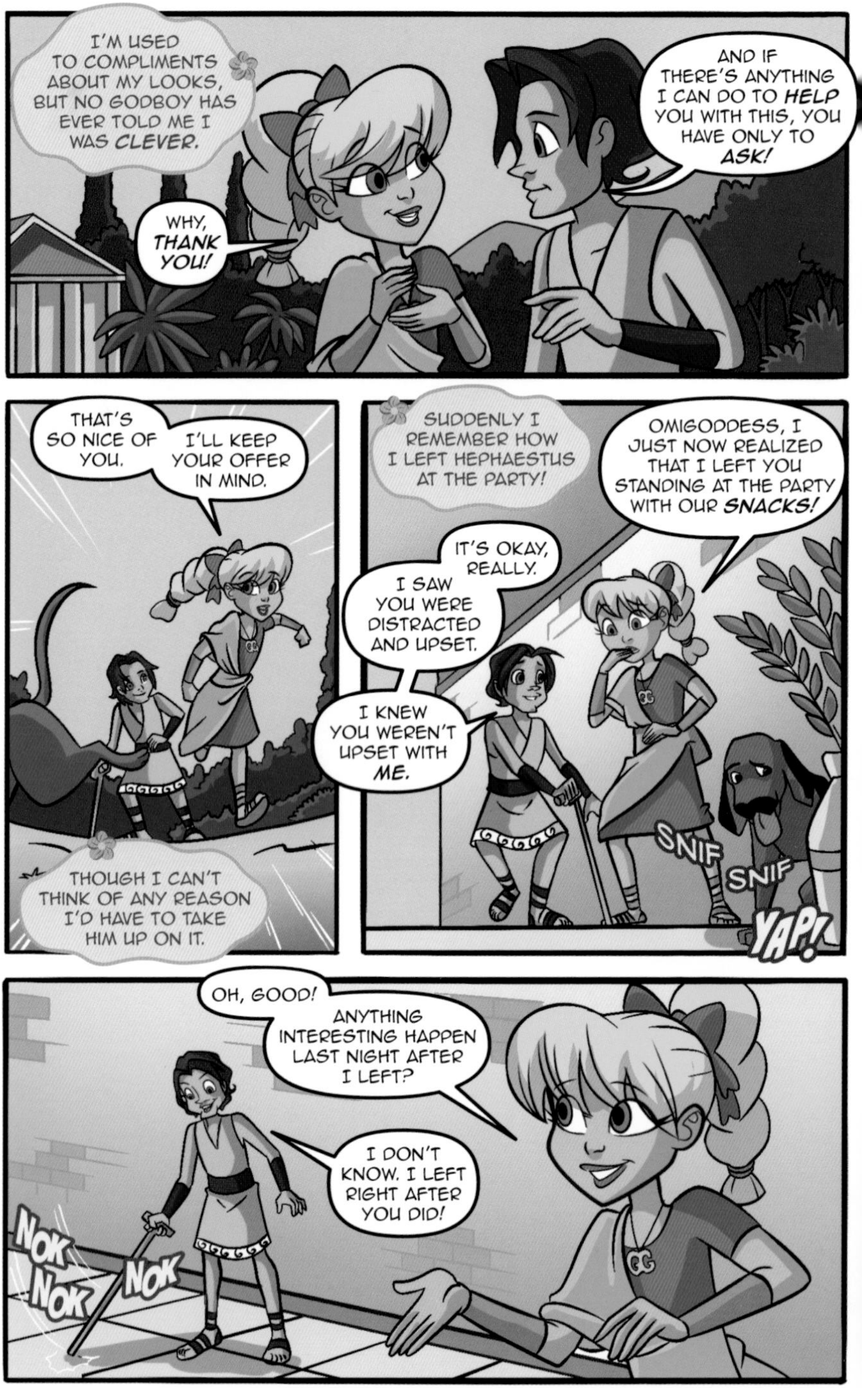

I'M USED TO COMPLIMENTS ABOUT MY LOOKS, BUT NO GODBOY HAS EVER TOLD ME I WAS *CLEVER.*
WHY, *THANK YOU!*
AND IF THERE'S ANYTHING I CAN DO TO *HELP* YOU WITH THIS, YOU HAVE ONLY TO *ASK!*
THAT'S SO NICE OF YOU.
I'LL KEEP YOUR OFFER IN MIND.
THOUGH I CAN'T THINK OF ANY REASON I'D HAVE TO TAKE HIM UP ON IT.
SUDDENLY I REMEMBER HOW I LEFT HEPHAESTUS AT THE PARTY!
OMIGODDESS, I JUST NOW REALIZED THAT I LEFT YOU STANDING AT THE PARTY WITH OUR *SNACKS!*
IT'S OKAY, REALLY.
I SAW YOU WERE DISTRACTED AND UPSET.
I KNEW YOU WEREN'T UPSET WITH *ME.*
SNIF
SNIF
YAP!
OH, GOOD!
ANYTHING INTERESTING HAPPEN LAST NIGHT AFTER I LEFT?
I DON'T KNOW. I LEFT RIGHT AFTER YOU DID!
NOK
NOK
NOK

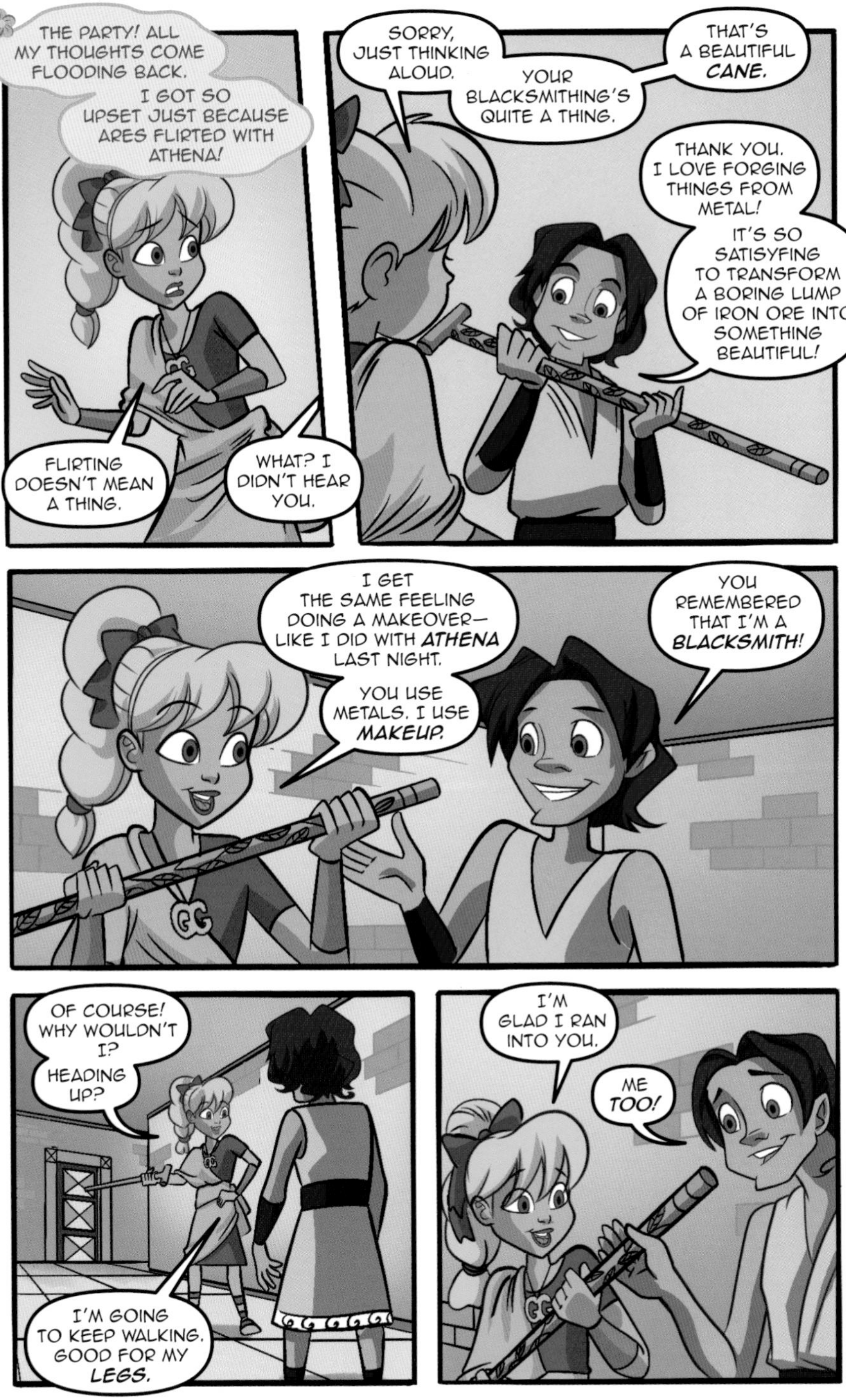
THE PARTY! ALL MY THOUGHTS COME FLOODING BACK.
I GOT SO UPSET JUST BECAUSE ARES FLIRTED WITH ATHENA!
FLIRTING DOESN'T MEAN A THING.
WHAT? I DIDN'T HEAR YOU.
SORRY, JUST THINKING ALOUD.
YOUR BLACKSMITHING'S QUITE A THING.
THAT'S A BEAUTIFUL **CANE.**
THANK YOU. I LOVE FORGING THINGS FROM METAL!
IT'S SO SATISYFING TO TRANSFORM A BORING LUMP OF IRON ORE INTO SOMETHING BEAUTIFUL!
I GET THE SAME FEELING DOING A MAKEOVER— LIKE I DID WITH **ATHENA** LAST NIGHT.
YOU USE METALS. I USE **MAKEUP.**
YOU REMEMBERED THAT I'M A **BLACKSMITH!**
OF COURSE! WHY WOULDN'T I?
HEADING UP?
I'M GOING TO KEEP WALKING. GOOD FOR MY **LEGS.**
I'M GLAD I RAN INTO YOU.
ME **TOO!**

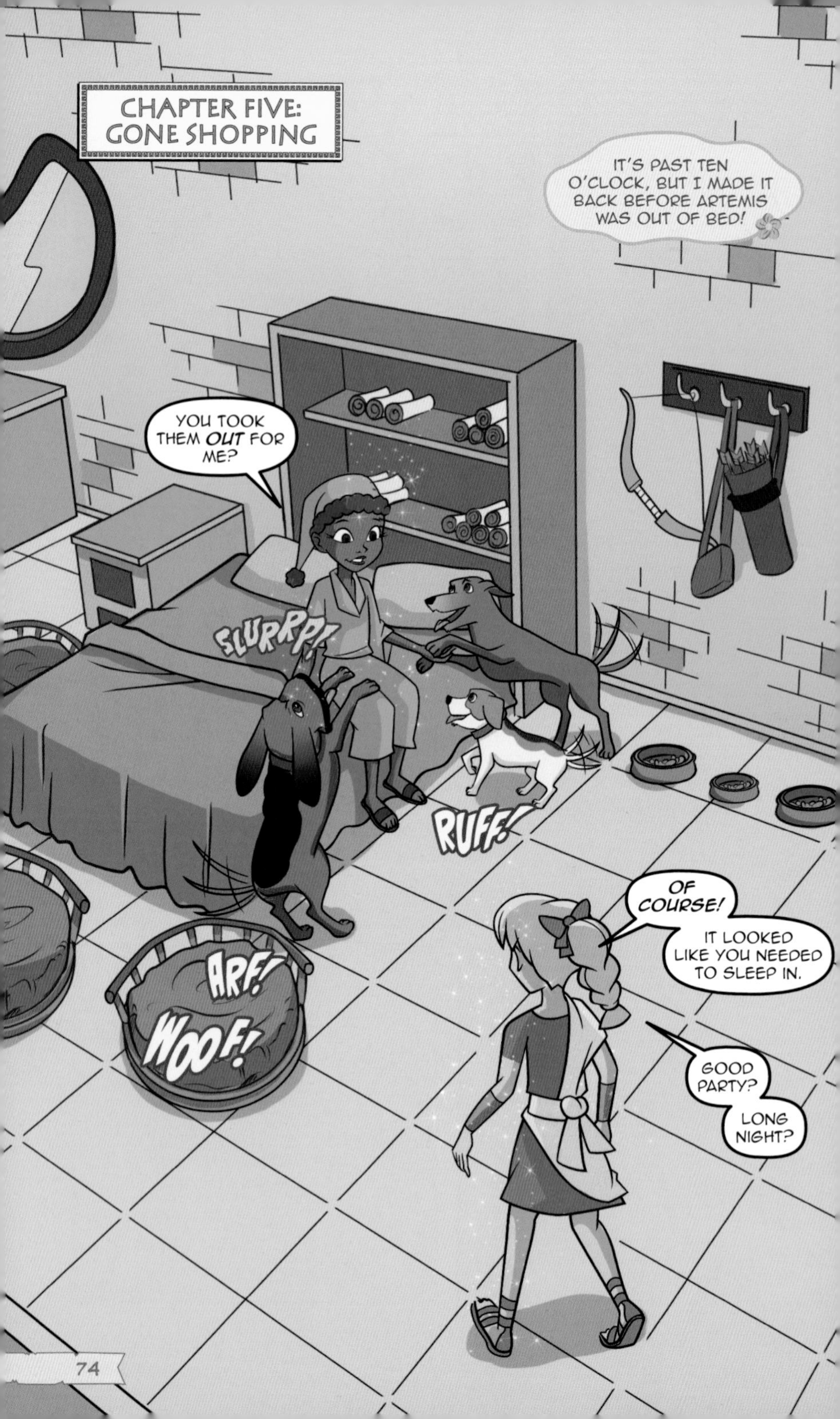
CHAPTER FIVE:
GONE SHOPPING
IT'S PAST TEN O'CLOCK, BUT I MADE IT BACK BEFORE ARTEMIS WAS OUT OF BED!
YOU TOOK THEM *OUT* FOR ME?
SLURRP!
RUFF!
ARF!
WOOF!
OF COURSE!
IT LOOKED LIKE YOU NEEDED TO SLEEP IN.
GOOD PARTY?
LONG NIGHT?

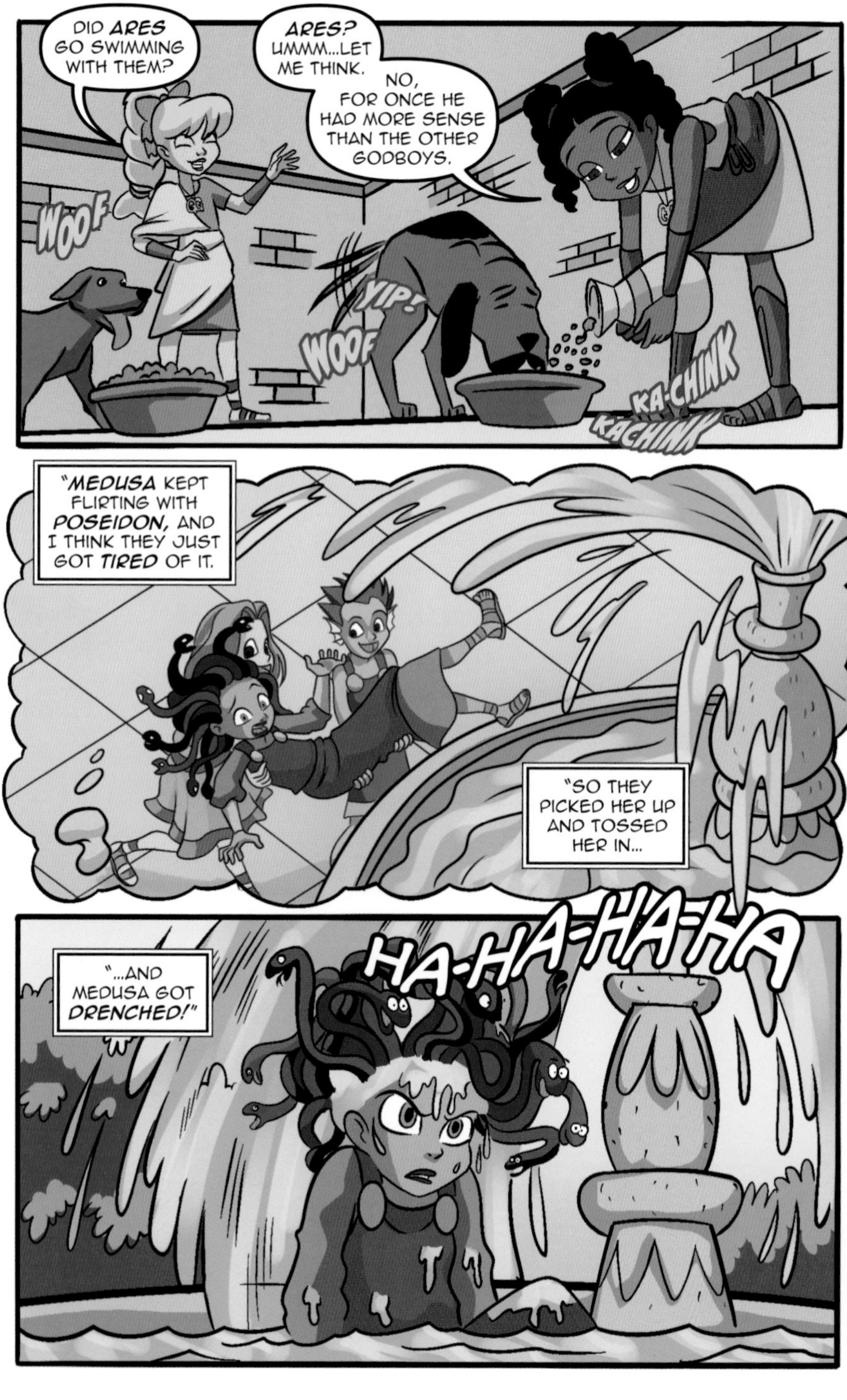
DID ARES GO SWIMMING WITH THEM?
ARES? UMMM...LET ME THINK.
NO, FOR ONCE HE HAD MORE SENSE THAN THE OTHER GODBOYS.
WOOF
YIP!
WOOF
KA-CHINK
KACHINK
"MEDUSA KEPT FLIRTING WITH POSEIDON, AND I THINK THEY JUST GOT TIRED OF IT.
"SO THEY PICKED HER UP AND TOSSED HER IN...
"...AND MEDUSA GOT DRENCHED!"
HA-HA-HA-HA-HA

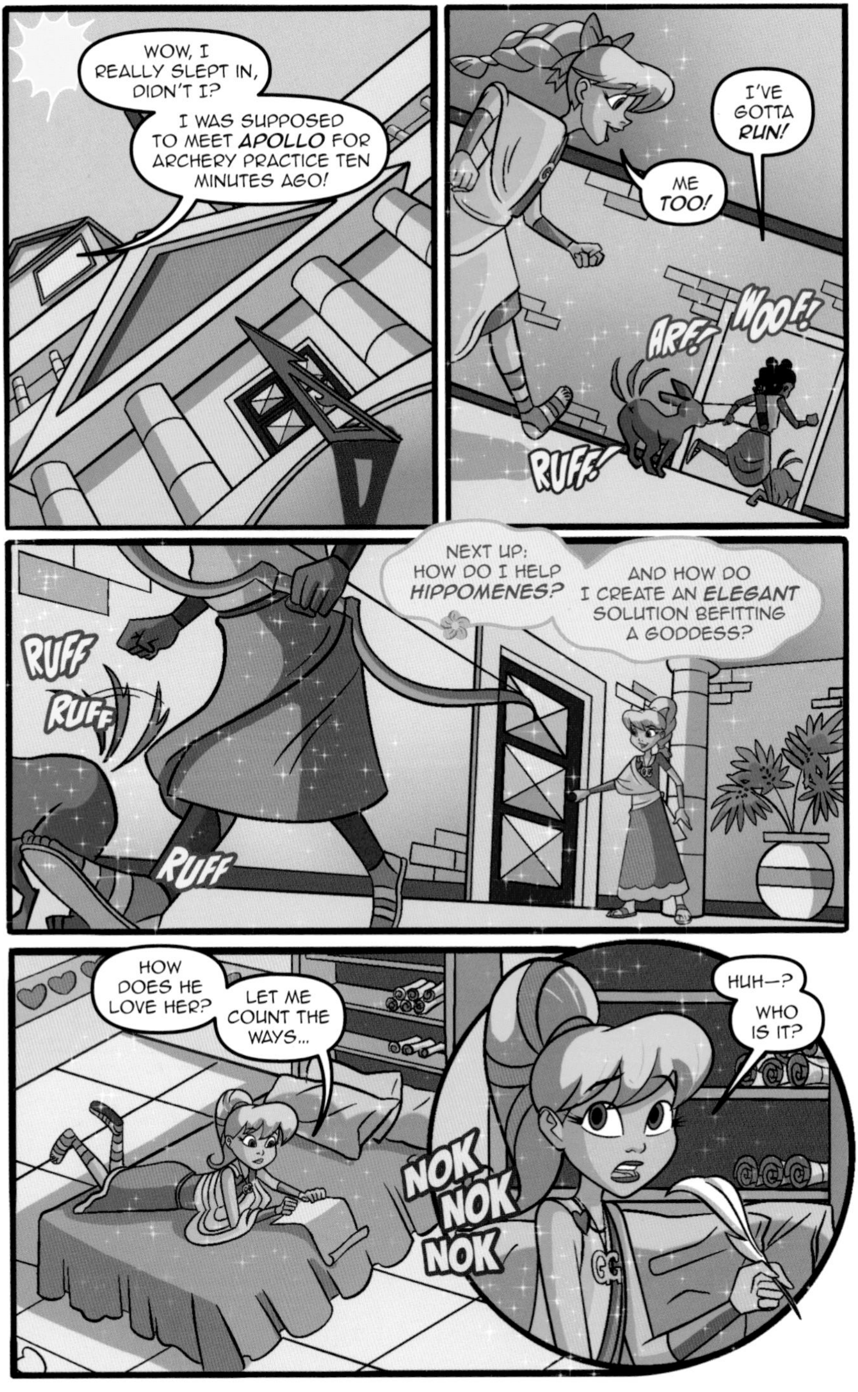
WOW, I REALLY SLEPT IN, DIDN'T I?
I WAS SUPPOSED TO MEET *APOLLO* FOR ARCHERY PRACTICE TEN MINUTES AGO!
I'VE GOTTA *RUN!*
ME *TOO!*
WOOF!
ARF!
RUFF!
NEXT UP: HOW DO I HELP *HIPPOMENES?*
AND HOW DO I CREATE AN *ELEGANT* SOLUTION BEFITTING A GODDESS?
RUFF
RUFF
RUFF
HOW DOES HE LOVE HER?
LET ME COUNT THE WAYS...
NOK NOK NOK
HUH—?
WHO IS IT?

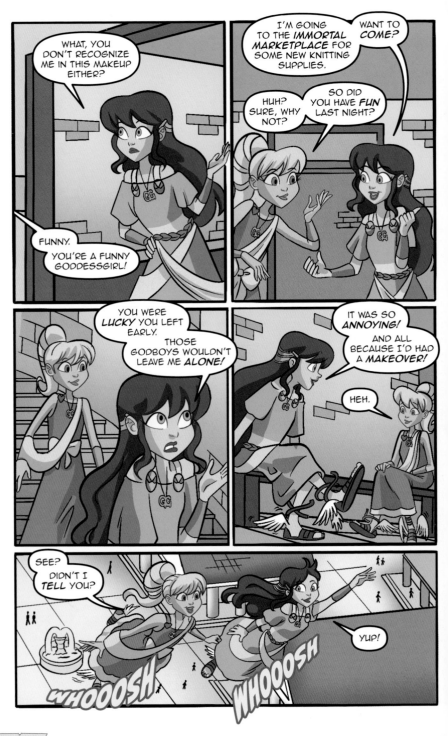

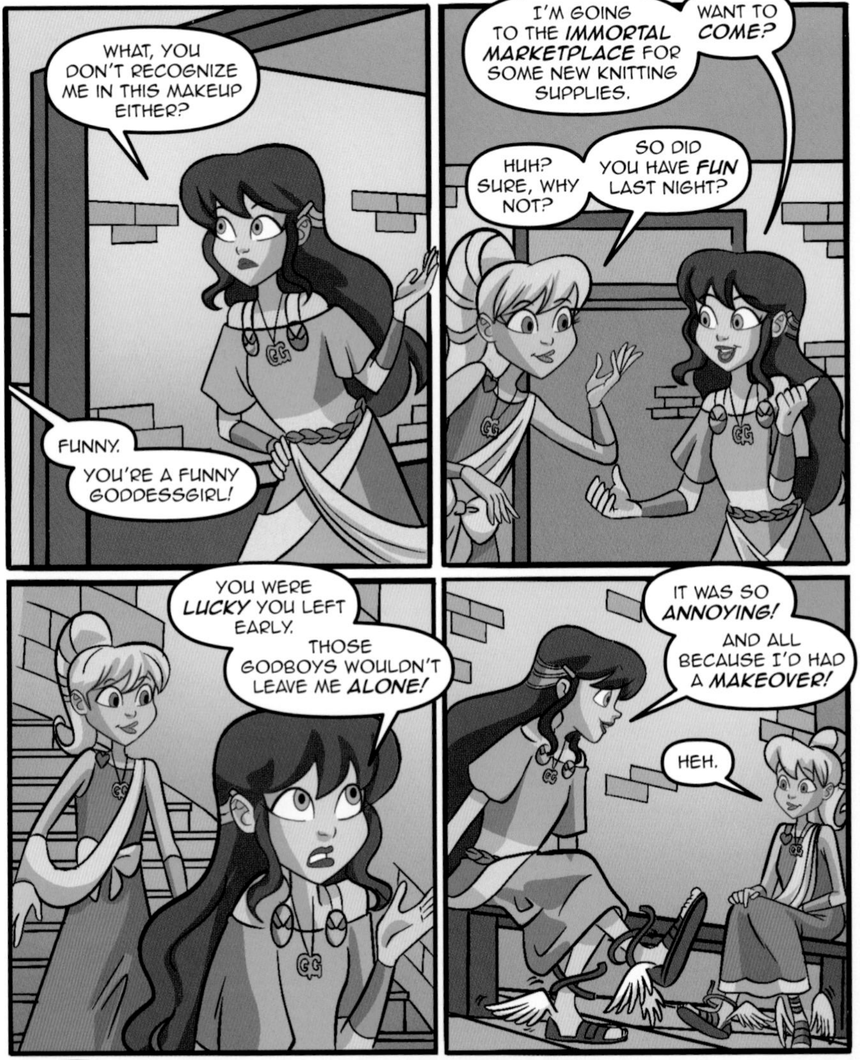
WHAT, YOU DON'T RECOGNIZE ME IN THIS MAKEUP EITHER?
FUNNY.
YOU'RE A FUNNY GODDESSGIRL!
I'M GOING TO THE *IMMORTAL MARKETPLACE* FOR SOME NEW KNITTING SUPPLIES.
WANT TO *COME?*
HUH? SURE, WHY NOT?
SO DID YOU HAVE *FUN* LAST NIGHT?
YOU WERE *LUCKY* YOU LEFT EARLY.
THOSE GODBOYS WOULDN'T LEAVE ME *ALONE!*
IT WAS SO *ANNOYING!*
AND ALL BECAUSE I'D HAD A *MAKEOVER!*
HEH.
SEE?
DIDN'T I *TELL* YOU?
YUP!
WHOOOOSH
WHOOOSH

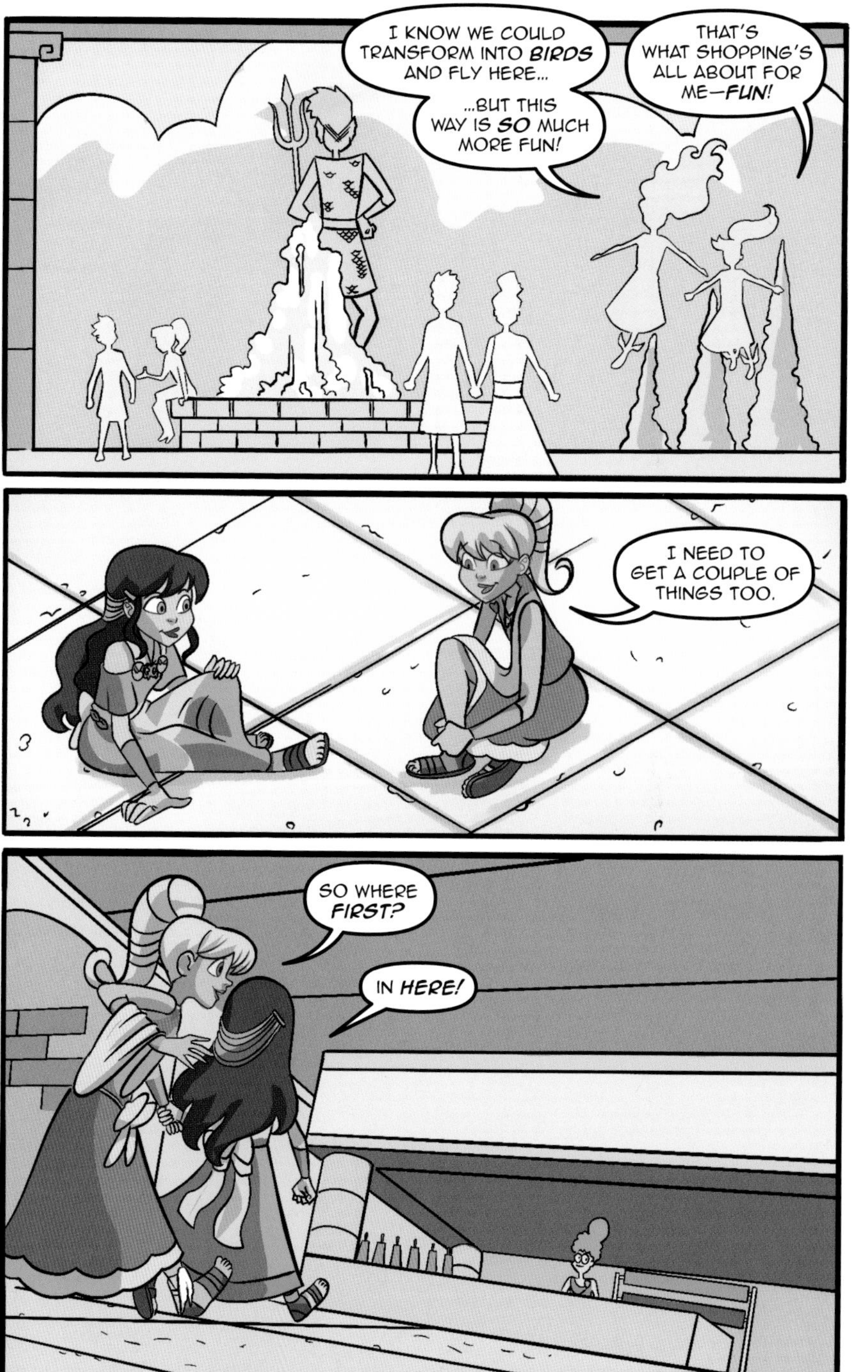
I KNOW WE COULD TRANSFORM INTO BIRDS AND FLY HERE...
...BUT THIS WAY IS SO MUCH MORE FUN!
THAT'S WHAT SHOPPING'S ALL ABOUT FOR ME—FUN!
I NEED TO GET A COUPLE OF THINGS TOO.
SO WHERE FIRST?
IN HERE!

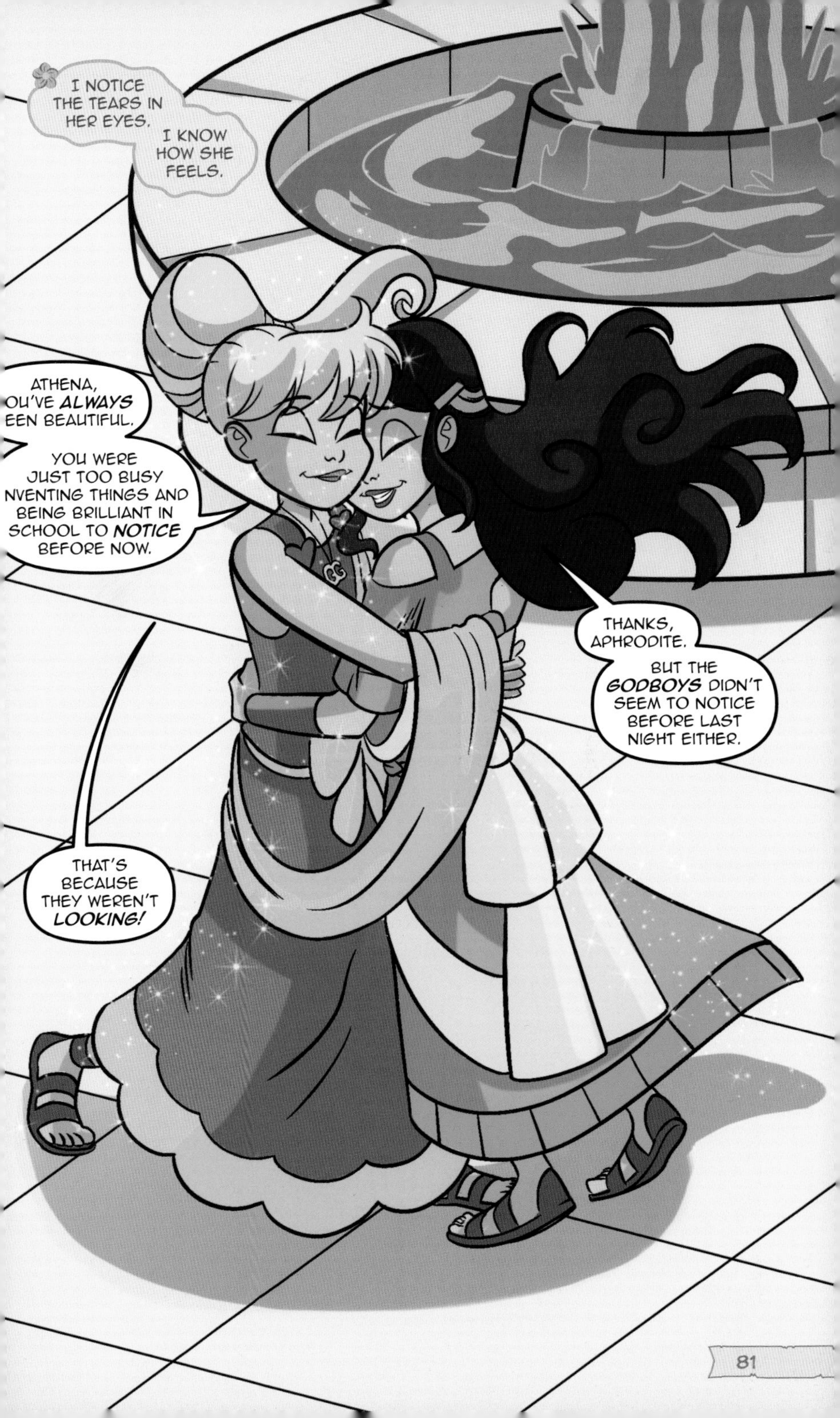
I NOTICE THE TEARS IN HER EYES.
I KNOW HOW SHE FEELS.
ATHENA, OU'VE ALWAYS EEN BEAUTIFUL.
YOU WERE JUST TOO BUSY NVENTING THINGS AND BEING BRILLIANT IN SCHOOL TO NOTICE BEFORE NOW.
THANKS, APHRODITE.
BUT THE GODBOYS DIDN'T SEEM TO NOTICE BEFORE LAST NIGHT EITHER.
THAT'S BECAUSE THEY WEREN'T LOOKING!

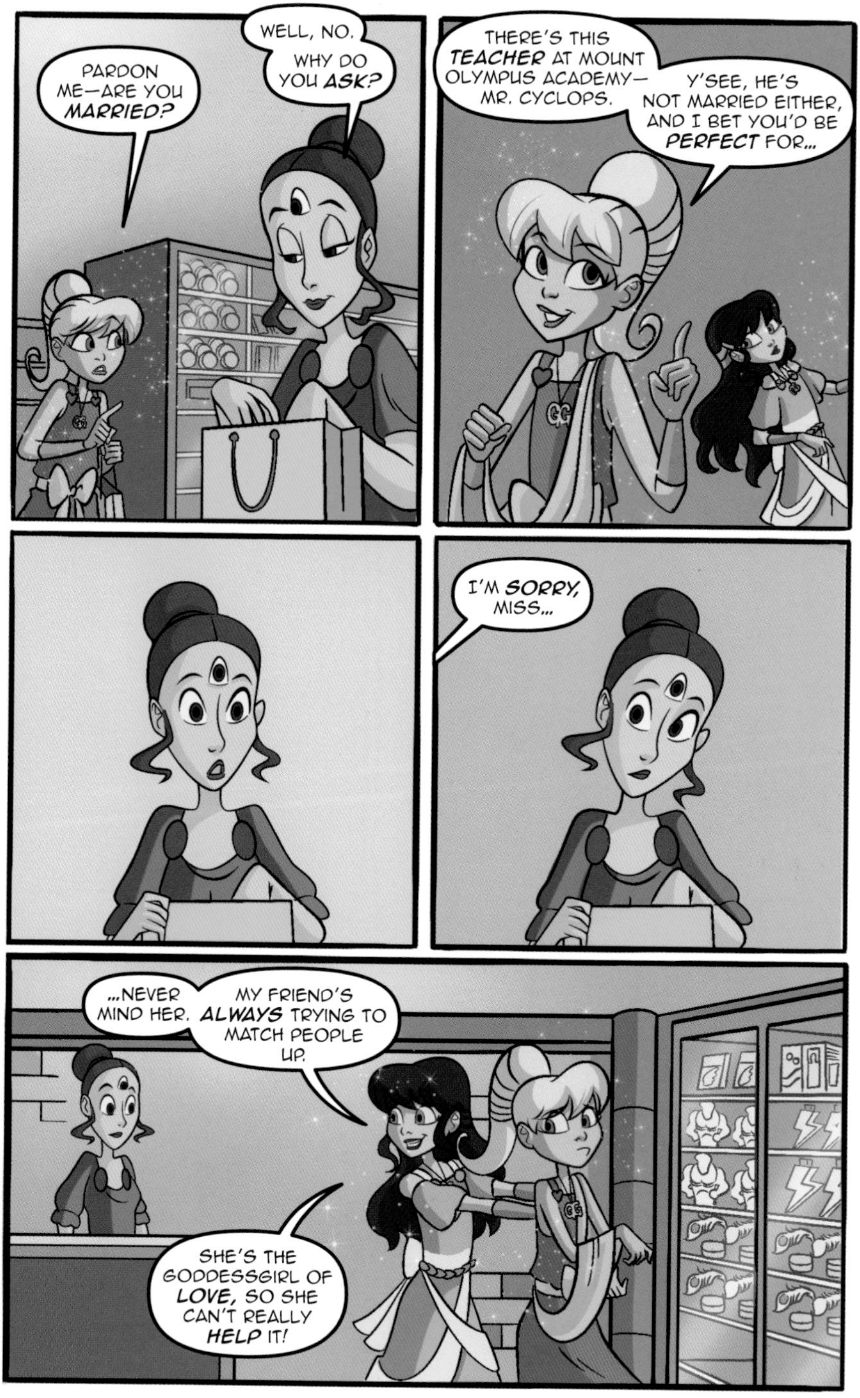
PARDON ME—ARE YOU MARRIED?
WELL, NO.
WHY DO YOU ASK?
THERE'S THIS TEACHER AT MOUNT OLYMPUS ACADEMY—MR. CYCLOPS.
Y'SEE, HE'S NOT MARRIED EITHER, AND I BET YOU'D BE PERFECT FOR...
I'M SORRY, MISS...
...NEVER MIND HER.
MY FRIEND'S ALWAYS TRYING TO MATCH PEOPLE UP.
SHE'S THE GODDESSGIRL OF LOVE, SO SHE CAN'T REALLY HELP IT!

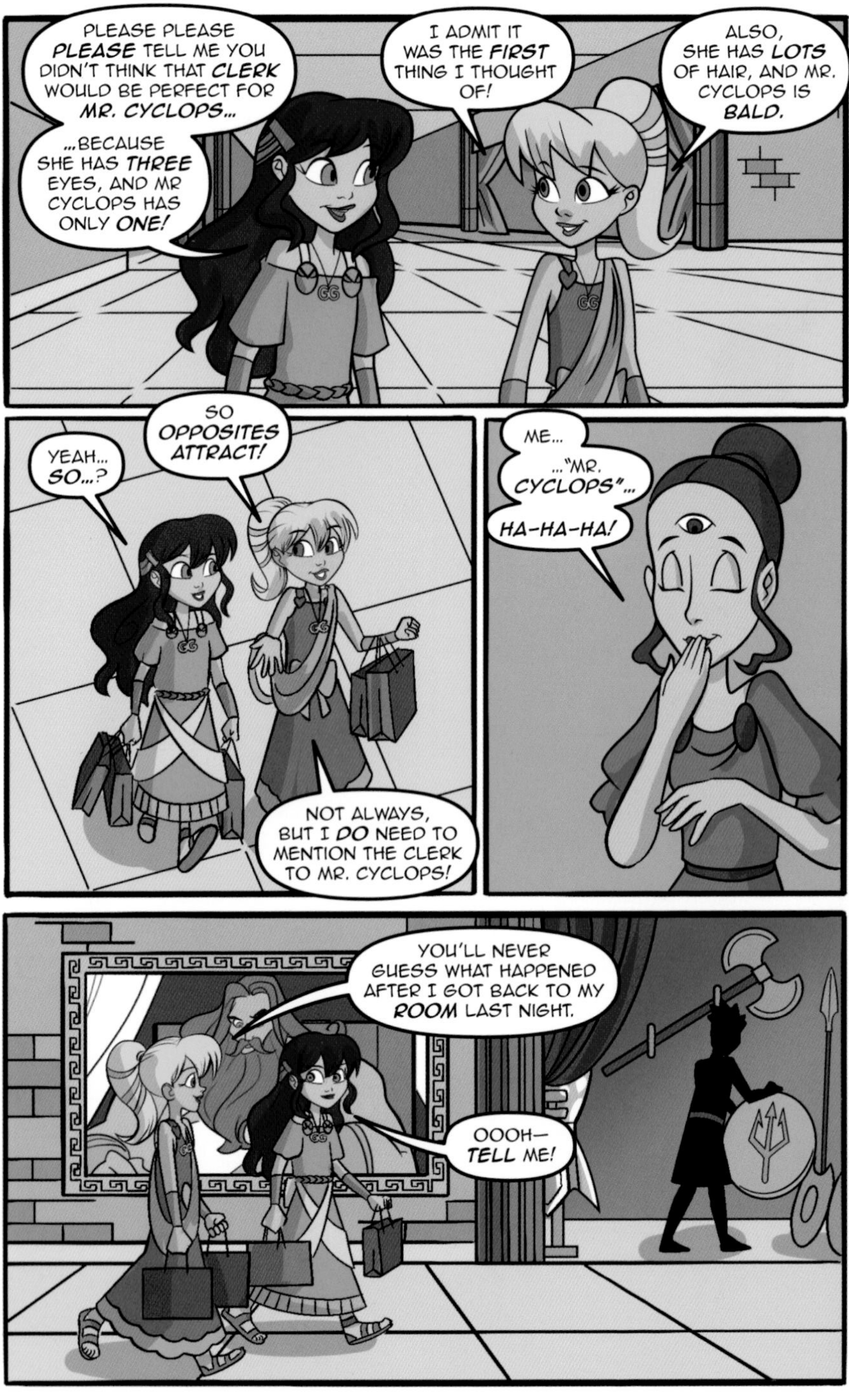
PLEASE PLEASE PLEASE TELL ME YOU DIDN'T THINK THAT CLERK WOULD BE PERFECT FOR MR. CYCLOPS...
...BECAUSE SHE HAS THREE EYES, AND MR CYCLOPS HAS ONLY ONE!
I ADMIT IT WAS THE FIRST THING I THOUGHT OF!
ALSO, SHE HAS LOTS OF HAIR, AND MR. CYCLOPS IS BALD.
YEAH... SO...?
SO OPPOSITES ATTRACT!
NOT ALWAYS, BUT I DO NEED TO MENTION THE CLERK TO MR. CYCLOPS!
ME...
..."MR. CYCLOPS"...
HA-HA-HA!
YOU'LL NEVER GUESS WHAT HAPPENED AFTER I GOT BACK TO MY ROOM LAST NIGHT.
OOOH— TELL ME!

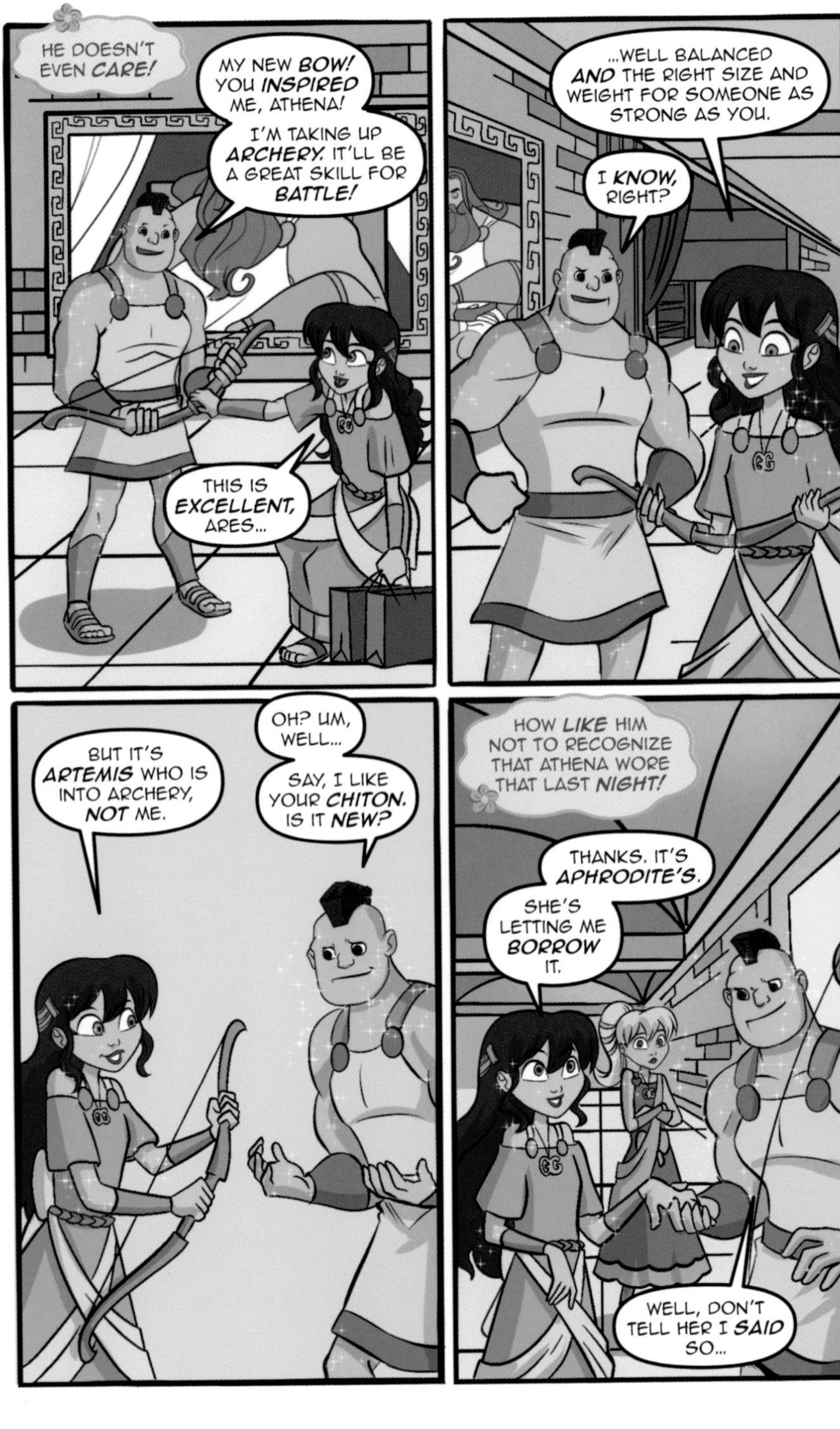

HE DOESN'T EVEN CARE!
MY NEW BOW! YOU INSPIRED ME, ATHENA!
I'M TAKING UP ARCHERY. IT'LL BE A GREAT SKILL FOR BATTLE!
THIS IS EXCELLENT, ARES...
...WELL BALANCED AND THE RIGHT SIZE AND WEIGHT FOR SOMEONE AS STRONG AS YOU.
I KNOW, RIGHT?
BUT IT'S ARTEMIS WHO IS INTO ARCHERY, NOT ME.
OH? UM, WELL...
SAY, I LIKE YOUR CHITON. IS IT NEW?
HOW LIKE HIM NOT TO RECOGNIZE THAT ATHENA WORE THAT LAST NIGHT!
THANKS. IT'S APHRODITE'S.
SHE'S LETTING ME BORROW IT.
WELL, DON'T TELL HER I SAID SO...

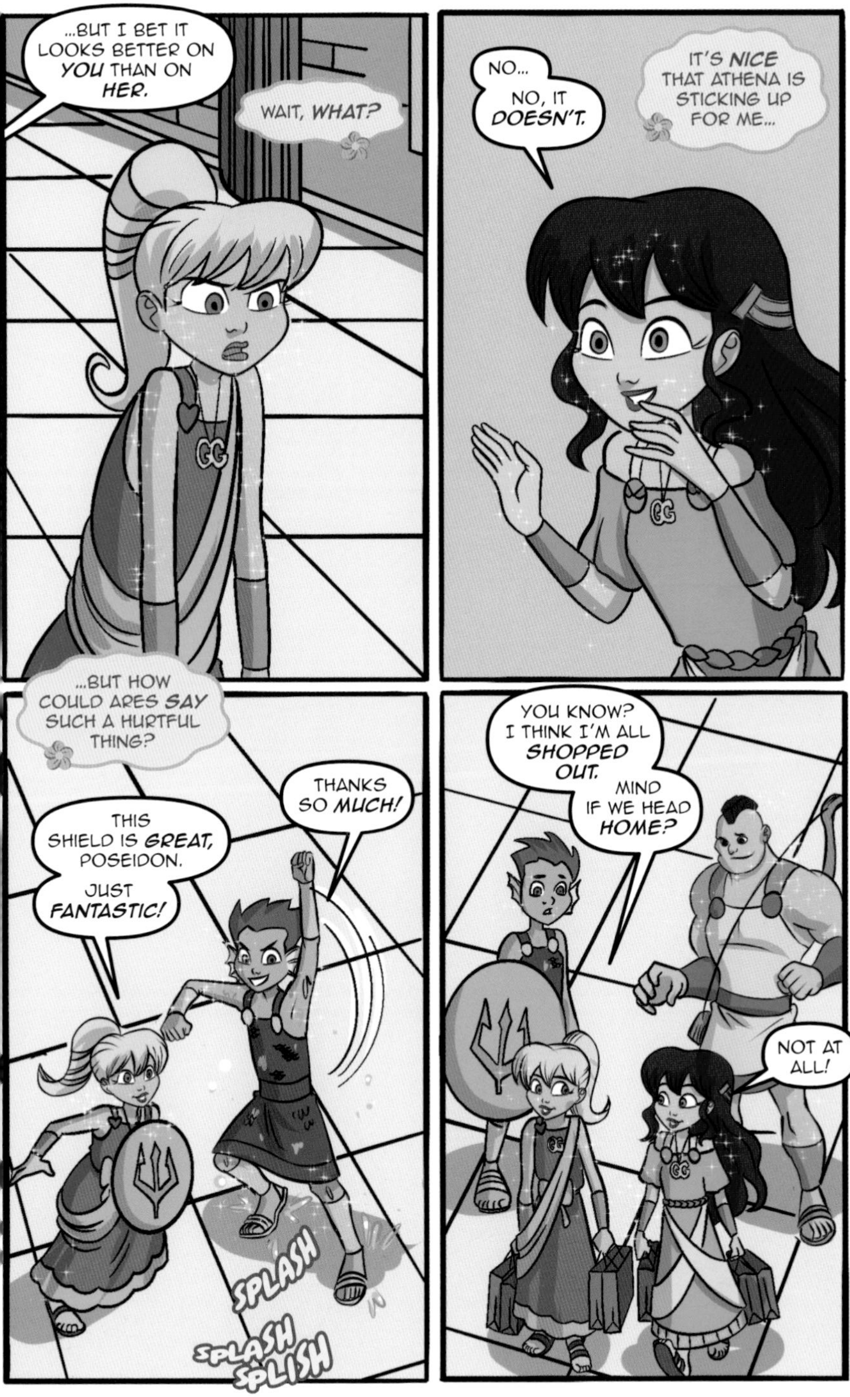
...BUT I BET IT LOOKS BETTER ON YOU THAN ON HER.
WAIT, WHAT?
NO...
NO, IT DOESN'T.
IT'S NICE THAT ATHENA IS STICKING UP FOR ME...
...BUT HOW COULD ARES SAY SUCH A HURTFUL THING?
THIS SHIELD IS GREAT, POSEIDON.
JUST FANTASTIC!
THANKS SO MUCH!
SPLASH
SPLASH
SPLISH
YOU KNOW? I THINK I'M ALL SHOPPED OUT.
MIND IF WE HEAD HOME?
NOT AT ALL!

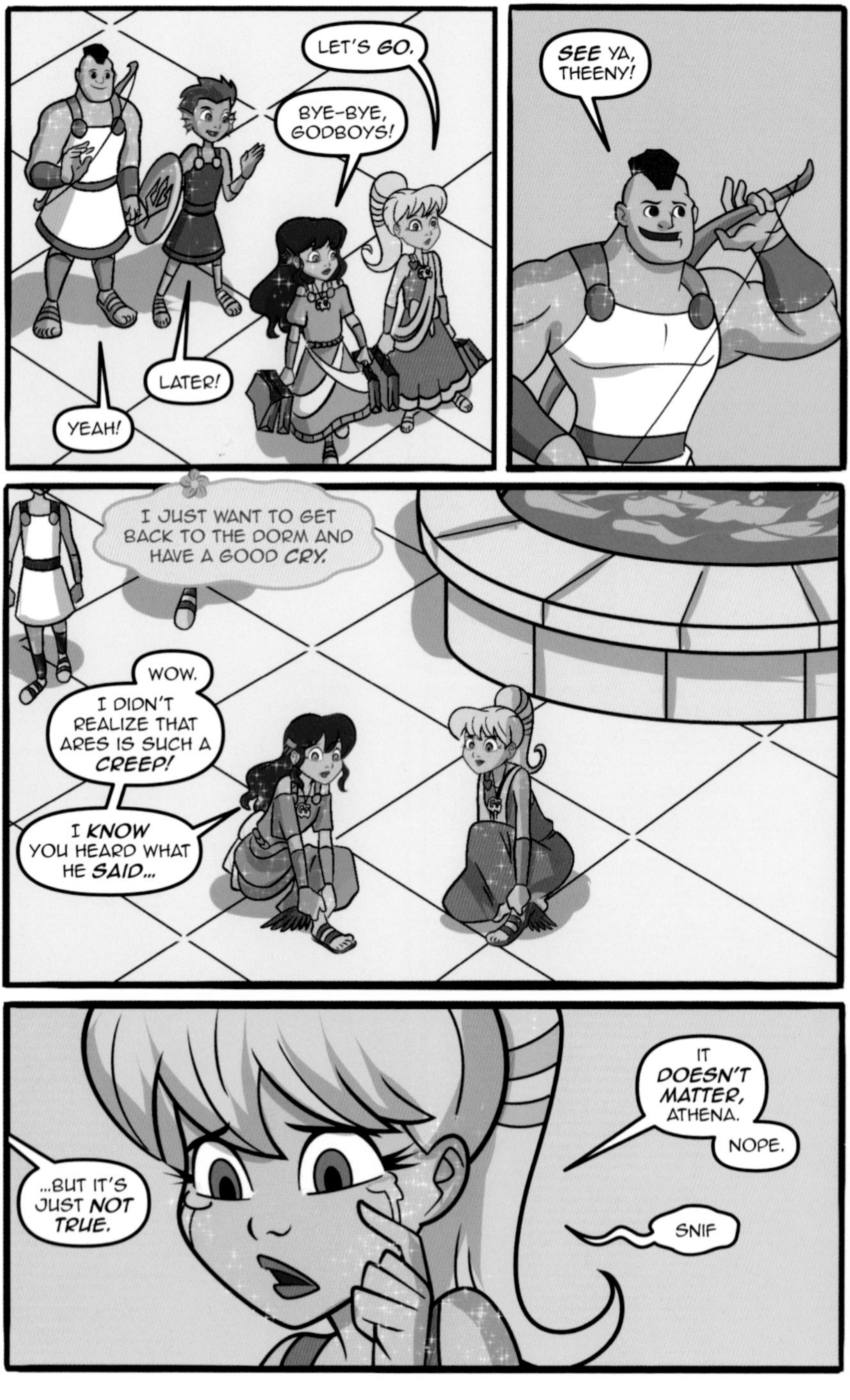
LET'S GO.
BYE-BYE, GODBOYS!
LATER!
YEAH!
SEE YA, THEENY!
I JUST WANT TO GET BACK TO THE DORM AND HAVE A GOOD CRY.
WOW.
I DIDN'T REALIZE THAT ARES IS SUCH A CREEP!
I KNOW YOU HEARD WHAT HE SAID...
...BUT IT'S JUST NOT TRUE.
IT DOESN'T MATTER, ATHENA.
NOPE.
SNIF

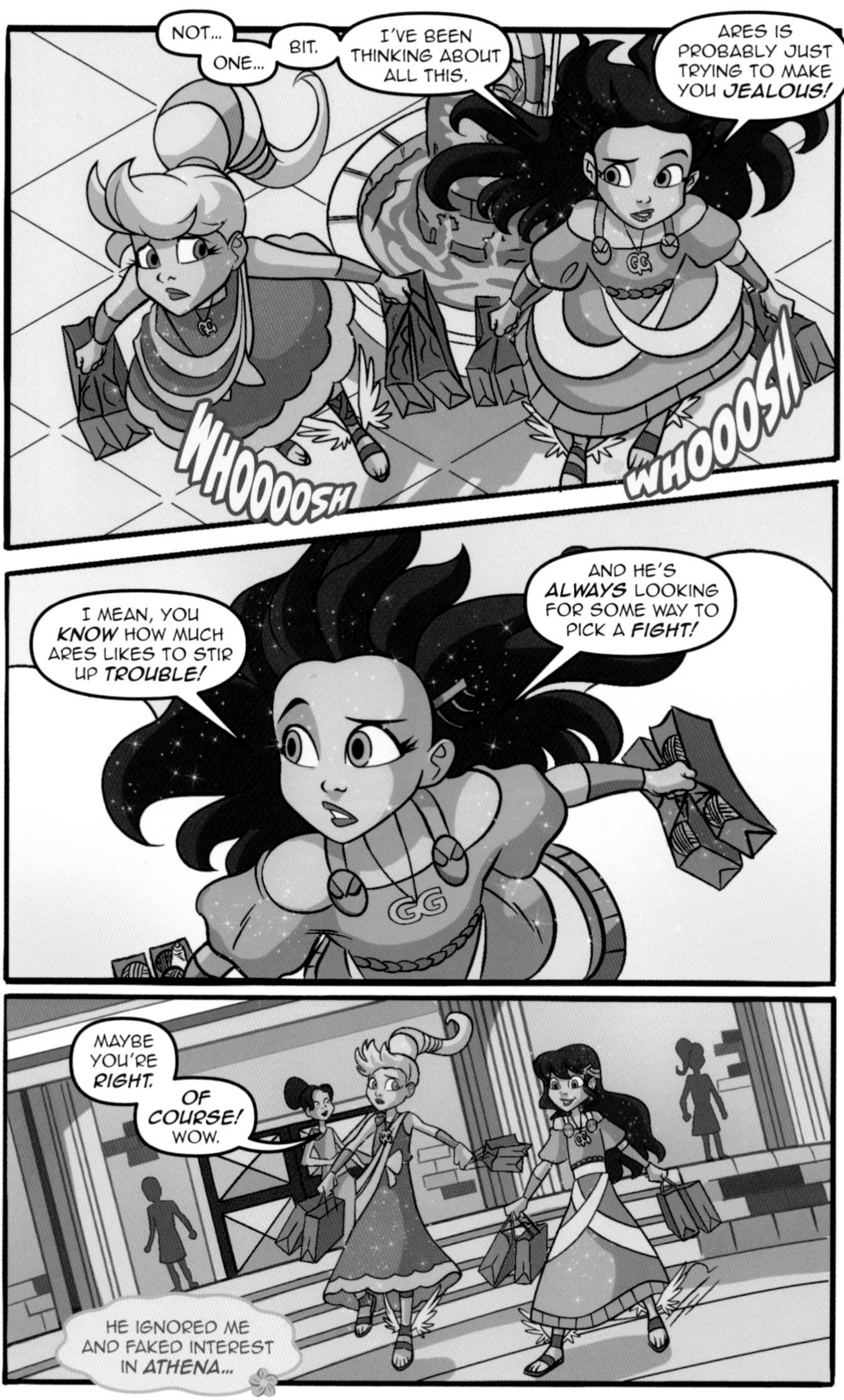
NOT... ONE... BIT.
I'VE BEEN THINKING ABOUT ALL THIS.
ARES IS PROBABLY JUST TRYING TO MAKE YOU JEALOUS!
WHOOOOSH
WHOOOSH
I MEAN, YOU KNOW HOW MUCH ARES LIKES TO STIR UP TROUBLE!
AND HE'S ALWAYS LOOKING FOR SOME WAY TO PICK A FIGHT!
MAYBE YOU'RE RIGHT.
OF COURSE! WOW.
HE IGNORED ME AND FAKED INTEREST IN ATHENA...

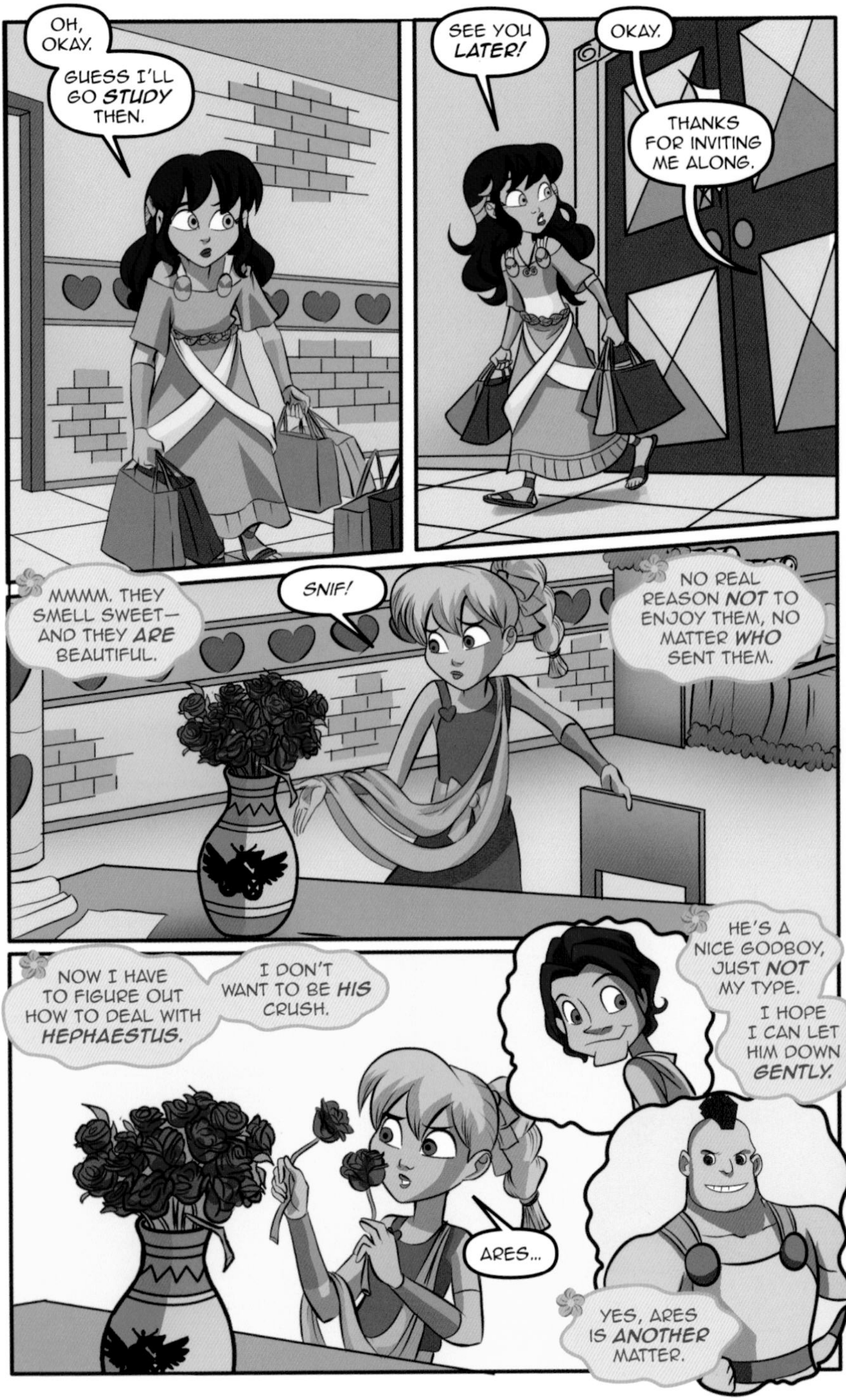

OH, OKAY.
GUESS I'LL GO **STUDY** THEN.
SEE YOU **LATER!**
OKAY.
THANKS FOR INVITING ME ALONG.
MMMM. THEY SMELL SWEET—AND THEY **ARE** BEAUTIFUL.
SNIF!
NO REAL REASON **NOT** TO ENJOY THEM, NO MATTER **WHO** SENT THEM.
NOW I HAVE TO FIGURE OUT HOW TO DEAL WITH **HEPHAESTUS.**
I DON'T WANT TO BE **HIS** CRUSH.
HE'S A NICE GODBOY, JUST **NOT** MY TYPE.
I HOPE I CAN LET HIM DOWN **GENTLY.**
ARES...
YES, ARES IS **ANOTHER** MATTER.

CHAPTER SIX: GOSSIP

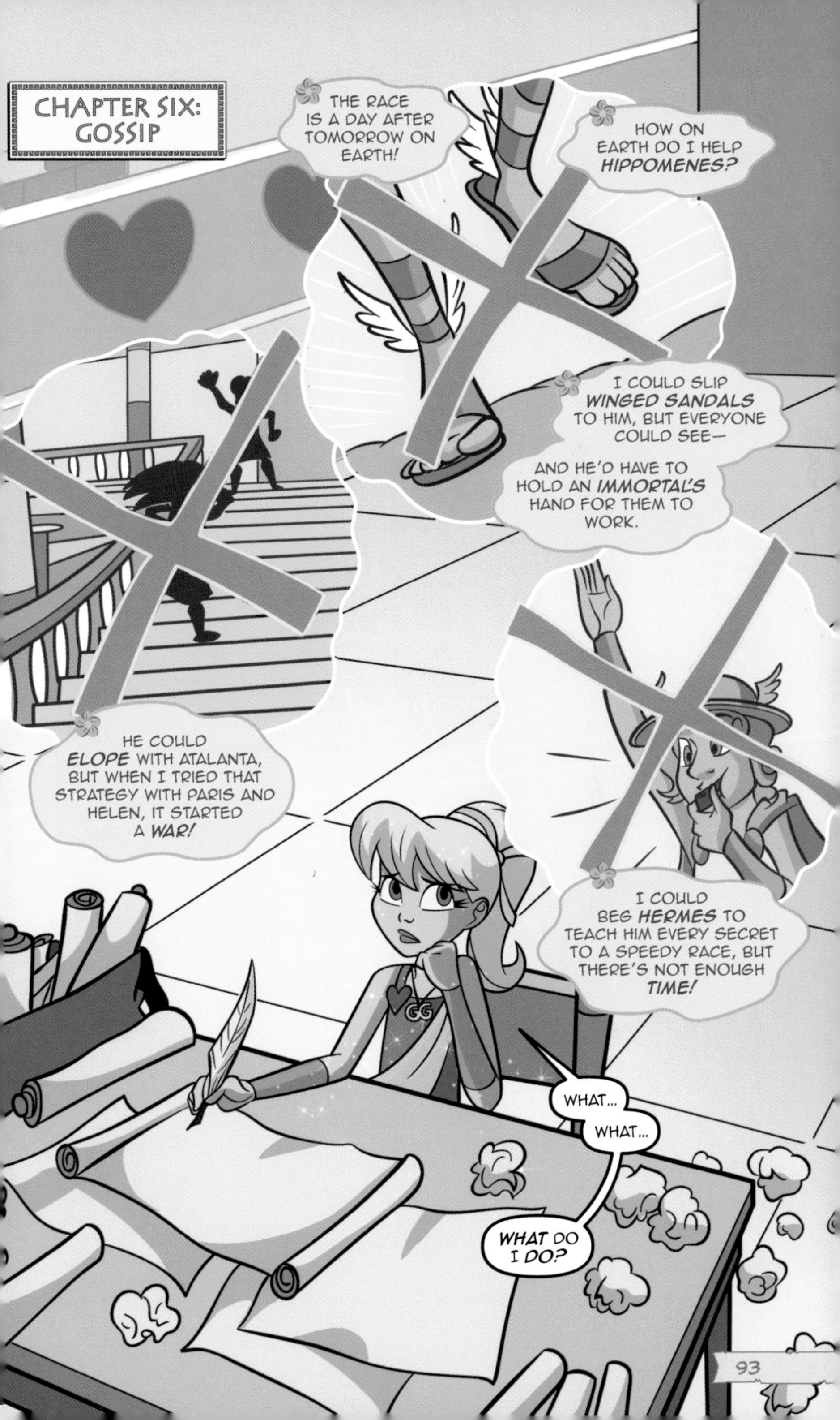

THE RACE IS A DAY AFTER TOMORROW ON EARTH!
HOW ON EARTH DO I HELP HIPPOMENES?
I COULD SLIP WINGED SANDALS TO HIM, BUT EVERYONE COULD SEE—
AND HE'D HAVE TO HOLD AN IMMORTAL'S HAND FOR THEM TO WORK.
HE COULD ELOPE WITH ATALANTA, BUT WHEN I TRIED THAT STRATEGY WITH PARIS AND HELEN, IT STARTED A WAR!
I COULD BEG HERMES TO TEACH HIM EVERY SECRET TO A SPEEDY RACE, BUT THERE'S NOT ENOUGH TIME!
WHAT...
WHAT...
WHAT DO I DO?

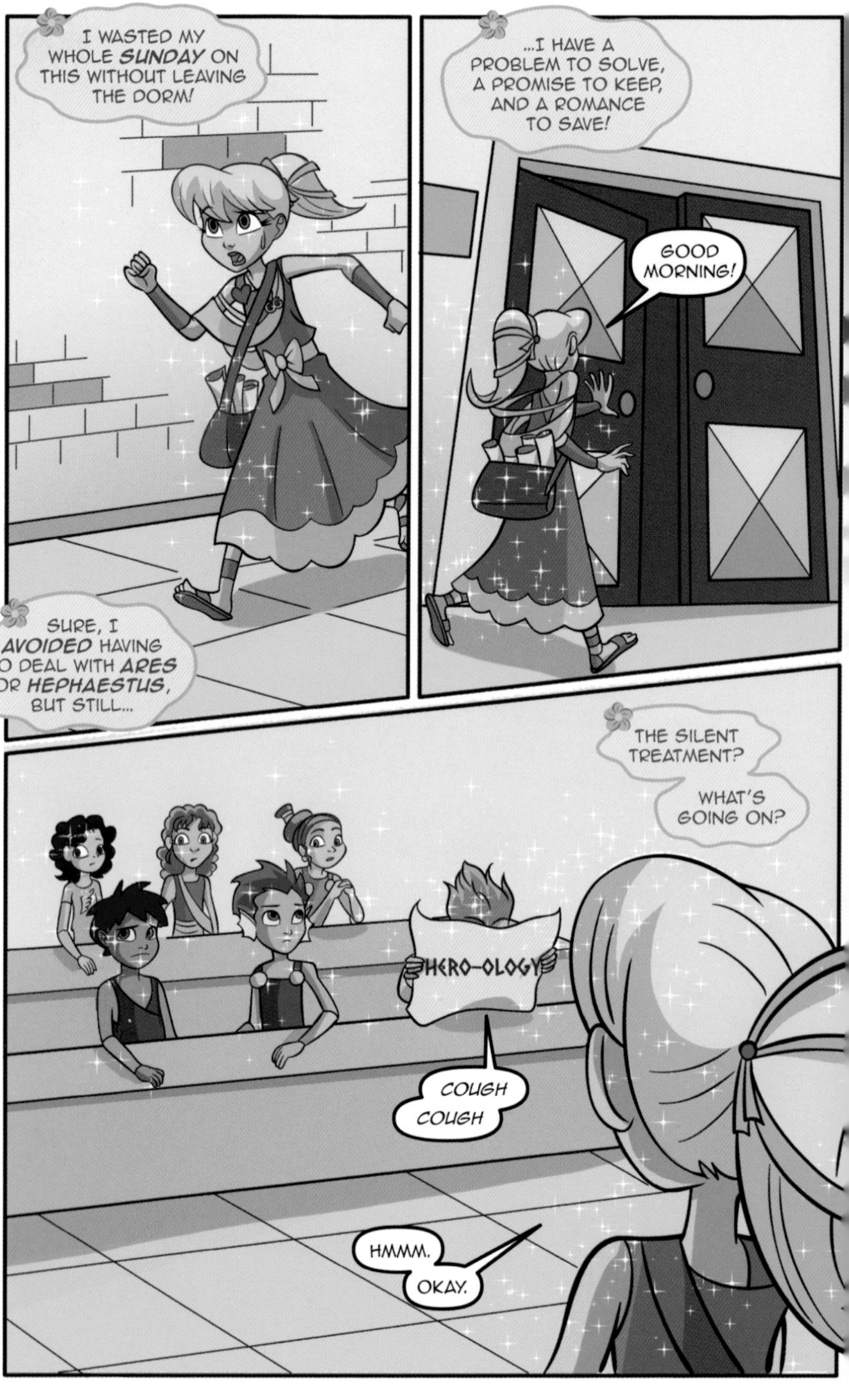
I WASTED MY WHOLE SUNDAY ON THIS WITHOUT LEAVING THE DORM!
SURE, I AVOIDED HAVING TO DEAL WITH ARES OR HEPHAESTUS, BUT STILL...
...I HAVE A PROBLEM TO SOLVE, A PROMISE TO KEEP, AND A ROMANCE TO SAVE!
GOOD MORNING!
THE SILENT TREATMENT?
WHAT'S GOING ON?
HERO-OLOGY
COUGH
COUGH
HMMM.
OKAY.

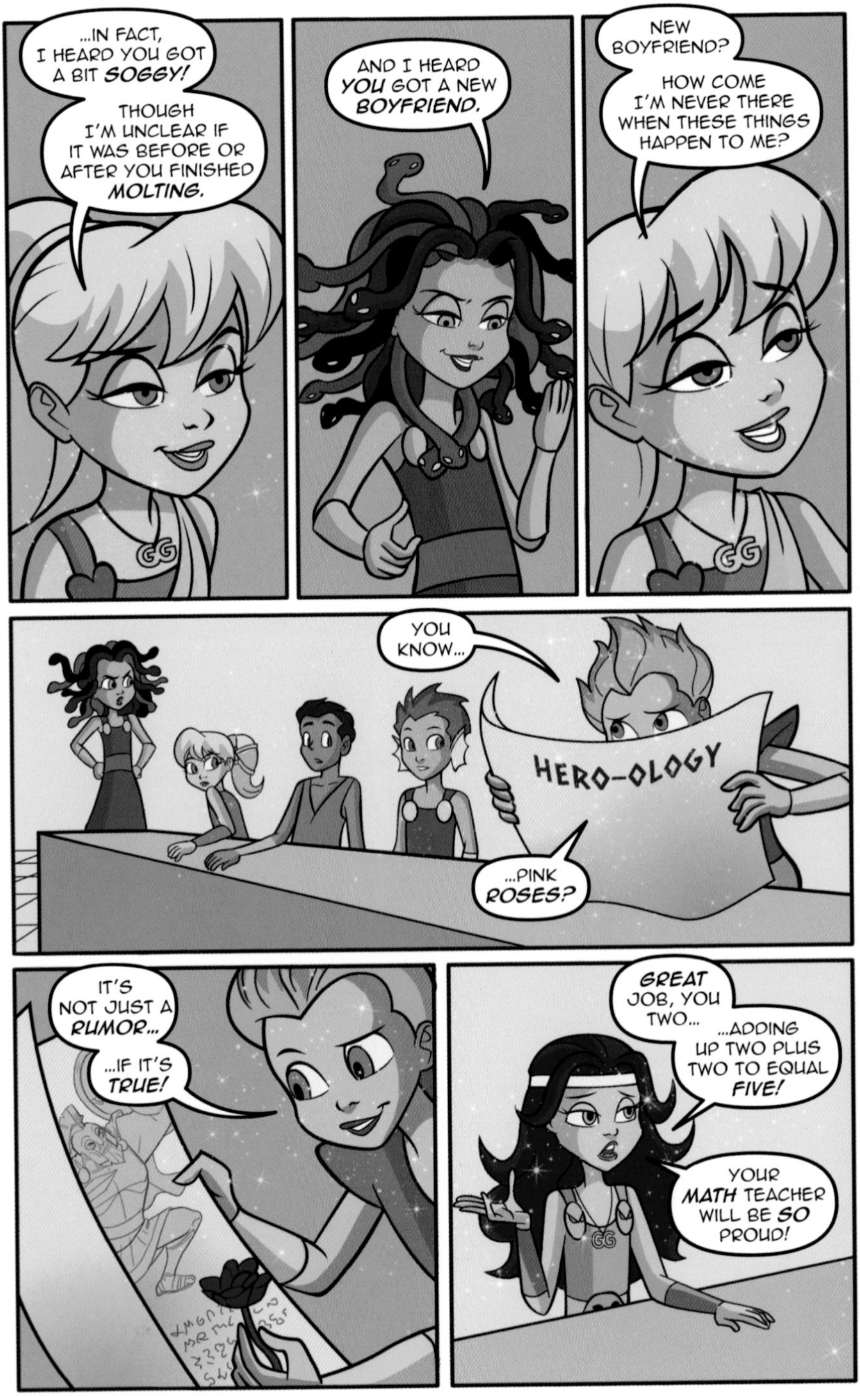
...IN FACT, I HEARD YOU GOT A BIT SOGGY!
THOUGH I'M UNCLEAR IF IT WAS BEFORE OR AFTER YOU FINISHED MOLTING.
AND I HEARD YOU GOT A NEW BOYFRIEND.
NEW BOYFRIEND?
HOW COME I'M NEVER THERE WHEN THESE THINGS HAPPEN TO ME?
YOU KNOW...
HERO-OLOGY
...PINK ROSES?
IT'S NOT JUST A RUMOR...
...IF IT'S TRUE!
GREAT JOB, YOU TWO...
...ADDING UP TWO PLUS TWO TO EQUAL FIVE!
YOUR MATH TEACHER WILL BE SO PROUD!

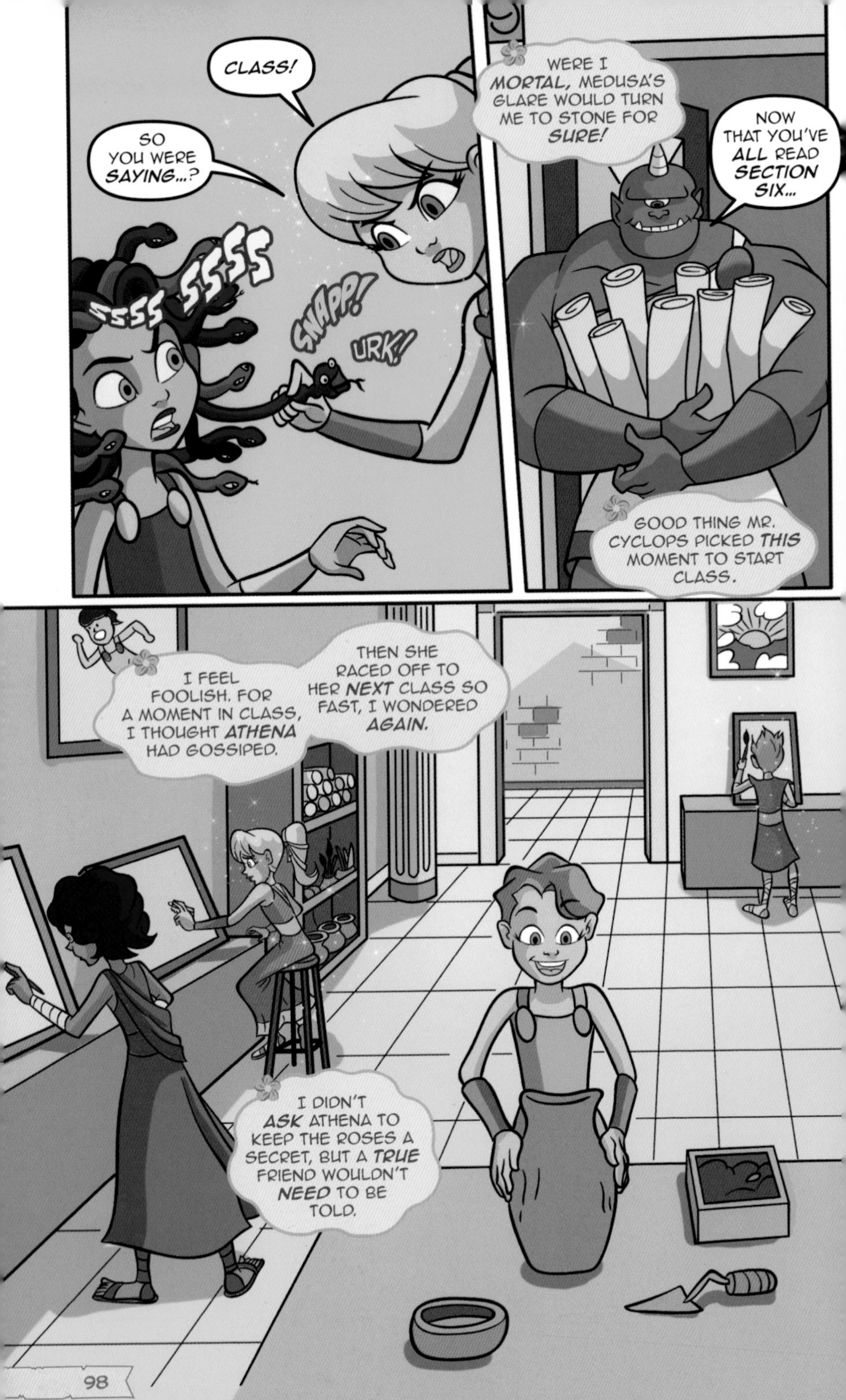
CLASS!
SO YOU WERE SAYING...?
SSSS SSSS
SNAPP!
URK!
WERE I MORTAL, MEDUSA'S GLARE WOULD TURN ME TO STONE FOR SURE!
NOW THAT YOU'VE ALL READ SECTION SIX...
GOOD THING MR. CYCLOPS PICKED THIS MOMENT TO START CLASS.
I FEEL FOOLISH. FOR A MOMENT IN CLASS, I THOUGHT ATHENA HAD GOSSIPED.
THEN SHE RACED OFF TO HER NEXT CLASS SO FAST, I WONDERED AGAIN.
I DIDN'T ASK ATHENA TO KEEP THE ROSES A SECRET, BUT A TRUE FRIEND WOULDN'T NEED TO BE TOLD.

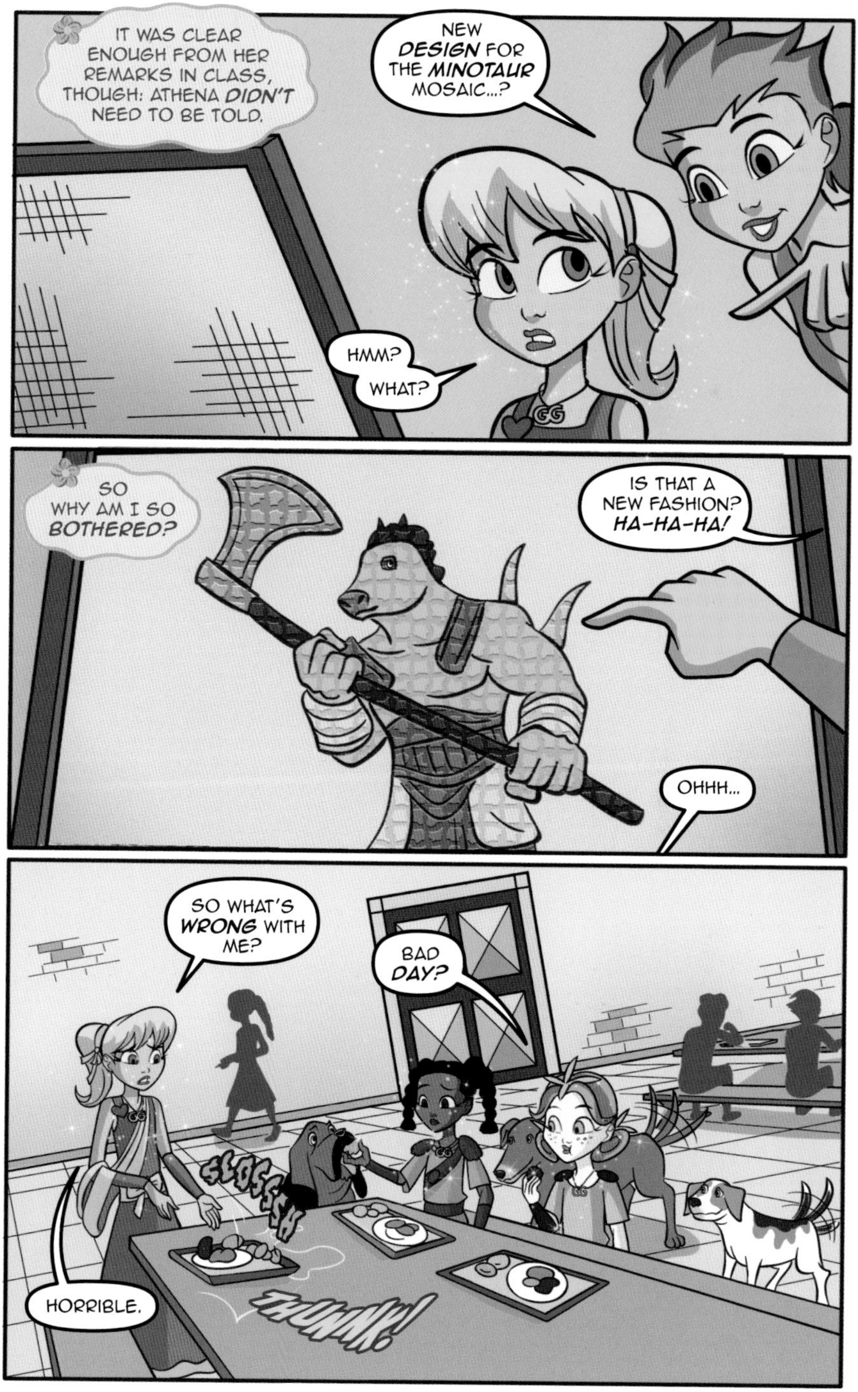
IT WAS CLEAR ENOUGH FROM HER REMARKS IN CLASS, THOUGH: ATHENA *DIDN'T* NEED TO BE TOLD.
NEW *DESIGN* FOR THE *MINOTAUR* MOSAIC...?
HMM?
WHAT?
SO WHY AM I SO *BOTHERED?*
IS THAT A NEW FASHION? *HA-HA-HA!*
OHHH...
SO WHAT'S *WRONG* WITH ME?
BAD *DAY?*
SLOSSSH
HORRIBLE.
THUNK!

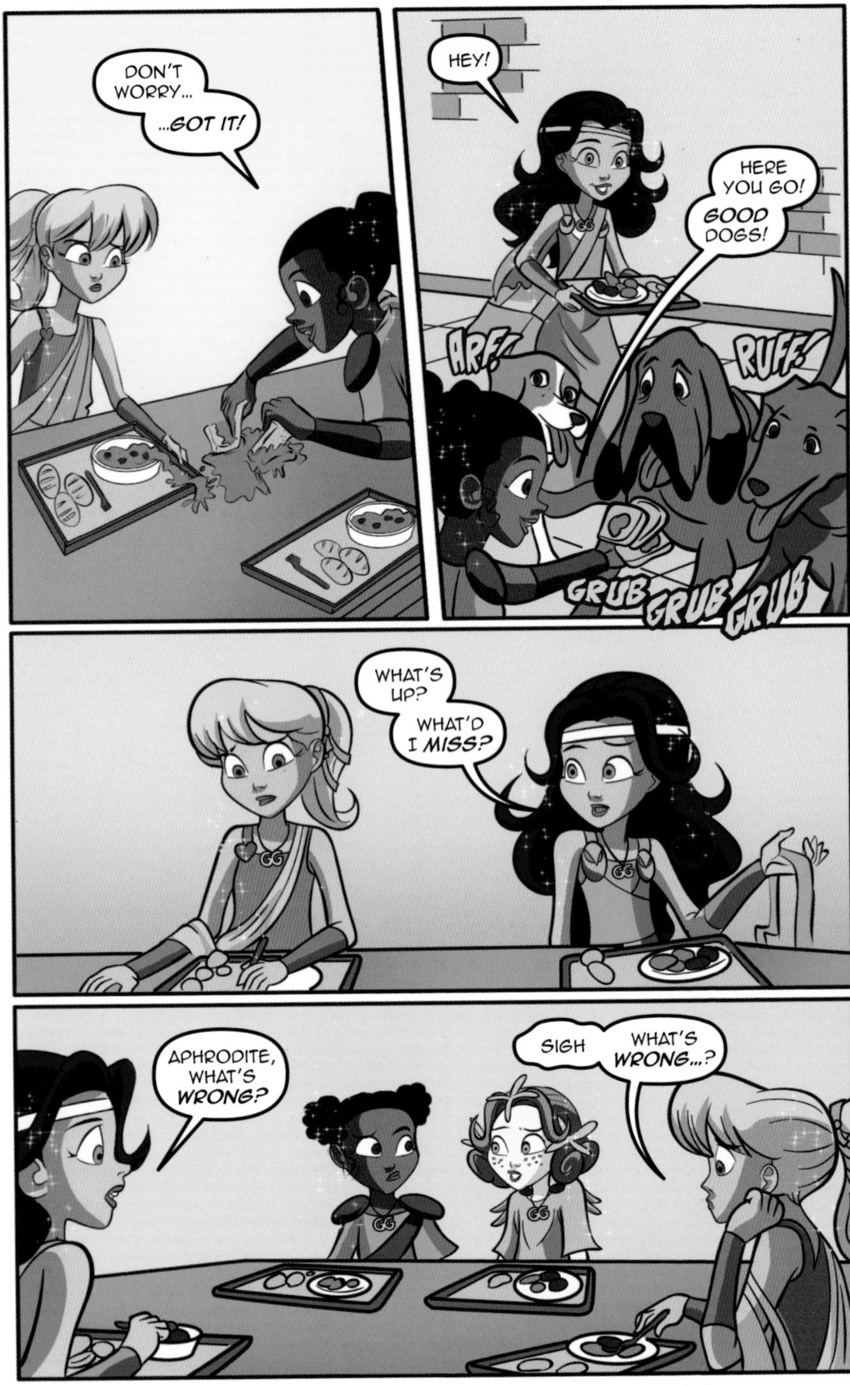
DON'T WORRY...
...GOT IT!
HEY!
HERE YOU GO! GOOD DOGS!
ARF!
RUFF!
GRUB GRUB GRUB
WHAT'S UP?
WHAT'D I MISS?
APHRODITE, WHAT'S WRONG?
SIGH
WHAT'S WRONG...?

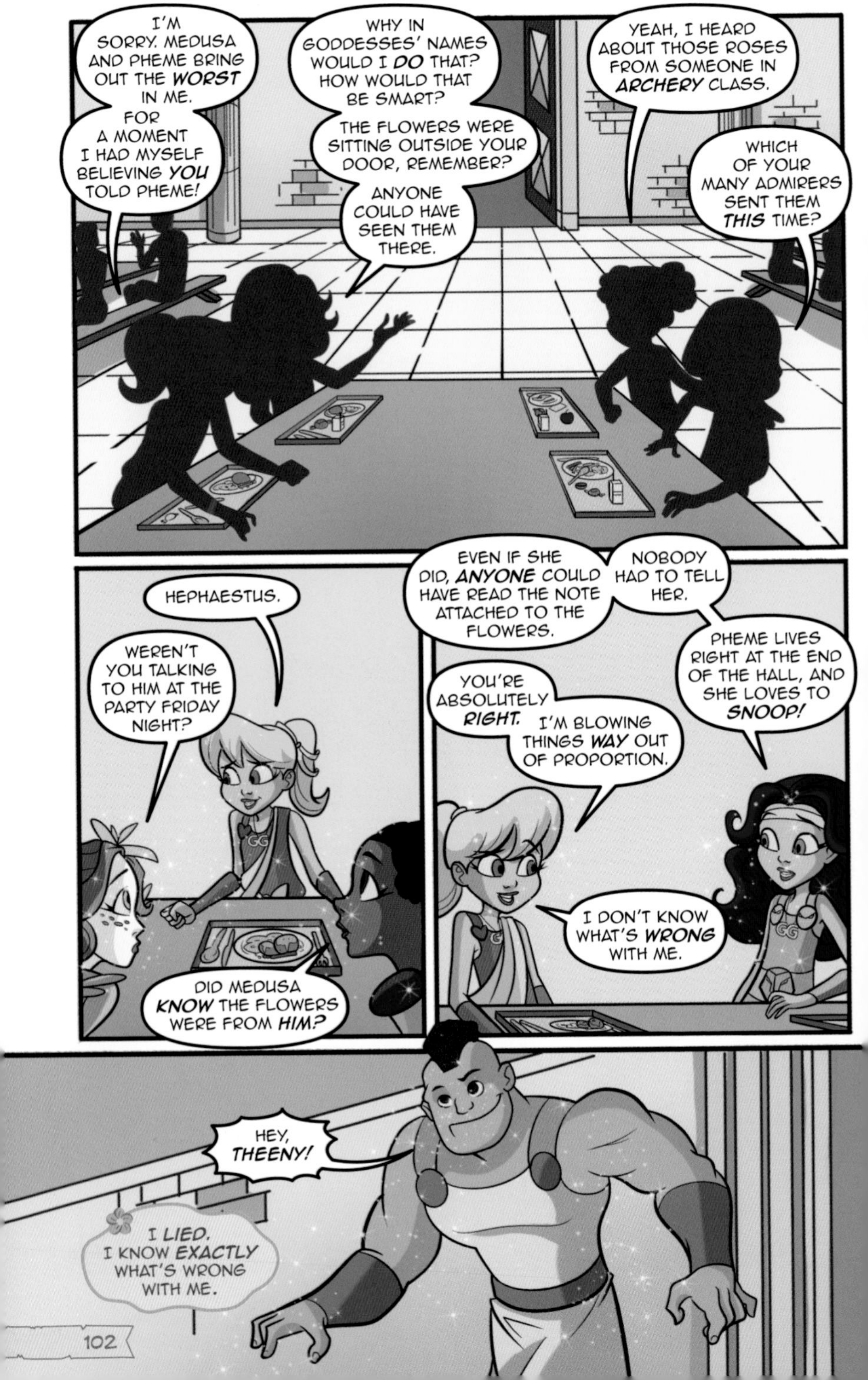
I'M SORRY. MEDUSA AND PHEME BRING OUT THE *WORST* IN ME.
FOR A MOMENT I HAD MYSELF BELIEVING *YOU* TOLD PHEME!
WHY IN GODDESSES' NAMES WOULD I *DO* THAT? HOW WOULD THAT BE SMART?
THE FLOWERS WERE SITTING OUTSIDE YOUR DOOR, REMEMBER?
ANYONE COULD HAVE SEEN THEM THERE.
YEAH, I HEARD ABOUT THOSE ROSES FROM SOMEONE IN *ARCHERY* CLASS.
WHICH OF YOUR MANY ADMIRERS SENT THEM *THIS* TIME?
HEPHAESTUS.
WEREN'T YOU TALKING TO HIM AT THE PARTY FRIDAY NIGHT?
DID MEDUSA *KNOW* THE FLOWERS WERE FROM *HIM?*
EVEN IF SHE DID, *ANYONE* COULD HAVE READ THE NOTE ATTACHED TO THE FLOWERS.
NOBODY HAD TO TELL HER.
PHEME LIVES RIGHT AT THE END OF THE HALL, AND SHE LOVES TO *SNOOP!*
YOU'RE ABSOLUTELY *RIGHT.*
I'M BLOWING THINGS *WAY* OUT OF PROPORTION.
I DON'T KNOW WHAT'S *WRONG* WITH ME.
HEY, *THEENY!*
I *LIED.* I KNOW *EXACTLY* WHAT'S WRONG WITH ME.

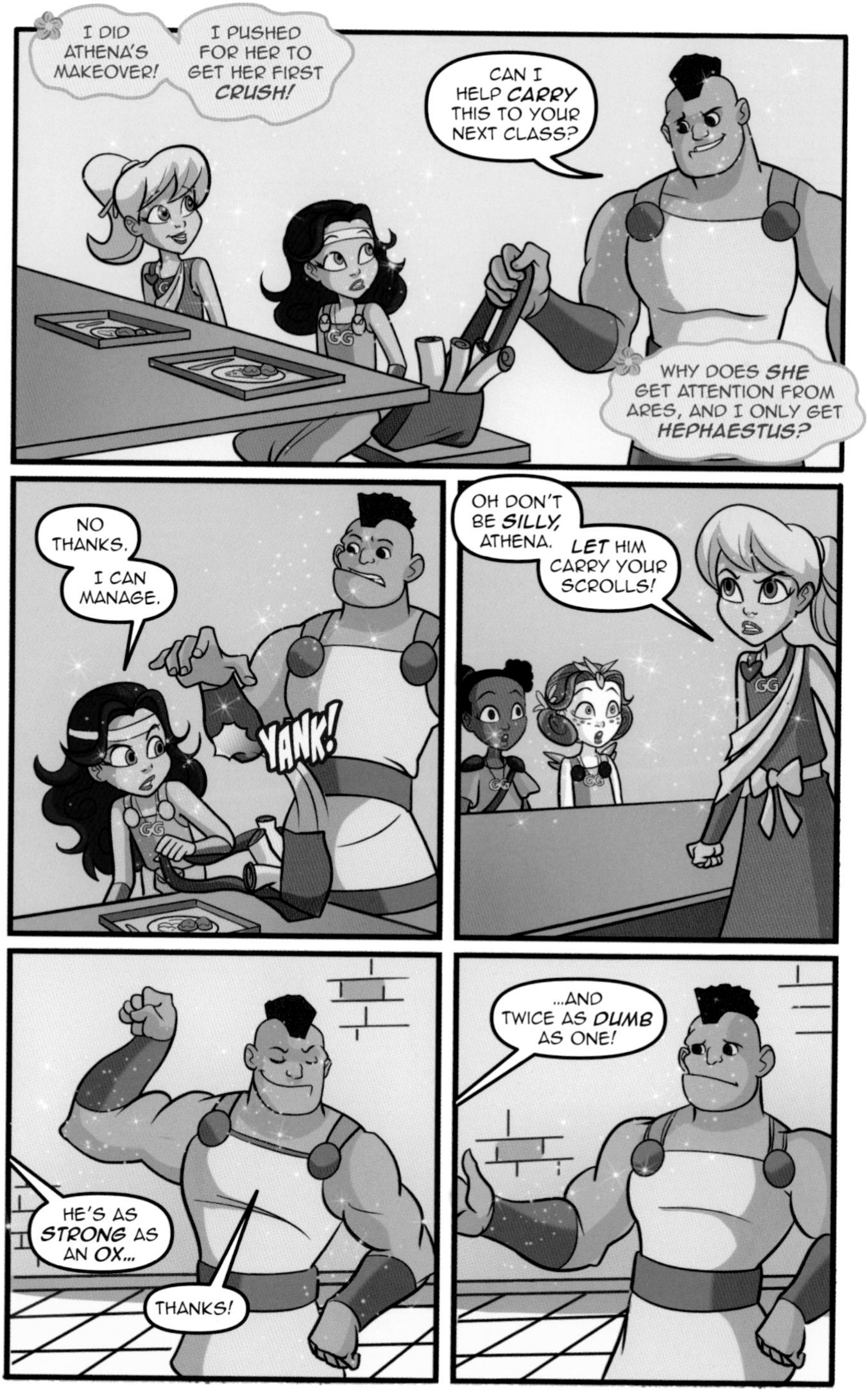

I DID ATHENA'S MAKEOVER!
I PUSHED FOR HER TO GET HER FIRST CRUSH!
CAN I HELP CARRY THIS TO YOUR NEXT CLASS?
WHY DOES SHE GET ATTENTION FROM ARES, AND I ONLY GET HEPHAESTUS?
NO THANKS. I CAN MANAGE.
YANK!
OH DON'T BE SILLY, ATHENA.
LET HIM CARRY YOUR SCROLLS!
HE'S AS STRONG AS AN OX...
THANKS!
...AND TWICE AS DUMB AS ONE!

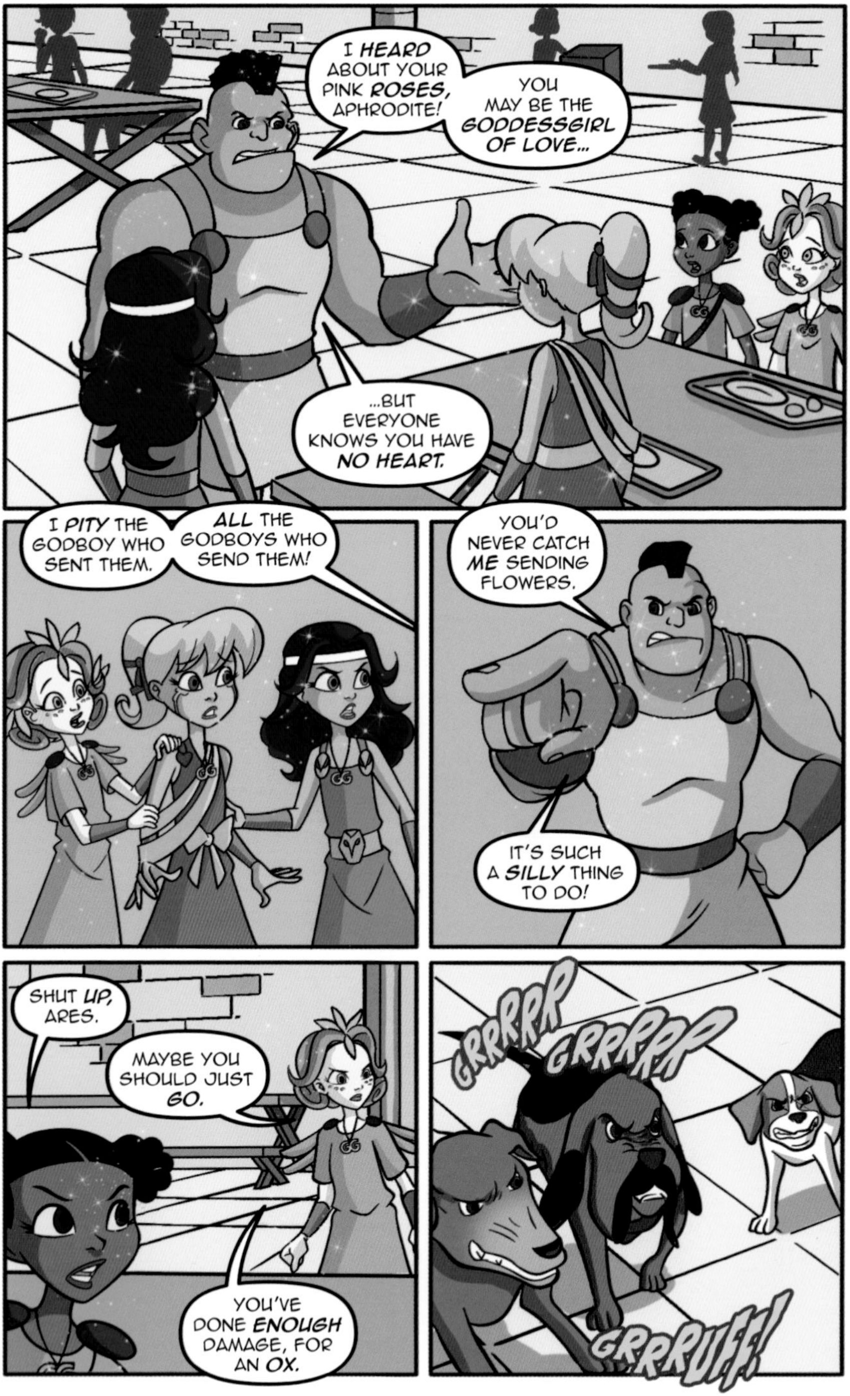
I HEARD ABOUT YOUR PINK ROSES, APHRODITE!
YOU MAY BE THE GODDESSGIRL OF LOVE...
...BUT EVERYONE KNOWS YOU HAVE NO HEART.
I PITY THE GODBOY WHO SENT THEM.
ALL THE GODBOYS WHO SEND THEM!
YOU'D NEVER CATCH ME SENDING FLOWERS.
IT'S SUCH A SILLY THING TO DO!
SHUT UP, ARES.
MAYBE YOU SHOULD JUST GO.
YOU'VE DONE ENOUGH DAMAGE, FOR AN OX.
GRRRRR
GRRRRRR
GRRRUFF!

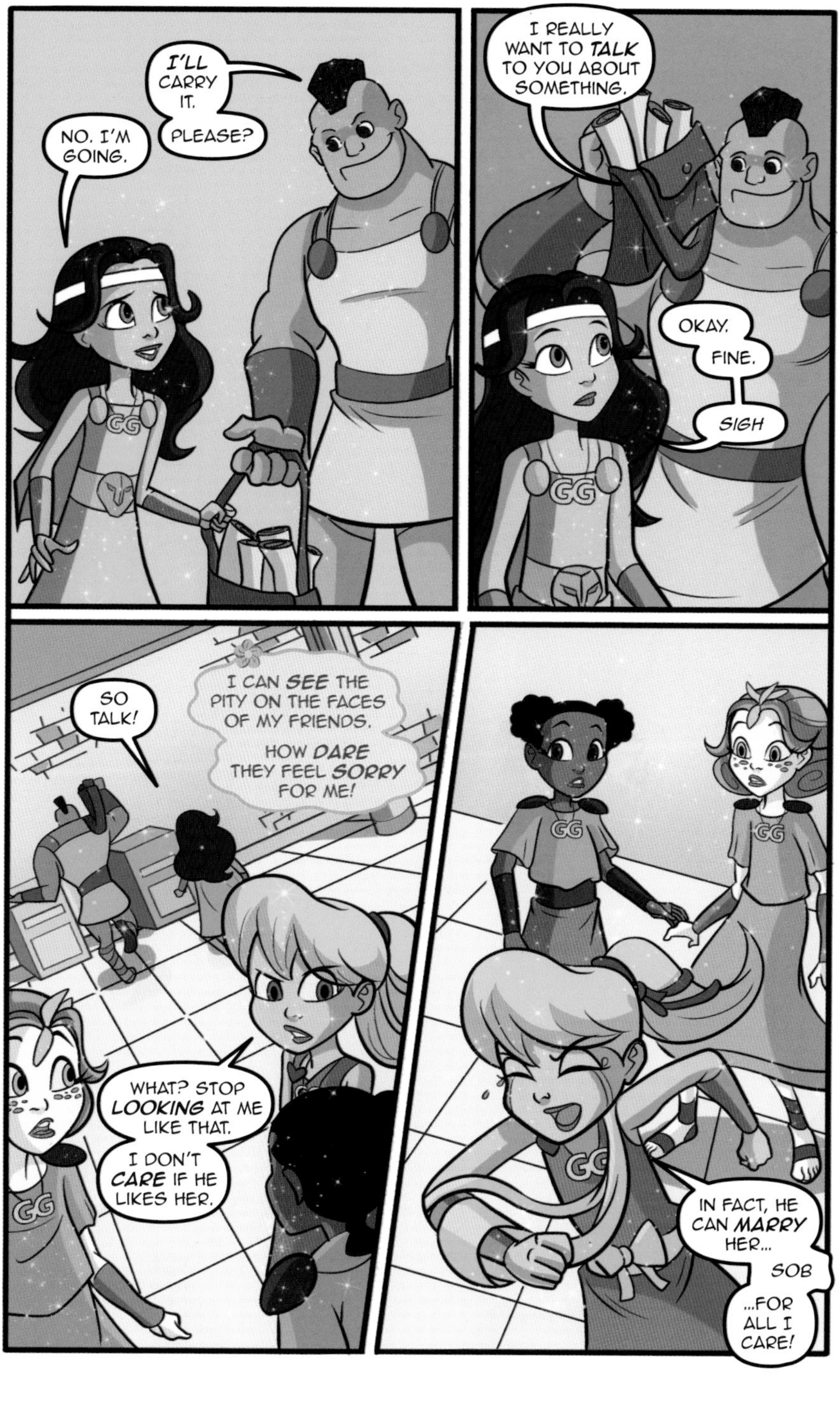
I'LL CARRY IT.
PLEASE?
NO. I'M GOING.
I REALLY WANT TO TALK TO YOU ABOUT SOMETHING.
OKAY.
FINE.
SIGH
SO TALK!
I CAN SEE THE PITY ON THE FACES OF MY FRIENDS.
HOW DARE THEY FEEL SORRY FOR ME!
WHAT? STOP LOOKING AT ME LIKE THAT.
I DON'T CARE IF HE LIKES HER.
IN FACT, HE CAN MARRY HER...
SOB
...FOR ALL I CARE!

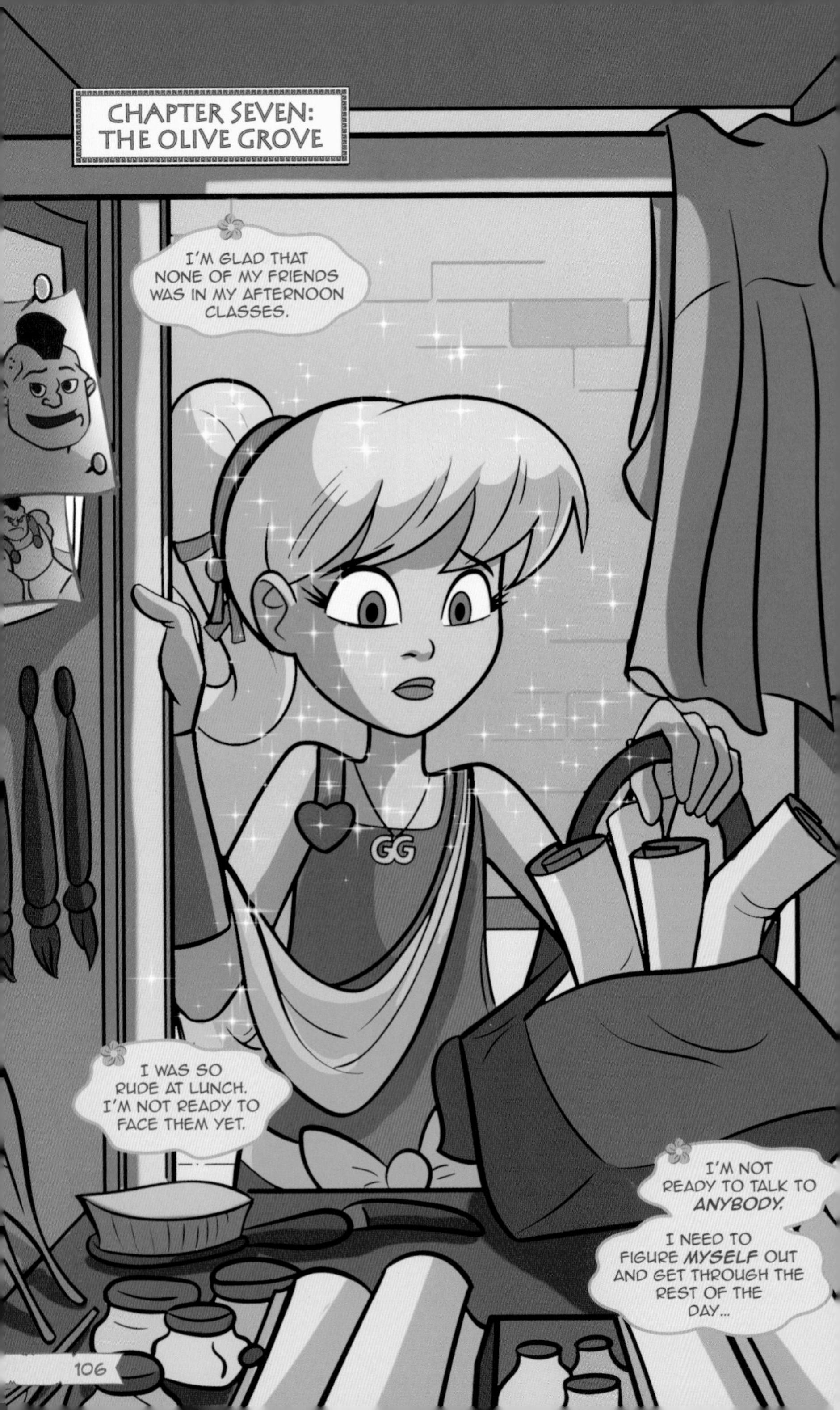
CHAPTER SEVEN:
THE OLIVE GROVE
I'M GLAD THAT NONE OF MY FRIENDS WAS IN MY AFTERNOON CLASSES.
GG
I WAS SO RUDE AT LUNCH. I'M NOT READY TO FACE THEM YET.
I'M NOT READY TO TALK TO *ANYBODY.*
I NEED TO FIGURE *MYSELF* OUT AND GET THROUGH THE REST OF THE DAY...

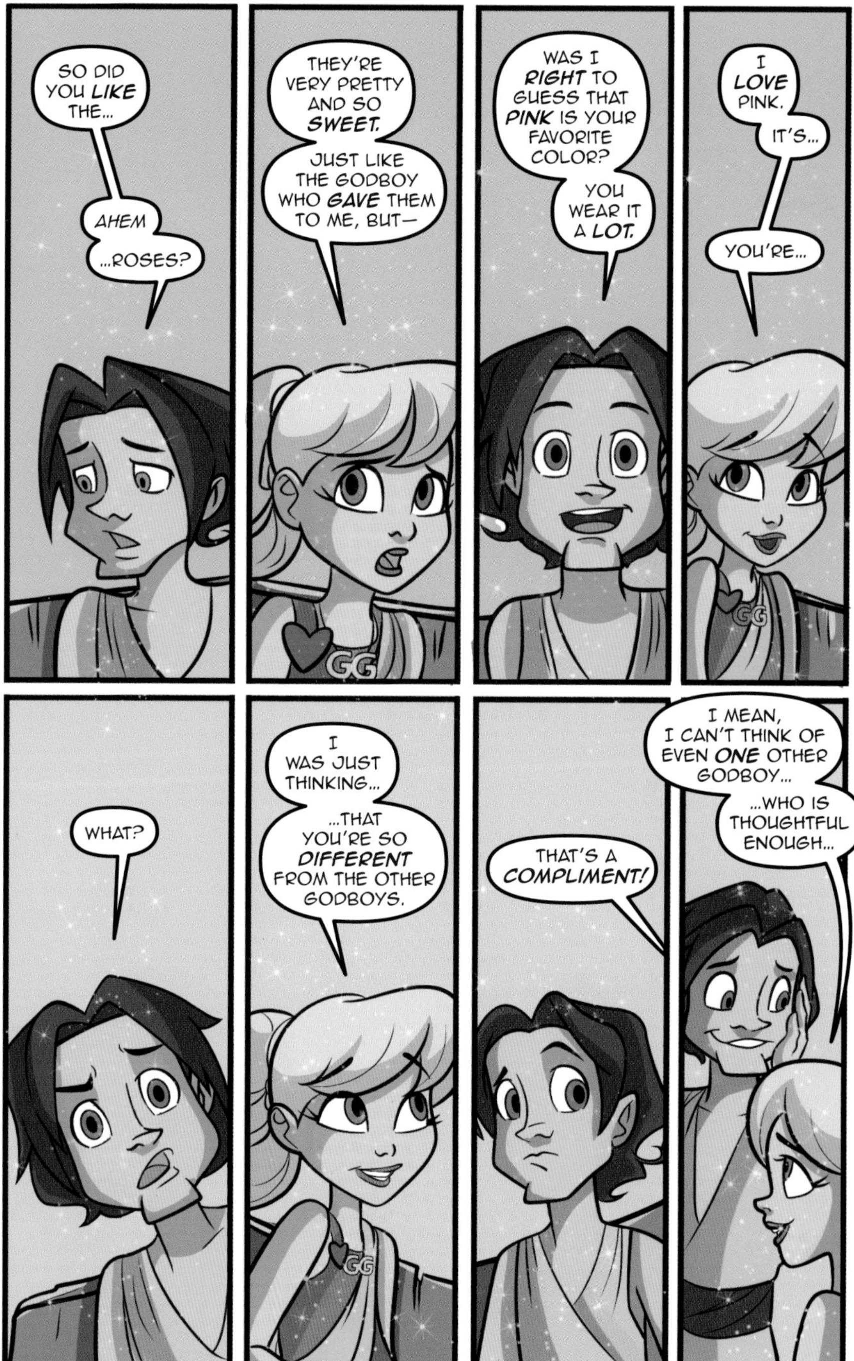
SO DID YOU LIKE THE...
AHEM
...ROSES?
THEY'RE VERY PRETTY AND SO SWEET.
JUST LIKE THE GODBOY WHO GAVE THEM TO ME, BUT—
WAS I RIGHT TO GUESS THAT PINK IS YOUR FAVORITE COLOR?
YOU WEAR IT A LOT.
I LOVE PINK.
IT'S...
YOU'RE...
WHAT?
I WAS JUST THINKING...
...THAT YOU'RE SO DIFFERENT FROM THE OTHER GODBOYS.
THAT'S A COMPLIMENT!
I MEAN, I CAN'T THINK OF EVEN ONE OTHER GODBOY...
...WHO IS THOUGHTFUL ENOUGH...

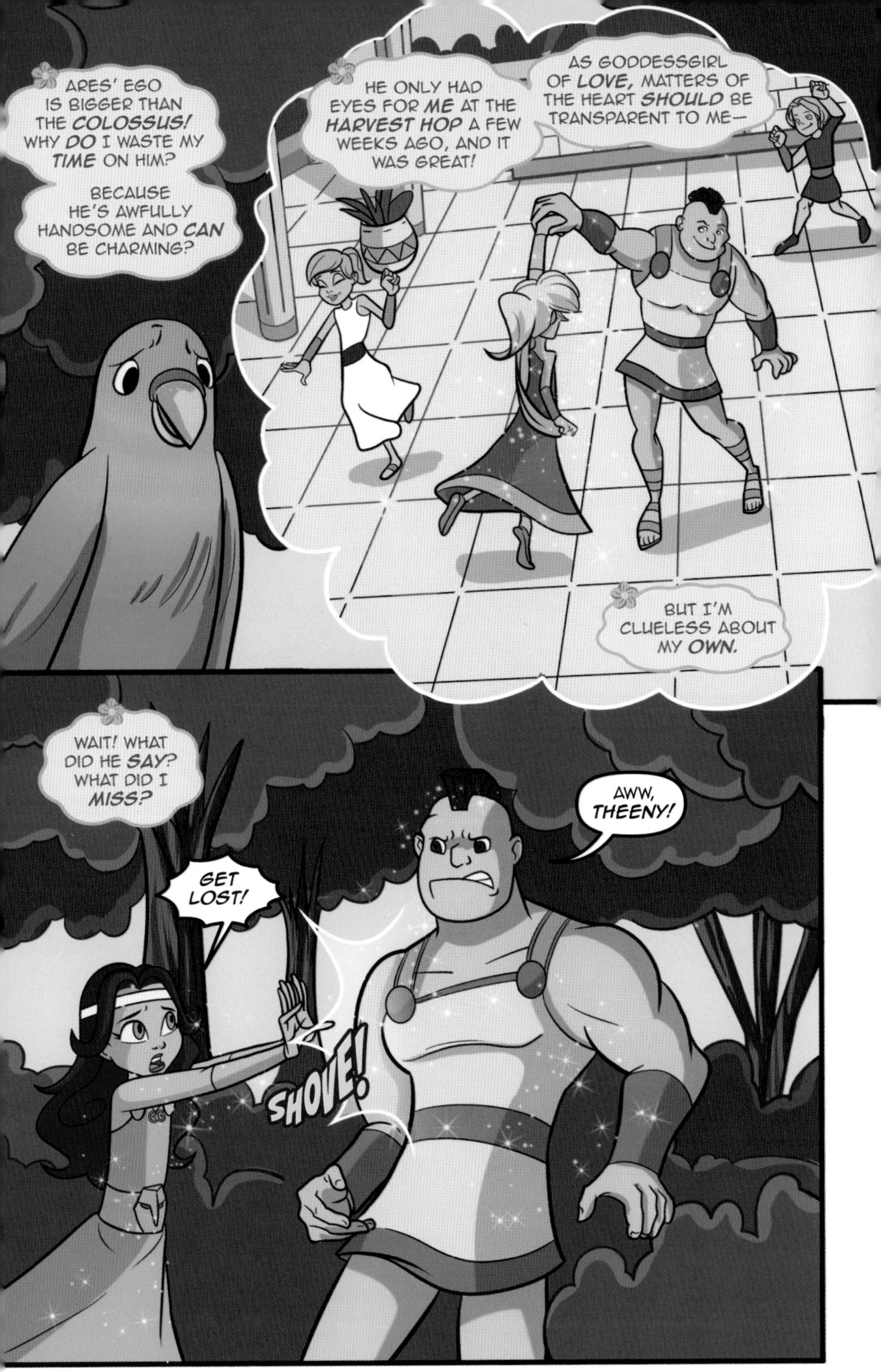
ARES' EGO IS BIGGER THAN THE COLOSSUS! WHY DO I WASTE MY TIME ON HIM?
BECAUSE HE'S AWFULLY HANDSOME AND CAN BE CHARMING?
HE ONLY HAD EYES FOR ME AT THE HARVEST HOP A FEW WEEKS AGO, AND IT WAS GREAT!
AS GODDESSGIRL OF LOVE, MATTERS OF THE HEART SHOULD BE TRANSPARENT TO ME—
BUT I'M CLUELESS ABOUT MY OWN.
WAIT! WHAT DID HE SAY? WHAT DID I MISS?
AWW, THEENY!
GET LOST!
SHOVE!

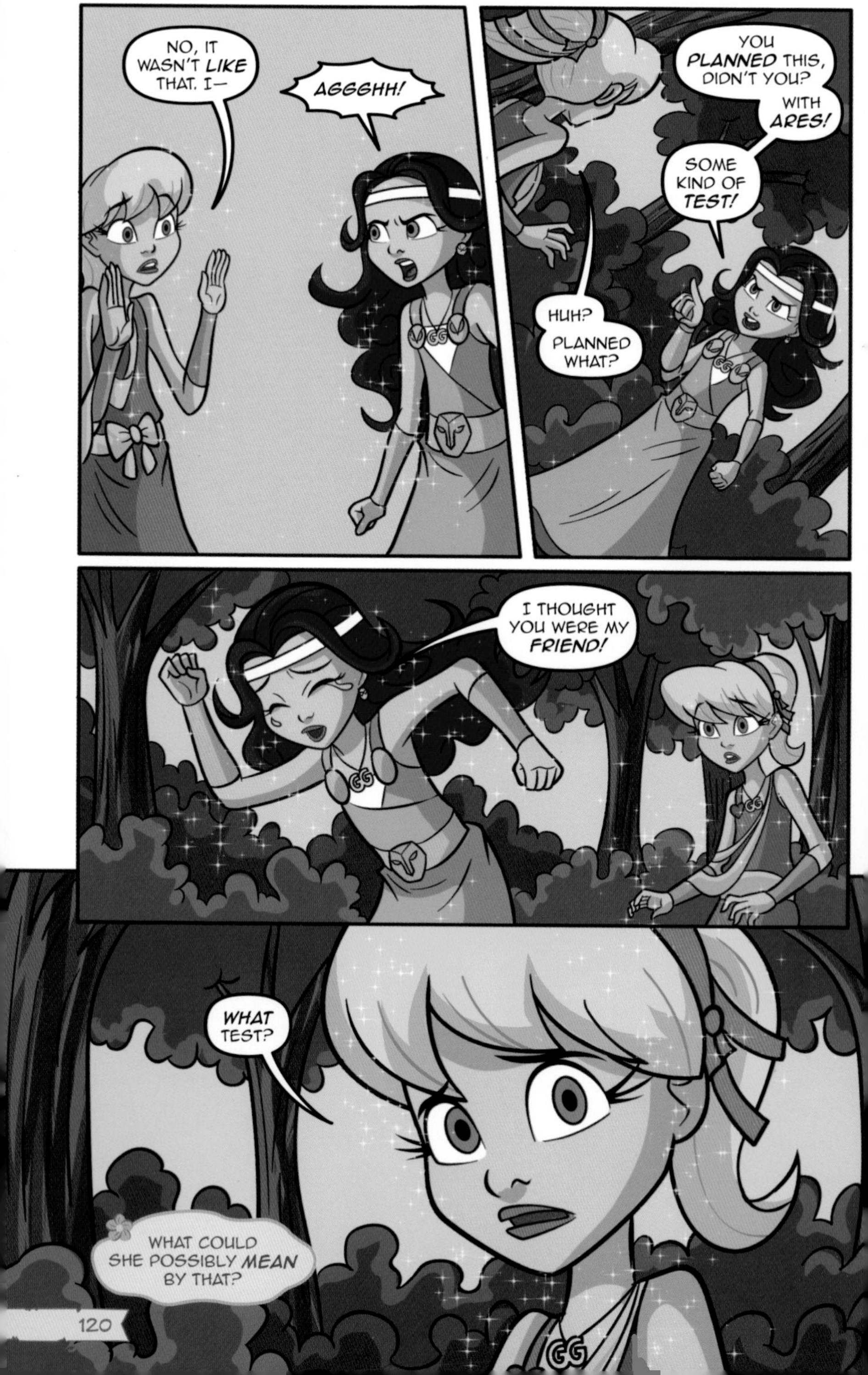
NO, IT WASN'T *LIKE* THAT. I—
AGGGHH!
YOU *PLANNED* THIS, DIDN'T YOU?
WITH *ARES!*
SOME KIND OF *TEST!*
HUH?
PLANNED WHAT?
I THOUGHT YOU WERE MY *FRIEND!*
WHAT TEST?
WHAT COULD SHE POSSIBLY *MEAN* BY THAT?

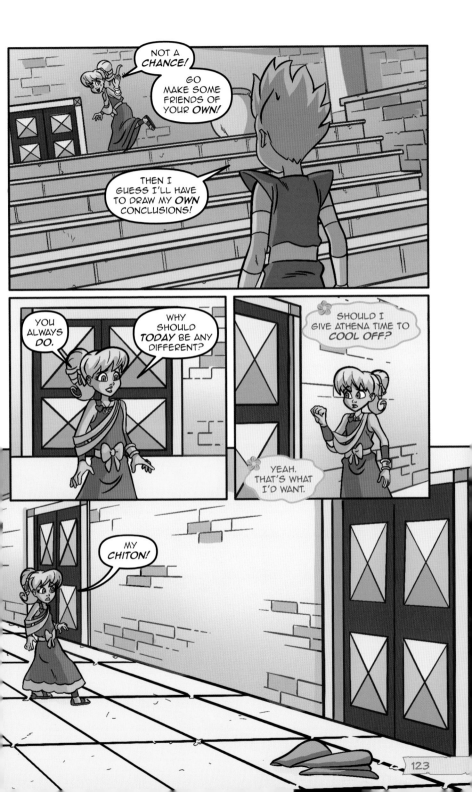

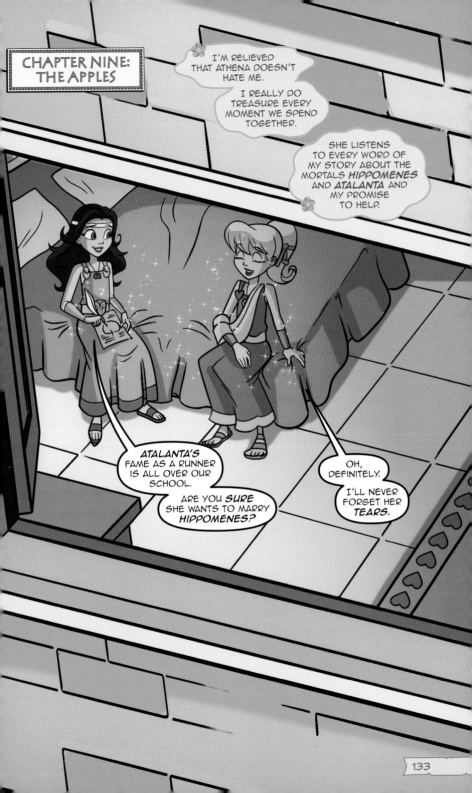

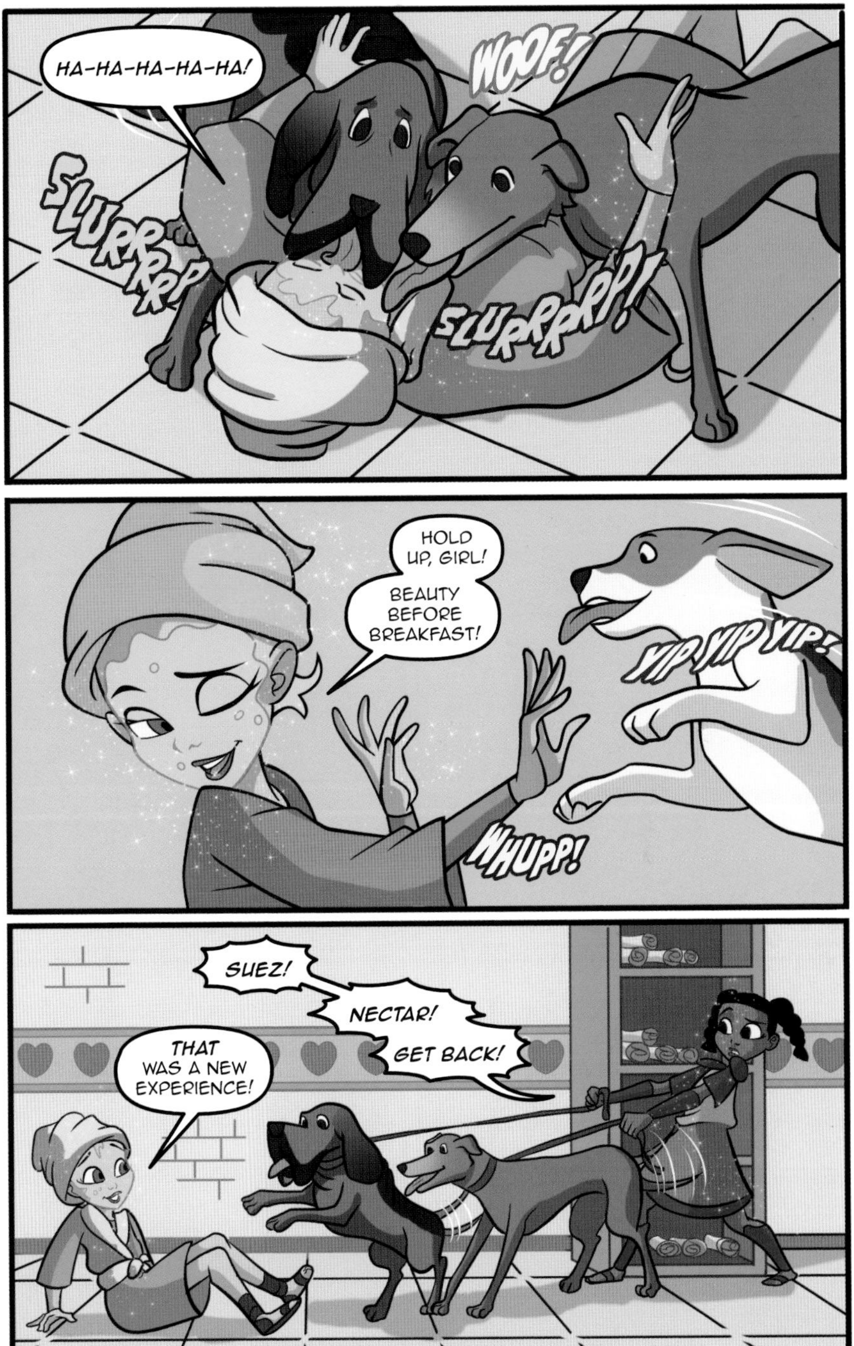

HA-HA-HA-HA-HA!
WOOF!
SLURRRRP
SLURRRRP!
HOLD UP, GIRL!
BEAUTY BEFORE BREAKFAST!
YIP YIP YIP!
WHUPP!
SUEZ!
NECTAR!
GET BACK!
THAT WAS A NEW EXPERIENCE!

149

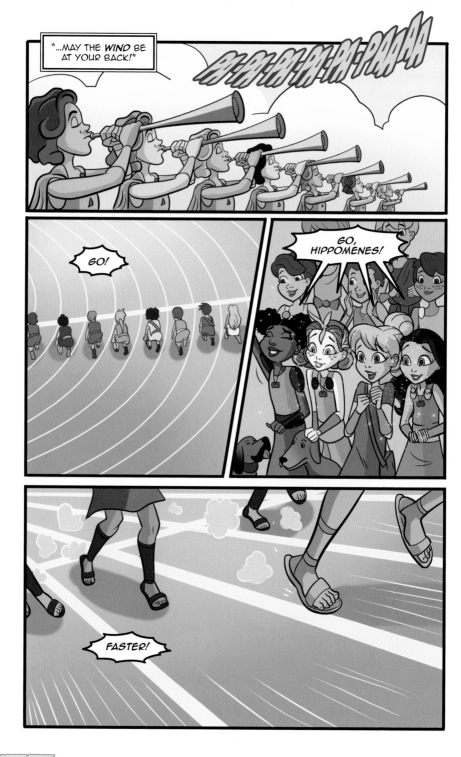

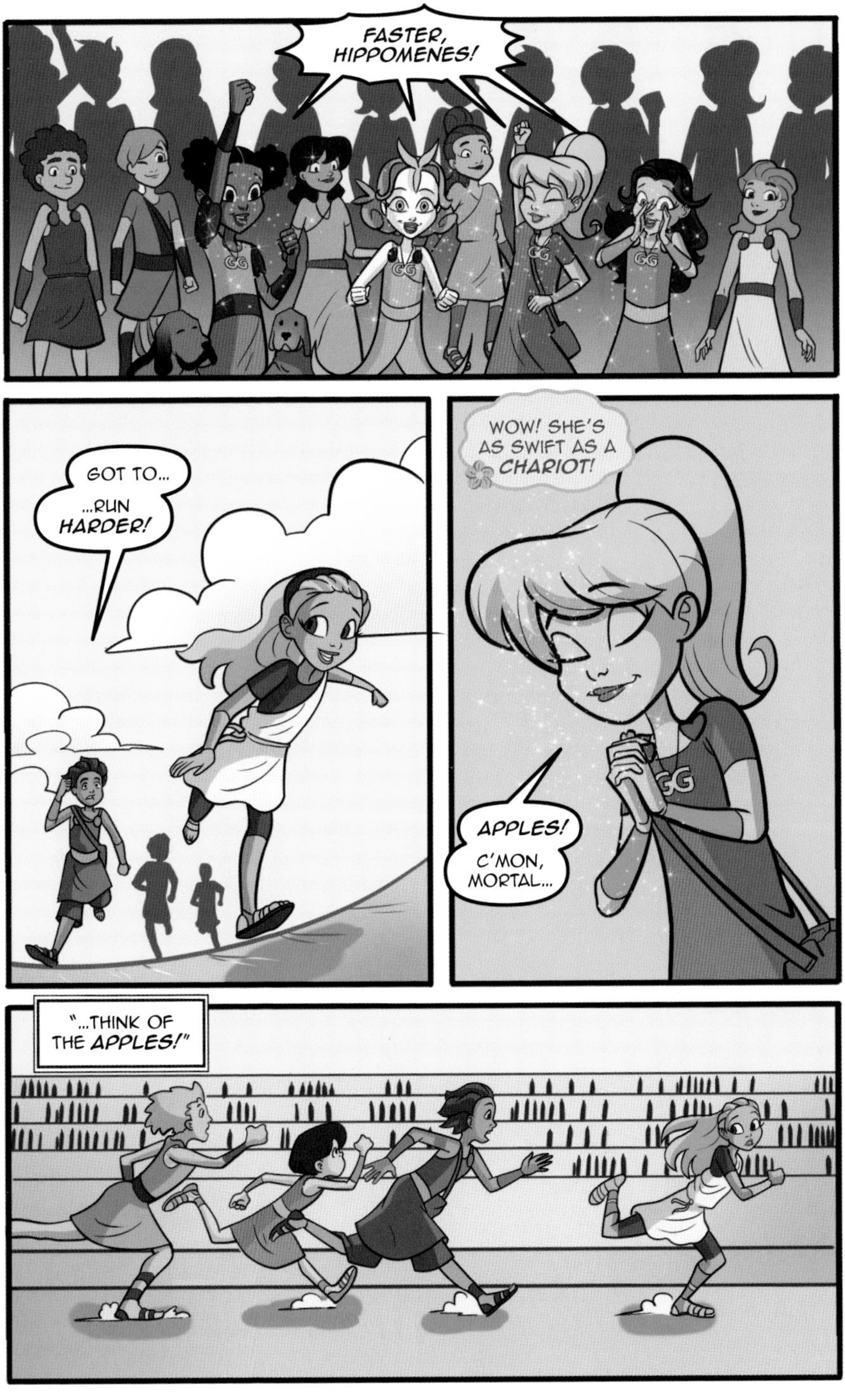
FASTER, HIPPOMENES!
GOT TO...
...RUN HARDER!
WOW! SHE'S AS SWIFT AS A CHARIOT!
APPLES!
C'MON, MORTAL...
"...THINK OF THE APPLES!"

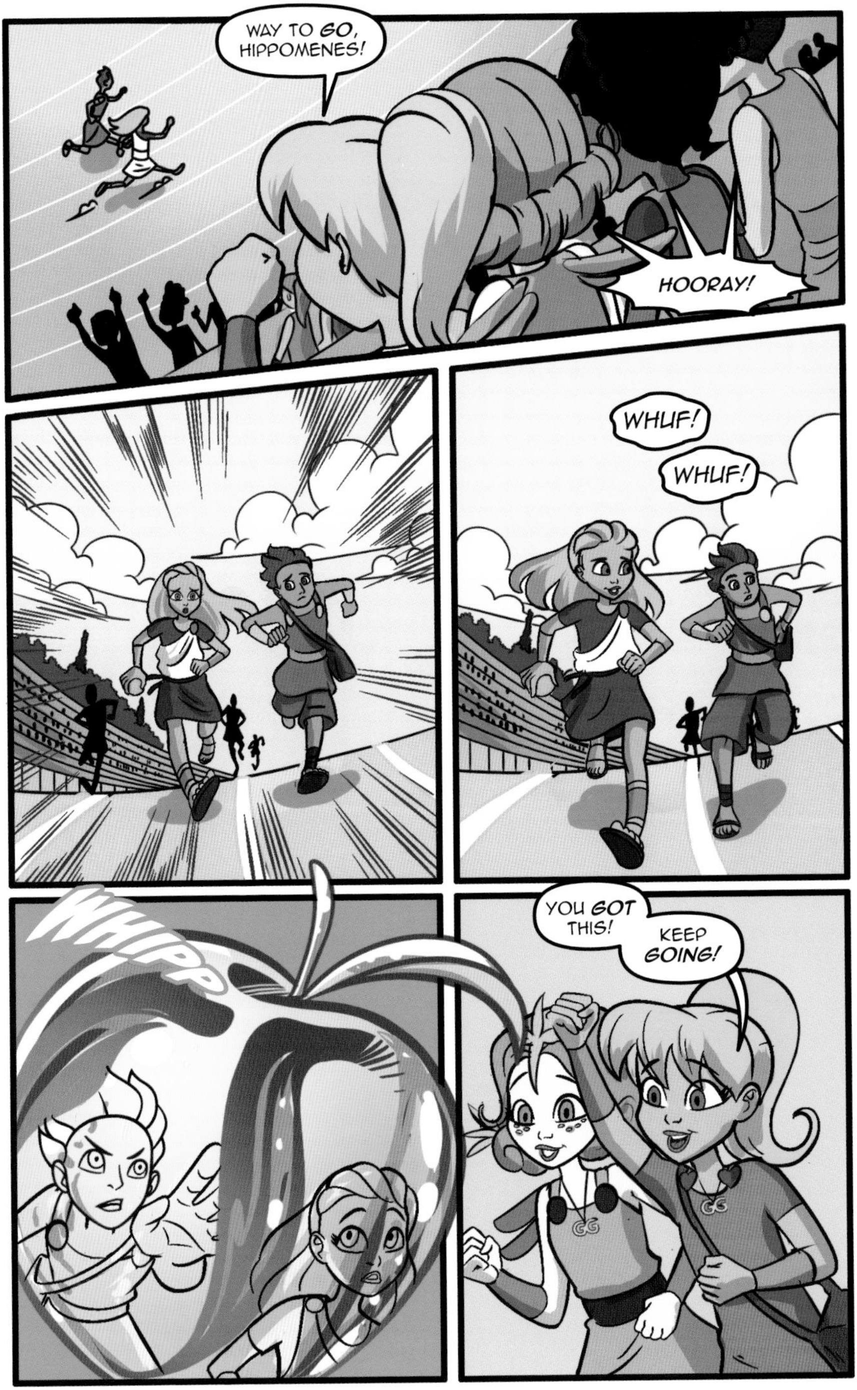

WAY TO GO, HIPPOMENES!
HOORAY!
WHUF!
WHUF!
WHIPP
YOU GOT THIS!
KEEP GOING!

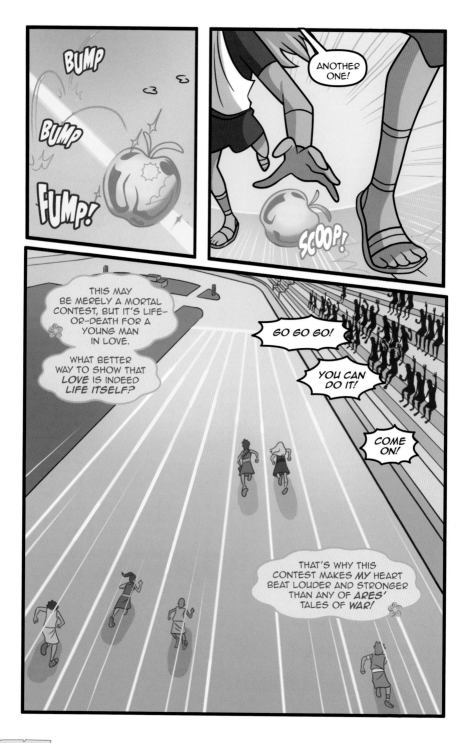

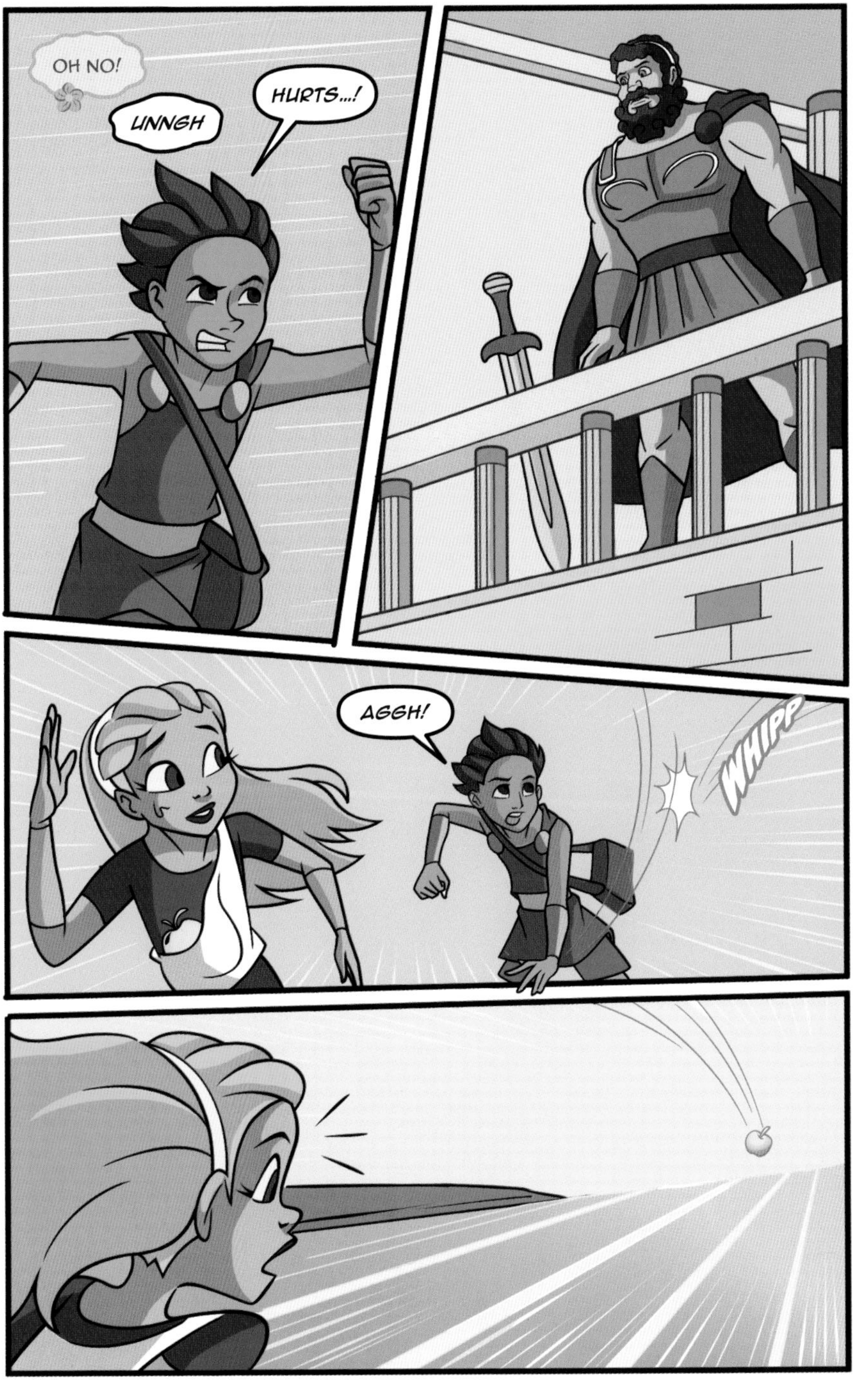
OH NO!
UNNGH
HURTS...!
AGGH!
WHIPP

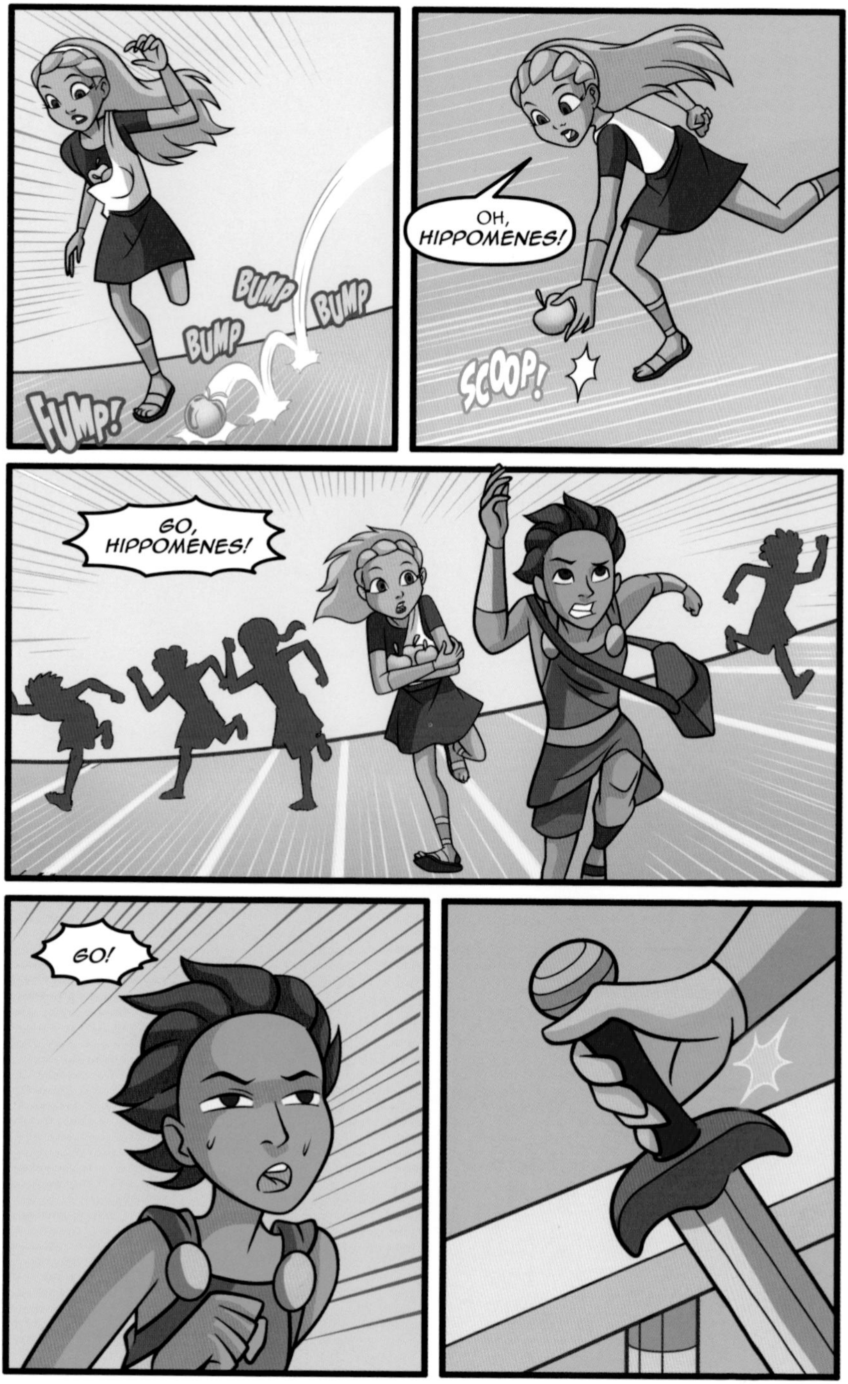
BUMP
BUMP
BUMP
FUMP!
OH, HIPPOMENES!
SCOOP!
GO, HIPPOMENES!
GO!

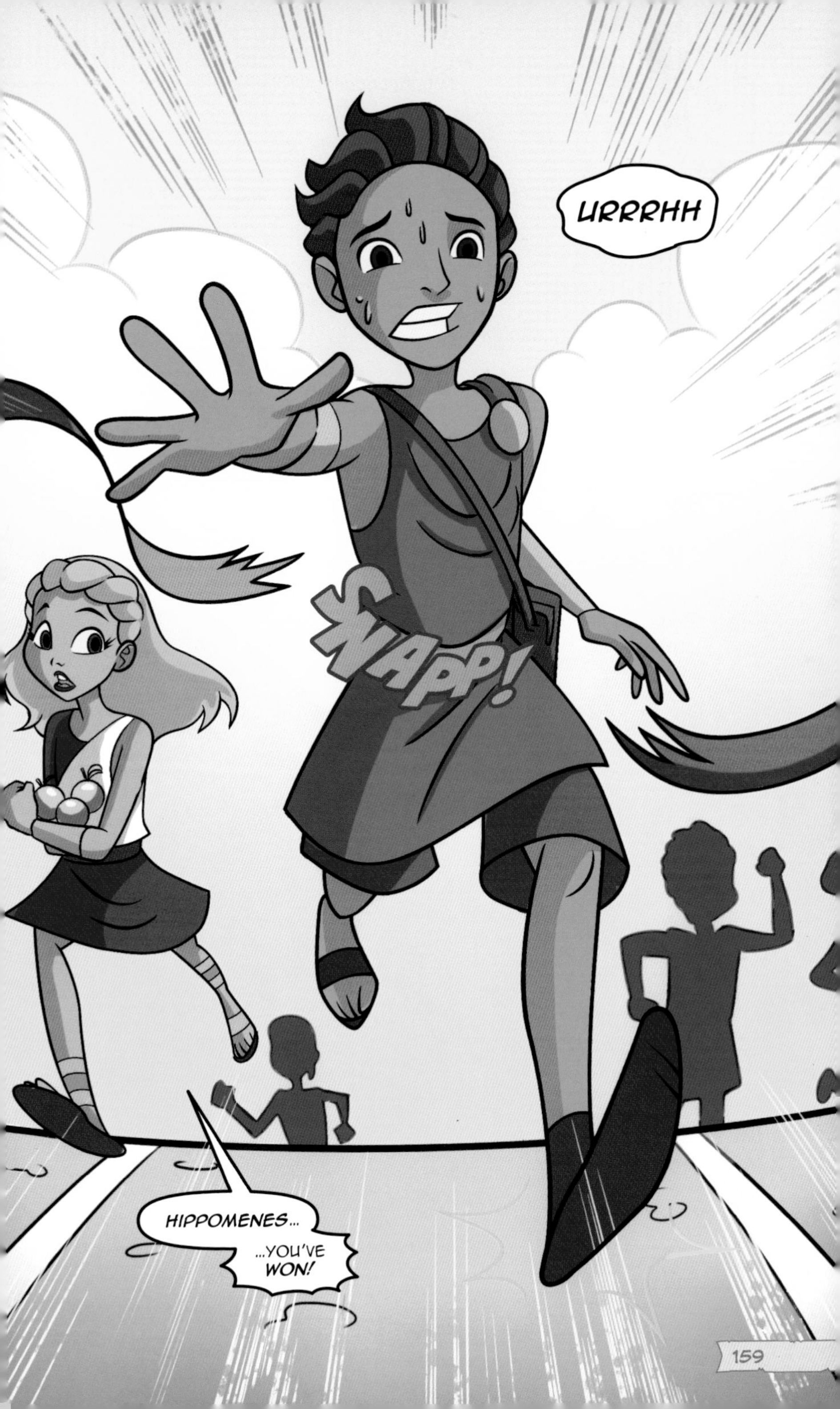
URRRHH
SWAPP!
HIPPOMENES...
...YOU'VE WON!

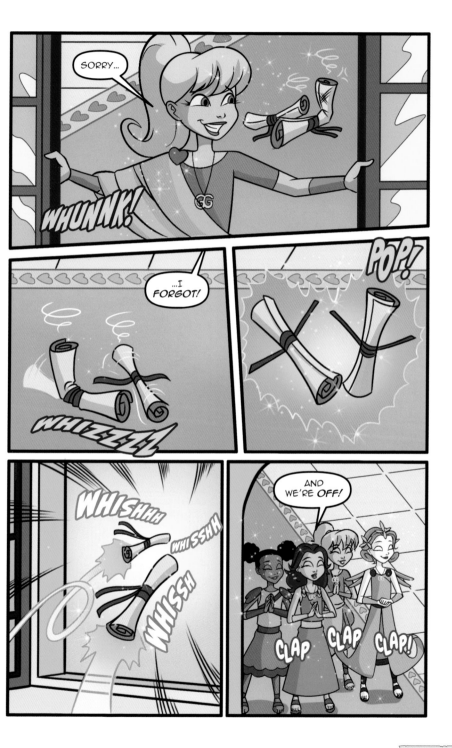

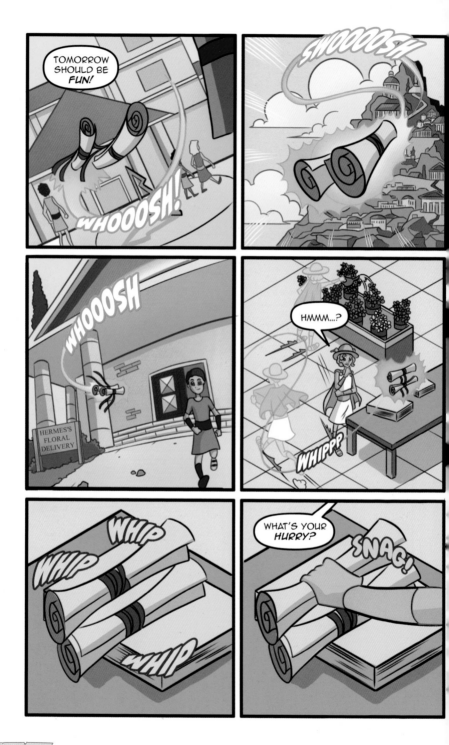

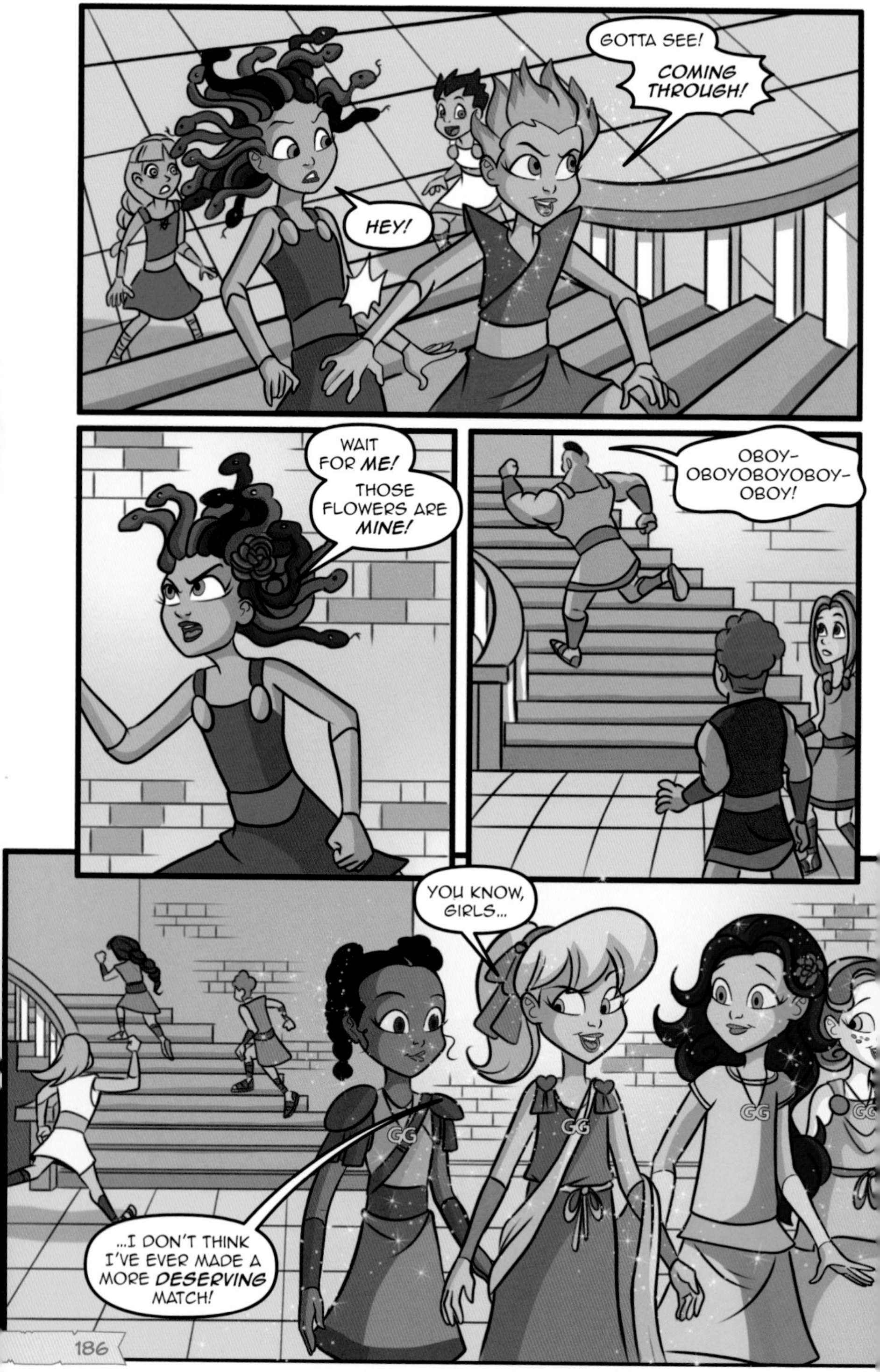
GOTTA SEE!
COMING THROUGH!
HEY!
WAIT FOR ME!
THOSE FLOWERS ARE MINE!
OBOY-OBOYOBOYOBOY-OBOY!
YOU KNOW, GIRLS...
...I DON'T THINK I'VE EVER MADE A MORE DESERVING MATCH!

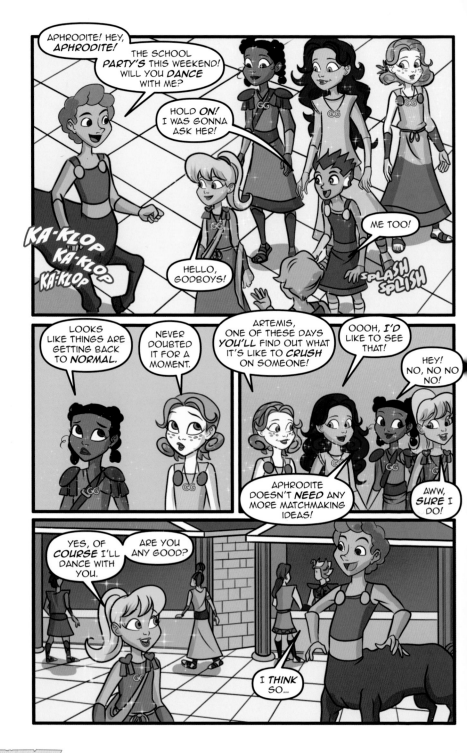